The Lost Lover

Also by Karen Swan

The Wild Isle series
The Last Summer
The Stolen Hours

Other books
Players
Prima Donna
Christmas at Tiffany's
The Perfect Present
Christmas at Claridge's
The Summer Without You
Christmas in the Snow
Summer at Tiffany's
Christmas on Primrose Hill
The Paris Secret
Christmas Under the Stars
The Rome Affair
The Christmas Secret
The Greek Escape
The Christmas Lights
The Spanish Promise
The Christmas Party
The Hidden Beach
Together by Christmas
The Secret Path
Midnight in the Snow
The Christmas Postcards
Christmas by Candlelight

The
Lost
Lover

Karen
Swan

MACMILLAN

First published 2024 by Macmillan
an imprint of Pan Macmillan
The Smithson, 6 Briset Street, London EC1M 5NR
EU representative: Macmillan Publishers Ireland Ltd, 1st Floor,
The Liffey Trust Centre, 117–126 Sheriff Street Upper,
Dublin 1, D01 YC43
Associated companies throughout the world
www.panmacmillan.com

ISBN 978-1-5290-8446-7 HB
ISBN 978-1-5290-8447-4 TPB

1 3 5 7 9 8 6 4 2

A CIP catalogue record for this book is available from the British Library.

Map artwork by Hemesh Alles

Typeset in Palatino by Palimpsest Book Production Ltd, Falkirk, Stirlingshire
Printed and bound by CPI Group (UK) Ltd, Croydon, CR0 4YY

Visit **www.panmacmillan.com** to read more about all our books
and to buy them. You will also find features, author interviews and
news of any author events, and you can sign up for e-newsletters
so that you're always first to hear about our new releases.

For Tash Christie-Miller
You keep getting better and betterer

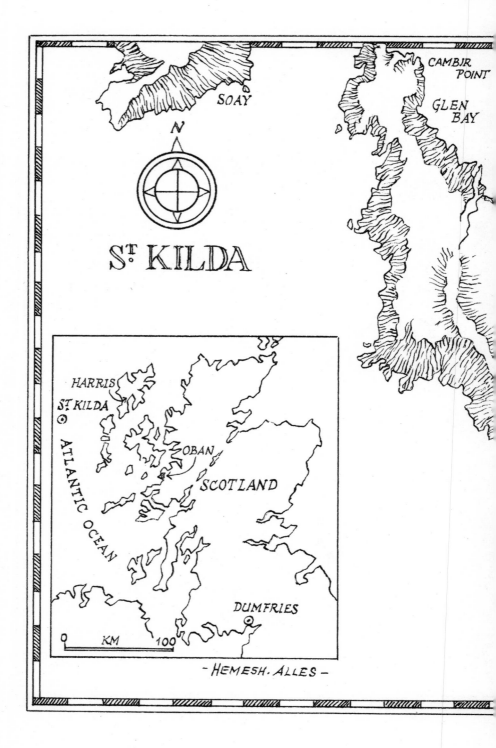

SOAY

CAMBIR
POINT

GLEN
BAY

N

ST KILDA

HARRIS
ST KILDA

OBAN

SCOTLAND

ATLANTIC OCEAN

DUMFRIES

KM   100

- HEMESH. ALLES -

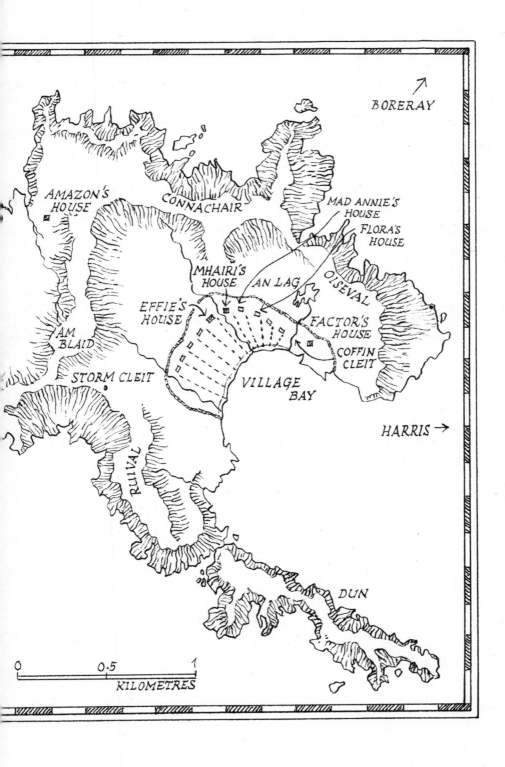

BORERAY

AMAZON'S
HOUSE

CONNACHAIR

MAD ANNIE'S
HOUSE

FLORA'S
HOUSE

MHAIRI'S
HOUSE

AN LAG

OISEVAL

EFFIE'S
HOUSE

FACTOR'S
HOUSE

AM
BLAID

COFFIN
CLEIT

STORM CLEIT

VILLAGE
BAY

HARRIS →

RUIVAL

DUN

0   0·5   1
KILOMETRES

Glossary

Characters

MHAIRI: pronounced Vah-Ree
CRABBIT MARY: Donald McKinnon's wife, crabbit meaning irritable or angry
BIG MARY: Mary Gillies
BIG GILLIES: Hamish, Mary and their children (as opposed to Effie and her father Robert Gillies; Robert and Hamish are brothers)

Dialect

BLACKHOUSE: a traditional, single-storey, grass-roofed dwelling
BLOODS: youngbloods; local youths
BLUFF: a cliff, headland or hill with a broad, steep face
BOTHY: a basic shelter or dwelling, usually made of stone or wood
BROSE: a kind of porridge
CATCH A SUPPER: to be scolded
CEILIDH: traditional Scottish dance event
CLEIT: a stone storage hut or bothy, only found on St Kilda
CRAGGING: climbing a cliff or crag; a CRAGGER is a climber
CREEL: a large basket with straps, used for carrying cuts of peat

CROTAL: a lichen used for making dye

DINNER: taken at lunchtime

DREICH: dreary, bleak (to describe weather)

DRUGGET: a coarse fabric

EEJIT: fool; idiot

EIGHTSOME: a Scottish reel

EVENING NEWS: daily walk down the street sharing news

FANK: a walled enclosure for sheep, a sheepfold

HOGGET: an older lamb, but one that is not yet old enough to be mutton

LAZYBEDS: parallel banks of ridges with drainage ditches between them; a traditional, now mostly extinct method of arable cultivation

PARLIAMENT: the daily morning meetings on St Kilda, outside crofts five and six, where chores were divvied up for the day

ROUP: a livestock sale

SMACK: boat

SOUTERRAIN: an underground chamber or dwelling

STAC: a sea stack (a column of rock standing in the sea) usually created as a leftover after cliff erosion

STRIPPING THE COW/EWE: milking a cow or sheep

SWEE: an iron arm and hook fitted inside a chimney for hanging pots above the fire

TEA AND A PIECE: tea and fruit cake

TUP: a ram; a ewe that has been mated with can be called TUPPED

WAULKING: a technique to finish newly woven tweed, soaking and beating it

He goes long barefoot that waits for dead men's shoes.

Old Scottish proverb

Prologue

26 October 1930

Casino de Paris

Flora sat on the slim perch, her legs reaching down in an elegant point as she swung back and forth, high above the stage. The jet beads of her bodysuit glimmered in the lights, the turquoise tail feathers behind her, resplendent. This was her favourite of all the songs she performed, the closest in nature to the melancholy ballads of home, and she felt her voice soar effortlessly, high above the flute and first violin. If she were to close her eyes, she might almost be able to persuade herself that she was still in the green, blanketing grasslands of St Kilda, where the sheep grazed beneath vaulted skies. She might hear the echoes of her girlhood friends, laughing in the byres; she might glimpse her parents walking to the tiny kirk as the pale sun set on another day; she might see her lover run up a frozen slope . . .

But this was no airy, stormy paradise. She was enclosed in a red velvet womb. The air was thick with perfume and smoke; taffetas ruffling as ladies stirred; gentlemen coughing in their starched shirts. Even in the darkness, Paris had its own signatures.

1

She swung higher in the jewelled birdcage, a whimsical creature enchanting them all. From this vantage point above the lights, she could look out upon the sea of faces and see every single pair of eyes trained upon her. She didn't need their applause; their open-mouthed wonder told her she was a star. All the pain, loss and heartbreak of the past months had led her here and now Paris lay at her feet, vanquished. But the dream she had stepped into was not her dream.

Her gaze swept lightly over the crowd like a chiffon scarf, falling suddenly upon a face she had never expected to see again. A man from her past, a lover from the mists, he walked inside her shadow, leaving footprints on her soul. He watched intently as she swung above him, a bird of paradise in a parliament of crows.

But he sank from her sight into the white glare of the footlights, gone again by the time she re-emerged.

Lost to her, he was the ghost she could not catch.

Just as she was the woman he could not save.

Chapter One

8 August 1929

Village Bay, St Kilda

Flora swept the hearth, the stone floor cool against her hands and knees as she tipped the ashes into the bucket. Even from inside the cottage, she was well aware of the progress the visitors were making up the street. She could tell from the ripple of excited voices and shy laughter that the villagers were performing the roles that had become something of a ritual whenever a tourist ship dropped anchor in the bay – Mad Annie and Ma Peg knitting socks at a ferocious speed as they sat on their stools; Crabbit Mary stoically carding the wool with her signature frown; Donald McKinnon and Hamish Gillies hauling boulders as they made repairs to one of the ancient cleits. The younger men made a show of strutting about with coils of rope looped over their shoulders, hands stuffed in their pockets, as if they might leap down a cliff at any given moment; time and tides permitting, they would hope to be urged by the visiting captain to give his guests one of their renowned climbing exhibitions. Only the dogs moved with any unselfconsciousness, but then, they cared little for the coins that crossed palms for these small displays of St Kildan life.

3

It had been a successful summer in that regard, the fine weather and calm seas bringing in the rich and the curious by the dozen, and the islanders had built up a small cache of coins that could be used at some point on the neighbouring isles. Though there were no shops or commerce of any kind here, over on Lewis, Harris and North Uist – some thirty-eight miles distant – there were markets, stores and farmers willing to trade, especially given that the landlord's factor was so intransigent on his punishing terms.

'Flora, quick now,' her mother Christina said, rushing back into the kitchen with a flustered look. 'Give me that pail, they're almost here.'

Flora sat back on her heels and saw her mother holding out the broom. 'How many of them are there?' she sighed, getting to her feet and swapping the bucket for the sweeping brush, knowing exactly what was to be done.

'Eight or nine, Old Fin thinks, but you know how his counting is.'

Flora moved past her mother and stood in the doorway, glancing down the wide grassy path towards the approaching party. Six people.

'Eeesht,' Christina tutted, reaching for the brush and trying to smooth the thick black braid that hung down Flora's back; she had taken little care with it this morning and fine wisps sprouted from her hairline. 'And, look, you've soot all over y' face.' Her mother reached up to smooth it away but appeared to succeed only in smudging it across her cheek. 'Och!'

'Not now, Ma,' Flora said under her breath. 'They're almost here.'

Her mother fell back into the shadows as Flora began to sweep the flat rock that served as their front doorstep. Her younger siblings were at their lessons in the schoolhouse, her

4

father and elder brother David up on Connachair, so the cottage was quiet and relatively calm for once.

With her head down as she worked, Flora saw several pairs of smart leather shoes step into her field of vision. She saw the sun glint off the nylon stockings one of the ladies wore, the swirl of punched leather decorating a pair of brogues, and she gave one or two more quick brushes before slowly straightening.

'Good morning,' she said politely, in English, for the tourists rarely spoke Gaelic, the language of the islanders. Six faces smiled back, that look of momentary surprise in their expressions as they took in the sight of her. It wasn't a phenomenon she could explain clearly. There were no mirrors on the isle, save in the reverend's house, and her only sense of herself was based off what she could glean from standing in the bay on a calm day, but there seemed to be something in the nuance of her features that set her apart – whether it was the curve of her appled cheeks, the fleshiness of her mouth or the flash of her green eyes she couldn't be sure, but people stared at her with an intensity that often seemed to embarrass them afterwards. Regardless, it had its benefits, and she allowed herself a small smile as she saw the older gentleman of the group reach for his camera.

'I say . . . would you be so kind as to oblige us with a photograph?' he asked. Grey-whiskered and pale, with a slight palsy to his hand, he held up the small box which had caused such fear when the first tourists began to visit. Flora remembered her own grandmother gathering her skirts and running back into the cottage in fright when one was first set on legs and pointed at her.

'Of course, sir,' she said, assuming her customary position on the threshold of the low stone cottage, her hands resting on the top of the broom, chin tilted slightly and her right hip jutting to ensure something of her shape was captured beneath her thick drugget skirt.

She didn't smile too brightly for the photograph, partly because the reverend didn't approve of 'overt' joy, but also because she was aware of the two young men in the party watching her. As was typical, they drank her in like a cool glass of water, eyes scrutinizing as if her beauty was a mathematical equation that could be solved if they just knew the formula. Without looking at either of them directly, she established that one of them was shorter and more immediately attractive, with bright blond hair, a cleft chin and an intensity of focus that bordered on impolite. The other was drawn in paler colours: light brown hair, hazel eyes, a close-clipped beard and a way of standing with his shoulders pulled back that suggested a restrained nature. As the camera flashed, she decided they didn't seem like brothers; something in the way they stood together suggested friendship, not brotherhood. The young women, though – eighteen and thirteen at a guess, standing close by one another, heads inclined in the same manner – had to be sisters?

'And perhaps another one with us all?' the gentleman asked.

'As you wish, sir.'

The man glanced across at the older woman she took to be his wife. 'It will be interesting to be able to show one of us with the natives, don't you think, dear?'

'Hmm,' his wife breathed, unsmiling. 'But then, who shall take the picture?'

Flora opened her mouth to offer her mother's services – it might mean another coin – but the brown-haired man stepped forward.

'I shall,' he said, one hand outstretched to receive the Kodak.

6

'But, James, then you shan't be in the picture,' the older of the two young women said.

'I think the world will survive that, Sophia,' he said simply.

Flora's eyes swept over the young woman who had spoken, as the group assembled around her. She was wearing what Flora knew to be called a cloche hat – very fashionable – and a lavender coat with a dropped waist and a pea-green ribbon detail; her shoes were cut low at the front and there was a thin strap holding them on. Flora remembered too late that she was still barefoot – the islanders only ever wore boots in the very deepest depths of winter, or when visitors arrived – and she tried to curl her toes under, certain they must be blackened with mud, dirt and soot.

The man called James seemed to see the movement because he glanced up from the camera momentarily, his gaze dropping to her feet and a tiny smile flickering over his lips before he lowered his head again and told them all to say 'cheese'. It was a custom Flora didn't understand – what did cheese have to do with a photograph? – and she simply stared straight into the lens, wondering what it was he could see in that dark circle. She felt aware of the blond man by her right shoulder, standing so close she could feel his breath on her hair.

The camera flashed again and she felt herself released.

'Thank you, miss. It's kind of you to oblige us,' the older man said, reaching into his pocket and pulling out a few coins. Flora eyed them dully as he counted them out. Money bought treasures back where they lived, but here it would go towards a hoe or a sack of potatoes.

'Yes, you're very kind,' the blond man said, catching her eye. 'What is your name, miss?'

She looked at him and saw her own usual confidence reflected in his eyes. She could tell he was a man also used to second looks and lingering stares, and she felt the energetic spar between them. 'Flora MacQueen.'

'Flora MacQueen,' he repeated, enunciating the words roundly as if liking the weight of them in his mouth. 'Well, Miss MacQueen, we shall be sure to tell everyone your name when we recount our travels and show them these pictures.'

'As you please, sir,' she replied. She kept her tone diffident, but it was difficult to look away from him, and the moment began to draw out. The women of the group had their backs to them as they trod carefully over the smooth stones onto the street, and as the stare held, Flora had to force herself to break it and turn from him, if only because she sensed her mother standing in the shadows. She knew she'd catch a supper if she was caught being bold.

'Come along now, Edward,' the older woman said, glancing back finally, and he – the blond man – smiled as if something had been confirmed for him. He tapped a finger to his temple, doffing an imaginary cap, as he took his leave from her.

'Thank you again, Miss MacQueen,' the older man said, tipping the coins into her hand.

'Enjoy your trip, sir,' she murmured, her hands clasping the top of the broom handle as, enviously, she watched them go. She felt their perfumed presence withdraw, leaving her alone on the stone step. Their privilege was careless and lightly worn in the short length of the young woman's coat and high heels; in the younger girl's dress embroidered with colours impossible to find here. She watched Edward's athletic stride as he sauntered off, his hands in his pockets, and felt something of her power return as he glanced back several times with a rapacious grin. James, the quiet one, didn't look around. His back straight, he walked on as if he'd never laid eyes on her; as if she was forgotten already.

8

She frowned, but when Edward looked round once more, he winked, his eyes sparkling with unspoken compliments that put the smile back on her face.

'How much did they give you?' Christina asked, emerging from the gloom a few moments later.

'A shilling and sixpence.'

'Generous,' her mother said. 'I hope they'll be as good to Ma Peg.'

Ma Peg fared as joint favourite on the island when it came to picture requests; her mother said it was down to their nominal matriarch representing the 'true' St Kildan spirit to the outsiders. In Flora's case, by contrast, it was generally thought she was so striking, the visitors needed evidence of it, proof almost, as if she were a siren or selkie.

'Hm, that young fellow was certainly full o' himself.'

'He's just confident.'

'Cocksure is what he is,' her mother muttered, taking the coins and disappearing back inside the house.

Flora followed after her, watching her drop the coins into the old glass bottle on the shelf that served as their bank.

'G'mornin'.'

They looked up as Effie swung in, the coil of rope looped over her shoulder like the rest of the craggers. Poppit, Effie's brown-and-white collie, lay down at the door, nose between her paws as she watched her mistress from the threshold.

'Eff,' Flora smiled, relaxing at the sight of her friend. She was dressed in her late brother's trousers and shirt, as usual, the cuffs rolled up and her skinny brown ankles sticking out. If Flora had thought her own feet were mucky, it was nothing to the state of Effie's. 'Where've you been? I didn't see you at the burn.'

'Feeding Tiny.' Tending the bull was a sought-after position, earning the keeper an annual one-pound sum which could be paid in cash or negotiated off the rents. It was a job that usually alternated between households, but ever since her brother John's death in a climbing accident two years earlier, leaving Effie as their family's sole provider, a tacit agreement had been reached among the village men that the role would fall to her each year. 'I saw the new boat come in.'

'Aye. You getting ready to go up to the Gap? They're big tippers, this bunch.'

'Maybe. Hamish says there's a big swell round the east side that's too rough for the smack just now. He's waiting on it to settle down first.' Effie paced the small room restlessly, unable to sit still. She was like a small squally wind, always blowing through houses and tearing over the moors.

'Well, then I hope it does, because having seen their clothes, I can assure you they'll not have sea legs. Anything short of glassy will be problematic for them.'

'Ugh, that would be so unfair,' Effie protested.

'Unfair?'

'Aye. You get coins to just stand there and look fine; I have to actually work for mine – *and* I have to depend on the weather in order for the tourists to row round to see it.' She gave a shrug. 'Not fair.'

'I'd hardly call it work!' Flora scoffed, refusing to be riled. Effie loved nothing more than a disagreement; she missed having her brother to scrap with, and her home with her lame father was always quiet, always still, these days. 'You're never happier than when you're swinging off your rope.'

There was a pause as Effie considered this. She was one of the finest climbers on the isle: strong but light, agile, dextrous and daring. Even though strictly speaking cragging was a man's job, in the Gillies household there was no one else to catch the birds and retrieve the eggs they depended upon, and neither Effie's pride nor her father's would suffer relying on the charity of their neighbours.

'Aye, true enough,' she conceded, letting her indignation go in the next breath. If she was tempestuous, she was also good-natured and never one to bear a grudge.

Flora's mother walked past them with the boiling pot. 'Chatting again, you two?' she tutted.

'Shall I take it for you, Ma?' Flora sighed, rolling her eyes. She was forever chided for being workshy.

'No. I've to speak to Big Mary anyway. But you can go down to the rocks and fetch me some crotal. I want to do some dyeing of the bolts today.'

'Aye,' Flora nodded. She pulled the lichen cutter from the clay pot; it looked like a regular spoon, save for having one half of the scoop sliced off to leave a sharp, straight edge for scraping. 'Come with me?' she asked Effie.

'Sure. I'm keeping out of Da's way.'

'His hip's bad?'

Effie rolled her eyes too in confirmation as they wandered back out into the sunshine together. Flora was unable to resist stealing a glance up the street to see where the visitors were now. She caught sight of them outside the MacKinnons', where Rachel, Mhairi's mother, was giving a spinning wheel demonstration.

Flora looked for the signature flash of Mhairi's red hair, but she was nowhere to be seen. 'No Mhairi?'

'Up at the lazybeds with Molly,' Effie said, glancing up the street too.

'Ah.' Flora's gaze snagged on the head of bright blond hair. He was far less interested in the spinning wheel than his

11

female companions – Mother? Sisters? – and was trying to engage the attention of one of the dogs instead. Flora smiled, seeing how he teased it with a buttercup stem, the dog resolutely ignoring him.

'Och, no,' Effie groaned, following her line of sight. 'Not another conquest.'

'I'd hardly call it a conquest, Eff,' Flora sighed, tossing her braid off her shoulder. 'He paid to take my photograph, that's all.'

'That's never all. I suppose he's in love with you now?'

'Not even close. We exchanged ten words. Less.'

'Mm.' Effie gave a tut and shook her head as they walked. 'He looks like trouble, that blond one with the—' She prodded her own chin with her finger. 'You know what Mad Annie always says: a dimple on the chin, the devil within.'

'Annie says a lot of things. Besides, I should be so lucky to experience his devilment,' Flora said with a wicked smile of her own.

'It's like a sport to you, teasing all these men.'

Flora gave a coquettish smile as she tossed her hair back. 'Well, I suppose it does provide a *little* amusement.'

'Ha. You won't be so amused when someone turns the tables on you one of these days.'

'Never.' She had no interest at all in any of the marriageable men on the isle, and the tourists were always gone from here far too quickly for any superficial attraction to develop into something more substantial.

They walked down the grass to the beach together. The tide was out, the waves slumping on the shore with a midsummer indolence, as if wearied by the endless sun. Flora looked out across the bay. It was the only viable landing point on the isle, the protected body of water created by the curving embrace of Dun, on the west, and the hulking shoulder of Oiseval Mountain on the east. The window between the two landmasses looked out to an empty horizon, only occasionally punctuated by a passing fishing boat or breached whale.

Flora sighed. An entire world existed beyond that blue line: a world where motor cars and talking pictures and electric lights were taken for granted; where people could buy their dinner and not hunt for it; where hair could be styled and coloured, and clothes didn't have to be made from wool they had woven, from sheep they had first plucked. There was a world beyond that blue line where ease and comfort and beauty were givens, not luxuries.

She looked more closely at the yacht that had brought in this Edward and James and the rest of their party. It was far from the biggest they'd seen, but it still glistened with the patina of moneyed privilege, and the chandlery clinked melodically against the masts as the boat rocked gently in the bay. It was a bright, warm day but there was a sharp, gusting wind that threatened to build.

They began working at the exposed rocks, Flora using the spoon, Effie using her nails to pull and scratch at the tufts of ochre lichen that trailed over them – her hands were incredibly strong from climbing. They stuffed what they could find into their deep skirt pockets as they chatted.

'Hm, slim pickings here,' Effie muttered after a while. 'Everyone's had the same idea.'

'Aye,' Flora agreed, sitting back on her heels. Her mother would not be impressed; there was barely enough here to steep in a pot of tea, much less dye a bolt of tweed.

'You'll need to go further out. Over there will be good plunder, I reckon,' Effie said, jerking her chin towards a point beyond the featherstore, towards the Oiseval headland. 'The rocks are too slippery for the likes of Crabbit Mary. She'll not risk her neck for some moss.'

'Come on, then,' Flora sighed, gathering her skirt.

But Effie shook her head. 'I'd better get back and check whether this climb is happening. We need the coins.'

They parted at the featherstore, Effie handing over her paltry harvest, and Flora made her way towards the rocks. The low tide meant everything was extra slippery, thick strands of frilled kelp draped on slick boulders, and she hitched her skirt up and scooted on her bottom to a point just above the water line. Humming to herself, she began to scrape and scratch again, oblivious to the crabs scuttling away and the fulmars and shearwaters wheeling overhead.

She had been working for an hour or so when she heard voices on the water and looked up to see the visitors being rowed to the yacht. Leaving already? She was disappointed.

Also surprised. She looked out to sea and saw the heave of a swell rising up, white horses in the open water beyond. If getting ahead of the rough sea was their intention, that time had already passed. Hamish Gillies and Norman Ferguson were rowing them out with their typical vigour, and she stopped working as she saw that mop of bright blond hair again; Edward was leaning back on his elbows, his face tipped to the sky as he basked in the sunshine. He looked like a man for whom life was jocular and affable. The higher-pitched voices of the younger girl and the young woman in the lavender coat came to her ear, though she couldn't make out their words.

Flora watched as they reached the vessel and their captain affixed the ladder. Embarkment was rarely an elegant process and she was vaguely amused as she saw the ladies flounder, arms outstretched, hands grasping as they squealed. Edward, by comparison, bounded aboard, disappearing below deck almost immediately.

Flora felt a stab of disappointment that he didn't even glance back to shore, as if for a final sighting of her. They were leaving early, far earlier than most visitors; the journey here was so long and arduous, most visitors were in no rush to get back on the water again for several hours, if not days.

'Oh . . . Miss MacQueen, isn't it?'

She whipped round, startled by the polished voice that – even without looking – she knew didn't belong here.

'Mr . . .' She stared back at the quiet man and realized she hadn't spotted his absence on the boat, her gaze fixed upon Edward.

'. . . Callaghan.'

'You're . . . but you're . . .' Confused, she swung a pointed finger vaguely between him and the boat.

'Yes. They've gone for a rest. It was a . . . difficult crossing.'

'Oh.' She looked back at the yacht, all passengers now on board and her neighbours rowing back for the shore. She realized her bare legs were on full display and she threw her skirts down with rare modesty.

He cleared his throat. 'Unfortunately, the captain doesn't think we'll be able to leave this evening after all, so they've decided to clean up and eat something before coming back to shore for a more . . . comprehensive experience.'

Flora's eyes narrowed at his choice of words. Comprehensive experience? Did they think they would be dining with Vikings? Walking with dinosaurs? Did they believe the islanders' hospitality was a given? Plenty of times unwelcome visitors had been left on the water, sometimes in the wildest of weathers, the village men refusing to launch the smack to bring them in. When the reverend himself had first arrived,

15

he'd fallen foul of Old Fin, castigating him for his pipe-smoking, and had had to unload his belongings himself in a rough sea when the other men had taken sides.

She sighed, feeling sanguine today and deciding to let his condescension wash over her instead. She glanced out to open water again. 'The sea does look restless.'

'Yes. The captain believes there'll be a window tomorrow.'

'To escape us?' She arched an eyebrow.

'Well, for the ladies' sake, we must err on the side of caution. I don't think any of them would describe themselves as adventurers.'

'How disappointing for you.'

He looked puzzled. 'That they're not adventurous?'

'That you're stuck here overnight.'

'Not at all. I'm rather pleased.'

'You are?' Flora tipped her head to the side, regarding him more closely. Though he had none of Edward's bold, flirtatious nature, there was a look of interest in his eyes that she knew well; it came and went like a sputtering flame, but it was there nonetheless. She preened a little. It had been a bruise to her ego to be overlooked by him earlier, but he probably understood he could never compete against his friend's charisma. 'And why are you so pleased about staying here?' she asked coyly, though she already knew the answer.

'Now I can look for some fossils.'

There was a pause. 'Fossils?'

'Yes, it's a hobby of mine,' he nodded, looking out across the rocks. 'Fossil-hunting.'

'. . . I see.'

'I expect you know the archipelago is part of a volcanic caldera?' His eyes gleamed with academic delight as he glanced down at her.

'Aye,' she murmured, although the details had never interested her.

'The volcano was active in the Paleogenic period, producing intrusive igneous rocks. By definition they're largely crystalline so I'm hopeful of finding some quartz or feldspar while I'm here.'

'I see,' she said again. Her voice was deliberately flat but he appeared not to notice.

'I asked one of your neighbours where I might find the best place for rockfalls and they said just below McKinnon's Stone, past the featherstore. Am I in the right place?'

Flora scowled at him – she had never spent a single moment of her life considering the rocks on her island home – as he stared back at her with a placid smile. How could he be so oblivious to her affront?

'McKinnon's Stone is further along, over there.' She pointed in the direction of the headland, completely dotted with rocks, boulders, chippings and scree. If it was a distinctive landmark he was looking for, he wouldn't find it.

'I see . . .' James Callaghan looked across for a moment. 'Over there, then . . . somewhere . . .' He looked back at her with a baffled smile that begged for more assistance, but she offered nothing further. 'Very well, then, I shall head in that direction . . . I apologize for disturbing you.'

'You didn't disturb me,' she muttered, turning back indignantly to the rocks at her feet.

'No?' He hesitated. 'What is it you're doing here?'

With a sigh, she reached into her bulging pockets and pulled out a clutch of ochre-coloured lichen. 'Fetching crotal for dyeing the tweed.'

'That sounds fun.'

She shot him a withering look. 'Not really.'

'Oh.'

She relented a little; her pretty pouts usually elicited a kind of desperation in men, but her tart manner was gaining no traction against his benign demeanour. He seemed genuinely oblivious to her sulk. 'It's getting harder and harder to find, is all,' she said. 'It takes a long time to grow, and we all need to use it for the rents.'

'The rents?'

'Aye, the tweeds we weave. People don't want brown cloth. The fashions are for colours now.' There was a little bite to the last words as she remembered the young woman's lilac coat.

'That must be quite a pressure, with it being a finite resource.'

She shrugged again as she began to scrape with the crotal spoon. What did he care? 'It's the same with the peats – getting harder to come by; but I'm sure we'll manage.'

The bell began ringing from the schoolhouse, signalling the children's dinner time. Flora's tummy grumbled but she was used to that and didn't stir from her position on the rocks.

He half turned away, then turned back again. 'Miss MacQueen, I wonder,' he mused. 'Would it be helpful if I were to pay you to be my guide in looking for this McKinnon's Stone?'

'Helpful?' Flora bristled. 'I don't need your charity, Mr Callaghan.'

'No, I know. I only meant, well . . . you'd be doing *me* the favour, actually. I've no more idea of where to look than I had before, and I wouldn't feel quite so bad for wasting your time if I were at least able to pay for it.'

She stared at him. He didn't seem to understand that most

men, desperate to find any opportunity to be with her, would gladly pay her to walk with them. Instead, he was paying her to help him find rocks?

'I'm afraid I can't. I need to bring this back to my mother.' She patted at her bulging pockets. 'She'll be waiting on it.'

'I see.' He looked back towards the village; the children were streaming out of the schoolhouse, eager for their dinner. '. . . Unless one of them could take it back for you?'

She looked over at the children, then back at him quizzically. 'I don't—'

'Quickly,' he said, with a click of his fingers. 'Before they're gone.'

Flora felt her temper flare at the gesture, his peremptory attitude; she was beginning to think she'd got him all wrong – he wasn't quiet but sullen; not restrained but haughty; not dignified but arrogant.

'Would a pound suffice?' he asked, noticing the flush spreading over her cheeks.

A *pound*? For her to take him to McKinnon's Stone? She didn't know what treasures he hoped to find there but she knew he'd be sorely disappointed; anything of value would have been discovered by the islanders long before now.

Not that that was her problem.

She turned back to the schoolchildren.

'Bonnie!' she called.

Her six-year-old sister turned at the sound, running over to them without a second thought. 'What is it, Flossie?' she asked in their customary Gaelic. 'Who is that?'

'A pompous, arrogant dullard,' Flora muttered back in the same, crouching down on her heels to Bonnie's level and pushing her hair back behind her ear. There was a smudge of chalk on her cheek and Flora wetted her finger to clean it off. There were twelve years between them, but Flora doted on her little sister.

'Why does he keep looking at you?'

Flora sighed. 'Because he's also rude.'

Callaghan intruded.

'Bonnie, is it?' he asked, enunciating the English words carefully and dropping down into a crouch. 'May I ask for your help?'

Bonnie blinked back at him, eyes wide, silent as he held up a silver sixpence.

'If I gave you my shiniest coin, would you take the crotal in . . .' He glanced at Flora. ' . . . Flossie's pocket and deliver it to your mother?'

Flora felt her cheeks burn. Perhaps he had simply, fortuitously, picked up the word 'Flossie' and understood it to be her nickname, but something about the look in his eyes told her he had understood her perfectly well.

She swallowed as she emptied her pockets, stuffing the crotal carefully into her little sister's cupped hands. 'Be careful, now,' she said. 'And watch your feet when you're walking. It's taken me over an hour to gather this – I don't want to see it scattered all over the street when I get back.' She kissed Bonnie on the forehead.

'What shall I tell Mama?'

'That I'm showing one of the visitors McKinnon's Stone. He's looking for fossils and he's giving me a shiny coin too,' she said clearly. It was important her mother knew she was earning money, or else she'd set the young men of the village after them. The matter of Flora's 'honour' was taken very seriously indeed.

'Yes, Flossie,' Bonnie said, wheeling on her heel and running off, patently taking no care at all about where she put her feet.

The Lost Lover

Flora looked back at James, to find him already staring.

'You speak Gaelic,' she said stiffly, after a moment's pause.

'Yes. My father insisted I learned . . . Surprisingly useful,' he said after a pause, no hint of levity in his voice.

She stared back at him, holding her chin a little higher. She would not apologize. She would not. He had been rude and insulting throughout their conversation. What did she care if he had caught her doing the same?

'Shall we then?' she asked, beginning to lead the way to the headland path.

He simply nodded in reply, though that ghost smile seemed to tiptoe behind his eyes again, determined not to be seen.

Chapter Two

They walked for a short stretch in silence, turning their backs to the village and heading towards the headland.

'Was it your father that I met earlier?' she asked in a tight voice.

'No. That's Mr Rushton. Gerald. And his wife, Virginia; and their two daughters, Sophia and Martha.'

She looked at him sharply – the omission was conspicuous by its absence. 'And what about Edward?'

His eyebrow inclined slightly as if the word sounded foreign coming from her mouth. Or perhaps he was amazed she had remembered. 'Edward is his son, yes. We went up to Cambridge together.'

'So you're a friend, travelling with them?'

'Yes.' His mouth parted as if he were about to add something, but the words appeared to fall back again in the next instant and she wondered what he had been about to say, what other titbits he would have added as to why he was travelling with this family. She wondered whether it had anything to do with Miss Sophia Rushton, she with her fashionable clothes and daringly exposed, slender legs. Flora had caught the way the young woman had looked at him on the street earlier, her pout that he wasn't to be in the family photograph. Was a union hoped for between the two families

– or already arranged? It was of no interest to her, regardless; she was simply pleased to learn that it was Sophia and Edward who were siblings.

She felt a ripple of anticipation at the prospect of seeing him again. There was so little that could count as excitement here and she yearned for an adventure of her own, a torrid love affair with a handsome stranger. All the young men on the island were either like brothers or simply not an equal match, for she had a quick wit to match her beauty and a fast temper too. None of them could handle her and everyone knew it. But Edward Rushton – he had a vitality to him that echoed her own, and she felt the primal pull towards him of game recognizing game.

'Will they stay aboard for long, do you think?' she asked, looking over towards the yacht as they walked. She had pulled slightly ahead of him where the path narrowed.

'I doubt it. Edward's a restless spirit. Easily bored.'

'Really?' The upward lilt of the question betokened her interest, she thought – an invitation for him to elaborate and reveal more about his friend; he must have witnessed the flirtation between them earlier? But instead he kept turning towards the looming cliff face as they walked, more interested in examining the bluffs. More interested in *fossils*.

Flora led him further around the shoulder of the headland until they left the bay – and the yacht – behind and were looking out across open water towards the distant isles of Lewis and Harris, hidden on the other side of the horizon. If they walked around further still, they would see the large neighbouring isle of Boreray, where the St Kildans grazed their sheep; no doubt James Callaghan was as interested in sheep as he was in rocks. She wondered how different, how thrilling, this walk might be if it was Edward here instead and not his awkward friend.

Presently she stopped and pointed upwards. 'Well, there it is – McKinnon's Stone,' she sighed, indicating an unremarkable sharp-angled boulder that pointed from the earth like a tooth, several hundred feet above them. She watched as James's gaze took in the somewhat underwhelming sight – he would never have found it alone and certainly not from down here. It was more marginally distinctive when seen from above.

They were silent for several moments and she wondered exactly what treasures he thought he might find here. Rocks were just rocks to her, something to sit on, to throw or to build up to create a shelter.

'How did it come by the name?' he asked, squinting against the sun.

'A series of unfortunate accidents for that family, in that spot,' she said darkly. 'They won't go near it now, though the last McKinnon as died there was at least thirty years past.'

He looked back at her, so tall that he seemed to peer down his nose at her. 'Are your people superstitious, Miss MacQueen?'

Her eyes narrowed again at his choice of words. Was he trying to offend her? '*My people* are sensible, Mr Callaghan. They don't repeat stupid mistakes. Death is far too easy in a place like this as it is.' She could hear her own mother's indignation in her voice.

'I can well imagine,' he agreed, scanning the immense, vertical sea cliffs and seemingly unaware of her arch tone. 'Although I suppose the upside of that is having a vivid sense – an appreciation, if you like – of being alive?'

He smiled so suddenly, the reflex so bright and unexpected, that she found herself unwittingly smiling back, all indignation momentarily forgotten; his eyes caught hers and she felt an intense 'locking' between them, as if they were only now seeing one another for the first time. He had none of his friend's dazzle, but she supposed he had a brooding intensity that was appealing in its own way. 'Maybe, aye,' she admitted, though she had never considered it before now.

He looked out to sea. 'That's an awareness I try to cherish in myself . . . although it's not always easy back home. Too much ready comfort dulls the spirit.'

'I think it sounds wonderful over there,' she sighed. She loved the idea of ready comfort.

He looked back at her, as if surprised by the sentiment. 'It has its charms, of course. Modernization is happening at a furious pace and there's no question it's making life easier for the many. But sometimes I wonder if with every advance we make in mechanization or technology, we lose something vital of ourselves? That connectedness with the natural world, our animal spirits? Whereas here, you're so free; it's you versus the elements. Versus Mother Nature. God himself.'

'*Him*self?' She gave a dismissive laugh. 'You think God is a man, do you? Mad Annie would take you to task over that.'

'Mad Annie?' He looked vaguely amused.

'One of the village elders. She doesn't believe in the patriarchy. She says women are superior to men.'

'How so?'

'She says our brains are sharper, we learn better, we tolerate pain better, we're more resilient and we can both give life and support life with our bodies. She says God wouldn't have given those superior gifts to women if God was a man, he'd have given them to men. Therefore, God is a woman.'

'I see.' He laughed, the sound buoyant and deep. 'And what does your church minister say to this?'

'Och, they have terrible fights over it, but they clash on everything,' she shrugged. 'Annie never goes to church anyway, so she doesn't care what he thinks. She does everything he deplores, I think mainly to spite him – she drinks whisky, smokes a pipe and spits like a camel.'

He arched an eyebrow. 'Have you ever seen a camel spit?'

'I've never seen a camel,' she admitted. 'But a fisherman told us about them once after Annie spat at his feet for flirting with her.'

'She didn't want him flirting with her?'

'She's a widow. She says she's done her time with men in this lifetime and deserves her peace.'

He laughed, again the sound earthier and more substantial than she would have expected for a man who liked fossils. 'She doesn't sound like she should be crossed. How will I know her when I meet her?'

'Oh, trust me – you'll know her when you meet her.' She pulled a face that made him grin again.

'I'll make sure to have my wits about me, then. And strictly no flirting.'

Flora managed to bite her tongue in time. Surely that was a joke? James Callaghan could no sooner flirt than she could fly.

She sat on a smooth boulder while he began to move around a small area below McKinnon's Stone. Squatting on his heels, he sorted through the stones that lay scattered, many of them fragments of larger rocks that had splintered on their fall from the bluffs. He examined each one closely, running his thumb over the surfaces, checking seams and fracture lines, before discarding them and moving on to the next.

She watched, somehow intrigued by his endeavours. His

26

profile was handsome and she felt it a pity that it was wasted on such an awkward man. He had moments of charisma, flashes of magnetism . . .

He glanced up, as if sensing her stare, before looking back at the stone held between his thumb and forefinger. 'You, er . . . you said earlier, you liked the sound of life on the mainland. I'm afraid I rudely cut you off with my interlocutions on the joys of life here. Have you been over to the mainland?'

'No.'

He seemed surprised. 'Really? Not ever?'

'Never. But I long to see it.'

'Hm; it might disappoint you.'

'No, never. I know it wouldn't.'

'How do you know?'

'Because sometimes the captains give us colour magazines that their passengers have discarded and my friends and I pore over them in the byres in the evening, when our parents think we're knitting.' She smiled, remembering Effie's shock at an illustration advertising ladies' girdles; such a contraption had looked more like some kind of advanced climbing sling to her eye, but Flora had simply loved how it transformed the woman's shapely figure into something even more nuanced.

'And what do you like about them so much?'

'We see the fashions and the make-up and the way the ladies set their hair.' She smoothed her own. 'Here, the wind is so fierce, we have to wear scarves to keep it from whipping us. The idea of hair that doesn't move . . .' She sighed wistfully, staring dreamily into the distance, just as a gust – as if taunting her – twisted around her and swung her thick braid.

KAREN SWAN

'I see. So you yearn for hair that doesn't move,' he repeated. 'What else?'

'Gramophones.'

'You like music?' He placed a stone upon another one and began rhythmically tapping it with a smaller, sharper one, like a tool.

'I love singing. Dancing, too, sometimes.' She watched him work.

'Only sometimes?'

'We can't do it much here, only in times of celebration. The reverend doesn't believe in too much festivity. He says it froths the spirit and wakens the devil.'

'Does he now?' James murmured, a slight frown on his brow, but not stopping his endeavours. 'How much store do you put by his words?'

'He's the most influential man on the isle.'

He nodded. 'Much to Mad Annie's chagrin, I should imagine.'

'Exactly,' she murmured, pleased he had heard the distinction. 'He's the most influential man and she's the most influential woman.'

'Well, then, perhaps she too would like life on the mainland.'

'Why do you say that?'

'Because that's the way the winds of change are blowing – more rights for the working man, and for women. The reverend would find himself with a smaller congregation on the other side of the water, I can assure you.'

'So then, now I want to go even more.'

He glanced up at her; it was like sunlight bouncing off water. 'I'm sure one day you shall.'

'Oh, I know I shall,' she said with certainty.

'You do?'

28

She nodded. 'I was born here, but I've always had a sense I won't die here.'

He stopped tapping and sat back on his heels watching her. 'A sense? But you maintain you're not superstitious?'

'Don't mock me!' she gasped, grabbing a clutch of moss and throwing it at him.

'Your words, not mine,' he smiled, ducking.

She laughed, before catching herself and looking away quickly. She felt embarrassed by her sudden burst of playfulness. It was childish and unsophisticated.

'If it's superstitious you want, then you need to meet Jayne Ferguson, Norman's wife,' she said after a moment.

He widened his eyes dramatically. 'Is she a witch?'

'Not exactly.'

'Not *exactly*?' A wry note spun off the words.

'She's got the gift of second sight. Well, they call it a gift, but it's more of a curse.'

'And what does the reverend make of *that*? Does he believe in the phenomenon?'

'It's not a matter of choosing to believe it or not. It's irrefutable,' she shrugged. 'Jayne's never wrong. When she has one of her dreams or visions, sure as eggs that person will drop dead within three days.'

James stopped knocking the rocks together, his amusement dropping from his face. 'How terrible for her.'

'It really is; it's a burden. She keeps to herself mainly. I think it's a way of protecting herself.'

'Does she ever reveal her dreams? It must be a terrible ethical dilemma?'

Flora shook her head. 'Never beforehand. Sometimes they're . . . so indistinct, she says she can't fully understand what she's seeing.'

'Does she actually see the death? The manner of it?'

'No.'

'That's a pity.'

Flora looked at him, appalled. 'Why?'

'Because then perhaps she'd at least have some ability to prefigure it and help alter that person's actions – if it was an accidental death, for instance. It would give her some agency. It must be terrible to have to be so passive in that circumstance, just some helpless onlooker waiting for it to happen.'

Flora considered the point for a moment. 'I'm not sure she would interfere, even if she could. Jayne would see it as meddling with God's plan.'

'She might be right.' It was a moment before James spoke again, and Flora could see he was troubled by this revelation. 'I'm surprised she ever leaves her bed.'

'She takes herself off, most days. She's quite reclusive. I think she fears any marked change in her day-to-day behaviour might give her away, and it would be so terrible to accidentally reveal to someone that she had dreamt of them. Can you imagine?'

'Her husband's certainly a brave man. I'm not sure I'd want to lie in bed night after night next to someone who might at any moment foresee my death.'

'Hmph.' She rolled her eyes. 'Norman would be the easiest to trick of anyone on the isle.'

'Really?' He had resumed tapping at the stone. From where she was sitting, Flora could see a small seam was beginning to widen. 'Why?'

'He's brutish and has all the subtlety of an axe. Jayne's so gentle and meek, he never even notices her. Sometimes I think she could die in her chair and he wouldn't notice until she didn't get up for his dinner.'

30

James chuckled, but winced at the same time. He tapped harder. 'You're a sharp judge, Miss MacQueen. Your own husband must have dancing feet, keeping on his toes all the time.'

'I have no husband,' she said simply. 'Nor will I, from here.'

'No? But there must be one man, surely, who is sweet on you?'

Flora stared at him in disbelief. Did he honestly think . . . ? But he was looking back at her with such earnestness, she couldn't find words to fit to her temper.

Suddenly the stone split open and he looked down; a second later, his face fell with disappointment. He gave a sigh. Whatever it was he saw there, it wasn't what he'd hoped for. This had all been for naught and it all would be. There was no treasure on these isles.

'I'm afraid I shall need to head back,' she said, primly gathering her skirts. She had never been so offended. How could he think she had any trouble finding a man to fall in love with her? It was *stopping* them from falling for her that was the difficulty!

'. . . Yes, of course,' he muttered, looking up after a moment and making to move as well.

'It's quite all right. You can stay here. I can make my own way back just fine.' She knew she sounded peevish, but she couldn't help it. He agitated her from one moment to the next and she wanted to escape him. She had done what he'd asked her to do, hadn't she? She'd guided him to McKinnon's Stone. Let him pay her and be rid of him.

'Well, I've not brought my tools with me, so I think any further exploration here will be futile without them anyway.' He rose to his feet and returned to the path, blind to the exasperation on her face.

He kept the conversation flowing on the way back, asking her questions about herself and her family as if he was genuinely interested, when all she really wanted to tell him about was the many declarations of ardour she had received in her young life: the boys who had threatened to throw themselves over the top if she refused their proposals; men who wanted to prove themselves to her in fearsome trials; poems that had been left on her windowsill; posies of buttercups self-consciously handed over on the way to kirk; all those rich tourists offering coins to have their pictures taken with her . . . She wanted to tell him of each and every one, and yet she sensed that even if she did, he would look at her blankly, completely unaffected. He simply didn't care one way or another. He didn't see her the way other men did. What little interest he had in her seemed to focus on her thoughts rather than her face.

They walked back alongside the bay and into the shelving embrace of the village.

'There you are!' a voice thundered, stopping them both in their tracks. 'I've been looking all over for you.'

Flora felt a rush of relief as Edward jogged over from the featherstore, looking dynamic and uniquely happy to see them. She watched as he approached, wondering if his call had been to his friend, or to her.

'Miss MacQueen,' he beamed, resolving the query at a stroke by taking her hand in his and kissing it. As if she were a friend. '. . . James,' he said, straightening up. 'We wondered where you were. Sophia was quite concerned.'

James frowned. 'I don't know why. I had told Martha of my plans.'

'Very last-minute, though. I'd thought you were coming to the boat?'

James shrugged. 'I was planning to, but then I remembered

something I'd read about McKinnon's Stone and decided this was my chance to see it for myself.'

'McKinnon's Stone? What about it?'

'I wanted to look for fossils there.'

'*Fossils?* Since when—?'

Flora turned back to James, interrupting the two men, her chin in the air. 'You promised me a coin, Mr Callaghan.'

She caught his gaze and it took him a moment to react. 'Yes . . . Indeed I did, Miss MacQueen.' He reached into his pocket and pulled out the promised pound.

Flora bit her lip; it was far more than she deserved for such a trifling favour. In thanks – and to give him an example of her feminine powers – she smiled her most dazzling smile, the one that made every man fall. Surely he would see now that her being without a husband was not on account of any shortcomings *she* might possess . . . ? If he was blind to her charms, then he was blind alone.

In her peripheral vision, she saw Edward smile, but James looked back blankly, her efforts like sunrays sinking into mud.

'That was a short rest,' James said to his friend.

'Well, you know me, old boy, can't sit around for long. Especially when we've seemingly found the homeland of the famed sirens.' He arched an eyebrow provocatively at her, not aiming for subtlety in the least.

Flora immediately stood a little taller, though she allowed the compliment to pass without comment.

'Did everyone come back to shore?' James asked, casting around the bay.

'Me and the girls. My parents are still resting.' He was talking to James, but Edward didn't lift his eyes off Flora once. 'Sophia and Martha are having some knitting instruction with one of Miss MacQueen's pretty friends.'

33

'Oh. Who?' Flora asked.

'I didn't catch her name. Light brown hair, and a freckle just there.' He pointed to the high curve of his left cheek.

'Ah, that's Molly.'

'You sound relieved.'

'Well, I am. If it was Effie teaching knitting . . .' She pulled a face. 'Let's just say her own father says her blankets are only fit for wrapping the dead.'

Edward burst out laughing. 'He sounds a very droll fellow.'

'Sharp-tongued, for sure,' Flora smiled. 'But it's water off Effie's back. She doesn't care a hoot for knitting, only cragging.'

'Do *you* crag, Miss MacQueen?' he asked, slipping one hand into his trouser pocket.

Flora tipped her head to the side coquettishly. 'Do I look as if I do?'

'Indeed no. You look as if you should nibble on cake while dripping in pearls, with baby cherubim singing to you.'

She gave an astonished laugh and they stared at one another for a moment, recognizing that they had broken past manners into open flirtation. It had taken mere minutes. This rich, handsome man was already in her thrall.

'I say, would you care to walk along the beach with me?' Edward asked. 'I appreciate it must be the dullest thing on earth for you; you've probably walked it a thousand times, but I don't fancy the look of those hills and I find myself wanting to know everything about you.' He crooked his arm, inviting her to slip hers through. 'I promise, I won't hunt for fossils.'

Flora gave a sudden laugh, amused by the tease. 'Well, if you promise *that*,' she smiled, accepting his arm and throwing a careless look James Callaghan's way. Was he in any doubt of her powers now?

'Before you go,' James said to her quickly.

She waited, triumphant at last.

'Would you tell me where I might find Miss Ferguson?'

Flora blinked, feeling the sting of obsolescence. He made her feel like a fly buzzing a horse. '. . . Third house on the right.'

'Much obliged, Miss MacQueen,' he smiled, continuing along the path. 'Enjoy your walk.'

Chapter Three

The tide was coming in, but it would be several hours yet before the water kissed the rocks that topped the beach. They ambled along the sand slowly, the water running towards their feet before pulling back with gentle hisses.

Edward was forced to break into a trot to escape the foaming frill. 'I fear I'm overdressed,' he said, glancing at her bare feet before relinquishing her arm and bending down to untie his shoelaces.

Flora buried her toes in the sand, aware that shoes (and lack thereof) were a signifier of the chasm between their positions in life, as he pulled off his socks and rolled up his trousers to keep the cuffs dry. It was strange to see a part of his body that had been hidden by expensive tailoring and she couldn't help but stare at his pale, soft skin. Ready comfort, James had said.

He looked down too and wiggled his toes playfully, as if reading her thoughts.

'You somehow manage to look majestic barefoot, Miss MacQueen,' he grinned. 'Whereas I feel rather like a boy in short trousers again.'

'Not at all,' she smiled as they resumed walking. 'You look like a true cragger now.' But any small, sharp stone was enough to hobble him, and she walked ever taller.

'I had thought the craggers would be the most exciting aspect of our trip.'

'Oh?' she asked after a moment, hearing the unarticulated 'but' hanging in the air.

'Yes. They're widely renowned, your men. Their abilities on a rope are admired much further afield than London.'

'Well, that's pleasing to hear,' she said, although she didn't think the men would care one jot what far-off strangers thought of their climbing abilities. 'The men do so love to have their egos stroked.' She deliberately didn't prompt him to complete his statement, and as they walked in silence for a couple of moments, she felt him glance her way a couple of times.

'Of course, now that I've actually arrived, I see that super-human feats of strength and agility are as nothing to . . .'

'To?'

A wave rushed in, covering his feet and splashing his legs, but this time he didn't run. Instead he laughed again. 'Well . . . to your beauty, Miss MacQueen.'

'Mr Rushton, please,' she murmured, looking away as if both bored and offended.

'No, I don't think you quite understand. I'm not trying to flatter you. Your face, to you, is, I'm sure, simply your face; but I am a well-travelled man and I have never, in my twenty-five years, seen anyone as captivating as you.' He had a guileless bounding energy to him, like the younger dogs.

'If you say so. Though of course we both know you have no way to prove such a statement; for all I know, you say such things to every island girl you meet.' Her eyebrow arched to a perfect peak as she watched him begin to protest. She cut him off. 'And besides, little merit is given to such attributes here. A fair face is no good against a winter storm or a failed harvest.'

'Ah – but a fair face can be the ticket to a good marriage.'

She didn't reply immediately, but her heart had skipped a beat at his quick words. 'A good marriage?' she queried.

'A financially advantageous marriage. You must know that we men are simple creatures, and the richer a man is, the simpler his needs? The world is modernizing at a furious pace and I'm of the view that the rich will only get richer, but when all is said and done, all any man really wants is a girl with a kind heart, soft arms and a pretty face . . .'

Flora stared ahead at the rocks, well able to imagine Mad Annie's response to those words. Or Effie's. Fists up or an arm wrestle would be likely.

'Rich men appreciate beautiful things,' he shrugged. 'It's our Achilles' heel.'

Our.

It wasn't lost on Flora that he had included himself in the summary, and the word shimmered as if the sun had bounced off it. He had thrown a hook into the water. But would she bite?

It didn't seem to cross his mind that she might be the fisher, and he the catch.

'What good would riches be here?' she asked, toying back, her words swimming around the bait. 'We have very little use for money on St Kilda.'

He stopped walking and turned to face her, seeing the provocative flash in her eyes. They both knew perfectly well no rich man would ever settle here. 'You are already too worldly for this small isle, Miss MacQueen. You have a sophistication that is apparent even barefoot in lumpen tweeds.'

'Lumpen?' she gasped with mock indignation. 'My father will take you to task for saying that.'

'Your father will never know,' he rejoindered, his own eyes flashing too.

So now they had a secret? Had she met her match? she wondered, allowing a small smile of surrender. This time.

They resumed their walk.

'You belong in the big, wide world, by the side of a man who can show you its true magnificence.'

'But where would I find such a man?'

She heard his low chuckle beside her. 'You may already have found him.'

'Really? Well, I shall take another look at Mr Callaghan, but on first impression, he didn't strike me as the Casanova type.'

Far from it.

He laughed out loud at her tease. 'I'm glad to hear it! And my sister would most certainly be.'

Flora glanced at him, her suspicions confirmed. 'Ah, I thought I discerned an intimacy between them earlier. So they are betrothed?'

'Almost inevitably.'

She frowned. 'But not . . . yet?'

'Not quite. But we have a few more days on board.'

Flora looked across at him. 'Is that why he was invited? To fall in love with your sister?'

'To *finish* falling in love with her. Frankly, the whole business has been dragging on for far too long. He's easily distracted, though, that's the problem. Gets bored.'

'Funny. That's what he said about you.'

Edward shot her a sideways look. 'Really?'

She shrugged. 'Is he aware of your plot?'

'He's an intelligent fellow; he's not *unaware*.'

'Does he love her?'

'They seem to enjoy one another's company.'

'And do you think your sister would be well suited to life with a man who hunts fossils?' she asked in a slight scoffing tone. 'She seems very fashionable – to me, at least. Won't he bore her?'

'Honestly? I've never heard Callie say a word about the things before today.' Edward shrugged. 'Although he is something of an adventurer – loves a mountain, can rhapsodize over a river – so why not a bunch of rocks, I suppose? He's forever falling out of Geographical Society dinners with talk of some trek or another. Sophia's been in love with him since she was twelve. Rather lacking in imagination, I'm afraid, my sister; it hasn't occurred to her to set her sights on anyone else. But there's no harm in that. It all works; Callie's a known entity.'

'A known entity?' It seemed a strange way to describe a friend.

'Yes. Our families are old friends; our fathers did something of a Grand Tour around Europe in their youth. And he's an enterprising fellow, Callie, so everything just . . . fits.'

She looked straight ahead as they walked, almost at the end of the beach now. The grey scree slopes of Ruival towered over them, the slap of waves hitting the rocks in the narrow chasm between Hirta and Dun, which had once been linked by a cliff arch.

'Fits,' she mused. 'Is that the polite way of saying he's rich enough to marry her?'

Edward chuckled. 'I'm afraid so. It's a bore, having to consider such things, but one must be practical too.'

'I'm sure.' She glanced across at him, catching his gaze as they turned back towards the village curving its gentle smile, puffs of smoke twisting from the chimneys and white sheets flapping on the lines. She could see her neighbours going about their chores, her eyes falling to the bright dots of foreign colour – lilac, chartreuse, begonia pink – outside the Fergusons' house.

'And what is Mr Callaghan's business?' she asked as they trod over their own footprints, heels over toes, the incoming tide pooling in the impressions of their ghosts.

'Well, *he* describes himself as an entrepreneur, but the family business is textiles. It's what brought us here, actually.'

'Oh?'

'We were moored at Uist and Callie mooted making the "quick detour" over here.' He grinned. 'Of course, there was nothing quick about it. Just ask my poor mother! We had never intended coming this far out, but the conditions were good – well, good enough, just about.'

'Why did he want to come here specifically? All the islands sell tweed.'

'Ah, but the quality of yours stands above the rest, we're told. Apparently it's softer than any others.'

She shrugged. 'Maybe. I've nothing to compare it with.'

'Well, he wanted to strike a deal for you to supply his family's company – that was the premise for it all.'

Flora felt her pulse quicken. The men were always complaining about the rates the factor paid them. Could this be a way to supplement their income? 'And did he? Strike the deal, I mean?'

'Sadly not. He spoke with the men when we landed, but it appears your landlord's quotas take almost all your capacity.'

'Aye,' she sighed. 'The rents have to be paid one way or another. Tweeds, feathers and fulmar oil are our main exports.'

'It's a shame. He was certainly disappointed – although *I'm* inclined to think the journey wasn't for nothing.'

41

'I'm glad you've enjoyed your visit here,' she said benignly, thwarting his attempt to flatter her again. If he thought she'd be seduced by vain compliments . . . 'We do seem to be getting so many more visitors these days. Our little village is attracting more and more tourists – gentlemen – like yourself.' She laughed. 'They do seem to love having their photographs taken here.'

'Really?'

'Oh, yes. Every other day it seems there's a new yacht dropping anchor . . . We get to meet so many new people. Occasionally some return again, but – well, that can be a little awkward sometimes. It can be hard to remember all those faces.'

He glanced at her, understanding her games in a way that his friend did not. 'Am *I* forgettable?'

'Utterly and instantly, I'm afraid.'

He laughed, throwing his head back. 'Well, then, perhaps I shouldn't allow you the opportunity. Out of sight, out of mind is a risk I'm not sure I'm prepared to take. Not to mention, I rather feel like I've discovered Magellan's lost treasure in finding you. It would be nothing short of a disservice to humanity to leave you here.'

She threw him a disdainful look. 'How so?'

'If I were to sail away from here without you, it would be like discovering the Blue Moon diamond, then kicking dirt back over her and resealing the mine!'

'You are absurd!' she giggled. 'And far too forward.' But she liked it, this confidence of his. She could imagine him commanding rooms, or a platoon; having the ear of important men and boasting a social circle that spanned presidents, minor princesses, magnates and high-stakes gamblers. His voice was variously inflected with fun, intimacy and serious-ness, depending upon the topic at hand.

'Forward? Have I offended you?' he asked, sounding not in the least perturbed by the idea.

'No, but you've known me for all of half an hour and you're already proposing to take me away from my home, my family and all of my friends.'

'You're right. It's absurd, isn't it?' He smiled at her and she had the sense that all the colours of him had deepened – his eyes were shining a more vivid blue, his lips were redder, his hair brighter – as if suffusing in the very essence of himself.

She looked away; she sensed he was used to winning people over to his ideas and plans, his energy, good looks and intense charisma making for a heady, seductive mix. 'You do believe in getting straight to the point, don't you, Mr Rushton?'

'I assure you, this is a new position for me to find myself in. Not to be immodest, but I rarely chase.'

'Chase?'

'Women.'

She tilted her head to the side and looked him up and down with a quizzical frown, as if the very idea was baffling. 'How so?'

He laughed again at the sharp barb of her verbal spar. 'Well, I would like to tell you it's on account of my wit, charm and dazzling good looks, but I suspect my family's fortune plays into my legend somewhat.'

Self-deprecation and a boast, all in one sentence. He was good.

'Mm. Well, if it's any consolation, I can sympathize.'

'You can?' he asked.

'Yes. We have a fine milking cow. Best on the island. Every-one wants her.'

His eyes danced. 'Is that so?'

'Indeed. I certainly think it was the driving factor behind Euan Gillies' marriage proposal this spring. His mother's had her eye on Eunice for a while now.'

He chuckled still. 'A mother's ambition is never to be underestimated.'

'Exactly. And I know y' mother's ambitions would be sorely disappointed by a match with the likes of me.'

'Not once she saw her grandchildren,' he said boldly, stopping in front of her.

She blinked but didn't step back, though he was in her personal space. 'I'm not the right *fit*,' she demurred. 'You've just said yourself how important that is.'

'For marrying off a daughter, yes,' he agreed. 'The first son and heir is given a little more . . . grace.'

'Grace,' she echoed, able to see at this close proximity the rapid rise and fall of his chest. He was a hunter, in full pursuit.

'Yes. Rich men and beautiful things, remember?' His eyes roamed her face with open admiration.

She looked away, though her own heart was pounding fast at their game. She knew she had to play this carefully. If he was quick to fall, he would be quick to pull back too. Overplay her hand and she knew he would lose interest. 'Well . . . I should want my own mother to see her grandchildren, too,' she said simply, looking out to sea and affording him a full look at her magnificent profile instead. 'In spite of how exciting everything sounds on the mainland, I'm not sure I could ever leave here.'

It was a lie, but it would keep him on his toes. Her entire world view had been informed by the stories of fishermen and the grey political establishment depicted in newspapers; but even these brief moments with him had brought alive a

44

world of characters and colours that had only ever existed in her imagination. She had always been able to glean and discern just enough from the fashions and deportments of the rich tourists to paint a picture of their lives in her own mind. Now here stood a man flirting with her and suggesting that she might *fit* into that world too. That he might bring her into it, beside him.

They were standing close to the shoreline, back where they had begun, and he bent down and pulled a small sprig of heather from the tall grass. He held it out as if offering her a rare orchid, and as she took it with a smile, she caught sight of something unfamiliar against one of the rocks.

'What's that?' she asked, pointing to a large woven container.

He thrust his hands into his trouser pockets, looking pleased with himself. 'That's my surprise for you. I thought we could have a picnic together.'

She looked back to him again. 'A what?'

'It's just a little something I got the skipper to arrange for me when we popped back to the boat just now.'

He had planned this?

'But what's in it?' she asked as they walked over.

He watched her, seeing her greed to know more, see more, do more. Did he sense he was her ticket off this isle? 'Tell you what – if you show me a pretty spot with a view, I'll show – and share – what's inside the basket. Agreed?'

Flora watched as he picked it up. From the way it sagged down from the leather handle, from the creak and groan of the woven receptacle, it was weightier than it looked. A small tinkling of glass came from within. Her curiosity was piqued.

'I think you will enjoy it,' he continued. 'We have picnics all the time on the mainland.'

A small fire kindled in her stomach, warming her bones. She had a sense of a door opening and his world gliding past in the frame – there, almost within reach, waiting for her. '. . . You do?'

'We do,' he smiled, holding out his hand for her as she stepped daintily onto the grass, both of them knowing he'd correctly baited the hook at last.

Chapter Four

The spot she chose wasn't especially high, but it afforded a dramatic view over the spine of Dun and out to open water. They were looking westwards, the sun tracking a high arc through billowing clouds and intermittently throwing down bright puddles, through which a few silhouetted seals slipped and played.

They were on the very edge of being in sight of the village now, right on the headland and perched on a flat, grassy area below the Ruival cliffs. It had been a short walk to get here, the ground plateauing after a steep scramble from beach to path. Flora had had to convince Edward to keep his shoes off and walk barefoot, for he seemed in a hurry to dress himself again, but the grass on this aspect was in fact not grass at all but a sea moss – the salt spray that was carried on the wind hindered grass establishment on this slope. It was so spongy and slippery that the leather soles considered smart on the streets of Piccadilly would be treacherous here.

'This will do nicely,' she said, angling them so that the wind would lift her hair back and off her neck, and not into her face. She dropped casually to the ground, no longer bothered about hiding her own bare feet – she sensed there was something in her undone wildness that excited him. She watched as Edward settled himself beside her. The basket – the treasure trove – was set between them and he unbuckled its leather straps.

Flora peered in, her eyes widening at the sight. Plates and glasses were tethered to the inside of the lid and in the well of the basket was a panoply of covered shapes. She was intrigued.

'For you,' he smiled, handing her a glass and pouring from a small bottle that had its own strap in the corner. 'You do like lemonade, I trust?'

'I've never had it,' she murmured, holding it suspiciously.

'Try. I think you'll like it – it's both sweet and tart at the same time.'

She took a tiny sip. It fizzed on her tongue and she startled a little at the unexpected sensation; fizzing wasn't something that happened here, but the taste was both pleasantly sharp and sugared. 'Mm.' She took another sip, feeling bolder now, as he unfastened the plates as well and handed one to her.

'Are you familiar with sandwiches?' he asked, unwrapping a linen napkin bundle secured with a length of string. Inside was a quartet of triangles of bread, padded with assorted fillings. 'We only have a limited selection, I'm afraid, on account of being at sea. It's a matter of what will stay fresh during the trip. We've got cucumber with mint, beef with horseradish – my personal favourite – and salmon mayonnaise.'

He held out the selection towards her and for several seconds, Flora just looked between him and the food. The arrangement of it, the smells, even the colours . . . A look of bemusement spread across his face. He couldn't possibly understand how overwhelming it was for someone who had only ever eaten boiled fulmar – or, on high days and holidays, roasted puffin – to be presented with such choice. There was

48

no variety to their meals here and there were certainly no embellishments.

'Go on, try one,' he murmured, nudging the bundle towards her again.

She reached for the triangle with the pinkish filling, her eyes closing as her teeth sank into the soft bread, a symphony of flavours exploding on her tongue. When she opened her eyes again, Edward was staring at her with a hunger of his own.

She chewed even as her mouth watered. 'What did you call it?'

'It's a salmon sandwich.'

'Salmon sandwich,' she murmured, staring sadly at what remained in her hand; it would be gone with another bite.

'Fear not, there's plenty more. Have another one.'

She took it from him, feeling a giddy rush of need. Hunger she was familiar with, but she had never known appetite before now. Eating the next one, she watched as his finger pointed at the rest of the food in the basket. 'We also have sliced chicken, potted meat and some cheese.'

'We make our own cheeses,' she said quickly, looking up at him, her mouth full.

He looked bemused again. Flora blushed, sensing an error on her part, but he had moved on in the next instant. 'Well, I'm sure they are far superior to these. Perhaps I could try some of your cheese when we return to the village?'

She nodded, looking eagerly back into the basket again, wanting more.

He laughed. 'I fear your eyes are bigger than your stomach, Miss MacQueen. You'll want to leave some room for the pudding.'

'Pudding?'

'It's a great treat under the circumstances – we have some sponge cake and jam tarts.'

'Sponge cake and jam tarts?' she repeated, the words unfamiliar and almost ticklish in her mouth.

'You've never had sponge cake?' He seemed surprised, pointing to the soft, springy dome.

'And so those are the jam tarts?' Her eyes scanned the glistening jewel colours: ruby red, golden yellow, emerald green. 'They're very pretty.'

He was staring at her, she realized, and she drew her excitement in like a fishing line; the more of her naivety she betrayed, the more imbalance of power she allowed between them. She decided to shift the subject away from her ignorance. 'Where did you set sail from, Mr Rushton?'

'Glasgow . . . And please, call me Edward.'

'Is that where you're from?'

He smiled. 'No. My family lives in London, but we stopped in to see Callie's new house first. He's rebuilding a property on Blythswood Square, following a fire; Sophia was keen to . . . cast an eye over it.' His eyes met hers and she caught the point immediately. The girl wanted to see where she would live. '. . . Another sandwich?'

Flora's hand reached without hesitation and together they ate, overlooking the sea. The gusting wind wasn't loosening its grip and the swell made for interesting viewing as the gannets dived like arrows, a minke whale further out blowing up sporadic spouts of water. She sipped lemonade, Edward refilling her glass without being asked and offering the sandwiches each time her plate was cleared.

So this was a picnic, she mused: being fed on the grass. Lunch with a view. She watched him lying back on his elbows, his legs crossed at the ankles. She suspected she had eaten far more than he and she was beginning to wonder if what he'd said about her eyes and her stomach might have been true. She felt the first tightenings of a bellyache.

Still, the jam tarts were winking at her. The ruby red one, especially, was crying out to be tasted . . .

'Please,' Edward said, seeing her avaricious glance and leaning over to reach it for her. He held it up to her mouth. 'You really must try one. They're delicious.'

Flora felt a small blush creep onto her cheeks as she nibbled it. It felt daringly intimate, being fed. 'Aren't you having one?'

'Perhaps in a few moments . . . Have another bite.'

Her eyes closed again, as rich colours translated into exotic flavours. She had never known food could be so pleasurable. A full tummy – fuel – was all she had ever expected from a meal before. How could she turn back now that she knew it could be this, too?

A slapping sound behind them made them both startle, Edward twisting sharply as they turned to find the end of a rope spooling on the ground. Flora looked up to a familiar sight – a spry figure bouncing off the cliff, bare feet scampering across the rock face; she grinned, feeling a spritz of relief that slightly surprised her. There was a pace to Edward's attentions that was necessary and yet disconcerting.

'That's it,' Effie called up, stopping casually on the bluff and watching as another figure – significantly larger and less agile – followed after her. 'Use your hands. Follow the crease to the left there . . . That's it. There's no hurry.'

'Eff?' Flora asked, not even having to raise her voice. This particular section of the rock face was perhaps a hundred feet high.

Effie glanced down, her feet planted on the rock wall as

she balanced on the rope. 'Hai!' she beamed, giving them a wave and seemingly forgetting she was dangling on a cliff.

'Is that a girl?' Edward asked, astounded. From this vantage it was admittedly difficult for him to tell – Effie was dressed in boys' tweed breeks and a woollen vest, her pale blonde hair twisted back.

'Aye, it's Effie Gillies,' Flora murmured. 'Don't worry, she's an excellent cragger. One of the best.'

'But what's she doing up there?'

Flora squinted to get a better look, but she knew exactly who she was seeing. 'Well, by the looks of it, she's giving your friend a climbing lesson.' And earning herself the coins she would be missing out on from the day's cancelled cragging exhibition; the swell wasn't going to drop today, that was clear.

They watched in silence as James, concentrating hard, slowly but surely descended the bluff. Flora forgot to eat, such was her trepidation as the rope spun and he missed a couple of what looked like easy footholds (or at least, Effie made them look easy); Edward too looked as if he didn't want to say anything that might distract his friend. But when James set foot on the grassy ledge several minutes later, he was beaming that surprising smile again.

'Well, that was . . . that was fantastic,' he panted, glancing bright-eyed across at Effie, planting his hands on his hips and looking up in wonder at the short but steep descent. He had taken off his jacket since he had left her earlier, his shirt-sleeves now rolled up, and a small sweat patch was beginning to bloom between his shoulder blades. His trousers were rolled up too, and he was barefoot – Effie would have insisted on it, Flora knew. It gave the climber far greater grip and manoeuvrability. He had strong forearms and ankles, she noticed, sitting behind him, and looked altogether a different beast to the buttoned-up, stiff fossil-hunter she had walked with earlier.

'You did well for a first-timer,' Effie said, shaking his hand in congratulations. 'We've not many easy drops here.'

'I'll admit, my stomach dropped when I saw you pop over the edge like that.'

'Aye, sorry, I meant to go slower. I forgot myself.'

James chuckled. 'Extraordinary. It really holds no fear for you?'

'Why should it?'

'. . . Fear of imminent death?'

'Och, no,' she demurred, as though there was simply no possibility of it.

'We always say Effie might fly if she fell,' Flora said from her spot on the ground, feeling a dart of irritation at their easy chatter. He'd been nowhere near as friendly or complimentary with her. 'She has such tiny, light bones, she's like the birds.'

James whirled around, looking in astonishment at the scene that had been behind him. 'I say, what are you two doing here?'

Had he really not seen them? Flora supposed he had been so focused on what was in front of him, above and below, he'd not had a chance to clock them behind him. Or perhaps he was not just blind to her charms, but to her generally.

'We're having a picnic,' she said grandly.

'Yes, I can see that.' His eyes fell to the part-nibbled jam tart on the plate in her lap.

'I've had Miss MacQueen in ecstasies over the tarts, Callie,' Edward said with a wink.

James gave no reply, but Effie fell to her knees and crouched over the basket. 'What's that?' she asked curiously, pointing at the sponge cake.

'Cake. Would you like to try some?' Edward asked, with yet more amusement.

But Effie pulled back and gave a wary shake of her head. Unlike Flora, she couldn't be so readily seduced by treasures from the Other Side.

'Are you sure? It's positively good for you to indulge once in a while. I'm sure the reverend wouldn't disapprove of cake.'

Flora watched from the corner of her eye as James unwound the rope from his torso and stood, looking around, on the grass beside them. She noticed that unlike Edward, he moved easily barefoot, oblivious to the stray shale fragments underfoot, his skin taut, the ankle bones broad. Unlike his friend, his clothes seemed to hide his masculinity, whereas for Edward, they enhanced the illusion of it. She wasn't sure which was preferable – to be less than you seemed, or to appear less than you were.

'I didn't know you'd gone to all this trouble,' James said, casting a glance in Edward's direction as he reached down into the basket and took a sandwich. He began eating it idly, as if it was no great treat, while he stood and took in the panoramic view.

'It was no trouble. Well, not for Cook. Of course I can't pretend *I* had anything to do with making it.' He gave a careless shrug. 'How are the girls getting on?'

'Knitting,' James replied, his eyes fastened on the minke. 'Terribly, I might add.'

'They can't be worse than me,' Effie sighed. 'And I've been doing it my whole life.'

'I don't believe you,' James smiled, glancing politely in her direction.

'It's true, isn't it, Floss?'

Flora nodded. 'I'm afraid so.'

'Are you a proficient knitter, Miss MacQueen?' James asked her, reaching down for another sandwich.

'Better than Effie, but I'm neither terrible nor good.'

'No? So what do you excel at, then?'

She looked up at him, at a sudden loss. Her greatest attribute was apparent to all but him.

'Getting out of chores!' Effie laughed, still distractedly eyeballing the food in the basket.

'As she should!' Edward rejoindered. 'With a face like that, she wasn't born to work!'

'I'm sure there must be more to you though than just a pretty face?' James asked with a frown.

Flora was surprised to hear him even concede her good looks, but before she could reply he looked away and she felt her cheeks burn. Usually she loved being known for dazzling people, but, for reasons she couldn't explain, with him it seemed lacking.

'That's an exciting-looking rock over there,' he said after a few moments, turning in a slow circle and indicating the cliffs to the west of where they sat.

'That's the Lovers' Stone,' Effie said with the merest of glances.

'The *Lovers'* Stone, eh?' Edward queried, rolling the words around in his mouth. 'You do love naming your rocks here, don't you?'

'Well, some of them are significant for us,' Effie said, perhaps a little more indignantly than she had intended. She wasn't accustomed to hiding her feelings. 'They can be place markers, or tributes to the dead, and they play a role in our customs.'

'Indeed,' James agreed hastily, as if apologizing for his friend's tactlessness; Flora had a sense he probably did that a lot. 'And which role does the Lovers' Stone play?'

Effie hesitated a moment, as if checking for mockery. 'If a man wants to take a wife here, then he has to stand up there on that ledge.'

'Really?' James sounded both intrigued and horrified. They all squinted at the silhouetted rock. It protruded up from the sheer cliffs in a stand-alone stack, a grassy footpath running behind it. The top of the stack was like a steeply angled table-top, with a short protrusion at the upper edge that nudged forward beyond the rest, overhanging the sea. The drop was several hundred feet onto rocks below. 'A fellow has to stand up there? That must be dicey with the winds, surely?'

'Aye, particularly when he has to do it on one leg,' Effie grinned.

'What?'

'He has to stand on his left leg, hold his right foot forward so it's extended over the edge into space, and then bend down and clasp the foot with both hands. Then hold it there to a slow count of ten.'

'You can't be serious?' Edward frowned.

'Why should I lie?' Effie shrugged.

'And that's done as an act of bravery?' James asked.

'Och, no,' she said with a dismissive frown. 'If it's bravery they're to prove then they'd go off Stac Briorach.' As if the plummet here was of no concern.

'What does this challenge prove, then?'

'Competence.'

James's eyes widened. 'Competence?'

'Aye. The challenge is an indication of his strength and agility, which is what you need if you're to be a good cragger. And you need to be a good cragger if you're going to provide for your family. A brave husband is no good here if he hasn't

56

strength and agility to back it up. He'll be dead in a day without either of those two things.'

'I see . . . But what if he falls?'

'Then you know he wouldn't have made a good husband,' Effie shrugged. 'That's why he has to do it *before* he can marry, you see? A weak husband is a dead husband is no husband at all, so why bother? Better to know before the ceremony. We can ill afford the lambs for the feasts as it is.'

Edward threw his head back and laughed. 'My God! It's fiendishly brutal, Callie, but you have to admire the efficiency!'

'Thank you.' Effie nodded with a solemnity that only amused him further.

'Actually, it's not entirely dissimilar to a courting ritual performed by bald eagles,' James said. 'They lock talons in the air and spiral downwards from the sky. The male is responsible for swooping the female back up, but sometimes he doesn't catch her in time.'

'And so *she* dies?' Effie asked.

'I expect so – but at least she knows he'd have made a terrible mate,' he shrugged.

Everyone laughed at the joke, Flora surprised by this sudden flash of humour, and James looked over at her as she folded with amusement. For a second, again, she felt that 'locking' between them, but then he looked back at the rocks the next moment, still fascinated. 'When was the last time it was performed?'

'Four years back?' Effie said, looking at Flora. 'Norman and Jayne?'

'About that,' Flora agreed.

He twisted back to them. 'And when was the last time someone fell?'

As if she had known the question was coming, Flora kept

her gaze on Effie, seeing the flash of pain dart across her fragile features. Her brother John had fallen two years previously – a chafed rope; her father had yet to forgive himself – but not from this spot.

'Not in our lifetimes,' she said quickly; truthfully. Effie wouldn't unburden her pain to strangers. Or anyone.

'The young fellows coming through must be terrified,' Edward said as James finally turned back to them.

'Actually, I think they're more terrified of succeeding than of falling,' Flora said, remembering her jam tart and picking at the pastry.

'How so?'

'Because then they'll have to marry us.'

'Is that so terrible?'

'We're none of us easy characters.' Flora rarely ventured into self-deprecation, but this time James Callaghan smiled at her words, and she felt a small bubble of pride, as if she had won it from him somehow.

'Nothing worth having is ever easy,' Edward said, leaning back on his elbows as he looked at Flora.

The others' smiles immediately faded and Effie caught her eye with a bored look; she reserved a special contempt for courtship and it was impossible to imagine her ever swooning in a man's arms. Flora suspected that like Lorna, their island nurse, Effie would choose spinsterhood over married life any day, for she valued her independence far too much.

'Out of interest, exactly how compulsory is this feat of competence for winning a St Kildan girl's hand?' Edward asked. 'Can't a husband's suitability be assessed by a different metric?'

He caught Flora's eye and she knew to what he was alluding. Fortune, perhaps?

'Rushton,' James said quickly, shooting him a dark look.

Edward arched an enquiring eyebrow, to which James responded with only a terse shake of his head. Edward sighed, letting the matter drop.

Flora stared at the jam tart in her hands, feeling humiliated. For a moment, she had let herself wonder whether there might be an arrangement to be made – they were attracted to one another, her beauty matched his fortune. It was an even trade. But with just a single word, James Callaghan had made it perfectly clear she wasn't the sort of girl to even flirt with, and she certainly ought not to have her hopes raised on any account.

Silently, Flora tossed the remains of the jam tart into the grass, several chunks of pastry breaking off. Moments later a fulmar swooped in, retrieving the major portion of the broken tart with nimble precision. Her exotic treat had become a seabird's pickings.

Flora looked away and out to sea, feeling the bitterness in her craw as she blinked back angry tears she would not allow to fall. The minke had disappeared now, sinking into the depths, but she fastened her gaze upon the seals still slipping through the waves, oblivious to the breeze in her hair and the eyes on her back.

Chapter Five

'Allow me,' Edward said, walking a few steps ahead and gallantly reaching back with his arm outstretched. Flora took his hand, though there was really no need. Although the ground through this section sat at a sharp tilt, with a near-vertical scree escarpment immediately below, she knew every inch of the path and was far more sure-footed than him; but she was beginning to discern that gallantry – and, crucially, *allowing* it – was an intrinsic part of high society life. Just because she was perfectly capable didn't mean she had to act it.

James, following several steps behind them, offered the same courtesy to Effie, but she pretended not even to see his hand as she swung her arms and marched like a toy soldier, ropes looped over her shoulder. To her, this was flat ground.

The picnic, Flora's first one, had been a great success – at least until James Callaghan's graceless arrival on the scene – and she had decided she liked them. Edward had told her about 'great spots' he knew along the river in Cambridge, of scenic viewpoints in Hyde Park and the Lake District, in the grouse moors of Yorkshire and rocky coves in Devon. Each place had sounded so different as he described them, a plethora of different landscapes for each season and every mood, and though there was something to be said for knowing her home like it was her own body – recognizing every crag and crevice, the temper of the wind and the pitch of the sun – life here was stifling in its smallness. What had always felt like a growing restlessness with her island home was beginning to feel suffocating.

'Floss! Eff!'

The call made both girls look up. They knew the voice well and were already, instinctively, scanning the bay for the familiar toss of red hair. They found it not on the street, aflame against the grey stone cottages, but on the beach.

'Hai!' Flora smiled, waving back at Mhairi, who was sitting on the rocks with her arms huddled around her knees. The sea-moss path sat eighty feet above the beach here and they had to walk a while for it to drop down.

'. . . Where were you? We've been looking for you,' Mhairi asked as they approached.

'We were having a picnic,' Flora beamed. The picnic basket was now significantly lighter post-lunch and Flora felt an urge to offer her friend some of the remaining cake. She liked the idea of being able to be generous. '. . . Have you met Mr Rushton yet?'

She saw the surprise cross Mhairi's face as Flora held Edward's arm a little tighter, though she was a composed girl and knew not to say the first thing that came into her head. 'Not yet,' she smiled. 'Good afternoon, Mr Rushton.'

'This is my dear friend Mhairi MacKinnon.'

'The pleasure is all mine, Miss MacKinnon,' Edward said, bowing his head just as the others caught them up. 'And may I also introduce my own dear friend, James Callaghan?'

'Ah yes, Mr Callaghan, I was just hearing about you,' Mhairi said brightly.

James looked surprised. 'You were?'

'Indeed. Miss Rushton was extolling your virtues. Apparently you are a . . .' She hesitated as she reached for the correct terminology. 'Keen shot and Cambridge Blue boxer.'

Flora knew that Mhairi had no more clue than she did as to what a Cambridge Blue was, but neither of them intended to highlight their ignorance.

'Hm. It sounds to me like she wasn't knitting hard enough,' James demurred.

'And did my dear sister have anything nice to say about *me*?' Edward asked with a mock-peevish tone.

'I believe we would have immediately moved on to that topic of conversation,' Mhairi smiled, hearing the joke.

'But . . . ?'

'But she felt a strong urge to swim.'

'Ha! A likely story,' Edward chuckled as everyone looked out to the water. The sea was far more protected here in the bay but nevertheless, the waves were breaking on the sand with something heavier than a slump now. 'Where is she, then?'

'She and Miss Martha are getting changed in the feather-store. It's more private in there . . .' Mhairi said, looking back along the beach. 'Ah yes, look, here they come now.'

Everyone watched as two figures made their way carefully along the sand, trying to dodge sharp stones; Flora suspected their feet were as fragile as silk. They were wrapped in light modesty robes, limbs pale, sunlight bouncing off their hair, and there was something in their deportment – a delicacy – that marked them out as rarefied, china dolls, even from a distance.

Flora kept her eyes on Sophia as they drew nearer. Gone were the lilac coat and flash of chartreuse dress; now she was draped in sapphire-blue cotton printed with large red flowers, her light brown hair released from her hat so that it spread over her shoulders.

'Ah, there you are!' Sophia called in a buoyant tone. 'We were wondering where you'd got to.'

'How was your knitting class?' Edward asked, reaching into his pocket for a cigarette.

'Tremendously successful!' she said confidently. 'Miss Ferguson was a delight, teaching me how to purl. I always used to go the wrong way but she showed me a little trick she uses and do you know, I think I shall be able to knit my own socks in no time.'

A smile played on her brother's lips. 'Excellent. Magnificent skill to have in your back pocket, should Lloyds make a misstep.'

'Well, are you boys coming in for a dip? The sun's so beastly hot; there's simply no respite, and not a tree anywhere. What's one to do for shade here?'

'Sit in the houses,' Effie said with a stony look.

'Of course,' Sophia smiled smoothly. 'But we can't expect to impinge on your hospitality *all* day.'

'Y' could always sit in a cleit.'

Flora tried to suppress a laugh, drawing a look from Sophia. The cleits – distinctive stone beehive structures with turf roofs – were used to store the salted carcasses of the fulmars, puffins and guillemots; fulmar oil was kept in barrels there, peats and occasionally – if they had any – harvested crops were dried inside too. They were useful stores but often smelly and, depending on the weather, either damp or putrid; certainly not the places for young gentlewomen to seek shade.

'Would any of you care to join us for a dip?' Sophia asked.

'No thank you,' Flora said, as Effie and Mhairi also shook their heads quickly.

'Oh yes – Miss Ferguson said none of you really swim.'
She looked back at the men. 'Isn't that extraordinary? They're
surrounded by sea but can't swim.'

'I'm not sure today's the day for it for anyone,' James said,
looking out to the water again. 'There's quite a swell out there.'

'Oh, it's perfectly all right in the bay. Papa said we could.'

'Where are they?' Edward asked, casting around for a
sighting of their parents.

'Taking tea with the vicar.' Sophia widened her eyes fractionally, just enough to signify a ripple of distaste.

'I still say it's too rough out there,' James frowned.

'Well now, you're not in charge of me *yet*, are you, James
Callaghan?' she purred, letting the robe slip from her shoulders to reveal her slender frame.

Edward shot his friend a bemused look at the riposte as
he took another drag of his cigarette, wholly unperturbed by
his sister's provocative display.

Flora felt herself taken aback. Sophia's bathing costume
was pale, almost the colour of her skin, and cut across the
hips in a sharp line so that up close it looked like she was
wearing a very tight, very short dress. From a distance, though,
it must surely look like she was wearing nothing at all? Flora
had never seen a bathing costume in real life before – only in
the advertisements in some of the ladies' magazines the fishermen would bring over for them – and it exposed so much
more than she might have expected. Almost as one, the St
Kildan girls looked towards the manse, where the reverend
lived; should he be looking from the window, he would surely
have a heart attack.

Martha, bored of waiting, tore off her green robe and, in
her navy costume, began racing down to the water's edge.
'Last one in's a sissy!' she called behind her.

64

With a laugh, Sophia broke into a pretty canter too, her hair swinging, long legs scissoring across the sand. Flora glanced across at James; he was watching through squinted eyes, his hands stuffed into his trouser pockets and an inscrutable look on his face.

'This is a terrible idea,' he muttered dourly.

'Don't worry, I'm their lookout,' Mhairi said to Edward. 'Mr Rushton insisted.'

'Yes, I'm sure,' Edward nodded. 'Father's very protective. I hope he's paying you?'

'Yes,' Mhairi smiled.

'Good; your time is precious,' he said, taking a final drag of his cigarette before letting it drop to the ground and stubbing it out with his foot. It took him half a second to remember he wasn't wearing shoes. 'Agh!' he yelled, hopping about in the grass and wincing with pain. 'Blast to hell!'

James laughed, allowing the others to follow suit.

'I need to go and stand in the shallows,' Edward groaned, and they all watched as he began to hobble over the boulders that separated beach from grass.

'Well, I'm going to head back home. I need to check on m' father,' Effie said, turning to James and pinning him with an expectant look.

'Indeed. Thank you, Miss Gillies,' he said, quickly understanding and reaching into his pocket, handing her a couple of shillings. It was far short of the pound he'd paid to her for doing much less, Flora noted. 'That was a fine climbing lesson. I consider it a great privilege to have benefited from your experience.'

'Any time, sir,' Effie said carelessly, throwing Flora and Mhairi a wink as she turned to set off over the grassy allotments towards the street.

But Mhairi had her attention on the water, and she gasped suddenly. 'Oh . . . Look out!'

Effie wheeled back round again.

'What is it?' Flora cried, turning to find Mhairi pointing towards the water. A set of larger waves – wake from a passing whaling ship, no doubt – was barrelling through the bay and about to hit the shore. Sophia was swimming towards it, but Martha had her back turned.

'Matty! Watch out!' James yelled, pointing behind her too. Sophia elegantly dived under the approaching wave but her little sister, unable to react in time, was wiped out by it.

'Oh no!' Mhairi cried, her hands over her mouth as the youngster's skinny body was pitched forward, tumbling over and over in the surf and leaving her sprawling in the shallows. After a few seconds, coughing madly, she managed to get to her feet – just as the next wave hit and she was churned up in the mêlée once more.

James jumped down to the rocks but Edward, already on the sand, had a good head start and began sprinting towards her. 'Matty, I'm coming!' he called. Within seconds he was wading through the surf, fully-clothed, his injured foot forgotten.

James stood motionless on the rocks, his eyes fixed upon the girl being thrown about like a rag doll in the water, as if she might disappear from his sight at any moment. Flora watched, her hands pressed over her mouth, seeing how Edward grabbed his little sister's arm – just as the next wave surged upon him too. He pulled her into him and quickly turned and braced, the wave breaking against his back, but the force threw him forwards too and they were both pitched into the surf. They disappeared under the surface for a few moments but soon burst up again, Edward holding his little sister aloft triumphantly as he began staggering back towards the shore.

'Dear God,' Flora murmured, watching as he moved them both out of harm's way, both of them coughing and spluttering. She was shocked by just how quickly things had taken a turn for the worse like that – but also at how quickly they calmed again once the wake dispersed. The subsequent incoming waves were already significantly less powerful.

Sophia waved at them happily from her point further out beyond the break, where the water looked almost flat. She appeared oblivious to the drama that had occurred behind her as she swam under and away from the wake. 'James! Come in too!' she trilled, kicking onto her back and making splashes with her feet. 'The water's lovely!'

Flora frowned at her ignorance. Did she think her brother was swimming in his clothes for fun?

James, still standing on the rocks, waved his arm at her. 'Sophia, come back in!' he motioned.

'Make me!'

Flora heard him groan as she watched the young woman flip again and begin to swim, her arms curving as she spliced the water with grace and precision. It was yet another difference between her world and theirs, another thing Sophia could do that Flora couldn't. She didn't need clothes to prove her privilege.

Flora watched as the young woman stopped, lifting both arms suddenly and diving down like the seals they had been watching earlier, slipping through the water with careless ease.

Edward and Martha had almost cleared the water now and they fell to their knees on the sand, the waves barely licking the soles of their feet as they both coughed. Martha especially had swallowed a lot of seawater and she kept retching, Edward patting her back, his own head hanging.

'We should help them,' Mhairi said, clambering off the rock.

'I'll go fetch Lorna to look them over,' Effie said, sprinting in the opposite direction.

Flora made her way down to the sand, able to pick up now on Edward's words above the waves.

'—want them seeing and making a fuss. You know how they are . . . Try to stand . . . That's a good girl.'

Martha got to her feet, her body looking limp and frail, hair hanging in whiplike strands. Mhairi rushed forwards with the rough towel they used for drying off after their evening baths. 'Is she all right?' she panted.

'She'll be fine,' Edward nodded. 'Just swallowed a bit of water.'

'Here, let's get you warm,' Mhairi said, enveloping the girl and rubbing her lightly.

'We should get you into your dry clothes. We've some bone broth on the pot back at ours,' Flora said to Edward. 'That'll warm her through.'

'Thank you,' he nodded, running a hand back through his hair. 'Sophia!' he called, turning back to his other sister. 'Come on, get out now! Fun's over!' He paused, a frown puckering his brow as he stared. He took a step back as he scanned the bay. '. . . Where is she?'

Flora looked out too in the general direction of where she had last seen Sophia as she dived down, but nothing broke the surface. No birds, no seals, no whales. No Sophia.

'Sophia!'

Their voices rose above the surf, a tint of terror in the word like glancing sunlight as they scanned for sight of her. The waves rolled in endlessly.

Dear God, where was she? Suddenly the bay felt vast and fathomless.

'There!' Flora cried, catching sight of something. What was it?

'What? Where?' Edward demanded, panic curling in the words as he couldn't see what she was showing him.

'There! There!' she cried as she began to race across the sand, her skirt hitched high to free her legs as she kept her gaze pinned to the slight discrepancy in the sea's skin. It wasn't a head she could see but . . . something was poking through the surface. Fingers? A hand? 'Can you see it?' She ran into the surf.

'Flora, stop!' she heard someone yell as she waded deep, up to her armpits, pointing desperately at the small dark discrepancy amid the blue. She didn't dare move her eyes lest she should never find it again, or it should disappear beneath the waves. She went a little deeper – too deep – and a small wave lifted her off her feet for a moment. Suddenly she felt the might of the ocean. She cried out.

Her feet touched the sand again—

'Get back!' James's voice was ragged with desperation as he sprinted up behind her. She could hear the thunder of water being displaced as he ran in in powerful strides.

'Flora, get back!' he shouted. 'I can see her! Get back!'

She did as he demanded, taking two steps back while she could, before the next wave came. He was almost upon her now and she dared to glance over; James's gaze was dead ahead as he blitzed past, arms pumping before he suddenly threw his arms forward and disappeared into the depths. Flora, standing on tiptoe and feeling the waves still trying to lift her off the sand, watched as he emerged again a few moments later in a streamlined fusion of opposite arm to leg.

He swam with power and focus and she remembered how he had watched Sophia intently from the rocks, almost as if he had known further trouble was brewing.

'Sophia?' Edward cried, wading up to his knees as he ran like one of the dogs in the shallows, darting from side to side.

Flora staggered backwards as she struggled to remain upright against the waves which tried to uproot her with every pass. The water was perishing and as she moved back to hip-height depth, exposing her torso to the wind, she began to violently tremble. James himself was barely more than a dark speck now, the rhythmic splashes bringing attention to his location as he motored towards a spot only he had fixed in his mind. In the next moment, he was gone too. Under.

Flora felt an arrow of fear as he was swallowed up, all trace of him wiped away. She waited, breath held, fingers pressed to her lips as seconds ticked past. They felt like minutes.

Too long . . .

She whimpered as her panic grew. Where was he? Why wasn't he surfacing?

Further along the beach she could hear Edward and Martha calling for Sophia *and* James now, but she dared not turn her head to look at them, nor to see if help was coming from the village. She couldn't take her eye off the spot where she'd seen him go under.

'There!'

Edward was pointing, wading out again, able to go further than her as he began to swim. She followed his direction of travel and caught sight of a dark shape heading for the shore – James, on his back, kicking furiously.

Relief broke through. It seemed an age before Edward met him and between the two of them they got to shallow waters where they could stand. With a shout of effort, James got Sophia off her back and the two men began to wade in, holding her under the arms.

Her head was lolling forwards and she looked lifeless. Drowned.

Flora felt her heart catch, cold fear beginning to course through her veins on this warm, sunny day. This couldn't be happening, surely?

She ploughed across the water – somehow, she had drifted at a diagonal to the men – and began to run back towards the beach. Martha was crying now, Mhairi trying to comfort her as the two men staggered out of the surf, Sophia limp as she was dragged between them, a dead weight in their arms. Edward was coughing, still struggling to catch his breath from his own dunking. As they came into the shallows, James swept Sophia up into his arms and ran the rest of the way with her to the dry sand.

He set her down on the beach and slapped her cheeks lightly a few times. 'Sophia! Sophia!' he cried urgently. 'Can you hear me? Wake up!'

The girl was pale and limp, her head lolling and her lips – to Flora's horror – tinged blue. She watched as James put a hand under Sophia's neck, angling her head back and pinching her nose with his right hand. Flora watched, dumbstruck, as he began breathing into her mouth several times, before interlacing his fingers and pressing down on her chest with his palms.

'What's he doing?' Mhairi asked her, a quaver in her voice.

Flora couldn't reply. She only knew that *he* knew exactly what he was doing. He moved with purpose and certainty, counting under his breath . . . Time seemed to drag, the wind growing cold.

Suddenly Sophia coughed, her body jerking into life and a trickle of water spilling from her mouth. Her eyelids fluttered once, twice, three times, her gaze fixing upon James hovering above her.

'Sophia?' he asked, his wet hair dripping onto her cheeks. He smoothed his hair back with a cupped hand, as if to save her from this too.

'James?' she whispered, blinking up at him, before noticing the other faces crowded around them and shrinking back. '. . . What happened?'

'You got tangled up in the kelp.'

'I . . . I did?'

'It's pretty thick out there,' he nodded. 'I had a devil of a time freeing your leg . . . You don't remember?'

Still she blinked, taking in his words, trying to find memories to match. 'So you saved me?'

'Well, I just happened to get to you first.'

'So you were watching out for me?'

'Well, I was just keeping an eye after the drama with Martha.'

Flora's eyes swivelled between them as she watched the interaction.

'Oh, James,' Sophia gasped, reaching for him suddenly and throwing her arms around his neck. 'You saved me!'

'Anyone would have done the same,' he said modestly, his voice somewhat strangled as she clutched herself tightly to him.

'But it wasn't anyone – it was you. *You* were the one looking out for me. You're my protector,' she said, before pressing her lips to his in a passionate kiss.

'Hey!' Edward said quickly, breaking them up almost immediately. 'Keep your breath for breathing, yes?' he said to her sternly. 'What would Papa say to this spectacle on the beach, in front of the entire island?' He looked around them at the gathering crowd as word spread throughout the village. 'We'll put it down to the ecstasies of being alive, shall we?'

'Indeed,' James said, pulling back and away. Recovering himself.

'Coming through!' a female voice said, and Flora looked up to see Lorna running on the sand, followed by some of the villagers. One of them was her elder brother David.

'Flora?'

'I'm fine,' she said quickly as he came over and checked her himself. In the corner of her eye, both Edward and James stared.

'What's happened?' Lorna demanded as she took in the sight of their five wet bodies, one laid out on the sand.

'Lorna's a nurse,' Mhairi explained quickly to Edward.

'She got caught in the kelp and was held under,' James said as Lorna crouched down beside the patient.

'For how long?' she frowned, looking instantly concerned.

'Two minutes, just over?'

Lorna did a visual assessment, before checking her vitals. 'Was she unconscious when you found her?'

'Yes, but I gave her the kiss of life and she revived very quickly.'

'Is she coherent?'

'Yes. Though she appears to have no memory of being underwater.'

'That's fairly common immediately after a trauma,' Lorna murmured, pressing two fingers on Sophia's wrist to take her pulse. 'What is your name, miss?' she asked the patient.

'Miss Sophia Cicely Frances Emmeline Rushton,' the patient replied in a breathy voice.

'Do you know where you are, Sophia?'

'On a rock in the middle of the North Atlantic . . .' She smiled. 'Also known, I believe, as St Kilda.'

'Indeed.' Lorna sat back, seeming satisfied with her condition and regarding her closely for a few moments, her gaze tracking between Sophia's left and right eyes. 'Well, it looks as if you've been lucky this time. Which one of you fished her out?' she asked, glancing between James and Edward, both sopping wet and shivering without even realizing it.

'I did,' James said quietly.

'You're the hero of the hour – you saved her in the nick of time.'

'It was pure luck, I assure you. It was Miss MacQueen who caught sight of her fingers breaking through the water.' His eyes met Flora's in acknowledgement and she realized he had gone back to formality again: she had been 'Flora' in the crisis, 'Miss MacQueen' now. But there had been something in the way he'd called her name, she thought, something in the way he stared—

Lorna got to her feet and brushed the sand off her knees. She looked back at Sophia. 'You'll need to come with me for a more thorough assessment in my surgery.'

'You have a surgery? Here?' Sophia asked, sounding impressed. Flora and Mhairi shared a look. It was actually the old blackhouse that sat next door to Lorna's cottage at the end of the street, just before the burn; but it was in better condition than most of the abandoned old properties and served as a useful space for wound dressings and the like.

'. . . After a fashion,' Lorna admitted. 'We'll need to get you into some dry clothes too.'

'They're in the featherstore,' Mhairi said, thumbing in that direction and looking ready to sprint. 'I can go get them?'

'Are they the clothes I saw you wearing earlier?' Lorna asked her patient.

Sophia nodded.

'Then they won't do; they're far too thin. Your body's had a severe shock and hypothermia's a risk. You'll need to keep your core temperature up. You'll need woollens.'

'But it's the middle of August.'

'And you nearly died, Miss Rushton. Your body doesn't care what the calendar says.' Lorna looked at Flora. 'Flora, you're about the same size and you need to change anyway. Once you're dry again, bring your Sunday best over to me.'

'But . . .' Sophia's expression was horrified as she looked between Lorna and Flora.

Flora caught her scorn and looked away. Yet again, without words, she was being told she wasn't good enough. She was lacking. 'Aye,' she nodded.

'Same goes for you two gentlemen – and her,' Lorna said, eyeing up Edward and James and Martha too; her frown deepened. 'Did she go in as well? Did she get caught under?'

'No. It's a long story,' Edward said quickly. 'But no – she's fine. We're all fine, just wet.'

'Hm, well, you'll need changing quickly. Every moment matters. Ask for Norman Ferguson and Donald McKinnon – they'll be able to help y' out with a spare change of clothes.'

'I'm sure that won't be necessary,' Edward said quickly. 'We can make our way back to the boat. We've plenty of things with us.'

'That may be, but you're not spending another twenty minutes on a sea crossing, in the smack, in freezing wet clothes. You can change first and then get back to the boat if that's what you want, but you're already shivering and the last thing I need is you all succumbing to secondary hypothermia – or worse. There's four of you and only one of me.'

'But—'

James put a hand on Edward's arm, stopping him from protesting any further. 'Thank you. We'll follow your instructions to the letter. The focus must be on making sure Miss Rushton is fully fit and well.'

Sophia smiled at his words, some colour returning to her cheeks.

'Come along then, Miss Rushton. Are you able to stand?'

'I . . . I'm not sure,' Sophia faltered, glancing at James again, and Flora guessed she wanted him to carry her all the way up to Lorna's cottage. Did she have any recollection of how heroically he had carried her from the sea? 'I do feel weak.'

James duly went to step forward but Lorna held up a hand, stopping him. 'Uh-uh, not you. Go find Norman Ferguson and change your clothes – he's your size,' she said warningly. 'David, Angus, you can help me transport Miss Rushton.'

Flora watched as her own brother and Mhairi's took Sophia by the shoulders and ankles and began carrying her over the beach like a sack of potatoes.

'Possibly I can walk . . .' Sophia said, her voice trailing off into the distance.

'I'll go to the manse and let the rev know what's happening,' Big Mary said, wringing her hands. 'Her parents were lunching there, I believe?'

Mhairi, still clutching the towel around Martha, began to herd her off too, towards the featherstore. 'Let's collect your clothes, then you can come to my house and see what we've got that's warm enough for you to put on. You know you're about the same age as my wee sister Christina. How old are you, pet?'

Flora hugged her arms around her body as she watched them go, scarcely able to believe how much had happened in a matter of minutes. She glanced across at Edward and James, both of them standing in sodden clothes, both shivering too and neither one of them aware of it.

'Jimmocks, Callie,' Edward said under his breath, watching as his sister was carried away. 'If you hadn't kept tabs on her like that . . .'

'It was Flora who saw her,' James said, looking over at her with an earnestness that suggested he would take no credit for the rescue. 'How are you, Miss MacQueen? Are you quite sure you didn't swallow any water?'

'I didn't,' she said.

'But you were out very deep – and you can't swim.'

'I'm fine.'

'You're frozen. You should change before you catch your death in this wind.' He looked at her with concern and she saw his hand shift a little in her direction, as if he was going to reach out to her.

'Catching death,' Edward echoed thoughtfully, a distant look on his face. 'It really is like that, isn't it? A ball that suddenly bounces at your feet. As if to say, "Your turn!"' He fell quiet again as the possibilities of what might have been impressed themselves on his imagination. 'It makes you realize how fragile life is,' he murmured. 'How fleeting . . . Life really can change in an instant.'

Flora heard the shift in tone and saw that Edward's eyes were upon her too now, burning with the ardour he had been trying to contain all day.

'We shouldn't allow ourselves to be distracted by things that really don't matter when in the end, all life really boils down to is being able to love and be loved in return.'

77

'Are you sure you didn't take a knock to the head too?' James asked with a scowl. His hand was back in his pocket now.

Edward laughed, his eyes still upon Flora. 'Quite possibly, but it might actually have knocked some sense *into* me!' He reached over and slapped James several times on the shoulder. 'And I don't care a fig for your modesty – you saved my sister's life, old boy!'

'Anyone would have done the same,' James demurred.

'No – you risked your life out there. The way you ran into the waves like that! You didn't give a thought to your own safety.'

James inhaled stiffly, his eyes flickering in her direction as if embarrassed that she was overhearing this exchange.

Edward arched an eyebrow. 'You know, my family will be forever in your debt now, Callie. Father will be at pains to thank you. I can say with some confidence that whatever you want will be yours for the asking. Anything at all.' He squeezed James's shoulder so hard that James looked across at him, and a silent message was communicated between them. 'So just ask.'

Flora watched as James looked back towards where Sophia was being carried away. All he had to do was ask.

Chapter Six

The girls convened in Effie's box room, pretending to be knitting, as they always did when they wanted to gossip. The day's excitement had been all the talk, even before the evening news, as word had spread quickly about the near-miss double tragedy. Mad Annie had been in a temper about it all afternoon, for she had been widowed when her own husband had drowned in the bay twenty-six years earlier; she had held a grudge against the sea ever since. The reverend, interrupted from his lunch, had insisted on saying prayers for the young lady in Lorna's surgery, which had only served to alarm her mother who, having been raised a Catholic, feared he was furtively delivering the last rites.

The visitors were back aboard their yacht now, light spilling from portholes to speckle the darkening sea. The sun had yet to set behind Ruival, but a slim lick of fire was beginning to sizzle along the horizon, the summer days so long here that nightfall was merely a moon's bounce of darkness.

It had been a volatile day in which lives might have been inexorably changed, as well as lost, and yet there had been nothing to suggest such alchemy in its inauspicious start as Flora had swept the hearth on her hands and knees that morning. Even if the Misses Rushton hadn't almost drowned, she herself had had her first picnic, eaten cakes and tarts and sandwiches – *salmon mayonnaise*, she repeated to herself, re-calling its exact shade of pink. She had drunk lemonade and felt bubbles fizz on her tongue. She had made a rich man fall into desperate desire for her, and a dour one smile (once, anyway).

The day had crackled with possibility, promise and threat – and yet now, at the close of it, what had really changed for her? She was still here, knitting socks with her friends in a room without windows. Edward Rushton wanted her, of that she was certain, but tomorrow they would waken to flat seas and he would sail away on the tide, her name forgotten by landfall.

Flora let her hands fall to her lap and pressed her head back against the rough wall, her eyes closed. She felt a heaviness in her chest she couldn't explain, an agitation in her bones that made her both restless and exhausted at once. What irked her? Why couldn't she settle?

'Look, she's dreaming on him,' she heard Effie say, then felt the kick to her ankle. She opened her eyes to find the others watching her.

'What?' she pouted, giving an irritable shrug.

'Did you make him fall in love with you?' Molly Ferguson asked. If it had been Effie doing the asking, the words would have been laced with sarcasm, but Molly's eyes shone brightly. She loved a love story; she was, herself, quietly falling in love with Flora's brother David, but she had yet to speak on it and few seemed to have noticed – certainly not her own abrasive brother Norman, nor Flora's parents. Flora herself had only guessed it when she had caught sight of a shared look in the kirk.

'I've known him less than a day,' Flora scoffed. 'And in that time, his sister almost died. There's barely been time to think, much less fall in love.'

'Aye, but there's nothing like a tragedy to focus the heart,' Molly shrugged, effortlessly turning a heel as she echoed Edward's own sentiments.

'Every time I looked over, he was staring at you,' Effie grumbled.

'He's devilish handsome!' Mhairi tittered. 'That smile! And his teeth are so white.' She sighed. 'I think it's the tow hair, though,' she mused. All the men on the isle were dark-haired and blue-eyed, and most grew thick beards. They were handsome but in an earthy, sullen way, never looking fully scrubbed, even on Sundays. Their bodies were stocky and muscular, with strong shoulders and broad hands like plates, though none were especially tall. Men like Edward Rushton – bright and polished, boldly coloured, with a jaunty nature – sat apart from them, as foreign in St Kilda as a parrot among the fulmars.

'I like his friend better, that Mr Callaghan,' Effie muttered. 'He doesn't talk drivel and he was fair decent on the rope.'

Flora thought again of James's ankles, though she had no idea why. She frowned, pushing the image away.

'He was all Miss Rushton could talk about when we were knitting,' Molly sighed. 'She's smitten, says she's been in love with him for years and has just been waiting to come of age so he can propose.'

'And what if he doesn't love her?' Effie asked with a wry look. 'She'll have been waiting in vain.'

'But he does love her.'

'Has he said that?' Flora asked, a little too quickly.

Molly shrugged. 'I don't know. But she must feel it's recip-rocated to say those things to a stranger, surely.'

Effie made a small sound that was neither agreement nor disagreement, her eyes flashing in Flora's direction. 'She seems a little silly for him, to me, that's all.'

81

'You don't know her,' Molly said loyally. 'We had a lovely conversation about the places she's visited and the book she was reading. She's almost finished it and she's offered to leave it for me – but you wouldn't know that, because you couldn't wait to escape the knitting lesson.'

'Aye! Because we were knitting! You know I'd rather chew my own leg. Besides, *he* was the one who couldn't wait. That Mr Callaghan was dead set on having some climbing instruction.'

'Tch, we could have done without the interruption,' Flora muttered. 'Throwing the rope down like that. Honestly Eff, of all the bluffs you could have chosen—'

'Wanting privacy, were you?' Mhairi winked.

'He was beginning to talk in a promising manner,' Flora shrugged. 'If we'd had a little more time to ourselves, who knows where it might have led?'

'Well, don't blame me,' Effie tutted. 'He was very specific about where he wanted to try and he said Ruival. I just wanted to earn my coins.' She gave a hapless shrug.

'Let me guess: he wanted to stop and look for *fossils* there?'

'No, I can't say he mentioned those—'

There came a knock at the door and all four of them looked up as Effie's father peered in. 'You're wanted, missy,' he said, looking across at Flora.

'Me?'

'Aye. Your father's here.'

Flora cast a frown at the others as she scrambled off the bed, carelessly dropping some of her stitches off the needle as she went and drawing a gasp from Molly, who tried to rescue them for her.

'Papa?' she asked, walking through into the Wee Gillies' main room. Her father was standing by the doorway, looking out across the bay. Had she forgotten to rinse a pot? Fetch a turf? Churn the cream? She was never knowingly diligent about her chores, but with all the day's disturbance, something must surely have slipped her mind. 'Is everything all right?'

Archie MacQueen turned and looked at her. Of all the men in her life, he was the only one who didn't seem to register her beauty; to him, she was simply Floss, his first-born daughter and second child, headstrong but kind-hearted, more likely to be found playing with the children than doing her chores; and, as he always called her in relentment, his songbird.

He gave a nod as if she had passed muster. 'You're invited for dinner.'

Dinner? She hesitated at the word. *Tea* wasn't for another half hour and didn't usually warrant an invitation.

'With them. On the boat.'

Her eyes widened and she heard the collective gasp at her back, the girls all gathered in the bedroom door. '. . . What?'

'Aye. The family wants to thank you for your help today.'

Flora blinked. She would hardly have described herself as a key helper in the rescue effort – finger-pointing had only done so much – but her heart soared as she understood what this really meant: James Callaghan might not be the only one for whom a near-tragedy would focus the heart. Edward Rushton was disregarding his friend's scorn too.

A smile escaped her as she automatically brushed her hand through her hair. 'And I can go?' she breathed.

Her father nodded, though he didn't look too pleased at her primping. 'Your mother doesn't trust them to return your clothes otherwise. She says you're to bring back Norman and Donald's things too.'

'Of course,' she nodded solemnly. It had been a source of smothered amusement watching the smart visitors climb aboard the smack in the St Kildans' tweeds earlier – lumpen, was it, Edward had said?

She turned back to the others with a rare moment of uncertainty, tucking her blouse into her skirt and tightening the waist. 'How do I look?'

'As bonny as the finch,' Molly beamed.

'But if I only had a dress—'

'A pretty face suits the dish-cloth, Floss,' Mhairi reminded her quickly. It was how she often consoled her when the rich tourists departed and Flora was left feeling their want a little too keenly.

'Ugh,' Effie dismissed with a roll of her eyes, crossing her arms over her chest.

'Hurry now,' her father said impatiently. 'Hamish is waiting at the jetty for us.'

With a parting look to the girls – each biting their lips, eyes wide – she stepped out into the evening. The moon was rising fast in the still-light sky. She pulled her shawl close around her shoulders, feeling the night's chill already drawing in.

Her father said nothing as they walked past the brightly lit cottages and the darkened factor's house towards the stone pier. He wasn't a man given to much conversation at the best of times but Flora wondered if he sensed something of the undertow to this mission, because he caught her by the elbow as they passed the featherstore, slowing their steps.

'Don't get your hopes up, lassie. They're not for the likes of us, and we're not for them.'

Flora swallowed and nodded, stung by his words; but what did her father really know? She had already drifted from the bedrock of her roots, the education into another life already

84

begun. Edward had indicated that he was a man who could show her another life. Might he now offer to give it to her?

The smack lilted on the soft waves, protected by the pier wall, and carefully they stepped aboard, Hamish nodding tersely in greeting as she settled herself primly on the bow. Within moments they were cutting through the water, the two men rowing in harmony and silence so that only the creak of the oars in their cups, and the sprinkling of droplets falling off the blades, could be discerned above the flurrying breeze. The waves grew bolder in the open bay, crested with sharp tips that occasionally caught the smack at the wrong time and splashed against her, but Flora scarcely noticed, her breath becoming more shallow with every stroke.

She kept her gaze fixed upon the yacht all the while. It looked like a bird, sleeping – the masts tucked and tightly wound, the creamy hull rocking back and forth on the anchor chain, everything in a state of slumber. But then came the sounds, low at first . . . music, drifting like a mist over the water . . . The two men swapped looks but Flora sat a little straighter, sensing beauty ahead of them.

In no time, it seemed to her, they were drawing alongside the vessel and Hamish gave a sharp call that drew a figure to the rails.

'Aye,' the captain said, raising a hand in acknowledgement and heading towards the stern. Moments later, a fixed ladder was lowered down and Hamish looped a rope around the bottom rung, tethering them together briefly.

'We'll be back for you when the moon hits Mullach Bi,' her father said, kissing her forehead once and looking pained, though not out of breath. 'So be ready.'

Flora glanced at the sky and saw it would take the moon two hours, or thereabouts, to track the path.

'And remember to bring back the clothes, or your mother will scalp you.'

'Aye.' She put a hand to the ladder and climbed upwards, not looking back.

The skipper got an arm to her elbow and helped her up with a roughness the Rushtons would never encounter. She righted herself quickly, striving for dignity.

'Good evening,' he said, looking back at her with black eyes and a scowl. It probably defied his belief that an island girl, dressed in homespun clothes, would be dining with them.

'Good evening,' she said after a moment, her gaze scanning the deck, though her head never moved. With relief, she saw there was no sign of her hosts and that she had another moment to compose herself. Soft light flickered from oil lanterns and she took in her first glimpses of life aboard a yacht: railings gleamed like gold, the wooden decking was the colour almost of Mhairi's hair, and thick white ropes – so unlike theirs used for climbing – were pulled taut in a web from the masts onto cleats. The back of the deck where they stood was an open space, with a small rowing boat tucked in at the end and a shuffleboard painted on the floor. A long table was bolted to the decking and covered by a fixed shelter that extended across to a double-height cabin which was just like a house upon the boat. To one side of a window was a door, to the other a staircase leading up to another level, winding around on itself like one of the shells that was occasionally washed up after a storm.

'You can go through,' the captain said, gesturing towards the cabin. 'They're having cocktails.'

Cocktails. Another new word.

He bounded up the staircase, disappearing from sight and

leaving her there; she stared at the door, wondering what she would find inside when even the outside was like a palace. Suddenly she understood why the visitors treated the villagers with such . . . bemusement. The life she knew, the only one she had ever known, must be as alien to them as this was to her.

She put a hand to the doorknob – solid, gleaming – hearing a staccato laugh on the other side of the door and a babble of voices all talking over one another. The door opened with a creak of the hinges and she stepped through.

'Ah, Miss MacQueen!' Edward jumped up from his seat, an elegant chair of a reddish colour she couldn't even describe. He looked delighted to see her, and infinitely more distinguished again now that he had changed into an ivory linen suit.

He rushed over to her and, reaching for her hand, pressed it to his lips. 'Thank you for agreeing to come tonight.'

She blinked at him, too dumbstruck to speak. This couldn't . . . this couldn't be a *boat*. Paintings in gold frames hung on wooden-clad walls that were so glossy she couldn't be absolutely sure that water wasn't running down them. Silk curtains hung at the windows, crystal lights shimmered; there was a bookcase, flowers in vases. Even a fireplace!

'My parents wanted to thank you for everything you did for Sophia today,' he said, leading her through to the area where everyone was congregated on long, soft chairs.

'But I really didn't do—'

'Nonsense. Had it not been for your excellent vision, James could never have found her, nor got to her in time.'

'Edward is right, Miss MacQueen,' his father said, stepping forward, taking her hand and bowing slightly so that his whiskers brushed her skin. 'There were many factors that came into play to protect our daughters this afternoon, and you were one of them. We're exceedingly grateful.'

'It was really nothing,' she murmured, looking over at his wife too who was sitting, pale-faced and clutching a glass, on one of the chairs. 'How . . . how is Miss Rushton?'

She looked around in closer detail now at the gathered faces all watching her and found Sophia in the corner of one of the chairs, surrounded by cushions. James Callaghan was sitting beside her, clutching a drink as well and looking distinctly displeased to see Flora, though he nodded politely in greeting. He too was wearing a light suit.

Sophia had changed (no doubt at speed) from Flora's Sunday best drugget skirt and cream wool blouse into a floaty primrose-yellow dress with a blue ribbon at the waist. She looked nothing like someone who had almost died that day. Were they celebrating already, Flora wondered, feeling again that tightness in her chest.

'I'm perfectly well, thank you. It's so sweet of you to ask,' Sophia purred. Her cheeks were pink, her eyes burning with almost feverish intensity, and her hair had been combed through and styled in soft waves. Too late, Flora realized her own hair was still in a braid from this morning. Babyish. Gauche. Inelegant. And as for her clothes . . .

'I'm sorry that I didn't . . . change,' she faltered as she looked back at the Rushtons in their finery, her fingers clutching her thin skirt. She had no other clothes, for her spare set was still drying by the fire.

'We gave you no time,' Edward said quickly. 'It was rude of us to give you no warning, but by the time we got our heads straight . . . Besides, you look simply sensational. I swear you could wear a potato sack and make it look like a Vionnet.'

She looked at him blankly. A what?

'Come, what's your poison?' he asked her, taking her by the hand and walking her towards a cabinet set out with sparkling crystal decanters. Instantly, she felt all eyes fine-tune upon their physical contact, and she sensed it had been a deliberate move on his part. 'Or shall I choose for you?'

She looked at him, knowing that he was saving her, that he had remembered – only fractionally too late – that the St Kildans rarely drank. She nodded and watched as he mixed a concoction of different liquids (and – was that an *egg*?) into a silver container. Covering it, he shook it extravagantly, while she stood there, silent and awkward. Music was playing quietly from . . . somewhere . . . She saw the gramophone in the corner and remembered her earlier conversation with James Callaghan in which she'd told him she longed to see one. And here it was. On a boat.

She watched as he poured the mixture into a glass, stirring it and handing it over with a smile. 'A White Lady cocktail,' he said.

'A White Lady cocktail,' she repeated.

'I did consider one called Death in the Afternoon, but given today's events, I don't think my parents would appreciate the humour.'

'Edward!' his mother scolded. 'That's not funny!'

'See? Come, sit,' he grinned, turning his back and winking at her, before leading her over to one of the long chairs. Carefully she lowered herself next to him; she was used to hard wooden settles but this was cloth-covered with feather cushions. The ground was covered with a soft, pale rug that extended to the walls, and she remembered her grubby feet were bare. She scrunched up her toes, trying to minimize contact with the floor, her gaze tangling with James Callaghan's as he clocked her private shame again. He had a knack, it seemed, for catching her out.

She placed the glass to her lips and took a sip, having to stop her face from registering every emotion of shock and surprise as the tastes hit. Unlike the lemonade, they were too complex to break down, her system immediately overwhelmed by the mix of sweet and sour, bitterness and syrup. It burned her throat – and yet she liked it.

'Good?' Edward asked her.

She nodded, the glass still at her lips.

'Drink it slowly,' James said quickly, from across the room. '. . . It's stronger than you think.'

Obediently, she lowered her hands, but she glowered at him, feeling a burn in her cheeks that he had shown her up and made a point of her lack of sophistication, even though it must already be perfectly apparent to everyone here.

'Ignore him. It'll help you relax, take the edge off. It can't be easy coming in here and joining people like us,' Edward said, shooting an annoyed look at his friend. 'Have another sip.'

She obeyed again, aware that the room had fallen into a stiff quietude since her entrance. Edward's excitement at seeing her again was evident – but had he forced her presence upon the rest of them?

'Where's Martha?' she asked, realizing the younger girl was absent.

'In bed, I'm afraid. Today's fright has wiped her out rather,' Mrs Rushton said.

'I'm sorry to hear that. It must have been dreadful for her.'

'To endure the waves herself, only to then have that ghastly wait as James saved Sophia . . .' Mrs Rushton pressed a hand to her heart and looked gratefully across at the hero.

James made a dismissive motion, shaking his head, but Sophia gazed at him with more than gratitude.

'I'm sure she'll have nightmares tonight,' Mrs Rushton continued, looking back at Flora. 'The water's so treacherous here. It's a wonder to me that more of your people aren't lost to it.'

'Well . . . we steer well clear of it, largely.'

'But you go out on the rowing boat.'

'Only in the bay, mostly. And it's only ever the men. They're strong, and they can read the conditions well. They won't even try if they don't like the look on it.'

'Mostly?' James cleared his throat as she looked over at him in surprise.

'What?'

'. . . You said they row in the bay mostly. Where do they go occasionally?'

She hesitated at his apparent interest, seeing a sharpness in his gaze. Was he trying to trip her up again? 'Well, the men make occasional trips to the other isles in the archipelago – mainly Boreray in early summer, to pluck the sheep.'

'That's four miles hence?'

'About that.' She was impressed he knew.

'That's a long way in a rowing boat.'

'Aye, but as I said, the men are strong and they check conditions first. They take no unnecessary chances.'

His eyes narrowed with seemingly further interest. 'Where else do they go?'

'There's a cave round the back of Dun where they tie up overnight for the ling fishing in spring.'

'Ling?'

'Aye, they can get a half dozen men sleeping in the boat.'

91

'That must be cramped.'

'Aye.'

She went to look away, but he didn't let her go, the questions still coming. 'Anywhere else?'

She felt pinned by his gaze. 'They go to Stac Lee for the gannet harvest in April.'

'Stac Lee? Now that's the needle-shaped rock, just outside the bay?'

'Aye. It sits between here and Boreray.'

James frowned, never taking his eyes off her. 'But it's sheer vertical rock. How do they land?'

'By jumping.'

He gave a shocked laugh, his entire body jolting like she'd jabbed him with a hot poker. 'They *jump* from the boat onto the stack? But what if they miss?'

'They don't,' she shrugged.

'But it's still one hell of a risk to take. One wrong move and they're certain to drown, surely?'

He spoke as if they had a choice. 'Well, we need the harvest. We can't afford to pick and choose,' she said grudgingly, not wanting to spell out how difficult it was to scratch an existence from this rock in the ocean. How appetite or taste had no consideration when enough was all that mattered. 'Besides, the risk is minimal now. Someone in the past managed to get an anchoring into the rock at the landing point. It gives the men something to hold onto, and their feet are used to gripping, of course.'

'Well, of course,' he echoed.

She looked away this time, knowing he was mocking her and hating how he seemed to unnerve her.

Everything was rounded here – no sharp corners, she noticed. Furniture bolted to the floors or walls, rails on every surface so that even in a storm this room would remain just as serene, just as tranquil. The Rushtons' lives had brushed against horror today, but no trace of it remained, and Flora felt like she had stepped inside a painting – into a world that was too beautiful, colourful and soft to be real. Were her friends really, even now, still sitting in Effie's room, knitting on the bed, while she sat here, sipping on a cocktail? How could two lives – so completely different – sit beside one another so closely?

She could feel Edward's eyes upon her, an intensity in them willing her to integrate and belong. Over his shoulder, almost as a mirage, she saw that door open again and the other world – his world – glide past. This was it, her opportunity. She had to . . . fit, somehow. Show him she could belong; become friends with his friends and charm his family. She sat straighter as she caught his gaze and she smiled at him, forced at first, but he beamed back so readily that it spread to her eyes and she felt herself relax.

He stretched an arm along the back of the chair, as if her confidence was contagious. 'We were, uh, just discussing the Glorious Twelfth before you arrived.'

'Oh?' She swallowed. Every new line of conversation threw her.

'Yes. Friends of ours have a grouse shoot in Yorkshire – we go every year, but Callie thinks he'll have to swerve.'

She swallowed again. 'Oh?'

'He's adamant he has to prepare for his beastly expedition to the North Pole,' Sophia complained, resting a hand on James's thigh. 'It's *so* unfair.'

'It's to Greenland, Sophia, not the North Pole,' James murmured, letting his gaze fall briefly to her hand before looking back at her again. 'And I really don't have any choice. Most of the expedition team have already left. It's bad enough that I'm having to join them in the Faroes as it is. The rest of the team left London last week.'

'Where did you say they're setting up base camp?' Edward asked.

'Forty miles west of Angmagssalik,' James replied, looking surprised by the question.

'Ah yes, that's the spot.' Edward looked over at her and gave a roll of his eyes. 'Rolls off the tongue, doesn't it?'

Flora smiled, but she was intrigued. 'What is the purpose of the expedition?' she asked him.

'It's called the British Arctic Air Route Expedition. We're investigating the possibility of a new transatlantic air passage between England and Canada.'

Flora didn't know much about air passages but she knew her geography, for there were maps hanging in the schoolroom. 'That's a long way.'

'It is. But that's the point. We're looking into the potential for a shorter route that connects the two via the Arctic Circle – namely the Faroes, Iceland, Greenland, Baffin Island and Hudson Bay, before coming to a stop in Winnipeg.' He traced a sweeping line in the air as if there was a map before them both. 'We're mapping two hundred miles of coastline. And surveying the least known part of the ice path along the east coast and central ice plateau of Greenland.'

'It sounds dangerous,' she murmured. James Callaghan, fossil-hunter, hadn't exactly struck her as an adventurer or thrill-seeker earlier; but then she thought of him cragging with Effie, barefoot; his strong ankles diving into the waves . . . He was more than he seemed.

'No more dangerous than people who can't swim leaping onto vertical rocks in the middle of the ocean, I'm sure,' he rejoindered. His eyes flashed with an inscrutable look and she couldn't tell if he was joking or not.

'It sounds fun to me!' Edward said. 'Lots of dog-sledding and larking about in seaplanes, from what I can make out.'

'Seaplanes?' she queried, but he just laughed, as if she'd been joking.

James caught her look of confusion but he looked away, choosing not to highlight her ignorance for once.

'How will you survive? What will you eat there? It's hard enough here, but on the ice . . .' She found herself fascinated by the idea of it. She wanted just to get to the mainland, but he was visiting a whole other continent.

'Provisions have already been taken out on the ship but we'll supplement with whatever we can hunt there – fish, seals, birds. We shan't starve.'

'How many are you?'

'Fourteen, which is a goodly number. We're not too large as to be unwieldy but we've a solid core of men to keep us going should sickness strike.'

'Is that likely?'

He shrugged. 'It's as likely there as it is here.'

His gaze was steady and he held himself almost preternaturally still as they talked, his attention wholly upon her even though Sophia's hand still lingered on his thigh. Something sat behind his eyes whenever they talked, but she couldn't pinpoint what exactly. Disapproval? Dislike? Disgust?

'Why are you going? I thought . . . I thought Edward said you have a textiles business?'

'Callie fancies himself both a businessman *and* an explorer,' Edward said dryly.

'If we discover the route is viable, then it will become my

principal business,' James replied in clipped tones. Flora sensed it was a bone of contention between them. 'I'd like to diversify my family's business away from just textiles. Commercial air travel is the future, and a transatlantic route will open up the world in a way that's been denied until now. No more week-long ocean crossings to New York. The world is speeding up. Efficiency is key . . .'

Was it? She listened, feeling intimidated by his careless knowledge. She had no idea that it took a week to sail to New York, or why anyone should even need to do that. The St Kildans only ever crossed to the other Hebridean isles when there was an urgent need for flour, or a doctor, or – following the smallpox epidemic of 1727 – more husbands. But it wasn't to her that his words were directed.

'. . . As I've told you countless times, Rushton, it could change the world.'

'*Could*, dear boy. Could.' Edward glanced at her. 'He's been after me to invest for months now.'

'It'll make you rich, brother,' Sophia said loyally to Edward, while smiling at James.

'We're already rich.'

'But a man can always be richer,' Sophia purred, crossing her legs.

'Well, I'll certainly drink to that!' Edward said, raising his glass and draining it.

James's eyes flashed, but he made no further comment.

'And you're *quite* sure it's not dangerous, dear?' Mrs Rushton asked him.

'Quite. We're well prepared and well equipped.'

'The team are using Shackleton's old vessel, Mother, the *Quest*,' Edward said, before glancing at Flora again. '. . . You know of Shackleton, the explorer?'

96

'Of course,' she lied, taking another sip of the White Lady.

'Poor chap. Still, he died doing what he loved, I suppose.'

'As long as *you* don't die doing what you love,' Sophia gasped, looking at James with alarm.

'I'm not planning on it.'

Flora gave a small laugh at his dry manner, but no one else joined in and she tried to turn it into a cough. The ghost smile hovered on James's lips again.

'Tell me, what do you love to do, Miss MacQueen?' Sophia asked her suddenly.

'Me?' Flora froze. 'I . . .' She faltered, glancing at Edward again and seeing the urge in his eyes that she find a way to connect with his family.

'She loves to sing,' James replied for her, meeting her gaze.

Sophia sat a little straighter. 'Really? . . . How would you know, James?'

'Miss MacQueen was my tour guide to McKinnon's Stone earlier. We chatted while we walked.'

'Oh. Yes, of course.' Sophia settled back, regarding Flora coolly as a small silence bloomed. '. . . Well, perhaps you would like to sing for us now?' she asked Flora, before immediately turning to her father with a keen look, as if he got the casting vote.

'Oh, but—'

'Why not? A little pre-dinner entertainment would be splendid, if you're quite sure, young lady?' he replied.

Flora hesitated. How could this have happened? Why had James put her on the spot like this?

'Go on,' Edward murmured encouragingly. 'Show them.'

'Very well, then,' she said quietly. She took another sip of her drink, then another – the alcohol infusing her blood so that she felt the loosening of her limbs and the relaxing of her spirit in this stiff space; it seemed to narrow the chasm between her and them, and she wanted more. Instead, she stared down at the ground as she tried to think of something short and fleeting to sing.

'Oh, you must stand. Do it properly,' Sophia urged her. 'I wish I could sing, but I just sound like a hippo with a sore throat whenever I try.' Her staccato laugh rose into the air, her hand touching James's thigh like a flitting butterfly.

Flora looked at her for a moment, sensing disingenuousness in her words despite the apparent friendliness. Miss Sophia Rushton had been raised as a cultured gentlewoman and Flora didn't doubt that singing, and no doubt playing an instrument too, counted among her many accomplishments. But, for some reason, she wanted Flora to have the limelight, to be on the spot.

She was expecting her to fail.

Flora handed her drink to Edward to hold as slowly she rose, smoothing her palms on her skirt. She could feel every set of eyes upon her but that, at least, was something to which she was accustomed, and she raised her focus to the painting above the fireplace as she began to sing.

It wasn't anything they would recognize, she was sure, for it was an old Gaelic ballad that her grandmother used to sing by the fire – winsome and forlorn, it nonetheless trickled over the octaves like a dancing wind, showcasing her range. Her voice was always a surprise, even to herself – rich yet light, she was capable of hitting the high, airy notes as well as sinking into deeper, lower caramel tones with ease – and she forgot her audience as she allowed the music to travel over and through her. It was the only time she ever escaped her body and became a soul.

She sang just three verses out of the six she knew, not wanting to go on too long, and the ending must have felt abrupt to her hosts because there was a long silence for several moments afterwards, as if they were waiting for more.

'Er . . . well . . . that's it,' she shrugged, sitting back into the chair again and seeing how everyone was staring at her, open-mouthed; Edward had a glazed expression on his face that only changed as she took her drink back from him. Instantly he began clapping.

The others followed suit, the ripple of applause fringed with swapped looks of surprise.

'Brava!' Edward cried, delightedly clasping her hand and again pressing it to his lips. 'Why didn't you *say*?' he asked, incredulous.

'Say what?'

'That you have a gift!'

'Oh,' she recoiled. 'It's no—'

'It most certainly is! You sing like an angel! A lark! Doesn't she, Mama?'

'I – indeed, dear,' she faltered, her gaze fixed upon their clutching hands.

'Quite exquisite,' his father added. 'Edward's right: you have a gift.'

'Thank you, Papa,' Edward said, as if the compliment had been aimed at him. 'Sophia?'

Sophia, mute for once, nodded vigorously, straining a smile.

'Callie? Don't you agree?'

There was a hesitation. James had been clapping politely, but with a look in his eyes that made plain he was tired of this charade of entertaining the island girl. 'Most pleasant,' he finally murmured.

Edward turned back to her. 'You see? Not only are you the

most beautiful creature I've ever seen in my life, but you're also the kindest, most talented—'

'Steady on!' James scoffed. The words seemed to take him by surprise as much as anyone, and he frowned into his drink.

A frown puckered Edward's brow too as a small silence bloomed, tension ratcheting between the two men as Flora saw a flash of temper cross Edward's good-natured visage. 'Actually, no, old boy – I don't think I shall. Not this time. It's never been truer that time and tide waits for no man and I know I'll regret it for the rest of my life if I don't speak from my heart now, while I have the opportunity.' He looked over to his parents as Flora saw James and Sophia swap horrified looks. 'Surely today was proof that tomorrow is not a given? How very different things might have been, but for a few quirks of fate that kept us just on the right side of joy.'

'Eddie, I'm fine!' Sophia protested with a weak laugh. 'Don't make a song and dance about it, please.'

'No. We were lucky, that was all, and we shouldn't assume happiness is our given, something to squander or take for granted. We have a responsibility to actively hunt our happiness down, and I know . . . I know I have found mine.'

He turned to Flora again, reaching for her hand, his blue eyes brimming with an ardour that took even her aback.

'Rushton,' James murmured, a growl in his voice that was exactly the same as the warning he had issued at the picnic earlier. Flora looked at him, locking eyes and seeing clearly all the disapproval he harboured for her.

But Edward would not be deterred. He squeezed her hand in his. 'Flora – I never dreamt when I came ashore this morning that my life could be turned around so completely in the course of a single day, but—'

A bell sounded. It rang like the kirk bell but was far closer, too close to have come from there.

'Aha!' Mr Rushton exclaimed, slapping his thighs. 'Is that the time?'

Flora looked at Edward in confusion. Were they to pray?

'Dinner is served,' Mrs Rushton said stiffly, waiting a moment so that her husband could rise first and then help her from her seat.

Flora watched as together they shuffled towards the door. Sophia, rising gracefully, smoothed her hair away from her face in a self-soothing gesture as she waited for James to put down his drink; they too moved as a pair, it seemed. There was a pause before he knocked it back and set the glass down hard on the table, his eyes locking with Edward's in silent disdain as he passed.

'Talk about saved by the bell,' Sophia murmured to James as they got to the door.

'Mm.'

Flora and Edward watched in astonishment as the party cleared the room within moments, his proclamations hanging in the air like an unfinished requiem. Nothing had been said by the others, but they both knew judgement had been passed.

Chapter Seven

Oil lanterns flickered on the deck as everyone took their seats around a table set with cut glass, polished cutlery and white linen. It wasn't a wholly unfamiliar scene to Flora; she had seen the reverend's table set up in a similar fashion once, when she had gone to collect a Bible one evening. The only difference was, this table bobbed and had a view out to sea.

Edward pulled out her chair for her before seating himself, James moving slowly around everyone and pouring drinks. He was being careful – the wind appeared to have got up while they were drinking their cocktails, and the yacht was rocking a little more than was fully comfortable. Spillage seemed more likely than not, but his hand remained steady.

Of course it did. She watched him, sensing that he never faltered, never fell. He was a man forever upright and composed. A man who always did the Right Thing.

'Some wine, Miss MacQueen?' he asked, coming to stand beside her, holding the bottle in a strange manner by its base. 'Or perhaps you'd prefer some water? That White Lady was rather strong.'

She bristled at the inference that she was losing her head. 'Some wine would be lovely, thank you.'

The hesitation before he poured registered his disapproval, as ever without words.

'What are we dining on tonight, Mama?' Sophia asked, draping the little cloth over her lap so that her dress was protected. Flora followed suit, also seeing how Sophia reached for the glass with her right hand and not the left. She was determined to follow every cue, to watch and learn, her instruction already begun . . .

She caught sight of the cutlery before her and frowned. What was this? She was used to knives and forks and spoons, but this equipment – it had teeth . . . and jaws . . . Not dissimilar to some of Lorna's medical equipment. She looked around the table in dismay; everyone's settings were identical.

'Lobster, dear. Mellowes said he took a chance and threw down some pots earlier. More luck than judgement, apparently.'

'I doubt that. I'd trust his judgement over anyone's when it comes to all things nautical,' Mr Rushton said. 'He's a first-rate skipper.'

James returned the wine bottle to a side cabinet fitted with two deep, round depressions. The bottle fitted perfectly, sinking in almost up to its neck, and Flora realized it had been built purely to house the wine. The boat had actually been built with wine-drinking in mind?

James came to sit in the empty chair beside Sophia, diametrically opposite Flora sitting beside Edward; Mr and Mrs Rushton occupying the heads of the table. A girl, roughly her age, appeared from the cabin, carrying a large tray loaded with plates. The deck tipped left and right as she walked and she was forced to counter-balance her arms to her legs. Flora watched, feeling nervous on her behalf, but she capably set the tray down on a collapsible frame that had been set up just behind Mr Rushton and began serving out. Her movements were timid and quick, her eyeline never rising above the tablecloth.

'Thank you, Tilly. This looks delicious,' Edward said,

smiling brightly at her as she placed his plate before him. The girl gave a shy nod, scarcely making eye contact, but Flora noticed that no one else deigned to speak to her as she moved around them like a benevolent ghost.

She disappeared back inside and Flora looked down at her plate with dismay: but for the potatoes, it was filled with vegetables she couldn't name and something hard-shelled. A crab, but not. How were they supposed to get *in*?

Mr Rushton cleared his throat and held up his glass in a strange, frozen manner so that everyone fell silent, all eyes upon him. 'Before we eat, I should like to raise a toast. To chance meetings' – he nodded his head towards Flora before looking back at his daughter, his smile growing – 'and good fortune. May we always be so blessed.'

'Chance meetings and good fortune,' the others resounded, holding up their glasses too for a couple of beats before taking a sip.

A toast, Flora repeated in her head, copying every move they made, half a beat behind.

She felt eyes upon her and found Edward watching, as if seeing her calculations for getting through this. He winked at her and she smiled, grateful he at least was making this as easy for her as he could. Their understanding on the beach earlier hadn't been forgotten, and he didn't look like a man ready to give up. Not yet.

Glasses were returned to the table and everyone picked up their cutlery, preparing to eat. They were covered by the overhead awning but the lively breeze still danced around them, invisible but bossy and rumpling Sophia's soft-set waves. Flora's heavy St Kildan braid, by contrast, didn't stir.

'Mm, I love asparagus and tomatoes,' Edward said appreciatively, his fork hovering momentarily over each vegetable and she realized he was naming them for her. 'And lobster is my absolute favourite.'

He picked up one of the implements – the one with the jaws – flexing it a few times in his hand before cracking one of the claws with it, then pulling out the soft flesh inside with a hook. Flora watched closely, her keen eyes missing nothing, before she repeated his action herself. Cracking the shell was no trouble for her – the St Kildans had strong hands as well as feet – and when she succeeded in not disgracing herself, she glanced over with silent delight. Edward winked once more, looking openly adoring, and she felt a wave of power that she could do this. Eyes were upon them, but she didn't need to look up to guess whose.

'What a pity this is our last night before heading back,' Sophia said, daintily cutting an asparagus stem. 'It's been such fun. I'm not ready to go back yet.'

'I'd be more than happy to stay for the week!' Edward said eagerly.

'James needs to prepare for his expedition, you know that,' Sophia said, glancing nervously in Flora's direction.

'I'm glad you've enjoyed the trip, Sophia darling,' her father said. 'And to think you said you had no sea legs,' he added, patting her hand warmly.

'Well, it's all turned out to be considerably more diverting than I expected,' Sophia replied, her body angling ever so slightly so that James's fork paused in mid-air before he bit into his lobster.

'. . . Where have you visited?' Flora asked cautiously, uncertain whether she was expected to contribute to the conversation or sit in silence. Their welcome couldn't exactly have been called warm and unreserved.

Sophia's eyes flitted towards her with a flick of irritation.

'Skye. Benbecula. Uist. Harris . . . We hadn't really intended going past the Minch, but James persuaded us to venture into open water and try here for a couple of days.'

'Well, it made sense to have a go, seeing as the wind was blowing in the right direction and conditions were fortuitous,' James shrugged.

'Not that fortuitous, my stomach recalls,' Mrs Rushton said lightly, a smile playing at the corners of her mouth.

'Indeed,' he agreed quickly, smiling back.

Flora watched him, the agreeable son-in-law ingratiating himself and proving himself as right for them as she was wrong. He was already part of the family. And yet . . . She watched him attack his meal. On the surface of things, he talked politely and pleasantly, carrying the conversation during any lulls and making light-hearted comments that drew smiles and groans as required. But watching him from the corner of her eye, she could see that he was drinking more than eating – and taking great pains to ensure everyone's glasses were always topped up.

Her gaze drifted across to Sophia beside him, winsome and radiant in her yellow chiffon gown, the sleeves fluttering in the wind. Sophia looked over at him every twenty seconds or so, permanently checking in on him, as if making sure he was still there. And the more she looked, the more James avoided her gaze.

He was nervous, Flora realized. And she could guess why. Everyone was expecting the proposal, but had Edward hijacked it earlier with his own attempted declaration to her? Had James missed his chance? The conversation had moved on since then to distinctly less sentimental topics, and Rushton senior was now holding forth on the Stock Exchange and somebody called Lloyd.

'You heard about Hatry's latest plan?' he asked the two younger men, chewing on asparagus. 'He wants to merge all the big steel and iron names into a consolidated concern. United Steel Companies, he's calling it.'

'Well then, that sounds like a pie we want a piece of,' Edward murmured, one arm laid out on the table, his fingers stroking the base of the wine glass. He glanced at her again, winking once more and making no secret of it. In the space of a half hour, it had apparently become standard communication between them. 'Don't you agree, Callie?'

'Actually I'm not so sure, no,' James demurred.

'Oh?' Rushton senior asked.

'There's a rumour going round that his so-called empire is just a house of cards.'

'*Rumour?*' Edward queried, faint mockery in his tone. Flora sensed a residual tension between the two men, their earlier discord not quite laid to rest. 'Since when did we pay attention to those?'

'I've some contacts in the Glasgow steelworks who are minded to think he's over-reached this time.'

Edward tutted. 'Never underestimate Cecil Hatry, I say. He's come back from failure and ruin more than once. The man's got vision and this is his most ambitious project yet.'

'I don't doubt it. But he needs the funds to finance something of that scale, and there are those who think his true wealth is inflated. Smoke and mirrors, if you will.'

'You really should stop being so timid, Callie,' Edward said breezily, reaching for his glass. Flora saw how James's jaw clenched on the insult. No man wanted to be called timid, especially in front of the woman he loved. 'Why should you put rumour ahead of solid business expertise and reputation? Papa's known old Hatry for years.'

'Well, socially at least, my boy,' Rushton senior murmured repressively. 'But you never really know a man until you do business with him.'

It was a subtle set-down of his son, and the men fell quiet.

'I don't think there's anything wrong with being cautious,' Sophia said primly. 'I'd far rather know we were comfortable and secure than live in terror thinking we might lose it all from one day to the next. James has exactly the right attitude, if you ask me.'

We.

Her meaning was perfectly clear as she looked upon him with adoring eyes, and Flora watched the opportunity open up for James's question again.

She waited – they all did – feeling the tension rise. Flora knew this was it, and even Mrs Rushton reached for her husband's hand. It was the last night of their trip. Surely it was now or never, regardless of whether Flora was intruding. It wasn't as if Sophia's answer was in doubt.

Just ask.

James lifted his glass to take another sip but found it was empty. He stared into the bottom for a moment before looking back up and finding all eyes upon him. His cheeks pinked and he glowered across at Flora, as if all this were her fault.

'My glass is empty,' he muttered, pushing his chair back so that it scraped on the deck. He retrieved the wine bottle from its custom-built spot and slowly went around the table refilling drinks, but his nervous agitation, hidden so well earlier, had broken cover.

Looks were shared as Sophia stared down at her fingers interlaced in her lap, and the moment – another one – began to slide away. Flora felt a pang of pity for her. The two women could hardly claim to be friends, but that didn't mean she couldn't sympathize with Sophia's predicament. In a funny sort of way, they both wanted the same thing: to marry into new lives.

Flora looked straight ahead as James came and stood beside her to refill her glass. The boat had drifted around its anchor chain and was now positioned to afford a clear view straight back to shore. She saw her home in a new way: humble, lonely, stoic. Her forebears had occupied this rock for over two thousand years and it provided shelter, community, love and warmth – but none of those things were exclusive to here, and they could be had in almost any other place with less suffering and a lot more ease. Sitting here now, sipping wine aboard a yacht, she felt sure that a life with the Rushtons – with Edward – would not be a misstep; that somehow, she belonged right here and not over there.

And yet it would always be home. There was comfort in the sight of the lights winking from the cottages, the curve of the street as it hugged the foot of the slopes of Oiseval, Connachair and –

She gasped, sitting back in her chair as she saw the moon shining fully upon the upper slopes of Mullach Bi; James jolted his arm away in reply, an arc of wine spilling from the bottle and spattering heavily across her clothes. She looked down at her blouse – ivory cotton trimmed with a red thread – now ruined with what looked like bloodstains.

'Oh!' she cried, jumping up. She had only three blouses and now one was ruined?

'You shocked me, startling like that,' he said quickly, blaming her. 'Here, wash it out before it dries—' And he reached over, grabbing a napkin, stuffing it in the water jug and beginning to blot her blouse.

Flora recoiled as the cold water seeped straight through onto her skin, his one hand on her back to hold her still and the other pressing against her chest as he soaked and dabbed the stains. He was stepping almost on her feet, he was so close. It took several moments of her standing there, frozen, before his fluster passed and he seemed to catch himself.

He looked down at her, flummoxed by the sudden predicament, before he instantly stepped away. 'I beg your pardon,' he muttered. 'I was trying to help.'

Flora, seeing that the blouse had been soaked through, pulled it quickly away from her body just as the maid came out.

'Tilly,' Mrs Rushton said with authority, less concerned about the state of the table than Flora's modesty. 'Can you please find a change of blouse for Miss MacQueen? Quick-quick, please.'

'Oh, I can just wear the one I loaned to Miss Rushton,' Flora said. 'I needed to bring it back with me anyway, and my father will already be on his way over to collect me. He said to be ready when the moon hit Mullach Bi.' She pointed towards the mountain. 'That was what surprised me, you see,' she said, glancing at James by way of explanation.

'Actually, Captain Mellowes just sent me through, Mrs Rushton,' Tilly said in a small voice. 'He's had to message the men ashore telling them not to make the crossing.'

'What?'

'The swell's too high, he says.'

'. . . He sent a message? But how? By carrier pigeon?' Mrs Rushton asked crossly.

'Morse, mother,' Edward said, pushing his chair back too and walking over to the railings as well. Unhooking a lantern, he looked down into the darkness.

'But . . . I have to get back,' Flora said with alarm, looking around the gathered company.

'No, not tonight, I'm afraid,' Edward said with a shake of his head, angling the lantern to catch the light best on the water. 'The skipper's right; it's got way up.'

'No, it'll be fine,' Flora protested.

'It's fine on *here*,' Edward said, replacing the lantern and coming back to the table. 'Because our long beam flattens out the worst of it – but your tiny rowing boat? It would be coming over the sides with every stroke. They'd be sunk before they were halfway here.'

Flora was appalled at the thought. 'But . . .' she faltered. What was she supposed to do?

'We won't steal you away in the night, if that's what you're thinking – although God knows I'm tempted to sneak the skipper some cash to try,' Edward said with a wolfish smile and that intimate wink again as he reached for his newly refilled drink. 'Don't worry. If it's too rough in the bay, it's most certainly too rough in open water. If you can't leave, neither can we.'

It was a slightly more reassuring thought. She looked back at the cabin. But where would she sleep? Out here?

'And Mellowes is certain of that, is he?' Mrs Rushton persisted, a look of slight panic on her face.

'Yes, ma'am,' Tilly replied.

Mrs Rushton inhaled deeply from her position at the table, looking pressed. It was several moments before she spoke. '. . . In which case, please make sure one of the berths is ready for Miss MacQueen. And avail her of some nightclothes and soap.'

'Very good, Mrs Rushton. Will you be wanting dessert?'

Mrs Rushton hesitated as she looked around at their

fractured party: Flora's arms crossed over her chest as she shivered in the night wind, Sophia's chin tipped down as she tried not to cry. 'No – I think, on reflection, we're all feeling a little fragile after today. Under the circumstances, it's probably best that we retire early. Especially with a day of travel ahead of us tomorrow.'

'Very good, Mrs Rushton,' the maid said again, scurrying off.

'Well,' Sophia said, into the silence that opened up. 'Today is just full of surprises, isn't it?' Her tone was light, but there was a slightly feral look in her eyes, her hands tightly clasped together. 'Wherever will it end, I wonder?'

'The weather can often cause problems here,' Flora murmured, feeling that this was all somehow her fault.

'Oh?' Mrs Rushton asked coolly.

'Aye. In the winter, the wind can be so ferocious, it can tear the roofs off. We have to have them strapped down – I don't know if you noticed?'

'No, no. I can't say that I did.' Mrs Rushton looked back towards the shore, a frown settling on her brow. 'You really do have a wild time of it here, don't you?'

Her disdain was clear and this time Flora didn't bother to reply. There was little point in defending her home when Mrs Rushton's low opinion was already fully formed.

She glanced over at James, still standing in the shadows and looking up at the stars. His fingers were tapping on the rails, his chest rising and falling so rapidly that he looked as if he was building up to something. Diving off the edge, perhaps? Or popping the question?

'We've a galley bunk where you can sleep tonight, Miss MacQueen,' Mrs Rushton said in a tight voice. 'I'm afraid it's not one of the staterooms. We're not quite fitted for larger

112

numbers, but I don't expect it'll make much difference to you either way.'

James's head spun round at the comment; Edward's too, but the older couple were already pushing back from the table.

'Well, goodnight all,' Mr Rushton said, bringing his gaze over to Flora. 'I expect Mellowes will have you rescued and repatriated at first light, Miss MacQueen, so we shan't see you. But it has been a pleasure to make your acquaintance.'

He nodded his head as he offered his wife his arm and they headed for the cabin. It was a summary dismissal, Flora knew that, clearly implying that they never expected – nor hoped – to see her again. In the space of twelve short hours, she had proved herself to be a dangerous distraction to their son.

Flora felt Edward's eyes settle upon her in the dark, but she didn't look back this time. It was clear his parents would not be persuaded; their relief that a disaster had been avoided with her tonight was palpable.

The four young people didn't stir as their elders left but there was a tension that could not be ignored. Sophia was staring over at James, tears shining in her eyes as she willed him to look back at her, to engage, to *see* her.

Flora frowned as she watched. Surely James could feel her distress? But he only looked ever more intently into the distance, as if imagining himself already long gone from here. Dreaming of his expedition, no doubt.

'Well . . . I think I shall retire too,' Sophia said finally, dabbing her lips with her napkin. 'It's been a difficult day.'

Her words seemed to resonate at last because James whirled round on his heel, looking at her with new scrutiny. 'Indeed. You've been through a terrible ordeal. Rest is the best thing.'

He spoke to her with such care, such respect . . . and yet so little actual feeling. As if emotions weren't hardwired into him but simply skirted the surfaces, clouds pushed by winds in a cool sky.

'Goodbye, Miss MacQueen – and thank you,' she said, looking shakily at Flora for a long moment before delivering a glancing shot at her brother. Her footsteps were light upon the deck, the door squeaking on its hinges as she disappeared inside.

And then there were three, Flora thought to herself. A strange, capricious mood was conducting in the air, an electric charge flashing at unexpected moments, like a storm about to break and setting everyone on edge.

James was still by the railings and appeared to be in no rush to go below deck. Edward pulled out a cigarette and lit it; he offered one to Flora, who declined, but James accepted. The two of them took their time enjoying their smokes in the fresh air, the lighted tips the only spots of brightness in the otherwise ink-black bay.

No one spoke, but nor did anyone seem to feel a need to fill the silence – it had an ancient quality to it, both comfortable and tense all at once. Men at leisure; old friends and a beautiful stranger . . . Flora instinctively sensed her part and remained enigmatically quiet.

She could guess at what James was doing: waiting them out. He disapproved of them, he had made no secret of that, and he was determined not to leave them alone for a minute. Edward seemed to realize it too, because he locked eyes with Flora as he finally ground out the stub of his cigarette in an ashtray, sighing deeply.

'Well,' he said. 'It's getting late. I suppose I should show you to your sleeping quarters, Miss MacQueen.'

'Thank you.' She took her napkin off her lap and dabbed her mouth just as she had seen Sophia do, though it had been

114

a while now since they had finished eating and Edward simply looked bemused by the gesture. Her cheeks flushed as she rose. 'Well, goodbye, Mr Callaghan.'

He half turned, his profile silhouetted in the moonlight. 'Miss MacQueen,' he nodded in reply. No platitudes from him that it had been a pleasure making her acquaintance. Certainly no compliments. It didn't surprise her, but it did somehow pain her.

Edward held the door open for her and she stepped into the cabin, following him down a turning staircase, the tension between them thick. For all their mutual hopes, the evening had been a series of frustrations, Sophia's as well as Edward's and her own. Everyone was against them – his family, his friend – but they each wanted something from the other that overruled those opinions.

The clock was ticking down; this was no time for faint hearts and half measures.

She watched his back as he walked ahead. 'I must apologize for the meagre quarters,' he mumbled, holding open the door so she could peer into the narrow room. She took in crisp cotton sheets, down pillows, a blanket, soft towel and a bar of soap; a cotton nightdress (one of Sophia's?) was draped on the bed and the Sunday best clothes she had loaned to Sophia were neatly folded in a pile, as well as Norman and Donald's. There was a small, round porthole giving her a view just above the waterline.

'Meagre? You forget who you're talking to,' she murmured.

'No, don't say such things. You deserve the master suite,' he said, looking pained. 'But short of throwing my parents overboard . . .'

She laughed, not entirely sure he was joking. 'I would gladly have slept on the deck and considered myself fortunate.'

'And I hate that you sincerely mean that. I wish I could be offering you something more impressive than this. If there had been some warning of the current predicament . . .' He pinned her with a desperate look.

'But how could there have been? Today has unfurled in ways none of us could have imagined.'

'It has, hasn't it?' he asked, looking back at her with a hunger that made her flinch. She wanted to escape into something better, but he . . . he just wanted her. She could feel his need to claim her. Possess her. He wasn't the first man to have looked at her in this way, but he was the first to have got her alone like this before. If her father saw . . .

'It's been beyond my wildest dreams, finding you here. How easily I might have gone through life without ever meeting you! The very thought of it fills me with horror now.'

'My mother always says what is meant for you won't go past you,' she said, gazing modestly down at her bare feet. They looked wrong again, buried in the plush carpet.

'I wasn't meant to go past you, Flora. Against all odds, we met and I couldn't . . .' He struggled for words. '*Un-know* now that you exist. Let me speak plainly – I'll never know a moment's peace until you're mine.'

His words were bold but exactly as she had suspected and she stared at the dirt on her toes, feeling her destiny inching towards her. She might barely know him, but he seemed even closer to a proposal than James had been at dinner: there were promises held within his words that he would take her away from here and introduce her to the wider world that she knew – that somehow she just felt – she belonged to. A crew cabin on a yacht was only the very beginning . . .

He reached for her hand, placing his other on her waist, and she knew he was going to kiss her. Her body stiffened.

The Lost Lover

For all her flirtatious manner, she had never been kissed before. She steeled herself and looked back at him, seeing the way his eyes roamed over her hungrily; she could smell the wine on his breath, his pupils dilated so that he had a giddy look, alcohol and lust making a heady combination. Could this be it? Her only chance at a life beyond St Kilda? Could she learn to love this man?

She lifted her chin, bracing herself as she felt the heat of him drawing near—

Someone cleared their throat.

James was standing on the small staircase, looking unapologetic as his eyes narrowed at the sight of them; it must have been quite obvious what was about to transpire but Flora, to her surprise, felt a jolt of relief that they had been interrupted. Edward's hand dropped down from her waist but he jerked his head in a dismissive gesture, as if motioning for James to leave so that they might continue unobserved.

James's eyes slitted further. All around them were closed doors – the captain had his quarters on the top deck, but Edward's parents had a suite at the far end which spanned the width of the boat. To the port side was Sophia and Martha's room – 'a twin' – and the starboard, another 'twin', which Edward and James were sharing. The cook, Tilly and Flora were in the crew cabins up the front. They were surrounded on all sides and neither she nor Edward could risk any one of the other passengers being made aware of this compromising situation. Something of which James was well aware.

'It's getting late,' he said coolly, his eyes firmly on his old friend. 'Time for bed, don't you think? It's been a long day.'

'Not long enough, if you ask me,' Edward muttered.

There was a pause, neither man moving. Stalemate.

'Still, we've a long day ahead of us tomorrow. We'll need

our rest.' James blinked slowly, his words as unhurried as his movements, and Flora realized he had absolutely no intention of leaving them alone. She looked back at Edward in despair; he might as well have been Mr Rushton himself, chaperoning them.

Edward seemed to realize it too because he gave a groan, his shoulders slumping. 'Very well, then. To bed.' He looked back at her, taking her hand and pressing it to his lips. 'Parting truly is such sweet sorrow, Miss MacQueen.'

Flora felt a jolt of panic at the words. Time kept stop-starting, some moments slipping by too quickly, others juddering to an abrupt halt, her future tossed back and forth like a ball juggled by seals. Thirty seconds ago, he had been on the brink of kissing her and perhaps making her dreams come true. Now he was saying goodbye. Though in her heart of hearts, she didn't know whether she was more disappointed or relieved at the interruption.

'Goodnight,' she replied softly, looking back at him with doe eyes that made him visibly shiver.

He leaned over and lightly kissed her cheek. 'Meet me on deck when they're asleep,' he whispered in her ear. 'I'll knock on my way up; wait two minutes, then follow.'

He pulled back, straightening up for the benefit of their witness. 'Goodnight, Flora.'

She gave a tiny nod of agreement as he walked backwards down the narrow passage, his palms on the shiny wooden walls, a smile in his eyes. Flora watched him put a hand to the cabin doorknob, throwing her a final wink before he disappeared inside.

James Callaghan said nothing at all, of course. A cursory nod was her goodnight and goodbye. He, for one, would never be back.

Chapter Eight

Flora stirred, locked into a deep sleep. In all her eighteen years, she had never slept in a room alone before, much less in one that rocked her like a cradle. The waves slapping against the hull were familiar, but so close to her ear on the pillow, lulling her back into the depths again . . .

A creak of hinges told her a door was being swung but she had heard it before and the echo of familiarity roused her again: words, faces, this place, drifted into her consciousness and she realized the ghost of a knock on her door still tremored in her mind.

Someone had knocked.

Blinking, she opened her eyes into a darkened landscape, a rippling moonbeam on water framed in a perfect circle . . . She gasped as everything came back to her.

Edward.

She had fallen asleep on top of the covers, she realized, waiting and waiting for a knock . . . What time was it? She looked out of the tiny porthole and saw that the moon had curved around the isle in an embrace, Connachair now basking in her glow and the sleeping village cast in a pale haze. Not a single light flickered from any of the cottages; not even Old Fin's, and he barely slept, often napping in his chair by the fire instead.

It had to be an hour past midnight, she guessed, draping her red shawl over the light cotton nightdress and scrambling off the bed. She pressed her ear to the door, listening for the sound of anyone else being up, but she could hear only distant snores and the groan of the yacht tugging on its anchor chain.

The door opened soundlessly, and she tiptoed along the corridor and up the turning staircase. All lights had long been turned off but as she carefully cracked the door open, trying to limit its creaks and groans, she saw the oil lamps on deck still flickering on a low flame, offering pinpricks of light. She stood for a moment, allowing her eyes to adjust; unfamiliar shapes hulked in the shadows. This was an alien landscape for a girl who had never spent a night off her isle before.

Pulling her shawl tightly around her shoulders, she padded silently out of the lee of the cabin, walking past the dining table onto the open deck where the shuffleboard was painted and the tender stowed.

No sign of him. Had she missed her chance? Again she felt a flutter of ambivalence – she could still go back to her cabin, let this moment pass – but if her heart told her one thing, her feet did another.

She turned and walked the other way instead, feeling the wind pick up as she passed by the cabin and stepped in front of it. Suddenly, a tiny light glowed ahead, dancing and seemingly disembodied in the darkness. Tendrils of cigarette smoke reached her, curling like cats' tails around her nightdress.

She watched him for a moment, still unseen. Over his shoulder, her village – her entire world – slumbered, unaware that her future stood on a precipice. Would he be her new horizon now? Could she trust her head, if not her heart?

She watched the cigarette tip dance, swooping up and down

in fluid arcs, as she silently walked over and tapped him on the shoulder.

He turned.

And she gasped.

'You?' she whispered. 'What are you doing here?'

'I could ask you the same thing,' James replied, raising the cigarette to his lips and drawing on it again. He offered it to her too but she shook her head, trying to understand how this could have happened. Where was Edward? She looked around them, searching for another inky figure, a dancing orange firefly on the midnight bay.

'He's fast off, I'm afraid,' he said, reading her mind. 'The wine always does that to him. He's snoring like a train – you might have heard?' He rolled his eyes. 'It can be somewhat testing, sharing a room with him.'

Flora looked back at him, sensing a difference in his demeanour – a casual diffidence that sat at odds with the po-faced earnestness he had presented all day.

'I don't know what you're talking about . . . I just came up to get some air,' she murmured, her hair blowing freely now that she had unbraided her plait. She saw his eyes watch it dance around her face before his hand rose to his lips again and he took another drag.

'Is that so?' he asked after a moment, openly sceptical.

'. . . Aye.'

'Trouble sleeping?'

'No, I . . .' She remembered she had been sleeping, deeply; that it was the knock at her door – as agreed – that had roused her. But if Edward was still asleep, he couldn't have knocked. She looked at James – *he* wouldn't have knocked for her, surely? If his plan had been to catch them together, the two

121

of them asleep in their cabins would have been just the result he was looking for. He had no reason to wake her.

'. . . Yes. Trouble dropping off.'

'Mm. I should imagine your mind was racing with all the possibilities my dear friend posited before you today.' He shrugged. 'I can see how it would be easy to have one's head turned by that. It's a lot to take in for most young women, much less—' He waved an arm in the direction of Village Bay.

Flora swallowed, feeling her indignation begin to flow. 'He has been nothing but kind and courteous to me. He has made no promises.'

'I'm very glad to hear it,' he said abruptly.

And there it was. The disapproval. She jerked her chin in the air at the outright slight. They were alone; manners held little importance for her now. Her eyes flashed and narrowed. 'I'm sure you are.'

Bemusement hovered in his eyes as he waited for her to speak, sensing too that they were past daylight decorum.

'You've looked at me like I'm the cat's stink all day. You don't think I'm good enough for the likes of him.'

'I've never said that.'

'But you think it. I can see you don't approve of me.'

'It's not you that I don't approve of. That's not how I feel at all. I just don't think you know him. You're strangers.'

'We spent the day together.'

'Then you're strangers who spent a day together. You still don't know him.'

She arched an eyebrow, challenging him with a fierce look. 'You have no idea how well I know him – you don't know what he talked about with me, or . . . or the things we did.'

There was a brief silence and Flora could see she had scored a point at last, a flesh wound. His eyes swept back up to hers and she felt again the locking of their gaze that she had experienced that morning. His mouth opened, but there was a pause before the words came. 'Edward can be . . . impulsive.'

'You say impulsive. I say he's a man who knows what he wants – and I like that. He wants to show me the world, introduce me to people. What's so wrong with that?'

'It's ridiculous. You're planning a life with him when you only met him this morning?'

'Time is a luxury we don't have.' She shot him another sly look. 'And besides, does that really have anything to do with it? By that reasoning you must be *wildly* in love with Miss Rushton, seeing as you've known her for years. And yet you let her go to bed crying this evening . . .'

James's eyes flashed at the sudden turning of the tables and she flinched a little as he took a final hard suck on the cigarette before flicking it into the air. She watched the bright stub dive in a high arc towards the water.

'You know full well you disappointed her by not proposing tonight,' she said defiantly.

'Yes, I do know,' he agreed. 'And it pained me to see, but I acted in her best interests. It wouldn't have been right.' His mouth had settled into a flat line.

'Because I was there?'

He looked at her levelly. 'Yes, in part.'

She swallowed. Though she had baited the answer, it still somehow hurt to hear it.

They were both silent for a moment, the wind making her nightdress flap like a skua's wings, and she saw his gaze fall to the outline of her body. He looked back at her.

'Believe it or not, I'm trying to help you. It would never work out with the two of you – back in the real world.'

123

'You don't know that.'

'Yes, I do.'

'You don't know me.'

'Don't I?' His eyebrow arched fractionally and she felt it again, that instinctive connection, a pull in her belly she couldn't understand.

'No.'

He looked away. 'Well, I do know Edward, far better than you, and I can say with utmost confidence that although he will promise you the world – and he'll mean it, while he's here – over that horizon, he's a different man, with far too many prospects. I told you this morning that he's easily bored. He would hurt you and I guarantee that within the month, he would abandon you. He's as quick to fall out of love as he is to fall into it. I've seen it happen many times.'

Flora stared back at him, stung by the wretched picture. Was that true? Would Edward forget her? Not keep his promises? Falter at the first real sign of his parents' objecting to their match? Abandon her?

'How can you call yourself his friend when you talk of him in such a way?' she asked instead.

He stared at his feet for a moment. 'Good question. I know I'm being hard on him. And over that horizon, I too am a different man; over there, I do not interfere with his carousing ways. I will defend him in almost every situation *because* he's my friend, and because the women he meets over there are perfectly able to understand what he is.'

What he is? She frowned. 'But I'm not?'

'I don't believe so, no.'

'You think me naive.' She almost growled the words.

'Yes.'

'I am no such thing!'

'Do you know what a playboy is?'

She stared back at him, glowering, before she was forced to shake her head.

'No, of course not. I doubt there are many of them here.' He sighed, looking back to shore at the slumbering village. 'Well, let's just say that with his money and "boyish good looks" – the *Tatler*'s words, not mine – he has his pick of romantic partners. No one is off limits to Edward Rushton. Even the prettiest, richest young ladies, with fathers in powerful positions, succumb to his . . . charms.'

'I don't believe you,' she said hotly, turning her face away from him.

'Ask Sophia's debutante friends. Or indeed, many of their mothers.'

Flora gasped, shocked by the insinuations and slanders. 'That's easily said,' she hissed. 'When you know he can't prove otherwise here.'

There was a pause as he watched her. 'Do you recall the girl who served us dinner?'

'Tilly . . . ?' Flora's mouth dropped open as she realized what he was telling her. She remembered how no one would even look at the girl. *'Tilly?'*

He stuffed a hand into his trouser pocket, watching as her mind raced. 'Many a thing drops from the man who often flits, Flora – isn't that the saying?' he murmured.

Flora took a step back, hardly able to believe her ears. How could she have been such a fool? To have been fed all those sweet, pretty lies and believed them?

She turned away from him and walked over to the bow rail, angry tears stinging her eyes. But if her pride had gotten the better of her in allowing her to believe that she could, in the course of a single day, tempt a handsome, rich man to propose to her – that she was destined for the life that was his birthright – then pride would also stop her tears from falling. For several minutes she stood alone, the wind making a sail of her dress and a pennant of her hair as she composed herself, looking back at her home, the place she belonged after all.

'Well, you must be very pleased to have delivered your message with such precision,' she said, gripping the rail a little more tightly as he came to stand by her.

'Not in the least. I take no pleasure from it,' he murmured. 'I'm only glad I was able to talk to you freely in time. I thought he'd never drop off.'

She looked back at him quizzically. '*You* were waiting for *him* to fall asleep?'

'Naturally. I knew he would propose meeting you here.' He shrugged. 'It was something of a battle of wills, but the wine got the better of him in the end. Usually does.'

Usually does? Flora frowned as she remembered how James had taken it upon himself to serve the wine at dinner. Had the measures been unusually generous? '. . . You tried to stop me from drinking any,' she recalled.

'Correct.'

'I thought you were suggesting I'd had too much, that I was behaving improperly.'

'Quite the contrary.'

'Excuse me?'

He glanced down at her. 'When you sang, it was beautiful to watch. You were enchanting.'

Enchanting. Flora savoured the word. She had been called beautiful many, many times, but enchanting? Never.

'I was simply trying to . . . protect your virtue. I knew what he might have suggested if he'd got you alone up here. And it wouldn't have been marriage.'

Flora stared at him in horror.

'You wouldn't be the first,' he shrugged. 'Or, worse, the last.'

She turned to face him, her elbow on the bow rail. 'So, you mean to say, all day you've been trying to *save* me from him?'

'. . . As best as I could. It's tricky, of course, when I'm his guest. But I didn't want to see you get hurt.'

He looked up at the stars again, and she stared at his handsome profile. If Edward wasn't the man she'd imagined him to be, nor was James. Neither of them spoke for several moments.

'Perhaps you ought to spend less time worrying about me and more time looking after Miss Rushton,' she said finally, pulling her thoughts back in again.

He looked down at his hands and she could see his jaw clench. 'Sadly, I think her brother should be warning *her* off *me*.'

'Why?'

'Because I don't love her.'

Flora's eyes widened. 'You don't?'

He didn't reply immediately, and she could see the pain on his face as thoughts travelled through his mind. 'I thought I did – or *could*, anyway. I have a great abiding . . . affection for her and I want to see her happy – but today I realized that I love her as a sister and nothing more.'

Flora stared at him, remembering the young woman's plaintive expression at dinner. 'But perhaps if you just give it time?'

He looked across at her. 'We've had plenty of that – as you pointed out yourself,' he said dryly.

'But she would love you enough for the both of you,' she argued.

'That would be unfair to her and wholly unreasonable.'

'But you're a perfect match! It all makes sense. You fit. You're the same sort and her family wants the marriage.'

'As I'm sure your family wants to see your marriage with one of the village boys. But can you make yourself fall in love with them?'

Flora was silent.

'No,' he said, answering for her. 'Exactly. The heart wants what it wants, Flora. Logic and *the right sort* has little to do with it.'

Flora caught the way he was staring at her, the way his body had angled in towards her as he spoke. *Today I realized . . .*

Why had he realized it today?

He turned to face her squarely, as if reading the thoughts in her mind. 'You asked me just now if your presence tonight stopped me from proposing to Sophia, and I told you that it did, in part. It wasn't because I was angry you were there, but because . . .' He sighed heavily. 'Because when you walked into the salon this evening, I knew that if I had proposed to Sophia, I would have been proposing to the wrong girl in the room.'

'*What?*' she whispered. She blinked as the moment stretched out, seeing now the look in his eyes. 'But . . . you don't even like me.'

'Would I have gone to all this trouble for someone I don't like? Besides, how could any man *not* like you?' He shook his head, looking irritated. 'You're dazzling Flora – beautiful inside and out.'

'But you didn't believe any of the boys here want me!'

He laughed, his face relaxing into a completely refreshed version of itself. 'Well,' he said after a moment, giving a guilty look as if conceding the point. '. . . I had to do *something* to keep you on your toes. If I had told you I thought you the most beautiful woman I'd ever seen in my life, I would simply have joined a very long list of men who had said exactly the same thing.'

It was true, she realized. 'So you were just pretending?'

'*Not* falling under your spell seemed to me the only way I could get your attention. How else could I compete against Edward? He's richer, funnier, more charismatic and more handsome.'

That's not true, she thought, staring back at him and seeing the fire in his eyes now; remembering his strong hands and feet, this man who was so much more than he showed.

His gaze ran over her face like musical notes on a score. 'I've been trying to get you alone all day, Flora.' His voice had softened, become more intimate, and she felt a rush of goosepimples brush along her spine. She felt disarmed by his confession. She had spent the day thinking he disapproved of her; that he actively disliked her. To have to turn it all on its head . . . Nothing had been as it seemed.

'So . . . the fossils?'

Another laugh. 'I don't give a damn about them. I did a geology course for one term but would struggle to tell a diorite from a peridotite. I just needed an excuse to talk to you.'

A ghost smile hovered on her mouth. '. . . And the picnic?'

'Our intrusion was no accident. Edward was furious with me for not going back to the boat this morning. When he saw me talking with you on the rocks, he guessed – correctly – that I'd bluffed him to go and be with you. That's why he got Cook to make up the fancy picnic.' He shrugged. 'I knew he'd up the stakes somehow. So I paid Effie to take me to where the two of you were sitting. If I couldn't prevent it from going ahead, I could at least sabotage it.'

Flora was amazed. She had picked up flickers of the tension

between the two men but she had thought it had been that they were fighting *because* of her, not *over* her.

James took a step closer. 'Look, Flora . . . Flossie,' he smiled, bringing back to mind his eavesdropping on her conversation with Bonnie that morning. 'I know this is a lot to be told in the middle of the night, and I know we don't know each other very well yet – but I also feel that somehow, we do . . . That our souls are not strangers.' And he pinned her with that look again, reaching out a hand and lightly tracing her jawline with his finger. The touch made her shiver. 'There's something here, between us, that I've never felt before – a spark – and I think you feel it too.' He locked his eyes upon her. 'Do you?'

She nodded, feeling helpless in the face of his plain words and bold plan. He didn't sweet-talk her like Edward, but there was something more compelling about his lack of guile. Edward might have seemed a prize to be won, but her attraction to James felt honest and real. He seemed to see her – truly see her, not just her pretty face – and she realized she wanted him to kiss her. Her gaze fell to his mouth. She really wanted him to kiss her.

'Then I'm . . .' He paused. 'God, don't look at me like that.'

'Like what?' She looked up at his eyes and he gave a small exhale as if trying to steady himself. He swallowed. 'I'm asking you to give us time to explore this. I expect Edward will come to your door when he stirs later. Don't answer it if he knocks. Don't marry him if he asks. Don't marry *anyone* . . . Give me some time.'

'But how . . . ? You're leaving in a few hours . . . You're going on your expedition and anyway within the month, the seas will be too high to get over here.'

'Then we'll write – as often as we possibly can. We'll share our stories and get to know one another across the sea, so that by the time I return from Greenland, I can come back here and take you away with me, properly. And then we'll know each other as well as if I had spent the summer here, walking with you every day – looking for fossils.'

The smile that played on his lips jumped to hers. 'How do I know you won't tire of me and disappear forever?'

He took a step closer to her. 'Flora, I would posit even the devil himself couldn't tire of you. You're a woman who could rob a man of his soul and he'd gladly give it up for a sweet kiss from you.'

Her gaze fell to his mouth again as she wondered what it would feel like to be in his arms, to be kissed by him . . .

He gave a tiny groan, as if she'd taken something from him, and as she looked up at him again, she saw the open longing in his eyes. She realized how close they were standing now, toe to toe, bodies almost touching. His eyes swept over her face as he placed his hands on her cheeks and bent down towards her, the very kiss already in the offing: her lips for his soul, their twin hearts conjoined.

Heart pounding, limbs tingling, her eyes closed as she waited to feel his lips upon hers. Her body felt electrified with yearning for his kiss.

But it didn't come – and the air between them grew suddenly frigid. Expansive.

'Wait!' she heard him exclaim.

Her eyes flew open just in time to see a fist fly and James was thrown back, sprawling on the deck. There was blood on his face and shirt, vivid scarlet even in the twilight, the vignette streaked with black as her hair flew in front of her face like Medusa's snakes, whipping and striking in the wind. Her white nightdress still flapped angrily, pressing against her body in one moment and leaping from it in the next.

Anger and rage swirled around them in a tempest and she already knew what she would see when she turned – wild blue eyes, angry reddened eyes, boring into her, lust turned in an instant to hate.

Chapter Nine

9 September 1929

The yacht curled into the bay at a clip, men scurrying aboard like ants and hauling down the billowing sails. Flora, standing on the ridge of the burn, watched as they collapsed like a sigh, the flying boat gliding to a graceful halt. Her finger twitched against her skirt, smooth skin against rough drugget, a nervous tic that almost always went unseen. As now.

Beside her, Effie, Mhairi, Molly and Lorna were watching the excitement too. It was just past the first week in September, and by anyone's reckoning they should have been cut off to all but the whaling boats by now; but a rare spell of fine weather had kept the seas flat enough that Donald McKinnon and Mhairi had risked a last-ditch passage across to Harris, returning only this morning. Donald, like the other men, fearing another hard winter and not liking the terms offered by the factor, had undertaken the journey to trade surplus feathers, tweeds and fulmar oil with a farmer there for tools. Mhairi had been obliged to accompany him to meet the man's son, with a view to possibly marrying him next year, for her own father needed to be relieved of the burden of providing for nine children. It was a fate awaiting all the girls of marriageable age, Flora knew – if they couldn't settle upon a husband themselves, it would be decided for them one way or another.

Mhairi had been an unwilling passenger but to everyone's surprise, the introduction had proved to be auspicious and she had disembarked only an hour ago with bright eyes and a new wildness in her spirit. Alexander McLennan, her intended, was handsome and fair, enterprising and clever, she said, and the girls had gathered her over to the burn where, hiding below its deep banks, they crowded round for details. Flora thought there was something different about her friend – a febrile, darting energy that couldn't quite land – but before she could probe, the dogs had begun barking on the beach. They were the islanders' alert to approaching incomers and often congregated at the water's edge several minutes before a ship or boat nosed around the headland; they were never wrong.

But no one could have anticipated this sight. Tourist boats and the schooners of the rich regularly dropped anchor in the bay in the months between early May and the end of August, but something of this calibre was unprecedented.

'I believe they call it a J-class,' Lorna said in amazement, still holding the sodden dressings she had been washing in the burn. 'It's a racing yacht.'

Lorna knew of such things, for she was a St Kildan by choice, not by birth, and she had spent the first twenty-four years of her life in Sutherland. Besides her medical training, she had a wider world view that the islanders – even the men – trusted and respected, and as such she enjoyed a prominent role in island life, helping Mhairi's father Ian with his postmaster duties too.

'Perhaps it's your sweetheart McLennan chasing after you, Mhairi,' Effie joshed.

'He owns a bicycle, not a boat,' Mhairi mumbled. Two

minutes earlier, owning the bicycle would have counted as a boast among a population with only some cows, a bull and several hundred sheep, none of which were reliable for transport – but things had already moved on, it seemed, and something of Mhairi's sparkle was lost.

'*Shamrock . . . Shamrock V*,' Lorna murmured, reading the letters stamped along the back of the shiny navy-blue hull.

A J-class racing yacht. It belonged to a world they simply couldn't fathom and as the huddle of young women slowly began to walk back to the village, Poppit trotting along the wall beside them, their eyes never lifted off it. The men were already on the beach and heaving the smack back into the water, woollen trousers rolled up to their knees and still wet from the earlier *sortie* as they jumped into their usual positions and began to row.

It was a morning of arrivals, it seemed.

'Who is it, do we know?' Lorna asked Mad Annie and Ma Peg, who were sitting on their stools outside Ma Peg's house and knitting at a ferocious speed. Their stitch rate always went up when something exciting was happening, their attention wholly on the object of interest, needles bobbing up and down in a frenzy.

'An eejit,' Mad Annie said dismissively, making clear her disdain of the New World vessel.

They passed Effie's cottage further down, where Robert was sitting on the wall. 'Do you know, Father?' Effie asked him. He was too lame to get himself in and out of the smack these days but he was smoking his pipe and, like the women, watching and tutting.

'None is scheduled to come by,' he muttered, looking concerned. The islanders knew from bitter experience that the capricious sea could take as quickly as it could give.

Effie indicated with a nod that she would hang back to stay with him, Poppit immediately settling herself down on the wall and waiting as well. She was Effie's shadow, companion and comfort, and Flora sometimes felt she would call the dog her best friend too.

They continued down past the other houses, the women and children gathered in doorways as they all watched the visitors being rowed back to shore. Even from a distance, the sharp lines of their felted homburg hats were distinct from the soft tweed berets of the island men.

It was no surprise to anyone that the reverend and his wife had come out to greet the visitors. When the whalers and fishermen came ashore, the reverend would happily accede to their superstition that it was bad luck to be greeted by a man of the cloth, but when visitors were clearly rich, no time was given to 'such fallacy'.

Flora's fingers twitched against her skirt again as the smack approached the beach and she felt an agitation rising through her that belied the stillness of her bones. She watched as two men jumped out and the boat was pulled ashore. One of the figures needed assistance with disembarking but the other leapt onto the stones with a dynamic vigour, and she felt her heart quicken. Immediately she quashed the thought, knowing it was impossible – he would be leaving for the Faroes any day, if he hadn't left already. But hope persisted even beyond logic.

It had been a month since James and the Rushtons left, and the days following had been long, lonely – and quiet. She had received a letter from him just a few days ago – and hastily wrote back by return – but he had offered no account of the journey home with his hosts, and she was left to imagine the tension aboard as both Edward and Sophia learned they had been betrayed at a single stroke. It must have been unbearable for everyone. Had the men fought again? Had Sophia wept? Had her parents cursed Flora's name? Not knowing was the worst thing.

James had reassured her, as they were roughly parted in the dawn light, that all was fair in love and that in time, the Rushtons would see this was all for the best; but in the nights that had followed since, as she waited for the passing fishing ships and their sporadic mail bags, Flora wondered if their disruptive – *inauspicious* – start would bring its own fate.

With the coming change in seasons and his own remote location as well as hers, she knew communication would only become more difficult and she still feared that with winter's protracted silence would come frustration, boredom, apathy and eventually, surely, abandonment. She had known him for only a day, after all, and it had hardly been love at first sight.

And yet . . . *Our souls are not strangers* . . .

The reverend stepped forward, a hand already outstretched in greeting as if to make the point that there was civilization even in this remote outpost in the middle of the North Atlantic. There was a pause as the figures, silhouetted against a sparkling sea, stood talking for a moment before a name suddenly carried on the wind.

'Lipton! Lipton!'

Beside her, Mhairi revived at the name as Flora felt herself sag – hope officially suspended – and the villagers began pouring forth from their homes. Sir Thomas Lipton had been their saviour eighteen years earlier, sending over emergency supplies of potatoes, meat, flour, sugar and tea – naturally – when word had lilted to the mainland that the islanders, during the brutal winter of 1911, were almost starving to death.

Flora's fingers curled inwards, her nails pressing sharply into her palms as she and Effie and Molly found themselves enveloped by the throng, everyone – including Mad Annie, who was never normally inclined to express happy delight – rushing past to greet their benefactor.

'Shall we meet him, then, Flossie?' Mhairi asked her, looping an arm through hers and leading her down towards the crowd now gathered outside Old Fin's house.

The islanders bustled and jostled around the visitors excitedly, everyone talking and wanting to get a look at the man who had saved them. The concept of millionairehood was alien to a community with a barter economy but as Flora tipped her head to catch a glimpse, something of his power emanated from the short, stooped, white-haired man.

'Ah yes, Miss MacQueen, Miss MacQueen,' he said, spotting her and somehow identifying her. He stepped forward, the crowd parting so that he took her hand in his own. 'I was told I would recognize you on sight.'

'Sir Thomas, sir . . .' Flora stammered, confused as he pressed the back of her hand lightly to his lips.

'I have with me someone who wanted very much to see you.'

What? She felt her heart quake again as he stepped aside and his companion, whose face had been obscured by his hat, looked up. Hazel eyes met hers once more.

'James!' she cried, her hands flying to her mouth. 'What are y' doing here?' Could it really be true? Her fantastical dreams were reality? Questions and confusion overran her thoughts. What about his expedition?

'I have something for you,' he said simply. 'Something you said you would like.'

She watched, open-mouthed, as he retrieved a smooth

golden barrel from his coat pocket. Her hands reached for it but she didn't dare to touch it in case this was a dream that, like a bubble, would burst on contact. 'Is it . . . is it . . . ?'

'Yes. I wanted you to have it before the winter comes in.' He smiled, seeming charmed by her shock. '. . . Take it.'

His fingers brushed hers as she took it – their first touch since that fateful night – and she looked back at him, their eyes alive. Was this truly happening? 'You came all this way to bring me a lipstick?'

He had asked her in his letter what she most desired from the mainland and she had said a red lipstick; to her, it embodied the glamour of the world to which he belonged, and she wanted him to think her naturally sophisticated in spite of her humble origins. But in truth, the only thing she had wanted from over there was him.

'My dear, he all but hijacked us in his determination to bring it to you,' Sir Thomas laughed as she pulled off the lid to reveal a bright, waxy vermilion stub. '*Shamrock* had just been sailed up to me in Glasgow from Pendennis, that I might give her a run before she's sailed over to Newport for the next America's Cup. Mr Callaghan, however, knowing of my long-held attachment to your people, convinced me a quick dilly over here would satisfy us both.'

The islanders huddled forwards at the sight of the lipstick, for the like had never been seen here before – but the minister recoiled at the sight of it as if it was the red devil himself.

'It is a fashion from the mainland, Reverend,' James said quickly. 'But I appreciate it may not be suitable for island life. It is simply intended as an aide-mémoire – something to remember me by.' His eyes met hers again and Flora felt the presence of her thirty-five neighbours drop away. As if *she* could forget *him*! He was the one who belonged to a world of countless pretty girls – he could meet a new face every day if he liked – whereas she was only ever surrounded by the rough boys of her childhood.

'Did you bring us some more brew, Sir T?' Ma Peg asked, less interested in love tokens than sustenance.

'Naturally, Ma Peg. Along with some other provisions I thought you might enjoy. I hope you don't mind the presumption?'

'Och, no, we'll indulge you!' Peg quipped with an almost flirtatious laugh. 'Shall we boil the pot, then? Tea and a piece?'

'That would be splendid, though I'm afraid we can dedicate no more than an hour ashore.'

An hour? No! Flora felt a spasm of fear twitch through her. James had been back for only a few minutes, but already the thought of letting him leave again was unbearable. She looked at him with open longing in her eyes. There was so much to say . . . The memory of their single day and night was all she had had to sustain her for the past month and she would lie in bed at night, re-remembering the sequence of events from the new perspective he had given her. Chasing her while giving no impression of there being a chase, his eyes silently following her every move from the moment she had set foot in the yacht's cabin, while Edward had paraded her as his own.

The girls had interrogated her, of course, on her return, and only Effie had seemed content with the men's reversal of fortunes. Both Mhairi and Molly had fallen – like her – for Edward's intense charm offensive, but from the start Effie had preferred James, with his self-effacing modesty and reserve. It had struck Flora as deeply ironic that the one girl determined never to fall in love had proved to be the best judge of men.

'My crew are on a strict timetable for the Atlantic crossing,'

Sir Thomas was explaining. 'My captain was quite displeased when I asked him to push back for a day to oblige our little outing.'

'How long did it take y' to cross?' Old Fin asked, his voice fading as the elders began to head for Ma Peg's cottage.

To Flora's relief, James made no move to follow. Rather, his gaze seemed to deepen in intensity, like a setting sun about to pat the sea, and they communicated without words all the longing that had been held in abeyance these past few weeks. He was a man well able to disguise his yearning, she knew that about him now; but standing here, nothing was hidden, and all the longing of that last night on deck was still there. He wanted her just as much as she wanted him.

He dragged his eyes off her. 'Mr MacQueen, I wondered if we might talk together, you and I?'

Flora's mouth parted in silent exclamation – what about getting to know one another through their letters first? – though a ripple went through the remaining islanders. There was a pause before her father nodded.

'I'll boil the pot too, then,' her mother said in a strained voice. 'Flora, y' can help me.'

Flora glanced over at Mhairi as her mother caught her by the wrist and began pulling her away. She widened her eyes and bit her lip, as if to convey her shock and excitement, but Mhairi didn't appear to see. She was standing motionless, staring as the men walked past the side of the house towards the grassy area at the back, headed by the stone dyke that encircled the village. It was always quiet up there.

'Did y' know he was coming?' Flora's mother asked in a low voice as they walked back to the cottage.

'No, Ma. It's as much a surprise to me as anyone.'

'You're sure? You had a letter from him just a few days ago.'

'He made no mention of coming over. I'd have talked him out of it if he had. It's an unnecessary risk just to bring me this.' Her grip tightened around the red lipstick.

'But he *didn't* come just to bring you that.' Her mother looked over at her and reached out a hand to smooth her hair. There was a nervous energy to her movements. 'You look feral again. There's dirt on your cheek and your hem's torn. I've been telling you to mend it these three mornings past.' Flora stood patiently as her mother began rubbing the dirt off her skin, fussing and tutting all the while. 'I'd no' be surprised if he thinks the better of it on seeing you.'

'Really?' Flora looked at her mother with alarm.

Christina MacQueen softened, cupping her daughter's cheek with a palm. 'No, pet. But there's many a gentleman likes the look o' you. Are you truly sweet on him too?'

'I am, Ma.' There had been no hiding her delight when the letter had come and she had told her mother some of what had passed between them – his request for time to get to know one another, for her to wait for him to return from his expedition. To not marry anyone else.

'But you scarce know him,' her mother cautioned.

'And yet somehow, I do,' Flora said, feeling flooded with emotion. 'We're new to one another but there's something . . . ancient between us too.' She had been so afraid she would lose him to time, but now she felt her future whispering to her on the breeze.

'Och, they're coming back,' her mother exclaimed, looking alarmed as she glimpsed a sight of the two men passing by the window. She licked her palms and smoothed her own hair down. 'They wasted no time, then! Straighten up, lass. Look smart while I greet him.'

Flora fell still as her mother walked over to the door. She

felt her entire life had been building towards this moment and she watched for their shadows to fall across the threshold.

She heard her father's voice first, stray words drifting through like feathers.

'. . . Callaghan . . . talked . . . a proposal for us . . .'

Flora bit her lip, scarcely able to believe this was real. A lipstick, and now—

'Archie?' Her mother's voice was shrill and alarmed. 'He wants to do *what*?'

'This is a wretched idea!' Flora implored her mother, panting, as she hurried to keep up.

The men had gone ahead, striding out with swinging arms, James's coat left draped over her father's fireside chair. As ever, the clock was ticking: time was against them.

'I think it's a smashing idea,' Effie said, practically skipping beside her as they skirted the hem of the beach.

'Your father said he insisted,' Christina replied grimly, looking as worried as Flora felt.

She glanced across the sea-moss slope towards the village; word had spread quickly, and the younger villagers and anyone able to move at speed were streaming down the grass allotments to join them and watch the spectacle.

They passed the bluffs where Flora and Edward had picnicked, but all Flora saw now was where James's rope had dangled down the cliffs as he had abseiled in, a smile on his face and sabotage on his mind. She remembered his interest in the Lovers' Stone even then, as Edward had lain, languid, in the grass. Had he been planning this all that time?

They arrived at the spot a few minutes behind the men. Flora's father was pointing out to James the idiosyncrasies known by the island men – the loose stone on the approach there, the uneven seam on the rock, the squally winds that screamed up the sheer cliff to the right.

James was rolling up his shirtsleeves. He had left his shoes and socks by her front door, and she was grateful that he'd had the foresight to acclimatize his feet for this venture by walking here barefoot. She stared again at his strong ankles, which had told her so much about him even when she hadn't asked, and she saw the dark hairs on his legs – a glimpse of a body still unknown to her. They hadn't even kissed . . .

She looked up to find him watching her. He smiled broadly and she rushed over to him.

'You don't have to do this.'

'I do,' he said firmly, tucking a stray tendril of hair behind her ear. 'It's important that I show your father I'm worthy.'

'But you are!'

'No, he only knows I'm rich, and those are two very different things. Besides, I want everyone to understand how serious I am about wanting this – wanting you.'

She stared at him, blinking rapidly. There were enough people here that she didn't want to make a scene – but she wanted to make a scene. Anything to stop him. '*Please* don't fall,' she whispered.

'I have no intention of it.'

'But it's so high. Your sort aren't used to it.'

He gave a low chuckle. 'Don't worry, I've been balance training since I left here.'

She was amazed. 'You have?'

'Walking a slack line.' He bent down and whispered into her ear. 'I refuse to die when I'm on the very cusp of making you mine.'

His words made her blush, and he winked as he drew back

again. How could she ever have thought him a man obsessed with fossils? His blood ran hot.

'Shall we do this, then?' he asked, turning to her father.

Flora watched, the small crowd cheering as the two men shook hands. Effie and Molly came over – Mhairi was resting after her arduous journey this morning. They each took one of her hands as James stepped onto the first rock. It wobbled, just as he'd been warned it would, and his arms shot out for balance.

'Tch, look at them,' Effie muttered under her breath. Flora followed her gaze to see Mhairi's big brothers, Angus and Fin, watching James closely with dark expressions. 'They look like they want him to fall.'

'Don't even joke about such things,' Molly hissed. 'They just don't appreciate outsiders coming in and taking the eligible girls for themselves.'

'They know full well I'd die an old maid over becoming a wife to either of them,' Flora muttered.

'Aye, but it's the principle they object to,' Molly reasoned. She was always reasonable.

James stepped forward slowly onto the initial slab. It projected upwards for a short distance before dropping by a foot to a lower slab wedged beneath it. This one rose sharply at forty-five degrees, for ten feet or so.

He walked carefully, keeping his chin up and his arms outstretched.

'This is madness,' Flora whispered, pressing her fingers against her friends' hands and feeling her panic rise. 'He doesn't have to do this.'

The girls squeezed back nervously too.

'It's not like he'll ever have to swing on a rope to provide for me,' she whispered, ever more desperate. Training or not, he might plunge to his death at any moment. 'We all know perfectly well I'll have a more abundant life with him on the mainland than I could ever expect here. He doesn't need to be agile or good on the ropes. This makes no sense!' Her voice was rising.

'Aye, but it's the principle of the thing,' Molly repeated, never taking her eyes off him. 'And principles matter.'

James had reached the pinnacle of the slab now and was standing on the narrow ledge that created a snub platform at its very edge. Flora couldn't breathe as she saw him lift his right leg several times, just an inch or two from the surface as if testing, before finally lifting it up and forward. She gave a small gasp as part of his body protruded into space above the sheer drop. Most people wouldn't even dare to sit on the Stone, much less endure this. Much less *willingly*.

She stared at his left ankle, willing it to remain rigid and stable as it wobbled on the granite slab; she felt her heart leap several times, nerves getting the better of her, but slowly, so slowly, he hunched over slightly, reaching with both hands to clasp the right foot in a fist. He was a tall man, with long limbs adding to the risks. If he should lose his balance now, with his weight straining forward, it would be a straightforward tumble into the depths.

Everyone felt the tension hum at this, the most dangerous point, as – with James locked into position – her father began to count, his voice low, the rhythm steady.

Flora stared at James's ankle, the only thing keeping him safe as he satisfied this stupid, reckless principle.

'Eight . . . nine . . . ten,' her father counted, nodding approvingly as James stood affixed as a tree, his shirt blowing in the breeze, the sun on his hair. 'You may release the hold, Mr Callaghan. The trial has been completed.'

Carefully, James released his foot and pulled it back, stepping down quickly so that both feet were planted on the rock again. A cheer went up from the villagers – even the MacKinnon brothers, somewhat begrudgingly – as he turned and staggered quickly down the steep slab. The men slapped his back as he made his way off the Stone and jumped onto the grassy path. Her father shook hands with him and gave a nod. 'We'll make a St Kildan of you yet, Mr Callaghan.'

'Thank you, sir. I should be honoured,' James grinned. 'Well, that's the easy bit done,' he said, drawing astonished laughs as he stood with his hands on his hips, looking back at the Stone with a satisfied sigh. 'Now for the hard part . . .'

'Aye,' the men agreed, their voices a low grumble.

'But are you quite sure about this, Mr Callaghan?' her father asked. 'A wild goose never laid a tame egg.'

There was laughter in her father's voice and James's eyes were bright as he looked over at her, an unstoppable smile upon his mouth. 'I've never been more certain, sir.'

He walked over, not wasting a moment as he dropped to his knee and pulled a box from his trouser pocket. Inside twinkled a gold ring with three sapphires. It was more treasure than the islanders had ever seen and yet, if he should have fallen, it would have been lost to the depths with him.

'Flora Rose MacQueen,' he said, his eyes fastened upon hers. 'I know it's fast, but when love strikes, a man doesn't need to buy time. And . . . well, frankly, the seas are against me.' He shrugged. 'Will you do me the honour of consenting to be my wife?'

She looked back at him consideringly, even while her heart somersaulted in her chest. It wouldn't do to be a foregone conclusion.

'. . . Can I think about it?' she asked with an arch look, jutting her shapely hip provocatively.

'Ha-hey!' the men laughed.

''Tis hard to hold a conger by the tail!' Angus MacKinnon yelled.

'Aye,' James laughed, refusing to get up from his knee. 'But my own dear mother always said the best apple is on the highest bough – so I will reach, even though I may fall in the trying.' His eyes never left her. '. . . Say you'll marry me, Flora.'

'Very well, then,' she beamed, unable to suppress her joy for a moment more. 'I will.'

Chapter Ten

They let the rest of the islanders pull ahead – and the islanders let them, striding ahead on the path. James's hand closed around hers as they walked back towards the village. They both knew they had only these precious few moments together before word of the engagement officially broke and the celebrations erupted; their joy would be claimed by everyone, and Flora wanted – needed – these few minutes with her fiancé before their happiness was public property.

They approached the shoulder of the headland onto the easterly flank but before she could round it and step into the shadow, he pulled her into him and kissed her deeply. Her first kiss, and she hadn't even seen it coming. In company, he was a model of decorum and restraint, but the private man had hidden depths and his duality excited her.

They were breathless by the time they pulled apart.

'Don't leave me here,' she breathed. 'Take me with you.'

'I wish I could, but it's impossible,' he murmured, though his eyes were burning into hers. 'I leave for the Faroes next week.'

'Next week?' she quailed. 'But . . . I thought . . . you being here after all . . . I thought you'd changed your mind.' She felt a kick of panic, fear rising once more.

'It's not something I can change my mind on. They're

already waiting for me as it is. Most of them arrived in the Faroes days ago.'

'But—'

'My departure has been delayed on account of some late deliveries, that's all. I'll be bringing them out with me, and then we're heading off to Iceland together.'

'Iceland.' These were all worlds she would never see.

'Don't look so worried,' he said tenderly. 'The sooner I go, the sooner I return. And this doesn't change anything, not really. We would have been separated over the winter anyway – and I don't have to stick the expedition out to the bitter end. I can be back by August.'

'August?' she cried.

'Or . . . or possibly July,' he murmured, smoothing her hair back from her face.

'But that's almost a year from now!' She pulled back from him; she couldn't bear it. She couldn't.

His hands reached for her again, warm and solid, soothing her. 'A year from now, life will be ours for the taking. And it'll be easy from thereon in – the difficult part was finding you,' he smiled. 'I may have had to come almost to the edges of the earth to discover you, but one sighting and I'd have rowed myself back here in a pudding bowl if I'd had to.'

'. . . I'm glad you didn't have to,' she said quietly.

'Me too.'

Almost another year here. Could she do it? She looked down at the jewels glittering on her finger, felt the lipstick weighty in her skirt pocket. Would they be enough? Talismans to keep her safe?

'It looks beautiful on you,' James murmured, looking too at the ring on her finger.

'It's the most beautiful thing I've ever seen.'

'It was my mother's. She died when I was seven and it's been in a vault in London ever since. I'd have been back sooner, but I had to go to London to get it first.' He reached for her hand and pressed it to his lips again; his eyes never left hers. 'It's been frustrating, all this to-ing and fro-ing, especially as I already knew before I left here the last time that I was going to ask for your hand.'

She was surprised. 'You did?'

'Yes. But I wanted to do it properly. And besides, back then . . . it wasn't the time, of course.' He cleared his throat and, for the first time, looked away.

'No,' she agreed, remembering that awful night and the thundering silence that had followed Edward's punch. '. . . How is he?'

He didn't reply immediately. 'He hates me.' He shrugged, though he looked pained. 'He hasn't spoken to me since.'

'Oh, James,' she whispered.

He shook his head. 'I don't blame him. He's entitled to be angry at me. I'd be the same if the shoe were on the other foot. Besides, I knew what was at stake – I was choosing between you and him. And I chose you.'

She watched him, seeing the sadness in his eyes neverthe-less. She felt responsible for it; she had cost him a good friend. 'And Sophia?'

His face dropped. 'Inconsolable, I'm told. Edward told her before I could, so God only knows how he broke the news. She locked herself in her cabin and they dropped me at first landfall.'

'Which was where?'

'Benbecula.'

The Outer Hebridean isle was closer to the mainland than

here, of course, but still remote – and a very difficult journey back without a boat. 'Surely not?'

'It was for the best,' he said quickly. 'Far better for everyone that we parted ways. There was no point in dragging out the awkwardness. I was week-old fish at that point.'

Flora sighed at the mess. 'She must have been so hurt.'

'Possibly.'

'Possibly? There's no doubting it!'

'Well . . . I'm not sure whether she actually loved me or just the idea of me. Sophia is used to getting what she wants, so it was a blow to her pride more than anything. But I never wanted to make her suffer, and she would have done if I'd gone ahead with it – being married to a man who's in love with someone else would have been a form of torture for all involved. This is better by far. She'll understand that in time.'

'It's all my doing, though,' Flora said quietly. 'You've lost your friends, we've hurt all these people—'

'You're not responsible – *I* did this. I made a choice, and I wouldn't change it,' he said, looking at her intently. 'Not a thing. What's between us is real. Make no mistake, you were a . . . a vanity project for Edward, something pretty on his arm. I stand by everything I said then. He was my friend for a long time and if I had believed for a moment that his feelings were genuine, then I . . . I hope I would have done the correct thing and stood aside.' He paused, his gaze burning, then clasped her face in his hands. 'No,' he murmured. 'No, I wouldn't. I'm not as honourable as that. I would still have fought him for you. I'd have fought anyone.'

Flora could feel the heat coming from him as she looked into his eyes, the press of his hands on her waist as the two of them stood barefoot in the grass. He was so sure of his convictions; his emotions were so . . . straightforward. He drew her in, kissing her again, and she felt the passion immediately surge between them. She wanted his lips, but also his hands too, caresses and sighs and everything she had read about in Big Mary's copy of *Jane Eyre*. She had never felt like this before, but she could see how it could swallow time, making hours feel like minutes – and by contrast, how his absence would make days feel like weeks.

A sharp whistle suddenly split the sky and they instinctively broke apart. She knew it was a warning shot from Effie; their absence had been noticed.

No. Not yet, she thought, clinging to him still. She needed more time. And yet, a month still wouldn't be enough. A lifetime . . .

He pressed his forehead against hers, his breathing coming hard, as if pulling back was an act of resistance. 'Floss . . . my Floss . . .' he breathed, his fingertips digging in as still they kissed.

For several moments they stood there, wrapped in one another's arms, together but apart. Close, but not close enough.

'We should head back,' she whispered finally, reluctantly, moving her fingers lightly over his cheeks as if trying to commit their contours to her muscle memory. 'Ma will be like the whale if we don't allow her to share the news.'

'The whale?'

'One went pop in the bay a few days past.'

'Oh.' He paused. 'It was dead first, I'm hoping?'

'Aye,' she laughed, liking his dry wit. 'The whalers tied it to the buoy out there in the bay, but they waited too long on getting back to it . . . You're lucky the winds have carried away the stench.'

He pulled a face at the thought. Exploding whales weren't a part of his reality. 'Well, I'd rather your mother didn't

explode on my account, so yes, we probably should get back.'
She laughed again as he took her by the hand and led her
round the headland.

The village was already abuzz with excitement. She could
see even from a distance Big Mary, Crabbit Mary and Rachel
MacKinnon carrying out the tripods for the hogget roast. There
would be music and dancing this evening; Old Fin would
have an opportunity to play his beloved accordion again – but
James wouldn't be here to see it. Aboard the *Shamrock*, the
crew were already making preparations to get underway again
and Sir Thomas, Mad Annie, Ma Peg and Old Fin were making
a slow procession down the street towards the pier.

They saw it all from this distant remove – the waves
pounding the shore, fulmars wheeling on the breeze, the dark
shadows of fluffy clouds speeding across the slopes as every
step took them closer to separation. James's hand tightened
around hers, their jubilation giving way to incipient despair.
Sweet reunion had been all too brief.

'You promise you'll come back for me?' she asked fearfully,
pulling him back again, out of sight. Panic came in waves.

'I promise.' He clasped her cheeks and kissed her once
more. Immediately her body sank against his, an unstoppable
force driving them together, his hands in her hair. It was cruel
that they had found one another in the dying moments of
summer, sharing mere moments in private, only to be forced
into a year's separation.

'But you might change your mind,' she gasped as he kissed
her neck, holding her so tightly that she was suspended on
tiptoe.

'Never. We'll write as much as we can, and . . .' He looked
back at her. 'I'll come back again if I can. I promise, I'll find
a way.'

The Lost Lover

But she knew it was a vain hope. He was sailing to the Arctic Circle via the Faroes and Iceland, then Greenland. He would be gone for months.

She could only wait, and hope, and trust that his word was as good as his kisses.

Chapter Eleven

13 December 1929

St Kilda slept. The boulders on the beach glimmered with ice and the land was pillowy with deep drifts, although the snow was pockmarked by dozens of footsteps to the cleits, the kirk and the featherstore. The villagers had been all but confined to their cottages for a month, give or take, only emerging in any numbers in their shawls and tweeds when the winds dropped and the snow clouds held long enough to collect more peat for the fires, or fulmar oil for the lamps. The cows needed daily stripping of their milk in the byres, of course, and Effie made a lonely figure as she trekked morning and dusk to the bull house, whatever the weather. But to all intents and purposes, the island was in hibernation. Winter here had neither subtlety nor mercy.

It had already proved that. The consequences of the sheep drama the preceding month were still being felt, and none could yet shake the pall of despair that had come from it. A sudden, severe blizzard, early on in the season, had blanketed the isle in drifts that came almost to the men's shoulders in places, and it had taken almost every able-bodied villager to help dig out the sheep stranded on the Am Lag plateau. Mhairi had almost been killed when a dugout collapsed on her and only the quick actions of Donald McKinnon had got her out in time, but by then, everyone had been soaked through and frozen to the bone. Several people had fallen ill with fevers afterwards but Molly had gone on to develop pneumonia and within the space of a few days, she had died.

It had been as swift and simple as that.

One moment she'd been here, the next she was gone: a radiant young woman snuffed out in her prime. No one had been left unaffected. Her brother Norman and his wife Jayne were grieving in their own, very different ways; Lorna was inconsolable, as if she were to blame. And Flora's own brother David, who had been in love with Molly and prepared to play the long game to win Norman's blessing, now quietly raged that his patience, respect and kindness had been rewarded in this way.

In the immediate aftermath, Flora, Mhairi and Effie had huddled together in the byres or in Effie's box room for comfort, knitting and talking in low voices. But somehow Molly's loss was felt all the more keenly when they were together – their quartet reduced to a trio – and gradually they had begun spending more and more time in their own homes instead. Effie read and painted; Mhairi distracted herself with looking after her siblings. But Flora, faced with David's despair as well as her own, had nowhere to hide, and she whiled away the hours by her window, as now, gazing upon a blank horizon, feeling caught in a half-life.

'Flora.'

The sudden rap at the glass made her jump and she startled to see Jayne, spectral, on the other side, looking back at her.

Flora frowned. Jayne was never one to strike up conversation without good cause, but she was especially reclusive at the moment; knocking on windows wasn't her style. Flora moved to open the window but the older woman simply shook her head and then jerked it in the direction of the street. A second later, she was gone from sight.

For a few moments, Flora didn't stir. It was all so odd. Surely Jayne didn't want her to go out there and follow her? Why not just knock on the door?

She got up after a moment, intrigued. Besides, what else was there to do?

'Where are you going?' her mother asked, looking up from her fireside chair. She was carding the wool, her husband weaving at the small loom that was usually stored in the roof rafters during the summer. Flora's brothers and sisters were down at the schoolhouse for the first time in weeks and a pot of fulmar broth was bubbling on the stove, ready for their return.

Flora pushed her feet into her boots. 'Out for some air. I've got to move. I'll go round the bend if I spend another afternoon in here.'

'You could always unravel those for me,' her mother said, pointing a foot towards a pile of jumpers that were outgrown and in need of reconstruction to bigger sizes.

'I will, just as soon as I've stretched my legs,' Flora said, wrapping two red shawls round her body in a criss-cross arrangement and shrugging on a tweed jacket.

'Tch, I keep telling you: the active mother makes the lazy daughter,' she heard her father murmur as she went to the door.

'Hush now. She's grieving, can you not see? She's not herself.'

'She's too much herself, if y' ask me.'

Flora closed the door behind her and stepped into the street, taking care about where she placed her feet. The stones were slippery and a deep lip of snow sat atop the wall. She looked around for sight of Jayne and found her several houses up, waiting in the gap between Ma Peg and Lorna's cottages.

'Jayne, is everything quite well?' she asked, walking on the snowy verge towards her. No one moved easily in their cumbersome boots at the best of times. 'Is it Norman?'

Norman Ferguson's tempers were legendary and when he raised his voice it could generally be heard from one end of the village to the other. He was fond of moving out of the cottage into the byre on the occasions Jayne found her voice and argued back, and would have to be cajoled home, days later, like a spoilt child. There had been no all-out fights yet, but since losing Molly he had been caught drunk several times, having stolen from the whisky barrel that had washed ashore two years back and was stored at the manse under the reverend's watchful eye. It was strictly to be used for high days and holidays only, and the last such celebration had been the ceilidh following the waulking of the tweed in the autumn; but the reverend had taken an unusually sympathetic stance in this instance. 'He's afraid of Norman, plain and simple,' Flora had heard her father say to Donald McKinnon.

'No,' Jayne replied, 'he's well enough today. He's down in the featherstore, doing an inventory of the oil stocks.'

She turned away and began walking between the cottages, towards the head dyke. She clearly expected Flora to follow her.

'Ah, so you just . . . want some company, then?'

Jayne smiled. 'Aye. Some company would be nice.' But she lapsed almost immediately into silence as they began climbing up the steep slope, leaving Flora puzzled. Never once in her nineteen years had Jayne requested her company for a walk.

'Can I ask you something?' Flora said presently, as they

crossed over the stream and started up the south face of Mullach Bi. Their breath was coming more quickly, more deeply, but they were fit and strong, well used to this terrain.

'Of course.'

'Did you see it?'

Jayne stopped walking. She knew immediately what Flora meant, but it seemed an age before she turned her head and looked at her. 'Aye.'

Jayne's visions – her so-called gift of second sight – were recognized and accepted by all the villagers, even the reverend, who was always the first to decry superstition. Few people dared to ask Jayne about them but Flora had a bolder spirit, an enquiring curiosity that meant she couldn't hold her tongue.

'And I prayed day and night for God to spare her.' Jayne gave a hopeless shrug, words inadequate in the face of such an unjust death. For all her gifts, she had no power to stop what she foresaw. She was a hostage to her own mind.

Flora swallowed. 'When . . . ?'

'When did I see it? A few days before. The night of the ceilidh.'

Flora thought back; it had been their usual celebration after waulking the tweed, a tradition that stretched back beyond all their lifetimes, including Ma Peg and Old Fin's. They had feasted on hogget and danced in the MacQueens' own byre; Flora remembered seeing Jayne dancing a little, enjoying herself. But then . . . she concentrated harder . . . she hadn't seen her much after the Eightsome.

'Did you know it was Molly? Were you certain?'

Jayne only nodded this time, a pained look on her pale features.

'Oh, Jayne.' The two women had lived together in the

cottage with Norman. How had Jayne kept such a horror from her? How had she eaten meals, talked with her, laughed . . . knowing what was coming? 'Do you think . . . ?' She could barely get the words out. 'Did she . . . did she suspect?'

Jayne shook her head quickly. 'I made certain of that. I could not have borne for her to know that terror too.'

Too. Flora watched her and felt a sense of the weight Jayne carried, the burden she could never share. To suffer in silence, knowing a loved one's death was coming in mere days and nothing could be done to stop it . . .

'She was so well, Flora . . . so s-strong . . . I couldn't understand how it would happen – not until the weather came suddenly in and the men began rounding everyone up to help.' Jayne swallowed, as if the words were hot coals burning her throat. '. . . When Mhairi was carried back, I thought at first I'd been mistaken. That I'd seen the wrong girl and – God help me' – she lifted her face skywards, her eyes closed – 'God help me, but for a moment I felt relief.' She looked across at Flora with urgency. 'I wanted no harm to come to Mhairi, you know that. But Molly – she was only my sister-in-law, but I loved her like blood.'

'I know,' Flora whispered, placing a hand on her arm. 'I know you did. And I understand why you thought that way.'

'You do?' Guilt played over her face like a shadow.

'Of course. Anyone would feel the same about their own.'

Jayne nodded but there was no real comfort to be had. They resumed walking, the snow crunching underfoot; on these higher slopes, it sat pristine and unmarked, virgin territory.

Jayne's words tumbled in Flora's head, thoughts dislodged by every footstep, and it began to occur to her that there was something else too that must have been terrifying for Jayne.

Her husband could sulk over a wrong look; to have lost his sister . . . She looked across at Jayne, always so forbearing. So discreet.

'Jayne.'

'Aye?'

'. . . Did Norman . . .' Flora hesitated over even using the word. 'Did he blame you?'

There was a hesitation. 'For not stopping it?'

'For not warning him.'

Jayne swallowed, her body seeming to deflate of air. '. . . Yes.'

Flora squinted. She hadn't heard any rows – and it suddenly didn't make sense. Norman Ferguson, an angry man, had lost his only sister; and every night he lay beside the woman who had foreseen it – a worry James himself had once articulated. She suddenly knew Norman wouldn't have let it pass unmarked. '. . . Show me.'

Jayne stopped walking again. 'What?'

'Show me how he blamed you.'

For a dizzying moment, as the two women held eye contact, Flora feared she had gone too far. No one ever pressed Jayne for details of her life; no one ever pushed for explanations. People kept their distance, afeared of her gift as if it could be summoned at will, a demon she could manipulate against her enemies. But Flora knew more happened behind their stone walls than in the other cottages. That Jayne was a keeper of all kinds of secrets.

'Show me.'

Slowly, Jayne pulled up the layers on her torso to reveal faint red marks across her ribs – marks like a boot print. But Molly had died a month earlier. Exactly how hard had he kicked her, for traces still to remain?

'Oh Jayne,' she whispered, tears gathering in her eyes.
'. . . Did you show Lorna?'

Jayne nodded. 'She's been very kind. And very discreet.
As I hope—'

'Of course,' Flora said quickly. 'I would never breathe a
word.'

'Thank you.' Jayne began walking once more but Flora
caught her hand and held it as they climbed together.

'You can always talk to me, Jayne – you know that? I'm
not superstitious like the rest.'

'I know that. You're fearless, Flora MacQueen.' Jayne
smiled, squeezing her hand and swinging their arms between
them.

They got to the saddle of the Am Blaid ridge and Flora
turned to look back down at the village. She felt glad to have
come out after all. The walk had warmed her in spite of the
perishing temperatures, and she felt a rush of love for this
snowy rock in the ocean, grey smoke twisting from every
chimney, lights glowing from the windows. Her home.

'Flora, come and see.'

She turned back to see Jayne standing a hundred yards
further up, right on the crest of the ridge. She was pointing
towards something in Glen Bay. It was one of those rare days
when the wind had switched direction, blowing straight into
Village Bay and whipping up waves that would make any
disembarkment impossible. But here, on the north coast,
protected by this very ridge, the sea lay perfectly at rest, a
banner of battleship-grey silk, rippling lightly below milky
skies.

'What is it?' Flora panted, gathering her skirts for the final
strides and coming to join her.

'It's the reason I brought you up here,' Jayne said, clasping her arm and holding her close as Flora tried to understand what she was seeing.

'What *is* that?' she frowned. She had seen aeroplanes, distant specks in the sky, a few times, but . . . this thing was floating on the water's surface, tethered to a rocky outcrop.

'I believe it's a seaplane,' Jayne said. 'I saw it circling, coming in to land earlier, when I was coming back with a peat. It would have been too rough to land on the other side.'

Flora hadn't heard the dogs barking on the beach for once. They warned of approaching ships, not planes. 'But who . . . ?'

Jayne looked at her and smiled. 'The letters B.A.A.R.E. were written underneath the body of it.'

Flora blinked. 'B . . . ?'

British Arctic Air Route Expedition. She gasped, her hands flying to her mouth. 'Surely not?' she cried, immediately scanning the wide bowl of the glen for a sighting of him. Where . . . ?

Then she saw it: a single track of footprints dotting the landscape from the rocky cove, all the way through to . . . She stepped forward and saw him in a dip, a dark speck in the snow, slowly making his way towards the ridge.

'James!' she called, hardly daring to believe her eyes.

He stopped and looked up, his silhouette visibly relaxing at the sight of her as she waved. 'Flora?!'

'He's really here? It's really him?' Flora laughed, looking across at Jayne.

'It really is.'

Flora pressed her fingers to her lips as she watched him break into a slow run. 'Who else did you tell he was here?' How long would they have together before the crowds intruded again? Had the reverend been alerted? He always liked to press the flesh of their well-heeled visitors.

'No one,' Jayne shrugged. 'And I won't be telling anyone, either.'

'You won't?' Flora looked at her in surprise.

'No. You've not had five minutes alone with him since he asked you to marry him and there's a long winter coming. Have some time together without everyone's fuss.' Jayne patted her arm and turned to take her leave.

'Jayne, thank you,' Flora called after her.

She smiled. 'There's been enough sadness here recently, Flora. As far as I'm concerned, it's about time one of us had a happy ending.'

Flora waited for him, shivering in the wind, seeing his power as he ran up the last of the slope, his bloody-minded determination to get back here one last time.

'I can't believe this is really happening!' she laughed as he drew ever nearer, still running until the very last step. 'You actually came back!'

'Didn't I promise I would?' he panted, eyes bright as he reached for her.

She stood on tiptoe to kiss him, feeling the warmth of his cheeks in her palms. He had the first shadow of a beard and his hair was longer than when she'd seen him in the autumn.

'You're crazy,' she whispered, running her hands over his face and in his hair.

'You're beautiful,' he murmured back, kissing her again and again, their passion surging like an underground spring. 'And cold! Flora, you're shivering.' Even just a few moments standing on this exposed hillside was enough to whip the warmth from her, but she didn't care. If it meant they had a few extra moments alone . . .

Without hesitation, he shrugged off his heavy shearling-lined jacket, seeming not to notice he was now in shirtsleeves. 'Come, we can't stay up here. Let's get you inside.'

'Wait,' she said, pulling back as he began to turn downhill, towards the ridge. 'I know somewhere else we can go . . . Somewhere private.' He looked at her. 'No one knows you're here. We don't have to go to the village. For once, we can be together, just the two of us.'

He looked uncertain for a moment and she saw a question pass through his eyes. She knew exactly what he was asking. 'Really?'

She nodded. She'd never been more sure of anything.

'Really,' she smiled, taking his hand.

Chapter Twelve

May 1930

Glen Bay, St Kilda

Flora hurried down from the ridge, heading for home, where stubby shadows slanted on sappy grass, and freshly scrubbed sheets and curtains flapped in the breeze as everyone spring-cleaned their homes after the long winter confinement. She had been in Glen Bay for two weeks now – Mhairi needed a companion as she tended the sheep flocks in the summer pastures – and to her surprise, she was missing the daily bustle and flow along the street, her neighbours' idle chatter and busy hands never stopping as life continued for them, uninterrupted.

The weeks were counting down quickly now to her summer departure, and it was as if she was suddenly seeing her home with fresh eyes. For nineteen years, she had followed the rhythms of island life without question or excitement; there was no novelty in pursuits which stretched back beyond the limits of her own memory. Now, though, she was acutely aware that everything she did would be for the last time: the gannet harvest, seeding the crops, lambing, hoeing the lazy-beds, waulking the tweed . . . Even just walking to the kirk

167

with Mhairi and Effie in the snow, scratching for lichen on the rocks above a stormy sea, seeing the pink thrift and buttercups bloom on the Ruival slopes, watching the wrens build their nests in the drystone walls – none of it would have a place in her new home.

But if there wouldn't be the same beauty there, hopefully the danger would be absent too. Death and disaster frilled the minutiae of their daily lives here and this morning had been no exception, with Mhairi sent into a wild panic as she milked the first of the ewes and caught sight of the semaphore over on Boreray. The girls had seen the boat going across only yesterday for the annual sheep plucking; the men were expected to stay over there for several days yet, but two huge cuts in the turf, visible across the water, had sent out a shockwave and a rescue boat had been quickly deployed by the remaining villagers. Two cuts signified injury – three, death – but they had no way of knowing who it was that was afflicted, and Mhairi wouldn't be calmed until they had news. It was down to Flora to get over here as fast as she could, her bare feet flying over the grass and dark hair streaming in the wind.

'Flora!'

Her name carried like a bird's call and she looked up to see Effie standing by the wall of the bull's house, waving wildly. She changed course, heading over to her.

'Where's the fire?' Effie grinned as they hugged in greeting.

'Uff,' Flora panted, exhausted by her exertions all over again and leaning back against the wall. She had lost more fitness than she had realized. 'I'm dead. She made me run the whole way here.'

'Mhairi did?'

'Aye.'

Immediately Effie looked worried. 'Why couldn't she run? Is she hurt?'

Flora quickly put up a hand. 'She's fine. But we were over on Cambir when we saw the cuts . . .' She looked directly at Effie. 'Who is it?'

'Donald McKinnon.'

'What?' Flora snapped up to standing again.

'He's got a head injury.'

'Is he going to recover?'

'Aye. He fell catching a sheep and cut his head, but Lorna thinks he'll be fine with some rest. She's going to stay with them for the next few nights too.'

'She is?' Flora was concerned. It must be a bad cut if Lorna was needed around the clock.

'Aye. Poor Mary's not up to much.'

'No,' Flora agreed, biting her lip. Mary's longed-for pregnancy was known, among the villagers, to be precarious, requiring plenty of bed rest. 'But he's definitely going to be all right?'

Effie grinned at her concern. 'Is absence making the heart grow fonder? Are you missing us over there while you idle the summer away?'

'Idle?!' Flora huffed, grabbing a stalk of grass poking from the wall and threading it through her fingers. 'We've three hundred sheep over there.'

'Aye, grazing and giving you no bother, from the look of things.' Effie's eyes twinkled with mischief.

'And what does that mean?'

'Just that you look bonny as ever. I thought it was hunger that had driven you back, but evidently not . . .' Effie teased, reaching forward to stroke her hair. 'The look of love?'

James flashed through her mind again, as he always did,

169

and she wondered what he was doing right at this moment – swooping in the skies in his Gipsy Moth seaplane, mapping and marking every jut and crevice of the Greenland coast? Or huddling in a tent pitched on the icy tundra, someone on watch for the polar bears? She had no way of knowing. Once he had left Iceland, as warned, all communication had ceased; no mail was possible from the wilderness. It would be months yet before he sailed back to London and some days it felt unendurable – she ached to hear his voice, to feel his touch.

'There's nothing bonny about spending a fortnight alone with Mhairi, let me tell you. She's grown up with her brothers telling tales about the McKinnon curse and dash if she doesn't believe it. She's frightened everything's going to kill her or her kin.' Flora rolled her eyes, moving the subject – and attention – back onto their friend, wishing she could tell Effie the whole story.

'Well, you can tell her it's all fine. No relatives harmed.'

'But Donald's not out of the woods yet?'

'No, but if Lorna thought it really bad, she'd have sent him to the mainland.'

'How?' Flora asked doubtfully, but as she looked up she noticed, for the first time, the yacht anchored in the bay. She gave a gasp at the sight of the elegant cruiser. How could she have missed it? It hadn't the racing lines of Sir Thomas's *Shamrock V* but it was a different beast to the Rushtons' boat James had sailed in on last summer too. Sleeker, with a graceful, curved hull and a triple mast, it sat comfortably between the other two vessels, at the very top of its class. 'Whose is *that*?'

Effie sighed. 'They're friends of MacLeod. The Earl of Dumfries and his son. They brought Mathieson over.'

'Eeesht,' Flora groaned, her mood immediately dipping at

the mention of him. The factor rarely improved anyone's day with his presence.

'I know. We thought we got lucky that the men decided to cross to Boreray on account of the weather and they took Mathieson with them, giving us some peace. Only . . . the next day, they're back again.'

'Bad luck.'

Effie shrugged. 'Worse for Donald.'

Tiny, the bull, gave a sudden snort and a few bucks as he trotted happily up the enclosure.

'He looks pleased with himself,' Flora murmured.

'He should be. He's had a long mating season,' Effie grinned.

'Men! Man or beast, they're all the same,' Flora joked back, reaching for Effie and pressing their heads together as she felt a sudden rush of love for her dear friend. Sometimes, the break between girlhood and womanhood hit her out of the blue and she felt a pang for those days before love had come into her life, when she had lived with a wide-eyed innocence that knew nothing of the obsessions to come. When she was with Effie she was reminded of their games in the grass, mischief-making in kirk, snorting with laughter in the byre in the evenings . . . But now, lambing in Glen Bay, she could only be sustained by thoughts of James. Her waking hours were dominated by a thin clutch of memories that played on a loop; her dreams were fevered, so that she awoke each morning tangled in her sheet and with a feeling of incompleteness.

She drew back and saw Effie give her a puzzled look, as if she sensed secrets. She looked as if she was about to say something but her expression cleared again in the next moment.

'Will you stay for dinner?' Effie asked instead. 'They'll be pleased to see you. Your pa had to skipper the boat back to Boreray, so he's worn out. David's still over there and your ma's upset by the fall.'

Flora bit her lip, pensive. 'If they see me, they'll make me stay. But Mhairi's got the jitters. She made me promise to come straight back.'

Effie scowled. 'I don't understand why, if Mhairi's got the jitters, she didn't come over here herself instead of sending you?'

But Flora was distracted. She had spotted Lorna talking to Crabbit Mary around the back of their cottage. The nurse was holding the stricken wife's hand consolingly as they spoke closely in what appeared to be low tones. Out of the patient's earshot? 'That doesn't look promising,' she murmured, feeling even more concerned.

'No,' Effie agreed.

'Perhaps I should stay a wee while after all, then. See if the situation changes.' She couldn't possibly go back to Mhairi with only half a story about Donald McKinnon's welfare: injured but recuperating was one thing, but Mhairi would need to know if he was thriving or languishing. Their love affair was a closely guarded secret but if he began to fail, she had a right to know, to be over here . . .

Flora looked back at Effie. 'Have I missed much?'

She expected a roll of her friend's eyes – how much ever happened here? – but to her surprise, Effie hesitated. 'There's been some excitement, aye.'

Flora brightened. She was thirsting for news, something to draw her out of her own head. 'Speak to me. Tell me.'

'I've been guiding the visitors while the men were gone.'

Flora's excitement abated. Was that all? 'Aye.'

'I'm being paid two shillings for my trouble.'

'*Two*?' It seemed a standard fee.

'And . . . we've become friends.'

'I thought you said they were lords?'

'Well, yes, but you wouldn't know it. Not really. There's no airs and graces when we're all out walking together.'

Flora's eyes narrowed. She detected an unusual hesitancy in her friend. 'And . . . ?' she prompted, sensing more. That look she had seen on Effie just now – had she been not sensing secrets, but keeping them? 'What else is there?'

'Miss Gillies! I've been searching for you.'

The shout startled them both and they looked up to find the factor striding towards them.

Flora gave a shudder of contempt. She had been locked in a battle of wills with him for several years now. When she was a child, he had paid her no attention, but as she grew into young womanhood and found her voice along with her curves, she seemed to levy a resistance in him that grew fiercer at every encounter. He didn't desire her, she knew that – she knew exactly how men looked at a woman they wanted – but she had come to realize that her beauty provided her with an advantage over everyone else that he considered to be his alone.

She had power. And that set them at odds.

It was her beauty that made people want to be her friend, to be near her, to look upon her. It was her beauty that made them want to help, oblige and please her. And it was her beauty that had first captured the attention of a rich, powerful, adventure-hunting fiancé. Her beauty would, a few months from now, propel her into a world far beyond this place and above the level of society he inhabited on the mainland. It had given her a power that had put her out of his reach. He couldn't threaten or intimidate her, and they both knew it.

'Eeesht,' she said under her breath. 'If it's not the devil himself. I'll catch you later.'

'Flora, wait,' Effie implored.

But Flora was already sauntering down the hill. 'Mr Mathieson,' she said breezily as she passed him with a swing of her hips, her nose in the air.

He gave a terse nod in reply and she could feel his eyes on her back as she slipped through the gap in the dyke and headed towards the cottages.

Lorna and Mary were still talking, heads bent together, the rest of the world shut out so that they didn't notice her approach until she was only a few steps away.

'Oh!' Mary startled, jumping back. '. . . Och, Flora, it's only you.' She pressed a hand to her heart as if to steady it. Her hand was trembling, Flora noticed, and she looked so guilty that even if Flora had not been privy to her secret, she would have known from her behaviour that she was harbouring one.

'Aye. I've come to check on Donald. I hear he's the one hurt?'

'Aye,' Lorna nodded, looking sombre.

'Mhairi sent you, did she?' Mary asked, and Flora picked up the thread of sarcasm in the words. The woman bristled with hostility, as if it was Flora who had stolen her husband from her.

'She was worried. It looks like she has reason to be?' Flora directed her question to the nurse. There was little point in entering into an argument with her best friend's lover's wife – this was not her battle.

Lorna stood a little taller, as if trying to assert her professionalism; this wasn't her battle either, but she had been drawn

174

into the secret on account of her medical expertise. Whatever her personal feelings about the love triangle, she could see that their arrangement – and so-called solution – wouldn't be possible without her assistance. If reputations were at stake, without Lorna, so were lives.

'He's taken a nasty blow to the head. Swelling of the brain is my main concern but so far he's alert to stimuli and lucid, so I'm confident he'll recover quickly with bed rest.'

'Confident?' Flora echoed. She needed cast-iron guarantees for Mhairi. 'But you're staying here overnight, so . . . you must have some concerns?'

'Let's say I'm cautiously hopeful, then. My staying over is purely precautionary. I'm expecting a full recovery but he's not out of the woods yet. Complications are always possible. I need to be on hand in case he deteriorates in the night, and of course Mary's condition precludes . . .'

The lie died on her lips and she gave a small, ironic smile. They had all become too well versed, too practised in the rehearsed narrative, to drop it easily. Mary was putting on such a convincing show of being pregnant that it was easy, even for those who knew otherwise, to believe it was true.

Lorna took a steadying breath, recalibrating her thoughts, her voice low. '. . . I just don't want to take any chances. Donald must not die. The baby will need its father. And Mary will need a husband to provide.'

Flora was silent for a moment at the unsentimental logic applied to his survival. 'Aye.'

What a mess it all was. She still didn't know how Mhairi could bear to go along with it.

Flora could still remember the wave of shock that had rippled through her as Mhairi had sat by the peat fire on their first night in Glen Bay and revealed to her the whole, scandalous truth. It had made Flora's own secret seem meagre by comparison. For Mhairi to fall in love with Donald, a married man, had been inadvisable to say the very least, but the catastrophe was far larger than just that: her betrothed, Alexander, Mhairi had finally admitted, was a brutish man at the mercy of his own carnal desires. Flora had recalled the unnatural brightness in Mhairi's eyes when she'd returned from meeting him in Harris. Her friend was terrified of becoming this stranger's wife – but the betrothal had been confirmed and it was unstoppable now. Donald couldn't simply divorce Mary and marry Mhairi, of course: the reverend would never permit it and the villagers would never accept their love.

But to give up their baby too – to relinquish it into the care of his unloving wife . . . ? That was the price Mhairi had agreed to pay for Mary's silence: she well knew the weight placed here upon reputation, family honour and sin. Mary would never breathe a word about the affair in return for raising their child as her own – and who would doubt it was hers? Her longstanding yearning to be a mother was well known among the villagers and the McKinnons' childlessness was commonly understood to be the reason for the enduring unhappiness of their marriage. This pact, such as it was, ensured reputations would remain intact for all parties. Vows taken before God would not be wholly sundered and life would continue upon its allotted path.

'It's the only way,' Mhairi had wept as the firelight flickered on her face. 'The baby will be with its father and no one shall ever be any the wiser.'

And so far, everything had gone according to plan. Donald had 'saved' his mistress by suggesting to the village's parliament that they trial two shepherdesses summering in Glen

Bay: freshly filled milk churns would be deposited at the Am Blaid ridge, the halfway point between the pastures and the village, and empty ones returned there each day. This would allow Mhairi's pregnancy to develop away from nosy neighbours – for if Mad Annie had a sharp tongue, she had even sharper eyes – and only Lorna and Flora would need to be brought in on the truth.

'So I can tell Mhairi he'll be well?' Flora asked the nurse. Donald's survival wasn't a matter of practicality for her friend. Their love was true. Honest. Real – Flora had seen it with her own eyes. Every day, at some point, Donald would steal over the ridge to spend precious hours with Mhairi, the two of them lying in the grass and talking intently even as the sands of time slipped between their fingers. They looked so right together; and yet here was his wife, maintaining an elaborate charade of a happy family-to-be in front of the neighbours.

'Barring any complications, he should be back on his feet within the week,' Lorna said.

Flora looked back towards the ridge with a sigh. Effie and the factor were still talking near the bull's enclosure. There was a stricken look on Effie's pale face.

'Good. I'll relay that to Mhairi then.'

'Aye, you can tell my husband's whore he'll live to see another day yet,' Mary said coldly as Flora went to turn away. 'He'll not die because I'll not let him. He made this whole sorry mess – and I'm going to make sure he damn well sits in it.'

Chapter Thirteen

Mhairi was already kindling the evening fire as Flora marched back down the slopes of Glen Bay. The valley was a wide, grassy bowl, dotted with cleits and sheep fanks and bordered on the eastern shoulder by the hulking mountain Mullach Mor. On the western flank, the headland of Cambir Point sat lower, stretching out into the sea like a cat's paw and looking onto the nearby isle of Soay. The glen was cleaved by a stream that fed into a narrow, rocky cove, splitting into two small waterfalls that splashed upon the emergent rocks there. Most of the year, except for a few stray days when the wind flipped to the south-east, the waves would pound the cove, inter-rupted in their march from the Arctic by the sudden obstruction of the archipelago. But during the summer months, the sea at large was sufficiently tame for Mhairi and Flora to climb down and wash in the waterfalls every evening, the waves merely pooling around their ankles on the granite slabs.

Their home for the summer was the souterrain known by the tourists as the Amazon's House, playing into the ancient legend of a fearsome huntress. There were several under-ground dwellings on the isles, usually just long pits dug a couple of feet below the ground and lined with stone slabs – they were ideal for sheltering in during harsh weather if an islander should happen to find themselves away from the village and an empty cleit. The men had stayed in one such on Boreray just these past few days for their sheep-plucking trip, for there were no trees to provide protection from the elements. The Amazon's House, however, was a far greater feat of Bronze Age engineering. It had a narrow entrance leading into an oval space that fed down into a larger circular chamber, with sleeping pods off the sides. It was just deep enough for them to stand, but it was dark and damp in there, no fires possible on account of the lack of chimney and restricted ventilation. For growing a baby, however, it was perfect. Mhairi said she had never slept so well, and Flora had to agree that the pervasive darkness of the souterrain made waking with the dawn strangely difficult.

Their days were passing with a pleasing rhythm of quiet industry as they milked the sheep, checked the lambs were putting on weight and monitored the late-tupped ewes. Sometimes the two of them talked or sang, but other times they moved around in companionable silence, each lost in their own thoughts of their coming futures and divergent fortunes. It was hard for Flora not to feel guilty at all the good coming her way and the tragedy facing her friend – waiting for it all to happen was possibly the worst part of all. With every sunrise and sunset, with every starlit sky that twinkled above them, the clock kept ticking, bringing them both closer to their fates.

Flora could feel her happiness growing inside her – she thought of James constantly, longing to tell him all her news – and she had to bite her tongue to keep from wondering aloud about their reunion, when she knew Mhairi was facing a desperate separation.

'Oh, thank God!' Mhairi cried, spying her and gathering her skirts as she walked awkwardly to breach the gap between them. Flora saw Mhairi's face fall as she approached, as if a sixth sense confirmed her worst fears. '. . . Donald?'

'Aye,' Flora nodded. 'But he's going to be fine. Lorna's looking after him. She's staying with Mary for the next few nights, just to see him through the worst.'

'Wh-what happened?'

'He slipped and knocked his head on some rocks – but Lorna is certain he's going to be well in a few days.'

Certain? *Hopeful* had been the nurse's word, but Flora couldn't bear to see the terror in her friend's eyes.

'I should go over there!' Mhairi gasped, her eyes wide as she looked over to the ridge, as if preparing to run.

'That wouldn't be wise,' Flora said, letting her gaze fall to Mhairi's swollen belly; she had another seven weeks before the baby was due but was beginning to show properly now and Lorna had warned her to expect a rapid growth spurt in the final weeks of the pregnancy.

'But he needs me!'

'Yes, but that's not possible right now.' Flora caught her friend's hand and squeezed it. 'You have to trust Lorna; you saw how she was after Molly died. She'll not let anything happen to him if she can help it.'

It had been almost six months now since the 'sheep drama', and their friend's death was still an open wound. It had hit Lorna particularly hard, and in the weeks that followed she had channelled her grief into anger, her shock into action. She had spent hours talking with the minister and the village elders, discussing – no, petitioning – the idea of an evacuation to the mainland. 'No one should die of pneumonia in this day and age,' she kept saying at dinner tables and on the street and at the burn, pale eyes blazing. 'We're vulnerable here when we don't need to be.'

Flora had assumed the villagers wouldn't take kindly to being told they were failing where their ancestors had succeeded – especially by someone who, like Lorna, wasn't a St Kildan by birth. But perhaps that was why her impassioned speeches struck a nerve, for she had never been low on grit. The facts were, the islanders had endured several bitter winters in succession where the crops had almost entirely failed and emergency provisions had had to be sent over by MacLeod. Added to that, the stories the fishermen kept bringing back of technology and fashions and medicines on the mainland, of new jobs and flourishing industries, had made the younger St Kildans start to dream of an easier life over the horizon – and survival here was dependent upon youth: strong, agile bodies that could haul and lower themselves on the cliffs, fast runners, strong lungs.

In the end a letter had been sent to Westminster requesting an evacuation, with an 'all or none' caveat pledged among the villagers. Nothing had yet been heard back, but nobody was holding their breath. After all, they had been requesting another boat, a radio mast and a regular postal service for years, and those meagre pleas had fallen on deaf ears.

'But she may not be able to help him!' Mhairi cried, unappeased. 'Molly needed a hospital and we couldn't get her there. The pneumonia would have been treatable on the other side. What if Donald needs the same – help there that we've not got here?'

'If she thought he needed to go over the other side, she'd have sent him, you can be sure of that.'

'How?' Mhairi's hands slipped from her grasp, fluttering skywards like startled doves. 'We've nothing here!'

'Actually, we do; it's why I've taken so long to get back. There's a sloop in the bay that just came the other day. If

Lorna needed it to take Donald to the mainland, do you think there's anyone brave enough to stop her?'

Mhairi blinked. 'No.'

'Exactly. He'll be fine. Stop worrying.'

With a gentle hand on her friend's back, she turned her to face downhill and they headed for their summer home. Mhairi took several deep breaths and shook her hands out, trying to calm herself. Flora could tell her friend had gone to a place deep inside her own head.

'But why were you over there so long?'

Flora looped her arm through Mhairi's, pleased to have an opportunity to change the subject. 'Well, it's quite the story. You won't believe your ears.'

'Tell me,' Mhairi replied, sounding intrigued.

'It belongs to the Earl of Dumfries. He's one of MacLeod's friends – sailed over with his son and they brought over the factor too.'

'Ugh, no,' Mhairi groaned, much the same way Flora herself had earlier.

'I know, and he's as odious as ever.' Flora rolled her eyes. 'The visitors, however . . . They're spending a week here, bird-spotting and catching eggs – and Effie's being paid to guide them.'

'That'll make her happy,' Mhairi murmured.

'Aye.' She leaned in closer. 'Especially as the son, Lord Sholto, is as handsome a man as you've ever seen.' Flora had met him with Effie on the rocks just before she'd headed back here; she had gone in search of Jayne, wanting confirmation that she'd had none of her foreboding dreams before she came back to Mhairi.

Mhairi looked at her in surprise. 'As handsome as James?'

Flora hesitated. 'Different. He's golden. Like a sun god.'

James could hardly be called a man of the soil, but he had a grit where Sholto had gloss. He was a man of action, industry and enterprise.

'Really?' Mhairi breathed, looking engrossed in someone else's story for a change. 'So don't tell me – now he's in love with you, and you're going to throw James over and marry him instead?'

Flora was indignant at the outrageous tease. 'No! No, I'm not, but not because of that.' She turned and looked straight at Mhairi. 'He's wildly in love with Effie. A blind man could see it.'

'*What?*'

'Aye! And she's in love with him!'

'No! Effie's in love?'

'Aye!'

'. . . Effie's in love?' Mhairi whispered as she began to see that Flora wasn't joking. 'But he's a laird, you said. An earl's son.'

Flora's own smile faded. 'I know. And I had to tell her it can never be.' She bit her lip. 'The way she looked at me, Mhairi, I think I broke her heart. I told her she can't stay in the village, not until he leaves again. She's going to come over here in the morning.'

Mhairi let her gaze travel skywards, instinctively reading the clouds and haze on the horizon and understanding what it meant: a storm was coming and the visitors would need to get ahead of it. Poor Effie was about to lose the man she loved too, but his departure would come in mere hours, not months.

'It's just all so quick!' Mhairi said, looking back at Flora again. They had been over here for only two weeks and yet something momentous had occurred. None of them had ever thought they'd see the day when Cupid caught their friend.

'But it is, isn't it,' Flora shrugged. 'When it's right, you just know.' They were back at the souterrain now and she poked the burning peat slab to get the flames leaping; Donald had brought the prized metal poker over for them 'for protection', though quite what dangers he thought they might face here, apart from the odd bad-tempered ewe, was a mystery. 'I wish I could have let her have her happiness, but you should have seen the way he was looking at her. And her at him. They're not fooling anyone. It's plain as day what's happening between them. She's an innocent. Eff's not like us, she doesn't have a mother to guide her through this; she might not realize the consequences . . .'

'No.' Mhairi looked away, her hands on her belly, and Flora knew what she was thinking – she had a mother and it hadn't saved her from her predicament. Her own love story had snuck up on her, a tap on her shoulder when she had been looking in entirely the opposite direction . . . Love didn't follow a rule book and when it came, it flowed like a flood, tearing your feet out from under you and washing you away. Knowing the rules was very different from being able to enforce them.

'But it's for her own good. She'll never see him again once he leaves here. She has to be realistic.' Flora could hear the anxious note in her words. She had done the right thing, hadn't she?

'Aye.'

'I warned her. I reminded her what happened to Kitty,' Flora said flatly. The fate of Flora's cousin was the cautionary tale flagged up to all the young St Kildan women after she had jumped from the rocks, pregnant and abandoned by the naval man she thought loved her.

Mhairi just nodded, looking saddened by it all. She knew

only too well that the right thing could still be the wrong thing – and vice versa. It was wrong that Donald was married to Mary and not Mhairi; it was wrong that Mhairi must marry a stranger and not the man she loved; and it was wrong that Effie must forsake a real love on account of class, money and station.

Flora reached around her waist and unknotted the red shawl. 'Here, thanks for this,' she said, handing it over and watching as Mhairi draped it around herself instead, the shawl covering the gap where her skirt could no longer close. It was harder now for Mhairi to see past her belly, and Flora bent down to help her fasten Donald's brooch to secure the layers of skirt and shawl together.

'There,' she smiled, straightening up again and meeting her friend's trepidatious gaze. They both knew it was a rudimentary patching, but for the moment at least, it was holding.

'Who's that?' Mhairi asked, looking up from her stool in the sheep fank and shielding her eyes from the sun as she watched the advancing figure on the slope.

Flora lurched up at Mhairi's question and followed the line of her pointing finger. 'At last! Better late than never,' she rejoiced. They had been waiting on Effie all morning but there'd been no sign of her, much to Flora's concern.

'No . . . I don't think that's Eff,' Mhairi murmured, her voice dropping off.

The two women stopped and waited, staring impatiently at the dark dot, willing it to reveal itself. Steadily the figure grew as it neared with every step, but the gait rapidly became distinctive. And there was no sign of Poppit.

'Oh no, it's Mathieson,' Flora groaned. 'What's he doing over here?'

Mhairi gave a sound of fright.

'Quick, we'd best make ourselves decent,' Flora said, picking up the filled pails and heading for the souterrain – but Mhairi stood rooted to the spot. 'It would hardly do presenting ourselves like this to him now, would it?' she pointed out.

The humidity was stifling and they were wearing just their slips for the milking, sweat beading at their brows. The sun had risen with a silent brilliance but as the day yawned, a storm had gathered its armies along the edge of the sky and the hot air was now turgid. Menacing towers of bruised clouds were billowing and spreading, rolling over the horizon like dark chariots, the breeze sucked away like the undertow of a tsunami, preparing to disgorge.

Mhairi jolted back to life and followed after her. The grass was spiky and dry underfoot and the sheep were listless. After the suffocating heat of the day, the damp coolness of the Amazon's House was a welcome relief and Flora dressed quickly, but when she emerged into the communal space a few minutes later, she saw Mhairi sitting on her sleeping shelf, still dressed in her slip. Her pregnancy could be largely obscured in the bulky layers of her skirt and blouse – the skirt was cut from a heavy cloth that hung away from the body and was so long as she stooped forward a little, the swell of her belly could still be disguised. The thin cotton slip, however, revealed everything, and Flora stared at her in surprise.

'Why aren't you dressed?'

'. . . I can't. I can't do it. He mustn't see me.'

'Of course you can. It'll be fine.'

'I can't, Flora. I can't lie to a man like him. He's too clever for me.'

Flora didn't reply immediately, not denying the truth in her friend's words. The factor was nothing if not astute. He had a sly cleverness to him, with watchful eyes and a sharp tongue. Flora knew how to make a man look where she wanted him to look, but Mhairi – never confrontational anyway – was neither confident nor wily enough to deceive him to his face. She would cower before his raptor's gaze and her secret would be out within moments; all this would have been for naught.

'Please,' Mhairi implored her. 'He's come down to check on the slops, it must be that he's here for. Won't you just show him yourself? Tell him I'm poorly.'

Was it the slops he wanted to see? Mhairi had been stirring them for him ever since the dead sperm whale had exploded in the bay last summer and he had retrieved the curious, stinking viscera, believing it to be a cure for his mother's gout. Twice every day, Mhairi had to refresh the water in the pail and stir the slops. It was an odious errand, but he was paying well and the money was welcome, for her father had ten mouths to feed besides his own.

'But you know he despises me. I won't flatter him and it only ever makes things worse.'

'No, he'll not do that now you're engaged. James is a powerful man, he knows that. Please . . .'

Still Flora hesitated – the stakes were high for her too, but she reminded herself that she had seen the factor just yesterday with Effie and the chance meeting had been uneventful. If anything, he'd seemed to make a point of not looking at her but *past* her, as if that would reduce her power.

'Fine,' she groaned. 'But you owe me.'

'Anything.' Mhairi handed back the brooch and shawl without needing to be asked, and Flora tightened it at her waist as she stepped back into the glare of the sun and waited for the factor by the smouldering fire pit.

187

'Mr Mathieson, to what do we owe the honour?' she asked, forcing a levity and welcome into her voice that she did not feel. It was one thing asserting her equality with him in the safe confines of the village, but over here, without the protection of her neighbours, she felt acutely aware of the power – physical as well as material – of the man. He was not tall or athletically built, like her fiancé; his bones did not speak to privilege and good breeding, but rather his was a body conditioned by the streets, fashioned from a hard childhood of neglect and beatings, where fists were used in place of words. Flora had heard he had been a fighter in his youth, and his physique bulged inelegantly with muscles that strained beneath his clothing. His skin was pocked with scars and his complexion often flushed, serving to highlight the coldness of his pale blue eyes. Flora guessed his age to be somewhere in the mid-thirties but she couldn't have said for sure – only that he was older than her, younger than her father. She swallowed as she felt his gaze settle on her, a gun upon the bird. 'This is quite a stroll, coming all the way over here.'

'Fetch Mhairi. I need to speak to her.'

The sharpness of his tone was startling and she sensed that the mitigating effect of the villagers' presence cut both ways: without them, she had no protection and he had no need of social niceties.

'I'm afraid she's resting,' Flora said quietly but firmly, summoning her poise. 'She's poorly.'

'God's truth,' he tutted, casting a blank gaze around the glen. 'Effie said the same.'

Flora's eyes widened in surprise. 'She did? When?'

'This morning.'

'Oh? We were hoping to see her today.'

188

'Aye, she said that too, but she's ditched coming to help you for learning to swim with his lordship instead.' He surveyed the bucolic scene of sheep grazing, the lambs skipping wanly in the heat. 'She's completely forgotten herself; her father's in a rage.'

Not just her father, Flora observed – his own lips had drawn white with anger. Effie had told her he'd warned her away from the high-born guests, saying she would embarrass his employer. 'Well, I'm . . . sorry to hear that.'

'Why? It's nothing to do with you,' he snapped. Was he fishing for an argument, she wondered, an excuse to raise a hand to her? She somehow knew that he wanted to; she felt his hostility like a bristling heat.

'I just meant, it's not nice to think of people being upset.'

He turned back to her, with a look that suggested it pained him to do so. 'Well . . . where are the slops? Fin MacKinnon told me Mhairi brought them over here with her.'

Flora gave a ready smile, relieved to get to the point of his visit. Soonest satisfied, soonest gone again.

'Aye, they're over here,' she said, pointing ahead to where Mhairi had carefully positioned the pail in a sheep fank, lest a boisterous lamb should accidentally kick it over. 'Mhairi's been diligent in turning them and keeping them in the sun. She goes down to the cove every morning and evening and refreshes the water. She's not missed a single day since you left last summer.'

Apparently this conscientiousness was insufficient, for his face folded into a scowl. 'The cove?' he cried. 'But the water's rough there! If they were to fall in, she couldn't recover them! They'd be lost to the sea!'

'Well, there's nowhere else over here where she can do it, is there?' she pointed out. The cove was the only sea access on this point of the island. 'But she's very careful. She lies on the low rocks as she does it and takes great care with them.'

They had reached the fank now and Flora stood back as he stood over the pail and peered in with strange intensity. It was hard to think of him as a good son and even harder to think these slops could ever help a physical malady. He dropped into a squatting position as he peered in, turning the water slowly so that it began to churn. Flora had seen for herself how they had changed in form from slimy entrails into something that was growing hard and pale, a snail turning into its own shell. The stink, though, remained as bad as ever, and Mhairi often returned with her eyes streaming from dry-heaving as she performed her duties.

To Flora's relief, he seemed pleased. 'Very well,' he said finally, rising again. 'You can tell her I can see she's been keeping to her side of the bargain. A few more months and I'll be able to take them back with me on the smack.'

'As you wish,' Flora replied, feeling grateful that in a few more months, she wouldn't be here to suffer his presence any more. In a few more months, he would be gone from her life forever and the days of standing beside a stinking bucket with a coarse, unpleasant man would belong to her past.

She realized the factor was staring at her and she straightened up, drawing herself taller so that there was barely two inches in height between them. 'What?' she asked.

'There's something different about you.'

His words chilled her blood as she felt his gaze absorb her with an interest that was notable by its absence on the other side of the isle. 'Really?' she asked, flashing him her most dazzling smile so that he might not notice the fear in her eyes. 'Perhaps it's the glow of love?' she asked, echoing Effie's own words. 'Have you heard I'm engaged? I'm to be Mrs James Callaghan in—'

'Yes, I heard,' he said, cutting her off abruptly. '. . . It's not that.'

Flora's heart rate escalated. The mention of James Callaghan had been intended as a warning shot, a reminder of the consequences that would follow, should he harm the fiancée of a rich, powerful man. But he seemed uninterested in veiled threats, his instincts leading him elsewhere.

She swallowed. 'My suntan, then?' She had read in a magazine one of the fishermen had brought over that they were becoming fashionable on the mainland. 'We're working outside here from dawn to dusk. Effie thinks we're lying about in the sun, but three hundred sheep to look after is a mighty number for just two of us.'

It worked, the factor lifting his attention off her and onto the white-dotted slopes. 'Yes, McKinnon told me about his new scheme,' he sneered. 'It sounds a ridiculous undertaking to me. You'll be half dead by the end of it.'

For once, Flora couldn't disagree with him – if the milking and the churn deliveries weren't gruelling enough, they still had some late-tupped lambing to get through. She was growing more exhausted by the day.

'Still, what do I care? So long as the rents come in on time, it's no business of mine how you divvy up the labour.'

Flora turned her head away at the slight, but remained silent. He turned to leave.

'Oh – Mr Mathieson!' she called after him. 'Could I possibly prevail upon you to carry two of the churns up to the cleit on Am Blaid? It would save us an extra loop there and back.' She spoke to him as a lady to a gentleman, though he didn't deserve the honour of being regarded as her equal.

The factor looked surprised to have been asked the favour and there was a moment of silence before he gave a sudden laugh. 'Does a man keep a dog and bark himself?'

'Excuse me?' Flora was so stunned by the insult she took a step back, as if pushed.

'Beauty won't boil the pot, Miss MacQueen, now will it?' he asked, his eyes narrowing as he diminished her with his words again. He had got a taste for her humiliation and he waited for her – dared her – to retaliate in her usual fashion.

But she didn't – she couldn't risk keeping him here for a second longer than was necessary – and his eyes narrowed as an unusual silence held. She felt his suspicion about her drift back again as he became predator to her prey once more, beginning to sniff, to circle, to close in on her fatal weakness . . . She made herself stand tall; still – a deer before the hunter – but as he saw that he had won, his interest faded. He relinquished his scrutiny, leaving without courtesy.

Flora watched him go, the adrenaline coursing in her veins at having allowed his humiliations, her dignity tattered and hanging like feathers at her neck. But her secret had held; that was all that mattered. Knowledge was power, and he was already dangerous enough.

Chapter Fourteen

Even below ground, the storm made itself felt, gales slamming against boulders and whistling through the cleits, rain falling like poisoned arrows and making the sheep skitter. The wind moaned past the open door, the entire sky a battlefield as the tumbling clouds were pierced with spears of lightning, cracks of thunder making her jump.

The weather had broken just as the sun set and Flora had retreated to her bed to reread James's letters. Mhairi – with a guilty conscience for throwing her to the wolf earlier – had insisted on taking the last of the milk churns up to the ridge, but that had been hours ago and Flora kept getting up and looking out for sight of her coming down the slopes. Where was she? Sheltering in a cleit until the rain lessened? This tempest looked set fast for the night.

'Mhairi?' she called with relief, as she saw something moving – lumbering – towards her at last over the grass. 'What took you so long?'

But Mhairi wasn't alone.

'*Lorna?*'

'Help me, Flora,' the nurse stammered, struggling to support Mhairi's weight.

'What's happened?' Flora cried, rushing out and feeling the storm grab her too.

'There's been an accident . . . Mhairi fell, badly. She's bleeding. I need you to help me get her onto the bed. Hurry now.'

Flora draped Mhairi's spare arm around her shoulders and together, scuttling sideways, they got her into the souterrain; protected from the wind, in the dim light, her face glowed a ghostly white. Mhairi could scarcely support herself as they dragged her through to the sleeping cell and Flora could see Lorna's arms shaking with the effort as they laid her down and got her legs up. Had she really just transported Mhairi down from the ridge all alone?

A groan escaped Mhairi but she seemed barely conscious, her eyes rolling back in her head.

'Bring me your blankets, clothes, anything we can use to elevate the pelvis. Quickly now,' Lorna said, reaching for the blanket on Mhairi's own bed and folding it beneath her buttocks. Flora flew back to her room and returned a moment later to find the nurse reaching for Mhairi's Sunday best shirt and using it to stem the blood flow between Mhairi's legs. Flora stopped short at the shocking sight – there was so much blood, Mhairi's legs lambent in the crepuscular light, her skirt pooled around her waist like an inky puddle.

Lorna took the blanket from her and used it to lift Mhairi's hips even higher.

'Get some rocks – the biggest you can carry. Carry *safely*,' she warned. 'I don't need yet another emergency on my hands.'

'Rocks?' Flora was confused.

'For resting her feet on. They need to be higher than her head.'

'Right.'

Flora ran back out into the night, the wind gusting her like

194

the wingbeat of swans, pushing her back. She scanned the ground by moonlight for a couple of smoothish boulders she could carry. She picked them up carefully and staggered back in. She could hear the nurse's distinctive clipped voice drifting through the underground chambers. There was nothing down here but soil and stones and yet Lorna's words held within them the education, wisdom and experience of city hospitals, and it was all the reassurance she needed. If Lorna was here, Mhairi's baby had every chance.

'Here . . .' she panted, setting them down.

'. . . Good,' Lorna said distractedly. She had her arm between Mhairi's legs, a look of concentration on her face. Automatically Flora fell still and silent, sensing the importance of her examination. After another minute or so she drew back, pressing the blood-soaked shirt to Mhairi's groin, and pulled her skirts back down. Lorna took off her gloves and set the stones under Mhairi's feet, wrapping them with the brown-and-white houndstooth-check lambing shawl she often wore, to soften the pressure against Mhairi's bones.

Flora watched in apprehensive silence as the nurse performed her medical observations, reading Mhairi's pulse, temperature . . . Mhairi was lying on her back, her gaze dully fixed on a point on the ceiling. She hadn't said a word.

'Very good, Mhairi,' Lorna said in a low voice finally, smoothing her hair back from her face. 'You're doing well.'

Flora winced at the sight of her friend, prone and pale. She shouldn't be going through this alone. '. . . Should I get Donald?' she whispered.

Both Mhairi and Lorna's heads turned at his name. The nurse gave a stern look. 'No – he's not well enough yet.'

Too late, Flora remembered Donald's own injuries from his fall on Boreray – both of the lovers wounded and stricken in their beds. Was it a coincidence that they should have been struck down within a day of one another – or retribution? How futile their efforts had been keeping their secret from the minister and villagers when God knew – he saw everything, and this was his judgement, surely?

Lorna stepped away from the patient and the two of them went and stood in the oval chamber, heads bent together. Lorna's expression was sombre, a deep frown between her brows. 'There's nothing more that can be done now. All we can do is wait.' The concern in her voice was distinct from the encouragement she had given Mhairi only moments before.

'. . . Haemorrhage?' Flora asked, her eyes wide, as she showed she knew and understood the grave risk to Mhairi's pregnancy. She had been a cautious student these past few weeks; Lorna, on her regular visits over here, was vocal on the risks faced by the expectant mother. Haemorrhage, convulsions and puerperal pyrexia were three of the Four Horsemen of Maternal Death. The fourth, abortion, was the only one Mhairi didn't need to fear.

'Yes, but it's slowed considerably. She'll continue to bleed a little over the next few hours but I'm satisfied she's clotting satisfactorily and it should stop very soon, especially now her hips and feet are elevated. Her waters are still intact and there's no sign of induction of labour, all of which is good. Most importantly, I've felt the baby kicking. You'll need to check for that every two hours, even if she's sleeping. Put your hand to the belly and feel around for movement.'

'Me? But where are you going? You can't leave us.'

'I have to get back to Donald. He's under observation too.'

Flora wondered how long it had taken Lorna to bring Mhairi down here, in the dark, in a storm, bleeding . . . She must have left the McKinnons' cottage at least a few hours ago now.

'There's nothing more I can do here for Mhairi at the moment. I'll come back again in the morning.'

'But—' Flora felt the panic surge.

'Mhairi's quite safe in herself, and so long as she doesn't move, I think the baby will be too. All you have to do is let her sleep and comfort her when she's awake. They've both been in distress but if she can remain calm, it will soothe the baby as well.'

'But . . .'

Lorna clasped her upper arms and squeezed them firmly. 'You'll be all right, Flora. You can do this. I have faith in you.'

Flora murmured uncertainly as she watched Lorna reach for her medical bag. It was always ready packed by the door of her cottage, filled with bandages, vials, needles and all manner of potions that were indecipherable to the villagers.

'I'll be back in the morning, all right? I'll check on the patient and bring Effie with me.'

'Effie?' Flora asked in another panic. Effie knew nothing of the predicament over here. 'But—'

'She knows now, Flora. She was the one who came to fetch me tonight.'

Flora frowned. What had Effie and Mhairi been doing together in the storm?

'And besides, you'll need someone to come and help you with the milking, seeing as Mhairi isn't to leave her bed.'

Flora nodded, feeling sick. It felt as though the ground was churning and not just the sky – as if greater forces were at work here.

'. . . Will you at least tell Donald about what's happened?' Flora asked, trailing after Lorna as she headed for the entrance.

'No. Not yet,' Lorna said firmly.

'But—'

'If he hears, he'll only want to come over here, and he's not strong enough for that yet.'

'But doesn't he deserve to know?' Flora pressed. What if Mhairi didn't stop bleeding? What if she did lose the baby?

Lorna turned back and pinned her with a sharp look. 'The state he's in right now, if he knows, the entire village will know. Is that what Mhairi would want?'

Flora swallowed. 'No.'

'No. It's in her best interests that we all act with caution and discretion. Mhairi has suffered a serious fall and I'm concerned about her; it's imperative she stays lying down – but I'm also worried for Donald, and it doesn't serve either one of them to be putting themselves through any undue stress. Rest is what will bring them all the best outcome.' She put a hand on Flora's shoulder. 'As soon as I think he's turned the corner, I'll tell him what's happened. Hopefully by then, I'll be giving him happier news with it too.'

Flora nodded as Lorna pulled her shawl up from her shoulders and tied it tightly around her hair – scant protection in these conditions. 'Sleep now, while you can. The most important thing is to keep her calm and off her feet. Bring her water when she needs it and check her belly every two hours for the baby's kicks.'

'And if there are none?' Flora asked, feeling the full weight of responsibility settle upon her shoulders. They were a two-hour walk from the village, and in the dark and in a storm . . .

Lorna looked back at her sadly. 'Then there would be nothing more we could have done for the child anyway. It's out of our hands. All we can do now is pray.'

Outside, the wind still howled, tearing up the sky and screaming around the glen as the nurse stepped out into wild night, her skirt immediately flapping and beating around her legs. Flora watched her go, a solitary dark speck on a starless night, on a rock in the middle of the sea. Within minutes she was out of sight. Flora stepped back into the souterrain, feeling the enormity of the burden upon her shoulders alone.

'Floss?' Mhairi's voice was weak and frightened.

Flora hurried back through. 'I'm here,' she said quickly. 'I was just saying goodbye to Lorna. She's gone but she'll be back over in the morning.' She crouched beside the sleeping ledge and clasped Mhairi's arm. '. . . How are you feeling?'

Mhairi closed her eyes. 'Better.' But her voice was flat and toneless.

'Lorna says it's imperative you rest. Completely. No getting up at all.'

'No,' Mhairi breathed. Even talking seemed to drain her.

Flora looked down at her friend's inert body. It was impossible to see the trauma beneath her clothes. 'The bleeding's still stopped?'

Mhairi hesitated, as if feeling for the sensation, before she nodded.

'Well, as long as there's no more, she thinks the baby will be safe.'

'. . . Really?' A tremor of hope flickered in the word.

'Aye. But no getting up,' Flora said firmly.

For several minutes, neither of them spoke as they settled into the reality of the night ahead of them. They were alone over here, two young women in the dark, and a baby fighting to survive.

'What . . . what happened up there?' Flora whispered.

She felt she could almost hear the thoughts whirring in her friend's head as Mhairi tried to make sense of the memories.

'I think . . .' she said haltingly. 'I think I walked in on Effie jumping the broom.'

'. . . *What?*'

A broomstick marriage was the age-old custom of their forebears when a ceremony needed to be held but no minister was resident on the island. It was recognized by the community, and there was a great romance associated with assembling a broom on an isle without trees: driftwood would need to be gathered, patience a virtue . . . But it had no legal status. As an educated man, Sholto would have known that; it was simply the perfect bluff: appearances without substance. 'She married Lord Sholto?'

'No.' Mhairi looked at her and there was suddenly an intensity in her gaze that was startling. '. . . The factor.'

Flora fell back, her back scraping against the wall, but she felt nothing. 'The f . . . ?' The word wouldn't come. 'Effie jumped the broom with Frank Mathieson?'

'He forced her to do it. He was wild, Flora,' Mhairi breathed, sounding distressed. 'Deranged! A madman! I never would have imagined he could be like that. He was attacking her.'

Flora's hands flew to her mouth. 'You mean . . . ?'

'They had been fighting. I think Poppit had bitten him . . . he almost killed Poppit.'

'. . . Effie and Mathieson?' Flora repeated, in shock. 'It makes no sense. He's twice her age! He's never . . . I mean . . . !'

'I know. She was horrified, Flora. Terrified. I don't think she had any idea he . . . thought of her like that.'

'My God. My God,' Flora murmured, trying – and failing – not to see it playing out in her mind's eye. She had seen the man's viciousness for herself today as he humiliated her for his own pleasure, but that he had actually *attacked* Effie . . . For all her friend's wiry strength and agility, Mathieson was twice her size, not just twice her age. 'Where is he now? Is Effie back home? Is she safe from him? We need to get over there and tell everyone what he did!' She went to spring up.

'No. No,' Mhairi said quietly. 'He's gone again. He left with the earl and his son. He came with them and he's set sail with them.'

'Oh.' Yet another heartbreak, then. Sholto was gone. Two tragedies in one hour. 'Poor Eff. All that in one night.'

'I know. Although right now, I don't think she can think on anything beyond Poppit being all right.'

'Of course,' Flora mumbled. She bit her lip, staring into space. '. . . It just makes no sense, coming out of nowhere like that. Why? Why *now*?'

Mhairi gave a sigh, a long-drawn-out exhale carrying a weariness that seemed to hail from her bones. 'I think it might have been because he knows he's going to lose her. Or rather, lose control over her.'

Flora looked at her blankly. 'Huh?'

'I met David on the ridge when I was bringing up the churns. There's been some news.' Her eyes met Flora's. 'They've granted the request. We're going to be evacuated at the end of the summer.'

Flora could feel the blood draining from her cheeks. 'What?? They actually said yes?'

'They did.'

Both women were quiet for a moment. Their own futures off the isle had already been decided upon, their fates set, but for their families, for their friends and neighbours, everything was about to change. For old and young, those for or against it . . . After over two and a half thousand years of continuous human settlement, St Kilda would finally fall silent?

'It means Mathieson is going to come back here again soon. The evacuation will mean things need sorting.'

Flora brought her attention back to Effie again and what this news meant for her. If Mathieson was coming back, then she wasn't safe. 'Then we have to tell people what he did. He can't just come back and—'

'No. Effie doesn't want that. At least, not yet. We need to talk to her first. She begged me not to tell Lorna that Mathieson had even been up there; he's made all sorts of threats against her father and she's terrified he'll act on them. We have to do as she asks. She made me say we'd just been walking and fell down in the dark.'

Flora frowned at the weak cover story. 'And Lorna believed that?'

'Seemed to.'

She dropped her head into her hands, scarcely able to believe all she had been told. A broomstick marriage; evacuation; the factor's violence against both Effie *and* Mhairi; Sholto's effortless departure; Mhairi's threatened pregnancy. Here they were, the two of them alone in a glen in a storm, and it felt as if the entire world was ending. Or their world, anyway.

'Everything's such a mess,' she despaired.

'I know,' Mhairi whispered.

Flora looked back at her friend. 'How did we get here, Mhairi?' she asked, her voice thick and eyes shining with tears as they clasped hands.

For a moment, Mhairi looked blank. But then she gave a shrug, as if it was obvious. '. . . Love.'

Chapter Fifteen

Flora was kindling the fire and boiling the pot when she saw Lorna and Effie's spry figures coming down the slope. The sun had only just peeped above the Mullach Bi peak and the air was unsettlingly still once more, the night's storm clouds darkening someone else's horizon. Flora watched as they drew ever nearer, arms swinging, Lorna's bag in her grasp; neither of them could have had more than four hours' sleep.

Lorna nodded at Flora in greeting as she approached, but she didn't stop. 'How is she?' the nurse asked, direct as ever and heading straight for the souterrain.

'As well as you could hope. She slept soundly.'

'And the bleeding?' Lorna asked over her shoulder.

'Seems to have stopped.'

'Good. Good.' The nurse slipped into the souterrain, leaving Effie and Flora together around the pit. Effie was pale and seemed somehow thinner than before, if that was even possible in the space of a day. Always skinny, she had never looked fragile – until now. There was a faint bruise on her cheek, some dirt still too, suggesting she'd been on the ground; images of the factor fighting her, overpowering her, filled Flora's mind.

What must she have thought as she saw the broom lying there, as his terrible intentions had been revealed, in the very moments before the man she loved was driven from these shores?

Her gaze rose to meet Effie's. 'Eff—'

'You should have told me.' Effie's voice was flinty and with a stab of shock and guilt, Flora realized Effie had discovered the truth of Mhairi's condition in the most terrible of ways. The deception had been revealed in a crisis – no time for explanations, no excuses given for why one of them had been trusted and the other left out in the cold. It was self-evident that Flora, being here, was on the inside of the secret. Complicit.

'Eff, I'm sorry,' she began, as Effie turned her face away. 'She made me swear not to tell a soul.'

'And I'm just anyone, am I?' Effie snapped. 'I considered you my sisters.'

'I am! We are. But . . .'

'But?'

'She's terrified, Eff. She didn't even understand what was happening until a few weeks past . . . She had no idea she was carrying a baby.' Flora looked at her, willing her to understand. 'It was actually Donald who first noticed the signs.'

Effie frowned. 'Donald?' Her tone was blank, but she could read Flora too easily and as she saw Flora's own surprise that the name meant nothing to her in this context, she suddenly understood it perfectly. *'Donald?'*

She almost spat the word, incredulous at the revelation, and Flora realized Effie must have assumed the baby was Alexander's; it was by far the more logical leap.

'They're in love.'

'Mhairi and *Donald*?'

'They're in love, Eff. Like you and—'

'Don't!' Effie hissed, a finger suddenly pointing to Flora's face, lips trembling. 'Don't say his name. It is not the same.'

Flora swallowed. Effie was a hothead but Flora had still never seen her so angry. 'They never meant for it to happen. There was never any sinful intention between them. They fell in love without meaning to.' It sounded so simple in theory. 'You can understand that, surely? It just happens – when you're not looking for it. Even if it's the wrong person . . . You know what love is now.'

'Except he's married! He took vows before God.'

'Aye.'

'And she's engaged!'

'. . . Aye.' Flora swallowed, not wanting to excuse, merely to explain. 'But Alexander's not . . . he's not what she made him out to be.'

Effie looked utterly disbelieving, as if nothing could excuse their transgression. And yet, Flora knew that if she repeated the story Mhairi had told her – if Effie understood there had been an obscenity, a sin against God—

'He's no gentleman,' she faltered.

'No gentleman? Of course not, he's a crofter!'

'Yes, but . . .' How could she say it? 'He's a brutish man. Donald tried to protect her from him and . . . But it was never about keeping secrets from you. Mhairi just didn't want you to be involved in something that would have troubled you; she felt that the fewer who knew, the better for everyone.'

'Lorna knows!'

'Because she's a nurse. If it wasn't for the baby coming, it would have remained a secret between just the two of them: Mhairi and Donald.'

'And Mary? Does she know what her husband has been doing behind her back?'

'Aye, she does now – and she doesn't care.'

'I don't believe that.'

'There's no love in that marriage, Eff. She won't lie with him. It's dead—'

'Won't lie with him? She's pregnant!' Effie blinked as she saw Flora's expression. '. . . What? Why are you looking at me like that?'

Flora froze, feeling the denial stick in her throat. 'I . . .' But the words wouldn't come.

The two women stared at one another. There had never been a moment in their lives that they remembered without each other; there was eight months between them and they were sisters in every way but blood. They could read each other, even without words, and Flora saw the first crease of a frown begin to fold between Effie's brows.

Effie gave a small sudden laugh, but there was no humour in it. 'Mary's pregnant!' she reiterated. 'I saw her when Donald was brought off the boat. I went to get her and I saw her with my own eyes getting off the bed . . .' Effie's voice trailed off and a silence followed. Puzzlement crossed her face. 'She was in discomfort, but she . . . she wouldn't let me near . . .' She looked back at Flora with fresh understanding. 'She's not pregnant?' she asked, pressing her hands to her mouth.

'No,' Flora mumbled, sounding choked. 'She's not.'

'So then the baby . . .' Effie looked ashen as the plan revealed itself and she looked towards the door of the souter-rain, where Mhairi lay in the dark, trying to hold onto her unborn child.

'Will go to live with its father after the birth and no one else will ever know.'

'No!' Effie protested fiercely. 'That's . . . awful! They can't take a baby from its mother!'

'Believe me, I feel exactly the same way. I can't even begin to comprehend how she could give up her own baby. I've been trying to get through to her every time we talk, but she's adamant, Eff: Donald's married and she's betrothed to Alexander. There's no other way forward that she can see. She says that knowing the child will be raised by its father will sustain her. She believes this is the only way she can repent.'

'By ripping out her own heart?!'

Flora held her hands out in despair. 'I'm still trying to talk her out of it, but you know how stubborn she is once she sets her mind on something.' She sighed. 'Her spirits are very low.'

Flora saw Effie's body slump at the words, everything making sense at last. '. . . So that's why she was in the panic about the cuts on Boreray. And the McKinnons' curse.'

'Aye.'

Effie stared at the ground, not speaking for a long time. She looked broken, just as she had after her brother John's death.

'How's Poppit?' Flora ventured. Mhairi had told her, as they had lain together in the dark last night, that the dog's leg had been broken as the collie protected both young women from the factor's attack. The dog's warm body had been Mhairi's only comfort as she lay on the ground, in the storm, waiting for Effie to come back with the nurse. After fetching Lorna, Effie had carried the dog back down to Village Bay and waited there, while Lorna had brought Mhairi back over here.

'Lorna's set her leg. She may end up with a limp but Lorna says it doesn't bother them so much as us.'

'No,' Flora agreed, trying to sound bright at the news. 'She's right about that. Three legs are no bother to them.'

'Aye. She's a faithful friend.'

The sarcasm told Flora she was not yet forgiven. 'Eff, Mhairi never chose me over you. Her reasons were . . . practical.' She watched, seeing how Effie's jaw had locked, stubbornly repelling her words, refusing to be consoled. She knew there was only one way she could make it up to her. '. . . Did you not think it strange that I should have volunteered when Donald first suggested two of us summer over here with the flock?'

Effie frowned at her words but didn't stir.

'Think about it – this is my last summer here. Before word of the evacuation came through, I knew I would be leaving here for good, leaving all of you, my family, behind . . . Why should I want to spend it then, with just Mhairi, over here?'

Effie looked back at her now, confusion blooming on her face.

'Why should I have worn my shawl around my waist, fastened with a brooch . . . ? Why do I look so *bonny*?'

Flora watched as Effie's mouth dropped open, followed by her eyes dropping down Flora's body. Standing upright, in the thick woollen skirt, she looked as she always had, but as she relaxed her muscles and cupped her arm around her belly . . .

Effie gasped, her eyes widening, and she took a step back. '*You* . . . ?'

'Six weeks behind Mhairi – but, aye, she and I are in the same boat.'

It wasn't strictly true. They were adrift on the same sea, but Flora wasn't facing anything like the rupture coming for Mhairi.

'Does James know?' Effie whispered, looking stunned.

Flora shook her head. 'Not yet. He's out of contact now until the summer.'

'But . . .'

'Don't look so worried. It's different for him and me – we can be married before the baby comes in September. He'll make an honest woman of me.'

'. . . Your parents?'

Flora dropped her head, ashamed. 'Donald's suggestion that I help Mhairi over here buys me time, that's all. The way I see it, the later I tell them, the shorter their shame. James and I will be married as soon as we're on the mainland and I'm hopeful that any scandal will be quickly forgotten once I'm Mrs James Callaghan.'

Effie didn't look convinced.

'Things are difficult now but we won't be stuck in this exile forever. We will all move on,' Flora said determinedly. 'Even Mhairi – at the very least she's going to be spared the shame I'll face.'

It was the wrong thing to have said and Effie recoiled, a small sound escaping her. 'You make it sound a mercy – giving up her baby to escape a scandal! You think she should be *grateful* she loses her child because then no one will know? None will talk?' She shook her head, eyes hard. 'What do you really care what the village has to say about this baby when you'll just move to somewhere people don't know you? You'll be five minutes off the isle and it'll be like it never happened! The world might burn down around the rest of us, but Flora MacQueen will step into her happy ever after, is that it?'

Flora was taken aback by her words. 'No, I didn't mean—'

'Aye, you did. You've got luck on your side, Floss. You always do.'

Flora watched as Effie angrily turned away from her, picking up a milk pail and heading for the nearest sheep fank, beginning the first of the day's chores. She felt unsettled by her friend's words, not because of the bitterness they contained, but the truth – because if there was one lesson Mad Annie had instilled in all of them over the years, it was that luck never gives.

It only lends.

Chapter Sixteen

July 1930

Flora waited at the milk cleit on the ridge, summoned there by Effie's distinctive dog whistle. The walk up had been slow, with numerous stops to catch her breath, and she watched with something approaching jealousy as Effie ran barefoot up the slopes towards her.

'Flora! Flora! He's back!' she panted, a stripling in the summer light.

'Who is?'

For a brief moment, Flora's heart leapt as her gaze swung to the bay for a sighting of a yacht. There had been so many dropping anchor in recent weeks – the calm seas and news of the islanders' imminent departure had created a sort of tourist boom, with well-heeled sailors coming over in search of St Kildan socks and postcards that were now of limited stock.

James wasn't due back in London for another month, but Flora indulged a fantasy that he would come back early and surprise her – on a yacht or on the *Seamoth* once more, circling the isle in a dazzling victory lap before he landed with a splash and took her away at last. It was a daydream that brought her comfort as the days and weeks wore on, the birth drawing ever closer, and she had almost convinced herself it was real; he really was coming to get her . . . But the only boat in the bay was the familiar *Dunara Castle* with its day-trippers.

'Mathieson.'

The fantasy burst as Flora heard the frightened tone in her friend's voice. 'Oh God,' Flora said, shielding her eyes as she looked down towards the village. It had been just over a month since his last fateful visit, Effie constantly on guard whenever the dogs began barking on the beach.

Effie panted, putting her hands on her knees and trying to get her breath back. There was a deep flush in her cheeks, a wildness in her eyes, and Flora knew her friend had run fast up these steep slopes, desperate to get away. The threat he posed to her was very real. What did he plan on doing now he was back?

'. . . Did he see you?' Flora knew they were both wondering the same thing – was he down there searching for Effie, right this moment?

'No. I was at the burn when I heard, so I called you and came straight here . . .' Effie shook her head, staring downhill anxiously. 'Do you think he'll leave again today too?'

'If we pray hard enough,' Flora murmured, but she knew that the evacuation gave him an excuse to be here, overseeing preparations. 'In the meantime, you should stay over this side with us.'

Effie looked at her, her gaze dropping to Flora's swollen stomach. There was no hiding her condition now and Mhairi's even less so. She shook her head. 'I'll only come by later if he doesn't leave with the *Dunara*.'

'But—'

'I don't want him having any reason to see you on my account.'

Flora hesitated, then nodded gratefully. 'But where will you go?'

Effie's eyes remained trained on the village. 'I'll stay high, maybe catch some puffins. That way if he does come up, I'll see him long before he sees me.'

Flora saw the sadness in her friend's face as she looked out to sea and knew she wasn't the only one scanning the horizon for boats carrying her lover. Lorna had told her and Mhairi of the pitiful sight of Effie standing by the post office every time a mail bag was brought over, waiting for a letter that never came. Sholto had left without a backward glance.

'How are you feeling today, anyway?' Effie asked, rousing herself from her troubles.

'Like the ewes – hot, bothered and heavy.'

'Mm, it'll soon be your turn.' Effie's initial shock and anger at her friends' predicaments had abated, although she still strongly disapproved of the McKinnons' plan. 'Remember to call if you need me. I'll raise the alarm with Lorna.' Effie had given them her smaller whistle, made from a puffin bone, to which Poppit was trained to respond. The dog's broken leg meant she couldn't run on the command of the three short pips as usual, and Effie herself certainly wouldn't hear it all the way over in Village Bay – but the dog would. Short of a force ten gale, Poppit would hear it almost anywhere on the island and Effie would know, by the prick of her ears and the cock of her head, that the alarm had been sounded.

'Thanks.' It comforted Flora to have it in her pocket beside her other talisman, the red lipstick. 'Look, I'd best get back to Mhairi. She's sleeping a lot and this heat's not helpful.'

'Aye, I'll see you anon.'

'But, Eff – stay safe, all right? Don't let him see you – but, if he does, make sure you're not alone with him. Not for a single moment.' Her friend nodded and they parted ways, Effie heading west for the encircling sweep of Mullach Sgar. The gradients were less severe there than below the drops of Connachair, and a track dotted the grass past the storm cleit, gradually dropping down to the Lovers' Stone headland and looping back into Village Bay past Ruival.

Flora picked up the empty churns, feeling all the weight of her bump as she walked back, enjoying the sun on her face and the ground firm underfoot. These were her final weeks in her home and she wanted them to be happy ones. Soon James would be back, their baby would be born and they would be a family. This life and, for all its hardships, its simple pleasures too, would be behind her, and she wanted to drink it all in while she could.

Mhairi was already sitting by the peat fire by the time she got back down, forty-five minutes later. To her surprise, Mhairi was draped in a blanket, her red hair wet.

'What's happened?' she asked, setting down the churns.

'One of the late-tups went into labour. I had to wash in the burn after the fluids went all over me.' She was shivering in spite of the intense heat.

Flora fell still. 'But . . . you shouldn't have done that.'

'I had no choice. She was breech, the first one was stuck.'

'You mean it was twins?' Flora asked. Mhairi had been determined they should lose no more sheep 'on her account'; over sixty had perished in the sheep drama last November, when she had been almost killed herself. Now that they were evacuating to the mainland and their sheep stocks were to be sold at market, every last ewe, hogget and lamb mattered.

'Triplets, but the last one died,' Mhairi shrugged. 'I've been lambing almost the whole time it's taken you to come back down.' She looked up at Flora with bright eyes. Too bright.

'It was as well I was over that way. We'd have lost the mother for sure if she'd gone into labour overnight. Another sheep down.' She shivered again, tucking her chin into her chest and clutching the blanket closer.

Flora nodded, but she didn't feel reassured by the so-called win. 'Sorry I was so long. I got chatting to Effie . . . Mathieson's back.'

'Again?' Mhairi looked alarmed.

'He came over on the *Dunara* so hopefully he'll be leaving with them too but we need to be on the lookout for him, just in case. Effie's hiding on the west slopes, so he may check for her here.'

'You don't think he'd try to . . .' Mhairi's voice faded out, as if she couldn't say the words. '. . . Again, do you?'

'It would be madness.'

'But he *is* mad . . .'

They both looked up to Am Blaid, searching for the devil himself dancing on the ridge.

'And if he doesn't go back on the *Dunara*?' Mhairi asked.

Flora bit her lip, hardly able to bear thinking about it. 'Then Effie's in for a very difficult few days.'

Flora felt herself pulled from her nap by a sudden breeze. She had been sleeping soundly, her weary body grateful for the middle-of-the-day respite – she could no longer sleep on her back, and sleeping on her stomach hadn't been possible for a long while. She stared at the stone wall inches from her face. Donald had come over with some dinner for them both and it was partly to give him and Mhairi privacy that she had come inside. She suspected he would have started on his way back to the village by now though.

She pushed herself up to sitting and sat there, drowsy, for

several moments before making her way outside. She stood by the entrance, blinking slowly and trying to summon the will to finish her chores. It was several moments before she realized what she was seeing, utmost fear arrowing through her veins.

'Mhairi!' The word was a hiss, Flora keeping herself hidden in the shadows.

Mhairi, sitting on the milking stool by the sheep fank, lifted her head and turned back at the sound. Flora frantically pointed up the slope at the sight of the factor, fast approaching.

Even from this distance, Flora could see her friend's body flinch in horror too and the ewe she was stripping bleated in protest, escaping with a kick and a wriggle as Mhairi struggled to get up from the low stool; but it took an effort now. She knocked over the pail in her haste, fresh milk spreading into the grass.

'Quick!' Flora urged her, but Mhairi twisted on the spot in panic as she took in the distance from the sheep fank to the souterrain, Mathieson fast closing the distance between them. His arms were swinging stiffly with his signature angry stride and she was fully exposed. There was no question of her being able to hide in time.

'Miss MacKinnon, I've been looking for you!' he called, long before he reached her.

They were menacing words from a man who, the last time they had met, had thrown her to the ground and Mhairi, with a whimper, stayed rooted to the spot. Flora could see her hands pulling into frightened fists as she debated, still, whether to run, before suddenly leaning on the low fank wall before her, elbows splayed across the top in an incongruously genial pose. 'I'm not hiding, Mr Mathieson. I've been over here all summer.'

Mathieson too seemed surprised by her demeanour; he stopped on the other side of the wall and stared. Had he wanted Mhairi to cower in his presence? Several moments of silence passed and Flora knew the details of their last meeting, up by the storm cleit on the night of the storm, were replaying through both their minds. He himself had no idea of how dangerous he had truly been that night, almost killing an unborn child. Had he come here to find Effie? Or to threaten Mhairi and assure himself of her silence?

'Have you come to count the sheep?' Mhairi asked quickly, offering him a third way. 'Because I can save you the bother and tell you myself if it will help you. You must be so busy with getting everything ready for the evacuation. Flora and I—'

'Yes, where is Flora?' he demanded.

Mhairi hesitated. Her unnatural pose, leaning forward, brought her into far closer proximity to him than she would ever be comfortable with. If he were to come around that wall . . . if he were to come in here, there would be no way for either one of them to conceal their heavily pregnant figures. 'Far end of Cambir Point, last time I saw her. One of the late-tups was getting into difficulty. We've had a few nights of it. Some breech births, but only one stillborn so far.'

Mhairi had never been a convincing liar but she was somehow holding her ground now.

The factor stood on the spot, perfectly still, as if he could detect the deception. Smell it. Slowly, he walked over to the wall where Mhairi was leaning and peered over it. She turned with him to look at the ground by her feet, her weight still carried forward so that the taut drum of her belly was concealed, for the moment, by her forward-hanging blouse and skirt.

216

'You spilled the milk.'

Mhairi nodded sombrely. 'Aye. She's troublesome, that one. Always struggles.'

Mathieson glanced sharply at her, as if it was Effie she had been describing. Flora felt sure Effie's ghost from that night was dancing in his mind – her fighting spirit, her loyal dog – but still he made no reference to what he had done, to what Mhairi had walked in on.

'I've come for the slops,' he said finally. 'Where are they?'

Flora gasped, realizing too late his reason for looking over the wall. Not searching for Effie after all, but –

She saw Mhairi flinch too. The slops had been kept in the milk bucket by that fank there all summer.

Until yesterday.

'The slops?' Mhairi's voice audibly quailed and the factor's eyes narrowed as her fluster returned.

'Yes, Miss MacKinnon. The slops. For which I have been paying you for the best part of a year to turn and cure in fresh seawater. The slops. Last time I was here, they were kept right there.' He pointed to the spot on the ground by her feet, white bleeding into green. 'Where are they?'

His stare grew darker and more intense as a long silence drew out. 'Miss MacKinnon?' The words were a growl.

'I . . . I . . .'

'Yes?' The sound was just a breath. Expectant. Menacing.

'I dropped them.' The words ran from her like a mouse scuttling across the grass – tiny and rapid, quivering with fear in the open air.

'You *dropped* them?'

'In the sea. When I was turning them the other day. A wave came in suddenly and took the pail from my grasp. There was nothing I could do. I'm so sorry.'

Flora, frozen too, watched on in utter horror. The factor's face was a marbled mix of contempt and rage. '. . . I don't believe you.'

'It's t-true.'

'No.' He shook his head, his lips drawn fully back in a snarl as he grabbed her suddenly, holding her jaw in one hand. 'You're playing me. I know what you're doing. Now the evacuation's happening, you think you can make yourself a fast buck . . .' He turned around on the spot, still holding her firm as his eyes darted everywhere searching for the bucket. Another pail was set by Flora's milking stool beside the other fank and he released her with such ferocity she cried out. He tore over to it, throwing it against the wall in a fury in the next moment as he saw it was empty.

He turned back to Mhairi, trembling with rage. 'Where are they?' he bellowed. 'I know they're here somewhere!'

'They're not, I swear!' she cried, holding up her hands defensively as he strode back to her in four paces. 'I'll give the money back to y—'

But the word was torn from her as he struck her hard across the cheek and Mhairi was knocked sideways by the force. She was on the ground, again. Beaten by him, again.

'Don't you touch her!' Flora screamed, bursting from the dwelling before she had time to stop herself.

There was a moment of stunned silence as Mathieson absorbed the new scene: both young women there . . . Slowly, his open mouth began to shape into a smile as their secrets were revealed in one swoop.

'Dear God!' he cried. 'So *that's* what it's all about!' He laughed loudly, throwing his head back so that the peals could echo and the longer he laughed, the more frightened Flora felt. Oh God, what had she done?

Her gaze fell to a point beyond his right shoulder, the world seeming to contract around the glen.

'Who else knows?' he asked finally.

'You can't!' Mhairi implored him, from her position on the ground, her cheek reddened from his strike. 'Please, you can't tell anyone!'

'Oh, I think you'll find I can do as I please, Miss MacKinnon.' His eyes travelled over her swollen stomach, then Flora's, taking in their relative differences in size. Flora's bump was still significantly smaller, but Mhairi had only a couple of weeks to go now.

He looked at Mhairi quizzically. 'Funny. I never took you for a whore, Miss MacKinnon. *Her*, yes—'

Flora gasped at his bare-faced insult. 'How dare you!' She spat at his feet but he merely laughed, as if enjoying her lack of decorum.

'Come now, what else should I call you? Do you think marriage will absolve you of your sins? You're a slut. A common prostitute, as I always knew you were. Oh yes – you were always destined to use your face and body to buy your way out of here.'

'You have no idea what you're talking about,' she sneered with all the contempt she could muster. 'Ours is a true love – but what would you know of that? No one's ever loved you! I doubt even your own mother could summon much affection for you. And Effie? She despises you – you *disgust* her . . .'

She felt herself grow as her words landed with gratifying force, his expression changing. She lifted her gaze off him again, feeling her confidence bloom.

'But when I see James again and I tell him all of the things you've said to me, the things you've done to my friends . . .'

She let the threat hang in the air, the words she had wanted to say before but swallowed back, now given voice.

For several moments he said nothing at all. He looked as stunned as if she'd landed a powerful punch on his nose. But then a look came into his eyes, one she knew all too well.

'He'll what?' A small smile grew with his confidence. 'Hit me? Have me fired?' He tutted loudly. 'No, no, Miss MacQueen. He won't be doing any of that. He won't be doing very much at all, by all accounts.'

Flora felt her blood run cold. What did that mean – by all accounts?

She saw the delight skip over his features at her ignorance. 'Oh – you haven't heard.' He feigned surprise. 'It's been in all the papers. Your Mr Callaghan's ship is caught in the ice. Held in a death grip, apparently.'

'What?' she whispered. She stared at him, completely unable to hide the terror she felt at his words. 'But . . . he's safe? They're all safe?'

'Who can say? They might already have frozen to death. Or starved . . .'

'Don't listen to him, Flora,' Mhairi said anxiously, staggering to her feet. 'He's lying! He's trying to frighten you. Word would have come if the worst had happened.'

Would it, though? How? She'd not received a letter from him since he left Iceland. He'd said they'd be uncontactable by all but radio communication – and there'd not been a radio mast on the isle since the end of the Great War.

Mathieson cast a disgusted glance towards her stomach. 'You've got to rather hope he does die. At least then he'd be spared the ignominy of knowing his child was born a bastard—'

Flora gasped as a roar swirled around the glen and Donald

suddenly leapt over the fank wall, launching himself at the factor. His approach back down the slope had been stealthy as he circled back, the factor's attention entirely occupied by the two women before him.

Both girls screamed, moving back as the men rolled on the ground amid a flurry of bone-crunching punches, grunts and curses. Limbs struck out of the mêlée every few moments – a thrown arm, a flung leg – as they flailed, one atop the other, striving for dominance. But Donald was still weak from his accident.

'Stop!' Mhairi cried, as the factor landed a swift uppercut to Donald's jaw and the two men were briefly parted. She looked around her desperately for something she could use to intervene. Donald was staggering, trying to rebalance himself, but the factor's hand was already pulled into a fist, his arm drawn back for the next blow.

Flora screamed – but this time it was Mathieson who spun, his arm suddenly hanging limp as he fell to the ground. A vivid slash could be seen at his shoulder, dark blood bleeding into his shirt.

Flora looked across at Mhairi, who was holding the metal poker, her eyes wide. It had a heavy, blunt tip, and further back, a smaller point that curved away in a hook; Flora saw that it looked dipped in blood.

Mathieson groaned, his skin a sickly grey as he rolled in pain.

Donald, getting his breath back, took the poker from Mhairi and crouched in front of the factor, his lips curled back as he lightly poked the tip towards Mathieson's chest.

'You wouldn't,' the factor panted, his eyes fixed upon it nonetheless.

Donald smiled. 'Why wouldn't I?' He still wore the shadows

of the bruises from his fall on Boreray, his shorn hair still growing back from where Lorna had had to shave him to clean the wounds. 'You tried to kill me.'

'No—' Mathieson panted.

'Aye, you did. You lied to the others while I was out cold, but I remember what went down – I never slipped.' His voice was a low rumble, like thunder, but he was calm now that the other man was on the ground and incapacitated. 'It would have been convenient for you, wouldn't it – getting rid of the person who was calling attention to your crooked ways?'

There was a short silence as Mathieson looked back at him with renewed fear. 'I don't know what you're talking about. I've a job to do and I do it.'

'No.' Donald shook his head. 'I'm onto you, Mathieson, and you know it; your thieving doesn't end with undercutting us. Even you wouldn't bother trying to kill a man over the price of wool. Which tells me that if you wanted me gone that badly, then I'm right. The only question is, how big is it, this racket you've got going?'

He prodded the factor lightly with the poker and the man groaned, trying to squirm away. But he remained tight-lipped, his eyes burning with hatred.

'You know full well that if I told the men what you did, it'd be more than a sliced arm you'd be going back with.' Donald spoke slowly. 'And we both know what would happen if I told MacLeod that his factor is robbing the tenants, trying to murder the men, striking the women, raping them . . . ?'

Mathieson's head snapped up.

'Yes – I know about Effie.'

'I never raped her!'

'Only because you were stopped.'

'She's my wife,' Mathieson hissed.

'In no one's eyes but yours!' Donald roared. 'You'll stay well away from her, you hear me? Your so-called marriage has no grounding in any law, certainly not God's. If you even so much as look in her direction, I'll use this poker on you and I'll not be so "polite". Do we understand one another?'

'Your threats don't frighten me,' Mathieson panted.

'Well, they should. Because the day we dock at the mainland, I'm going to the police constabulary and giving them everything I have on you. And then you won't just lose your livelihood and your reputation, but your freedom too.'

'They'd never believe a peasant like you! You're nothing. You're no one.'

'You think I'm not capable of outmanoeuvring a man like you, Frank?' Donald asked, dragging the metal tip over Mathieson's chest, jabbing it lightly. 'You don't think I've outwitted you already?'

He watched as the factor looked back at him in confusion. '. . . What are you talking about?'

'I just got back from Harris yesterday. I had an interesting meeting with a buyer there.'

'A buyer? For what?' His eyes widened as he joined the dots. '. . . Where is it?' He tried to sit up, but Donald simply prodded his arm with the poker again and he fell back with a cry of pain.

'Uh-uh-uh. The ambergris money is mine. All mine.'

Mathieson gasped at the correct classification of the slops. He looked around them at the numerous cleits dotted about. Were they here somewhere?

'Don't waste your time,' Donald said. 'The deal is already done.'

'W-who?'

But Donald just tutted and pressed a finger to his lips.

'. . . Why are you telling me this?'

'Because I want to be sure we understand one another. We are equal. I have something over you. Just as you have something over me.'

Mathieson's gaze swept over Mhairi and Flora, a look of disgust at their swollen stomachs. 'You mean you want my silence?' he panted, still clutching his arm, beads of sweat at his brow.

'No. I *expect* your silence. You won't breathe a word about anything of what you've seen here: not Mhairi's condition and not Flora's.'

Mathieson spat savagely at the ground, incensed. 'Why are you so concerned about these little whores, anyway?'

Donald struck his arm hard with the poker in reply, making the factor howl with pain. He raised his arm for another strike—

'Donald, don't!' Mhairi implored, stepping forward.

Mathieson stared at her, seeing her concern – seeing how she watched Donald constantly. He looked back at Donald in disbelief. 'It's *yours*?' He gave another cold laugh. 'You dog!'

Donald struck him again, hard, a spray of blood flying through the air and spattering on the grass. The factor cried out but Donald said nothing; there was a coldness now to his violence, his anger spent. 'We're going to start a new life together on the mainland, she and I, thanks to the money from the ambergris. Thanks to *you*, I suppose, Frank . . . Mary will be provided for, too, so don't think you've got any leverage over me there. *I've* nothing to hide, but I'll spare Mhairi any unnecessary pain.'

The windfall had changed everything for them, Donald finally persuading Mhairi that the money and the evacuation combined offered them the future they craved: becoming a family.

'But I'll do it in my time, on my terms and you . . . you won't know what's hit you if I see so much as one wrong look or hear one wrong word. Do we understand one another?'

He didn't blink until the factor nodded. 'Say it,' he demanded, kicking at his leg.

'Yes . . . Yes, we understand one another.'

The two men maintained eye contact as Frank's feet scrabbled against the ground and he slowly got up. He had to clutch his useless arm against his body and when he stood, he was stooped, his blood pressure low as the bleeding continued.

'How the hell am I supposed to explain this?' he demanded, looking down at himself. Blood had soaked his shirt and jacket.

'Tell Lorna a gannet attacked you,' Donald shrugged.

'She won't believe that!'

'Of course not. But nor will she care. You've no friends here, Mathieson; the sooner we're all shot of you, the better. Now go – and don't show your face over this side again.'

The factor stared at the three of them, his gaze falling to the women's stomachs a final time before he turned and limped away.

Donald put his arm around Mhairi; she was trembling violently and he pulled her into him as they watched him go. 'Don't worry. You'll be safe now,' he whispered, kissing her hair. 'He can do you no harm without hurting himself more.'

Flora stood apart from them as she watched the factor stagger back to the village. Destruction always seemed to trail in his wake, his fists a weapon, his words poison. He was down for now, it was true – but was he really out? The man who is born to be hanged will never be drowned, after all.

But she didn't care about his fate. Nor his threats. Let him say what he wanted if that was how it was to be. She just needed to know the truth about James.

And there was only one person who could help her with that.

Chapter Seventeen

'Flora.'

The word was a whisper, treading through her dream. James was leading her by the hand towards the cleit, his sheepskin flying jacket draped around her shoulders, her blouse unbuttoned. He was looking at her with a new intensity, his lips reddened from their hungry kisses.

'Flora,' he groaned, as they stepped out of the wind and she pressed her body to his again, for warmth, for love, for all the things she had never known until he had come into her life. His hands were heavy upon her hips, holding her close as he kissed her and she wound her arms around his neck, wanting to be closer still.

A moan escaped her as his hands and mouth travelled over her and she was no longer aware of the biting December chill. It could have been a sunny July afternoon in his arms, his hot breath the summer breeze upon her skin. Her fingers brushed the hair on his chest as she felt her skirt released and it dropped, billowing, at her feet.

'I couldn't wait,' he murmured, his hands in her long dark hair and pulling back her head to expose her throat. 'I had to see you one last time . . .'

'I miss you,' she whispered. 'I think of you every minute. I don't know how I can bear it.'

'I know. I feel it too. But we endure this now and then we'll be together always.'

'But it's too long. Another eight months . . .' Her breath hitched as his hand dipped between her legs, making them both groan. Her body instinctively arched, reaching for him, and he pulled her onto the ground, kissing her deeply until she no longer knew where she ended and he began. She felt their boundaries blur, their bodies becoming one—

'Save me.'

The words tripped her up, jogging out of synchronicity the pleasure that was rolling up her body in waves. What?

'Flora, save me.'

She wasn't rolling, she realized, but shaking. Pressure on her arm—

'Flora! Wake up!'

Flora's eyes flew open and she saw Mhairi standing over her, her head hanging. She was panting heavily and the dream – the memory – was whipped from Flora in a flash as she awoke fully.

'The baby's . . . coming.' Mhairi's voice was hoarse.

'But . . .' Flora felt a frisson of fear. It was seventeen days too soon. They weren't ready for this.

Too bad. Mhairi's body tensed suddenly, her head throwing back in an agonized silence that seemed to stretch out before a cry came to her throat. It was animalistic, a deep and ancient sound.

'Lie down,' Flora said, jumping up and pulling the blanket off the fulmar-feathered mattress.

Mhairi moved with agonizing slowness, crawling on all fours. Flora expected her to lie on her side but instead she sat back on her heels, her weight propped on her hands. From this angle, Flora could see that Mhairi's chemise was wet and

228

she knew the waters had broken, that the birth was an unstoppable force now.

'I'm calling Lorna,' Flora said, grabbing her skirt and reaching for the small bone whistle.

'Don't leave,' Mhairi begged, her voice a rasp.

'I'll be right back, I promise. We need her here as quickly as possible.'

Flora staggered from the chamber and through the souterrain, out into the bright night. The sky glittered, strung with stars that dangled and gleamed in a velvet canopy, the moonlight casting a silvered wash upon the sea. The sheep were silent and Flora saw Mhairi's red shawl sprawled like a bloody puddle on the grass; she must have come out here for some air and dropped it on her way back inside.

Flora looked up at the dark ridge, the wall that separated them from their families and neighbours, the barrier that had kept their secrets. But now it impeded the help they so urgently needed. It was the middle of the night. Lorna and Effie would be asleep, Poppit too.

She blew the whistle sharply three times, though the pitch was almost out of her hearing range. 'Short pips,' Effie had instructed her bossily. Flora stared into the darkness after a call she could not hear, for help she could not see. Suddenly the glen felt vast and impermeable and she, as fragile and insignificant as a flower in the grass.

She waited for a minute, then blew again. *One – two – three.*

She prayed Poppit would hear her; that right this moment she had lifted her head from her paws, her ears cocked, and was limping to her mistress's bedside. A cold wet nose on warm skin making Effie jump, scold and understand . . . Waken Lorna.

But if she didn't . . . How long would Flora hold out hope before she realized it hadn't worked, that they'd all slept through? Was she going to have to help Mhairi through this alone?

Another cry came from the souterrain, a lupine howl, and Flora ran back through, holding her own heavy bump. They needed Lorna more than ever before: nurse, ally, friend.

Their hour of need had come.

But would she?

The day was awakening, the sheep beginning to bleat and call, birds shrieking on the dawn thermals. It was a bright, beautiful morning and Flora sat on the milking stool, feeling the warmth spread on her tired face.

The night had been long. Endless.

Friendless.

Their plan hadn't worked. Perhaps the wind had been in the wrong direction; perhaps Poppit had slept too close to the crackling fire to hear the pips.

They'd had to do it themselves – the pushing and straining, the constant encouragement in the face of overwhelming pain and fear. 'When will it end?' Mhairi kept asking her, begging her, hair plastered to her face, tears streaking her cheeks and Flora's too.

She watched as the three figures ran down the slope, ants on a wall. It was still early enough to hope that no one else had seen them, for the bag in Lorna's hand always denoted a medical event. The bone whistle lay idle in her palm. She had been blowing it, three pips and a break, for almost two hours now as mother and baby lay on the mattress inside the cool, dim stone womb.

Flora rose as they approached.

'Where is she?' Donald asked, strides ahead of the women, as they galloped into the bowl of the glen.

'Donald—' she began, but it had been a rhetorical question and he dashed straight into the souterrain, bending low, his broad shoulders scarcely fitting through the narrow opening.

'How is she?' Lorna panted as she and Effie brought up the rear. 'And the baby?'

Flora swallowed, then shook her head – just as a cry bellowed out. Fresh tears streaked her cheeks. 'She never drew a breath.'

Lorna visibly paled before her eyes, Effie gasping with such horror that she staggered backwards again.

The nurse took in the news, swallowing hard several times as she stared at the ground. Another villager – lost. The last St Kildan, dead before she was even born. Was it not the perfect allegory for leaving here? Everything she had been arguing for?

Lorna steeled herself and dipped into the souterrain after Donald. Effie began to cry, her face hidden in her hands, but Flora couldn't console her; she couldn't move. What she had lived through tonight . . . it had been the stuff of nightmares, the two of them underground, like animals, in the dark, screaming, whimpering. All that suffering, all these months of solitude and hiding and hardship – and for what?

She heard a sound and Donald came back out, cradling the infant in his arms. A low moan left his body as the sun hit the child's body for the first and last time. She had a thatch of thick black hair, a wee pointed chin and ten wrinkled fingers and ten toes. She had been perfect except for the fact that she would not breathe, and Flora watched sorrowfully as Donald mourned his daughter, as small as a kitten in his arms. He held her like she was made of glass or rainbows, his tears splashing onto her cold cheek as he rocked her fruitlessly.

It was a while before Lorna re-emerged. She looked ashen,

visibly shaken by the unexpected loss, and Flora wondered if she felt guilty for having slept so soundly while they suffered.

Lorna came over to where Flora stood. 'Was the cord wrapped around the neck?' she asked quietly.

Flora shook her head.

'Did the baby get stuck?'

'She slipped out easily.'

Lorna frowned. 'She was fully grown . . . A healthy foetus. I don't understand.'

'. . . I think perhaps I do.' Flora lifted her gaze to meet the nurse's. 'Mhairi birthed some of the lambs the day before last.'

Lorna's eyes widened. *'What?'*

Donald stopped rocking at the sound of the sharp word and looked over at them. Both women stood frozen as he turned and retreated into the souterrain.

'One of the late-tups was in distress and she said it was the only way to save them,' Flora murmured.

'But . . . the infection risk—'

'Puerperal pyrexia, I know.'

'I warned her – both of you – about the risk of miscarrying,' Lorna protested. 'The two of you shepherding here was a ruse, not an actual obligation. You've got the whistle! We agreed Effie would come to deliver the lambs.'

'I was all ready!' Effie agreed urgently.

Flora arched an eyebrow. Precious good the whistle had proved to be. '*I* know that – but after the sheep drama, Mhairi was adamant we couldn't lose any more for the roup,' she said tonelessly.

Lorna raised her hands to her head and grabbed her hair, tipping her head back and squeezing her elbows almost in front of her face in frustration. A baby had been lost on account of selling sheep at market? 'My God, this can't be happening,' Lorna whispered. 'We were there! We'd got through it! The ordeal was done.'

Flora watched her as she paced, holding her head in her hands, and she realized the strain this deception had placed on the nurse – all the secret visits over here, teaching where she could, making emergency plans . . . And still they had failed, toppled at the last hurdle.

'How is Mhairi now?' Effie asked, roughly wiping her cheeks with the backs of her hands, leaving red marks on her skin.

Lorna was quiet for a moment. 'She has a slight temperature, which is down to the infection, most likely . . . but she's passed the placenta and there's no need for stitches.'

'Is she talking yet?' Flora asked. It was the silence, the deafening silence, which had been the hardest to endure.

Lorna shook her head. 'Not yet, she's in shock.'

Flora looked away. So was she.

'How long will that last?' Effie asked.

'There's no way of saying. She's gone through a trauma. How long is a piece of string?'

'She needs her mother,' Flora said quietly. 'We need to get her back over the other side.'

'Absolutely not.'

Flora looked at her in surprise. 'She's just lost her baby! She needs her mother! She's not capable even of talking, Lorna. She's *devastated*.'

'Aye, and she'll still be devastated in her mother's arms. Nothing will change this awful, awful predicament,' the nurse said, ever pragmatic, ever logical. 'But it can still get worse for her from here. If people find out about the baby, about the

deception that's been going on over here for *months* now . . .
Does it help her to add shame to her grief?'

Flora looked away. To know that she too was going to have
to endure the same horror in a few short weeks . . . She wanted
to get off this island, out of her skin. She couldn't be here, be
herself, another moment. '. . . Well then, Eff will have to stay
here with her – because I can't. I need to go to the mainland.
I can't have my baby here too. I won't.'

Both Effie and Lorna stared at her, seeing now her fear too.
Mhairi's baby was dead, but her own trial was yet to come.
What mischance awaited her?

There was a silence.

'If you go over there, even if you go straight to the jetty
onto a ship – everyone will still know,' Lorna cautioned.

'Let them! I don't care any more!'

'You don't care about your family's honour? You'd have
them leave St Kilda under a cloud? That's to be the MacQueen
legacy – a bastard child born in the shadow of the evacuation?'

Flora gasped at the nurse's bold words.

'James is sailing back right this moment—' Lorna continued.

'Is he, though?' In spite of Lorna's protests that she'd heard
and read nothing about the *Quest* becoming stranded, Flora
couldn't shake the factor's taunts. He'd found her worst fear
and pounced on it.

'Yes! Frank Mathieson's a liar! He'd say anything to hurt
you. Don't let his poison into your veins. James is coming
back and he can make an honest woman of you within hours
of setting foot on the mainland. Don't act in haste, Flora. Don't
undo everything you've striven for these past months.' The
nurse put her hands on Flora's shoulders, pinning her gaze.
'I know you're upset. It must have been awful for you, trying
to help as you did. I can well imagine how frightened you

must have been. But Mhairi's baby didn't die because we didn't have the right medical care . . .' Her voice dropped almost to a whisper. 'It pains me to say this, but the baby died as a result of her own actions. Even if she had been on the mainland, by the time the baby's distress came to light, the bacteria would already have been in her bloodstream . . . Mhairi's choice killed her unborn child and she's going to have to live with that knowledge. Somehow.'

Effie turned away, her face in her hands, her head shaking at the words, at the calamity that had befallen them.

'I'm asking you to think this through, Flora, for her sake as much as yours. Money can whitewash a scandal on the other side; *you* may get away with it if James comes back and marries you quickly – which I believe he will. But Mhairi doesn't have the protection of a rich fiancé. She won't ever escape it. Mud sticks. This will follow her wherever she goes. What if Alexander McLennan was to hear she'd borne another man's child? Do you think he'd spare her the rod?'

The nurse was unaware of the late change in Donald and Mhairi's plans – what would come of their shared future now? – but Flora still looked away, guilt-ridden that she should escape as Mhairi suffered on every count.

'For her sake, can you not stay another few weeks while she recovers from this? I know a day to come seems longer than a year that's gone – but she needs you. You're strong and your future is assured, Flora. You wouldn't make the same mistakes she has.' Lorna's grip tightened on her arms. 'I *will* protect you, Flora, no matter what. I'll come over here every single day and I'll make sure your baby survives, if it's the last thing I do.' She was grim-faced. 'A month from now, you'll be a mother and a wife, living on the mainland with the man you love. This will all be in the past – for both of you; if we can protect Mhairi's reputation, then she has the chance to move on from this as well.' Lorna leaned forward, catching Flora's gaze with her own. 'What do you say? Shall we all look after each other in these last few weeks?'

Flora looked at Lorna, then Effie. They were a sisterhood, weren't they? They always had been, always would be.

Her heart was pounding, but she nodded. Just three more weeks; she could endure that.

Chapter Eighteen

The isle was already slipping into her autumn colours, the days growing shorter, the sun less buoyant in the sky. Evacuation was only three days away but the weather was still fine, a rare blessing as they all prepared to leave their home for the final time. Tomorrow they would begin to bring the sheep back over the ridge in small flocks, containing them in the sheep fanks over in the Am Blaid saddle between Connachair and Oiseval, before boarding them straight onto the *Dunara Castle*, which would sail the day before the villagers, laden with the livestock and furniture.

There had been no possibility of leaving Glen Bay before now. Mhairi's milk had come in hard, making her weep with pain without a child to suckle; and when it had finally gone again, she had cried harder as the last vestige of motherhood ebbed away. It felt cruel that her figure looked girlish again so soon, shrunken all the quicker by her absent appetite. No mark had been left on her body and there was no baby to hold. It was almost as if the pregnancy had never transpired at all.

Mhairi's shock was profound, her guilt even worse; she was barely speaking and was eating just as little. Donald would sit with her, forcing her to swallow some broth, which was all she would take. He was riven with grief too; Flora didn't think she'd ever seen a more heartbreaking sight than him digging a tiny grave for his lost daughter, the five of them standing around a mound barely bigger than his foot, offering prayers to a god who had cast the most terrible judgement upon them.

Flora wondered how the other villagers hadn't noticed his stooped dejection and haggard expression but Lorna maintained everyone was distracted with their own business for once, packing up their belongings and cleaning their houses as if new tenants were coming in; the children had even been tasked with lifting the remaining potatoes from the lazybeds. Only Jayne, according to Effie, moved with her usual detachment, knitting on the rocks and driving Norman to despair.

'There y' are!'

Flora turned on her back to find Lorna heading over the grass to her. She had proved true to her word, tending to the two young women daily, registering temperatures, pulses and mood. She had taken to wearing the brown-and-white houndstooth lambing scarf, slung diagonally across her body and discreetly filled with her basic medical instruments – thermometer, stethoscope and some calming tonics for Mhairi's nerves – for striding over the ridge with her medical bag every day would surely have raised suspicions.

'I've been looking for y' all over.'

'Oh, it's you, Lorna,' Flora said wearily, using her arms to shift her position until she was sitting up. 'I wasn't expecting to see you again today,' she frowned. The nurse had already been over that morning, at sunrise.

'What are you doing all the way over here?' Lorna asked, ignoring the comment.

Flora shrugged. She was on Cambir Point, looking out to sea, a twenty-minute walk away from the souterrain. She had taken to coming here when Mhairi's spirits were especially low; several times she had caught Mhairi staring at her stomach with a look of utmost sorrow, and Flora felt riddled with guilt that her friend was suffering while her own baby continued to grow. It was a torture for them both.

'Just getting some air,' she muttered, as Lorna crouched beside her and reached for her wrist to take her pulse. Flora didn't even think about these tiny assessments now, they were so frequent.

'Are you feeling well in yourself?' the nurse asked.

'Aye.'

'. . . No headaches, bleeding, swelling of the feet, itching . . . ?' Lorna asked, putting a hand to her forehead, before pulling out her implements and getting more thorough readings. Again.

'No. I'm just tired.'

'That's to be expected now you're into the last month. There's a lot of growing that comes in the final weeks.'

'Aye.' Flora sat patiently as Lorna palpated her belly, listening for a heartbeat, checking her ankles for fluid retention . . .

'No contractions yet, I hope? Feelings of tightness, a need to bear down?'

Flora shook her head, puzzled by the nurse's overly-close attentions. Her anxiety at losing another patient was no secret but even so, this behaviour seemed extreme. 'Is there something you're worried about, Lorna?'

'Me?'

'Aye. Something you're not telling me? You checked me over just a few hours ago.'

'Och, I know, but . . .' The nurse sat back on her heels, biting her bottom lip, and Flora saw she was nervous; that she couldn't meet Flora's eye.

Immediately she stiffened. 'There *is* something.' She had

felt it. Felt it instinctively. 'Is it the baby? I felt it move just a few minutes ago!'

'No, no, it's not the baby,' Lorna said quickly. 'I just wanted to get a . . . baseline reading, before I . . .'

'Before you what? What's happened?'

Lorna stared at the grass for a moment before she raised her eyes. She reached for Flora's hand and clasped it between her own. 'Flora, there's been some news and I . . . I need you to prepare yourself. I'm afraid it isn't good.'

Flora felt her body go cold, her hands automatically drawing back and clutching her stomach as her mind raced ahead to the worst-case scenario, the one she had been fearing these past few weeks, ever since Frank Mathieson's heartless taunts. The one everyone had told her wouldn't come to pass. '. . . James.'

Lorna's mouth opened but there was a lag before her voice came. '. . . Mathieson wasn't lying about the *Quest* being stuck in the ice.'

'But you said . . . ?'

'I know. I was trying to protect you, Floss. I knew you'd only fret if you knew the truth. I kept hoping that . . . they'd get through it somehow. That it would all be passed by the time we got over there.'

'But . . . ?' Flora could hardly breathe.

'A fishing boat's come in this morning and the skipper says . . .' Lorna looked broken by the news. 'He says word on the shipping wires is the ice moved . . . squeezed, and the hull was breached—'

'No,' Flora gasped, her eyes wide as she envisaged the scenes: polar seas engulfing the vessels, men thrashing in fathomless blue water . . . James sinking . . .

'He's feared lost. They all are. I'm so sorry.'

Flora shook her head, refusing to believe it.

No.

She looked out to the horizon, crisp and darkly delineated against a bright sky. He couldn't be down there . . . He just couldn't . . .

No.

'Flora, try to stay calm.' Lorna's voice was distant, as if she'd fallen down a drop. 'Flora – Flora, are you hearing me?'

For a moment Flora had a sense of herself, hunched on all fours, her head hanging as a dull pain radiated through her bones. She felt she might disintegrate into dust, this agony obliterating her into tiny particles the wind could blow and scatter.

'Try to control your breathing for me. You're hyperventi-lating, Flora . . . Flora? . . . Breathe slowly . . . *Slow*-ly.'

'It's . . . it's not true,' Flora moaned, beginning to rock and sway. 'Oh God, tell me it's not. Tell me . . .' Sobs burst from her, violent and gushing, as she keened forward, her head touching the parched ground. She could feel the solid weight of his baby curled up inside her, limbs twitching and stretching out, impa-tiently awaiting birth – just as his own life force was extinguished and he fell into eternal stillness? 'No, no, no . . . !'

'Here, take this.'

She felt hands grasping her chin and she looked blindly across as Lorna spooned some soothing tonic into her mouth; she spluttered, almost coughing it up again, but Lorna held her jaw shut, forcing her to swallow. It was bitter and rancid, but it had been the only thing to keep Mhairi calm these past few weeks. Now it was Flora's turn.

'Flora,' Lorna's voice remained steady. Low, by her side. 'I'm so desperately sorry. I wish I could change it for you – but you need to think of the baby . . . Are y' hearing me? . . . Y' must calm yourself for the baby's sake.'

241

'This can't be real!' she wailed. A year she had waited for him! A year of holding him in her mind's eye and her heart, waiting and hoping for their life together to begin . . . only for him to be snatched away in these dying hours?

'It's all going to be fine—'

'No! It'll never be fine again!' A sound escaped her like her soul was splitting in two.

'You *will* survive this, do you hear me?' Lorna said firmly. 'You're strong, Flora. And young.'

Flora knew what she was really saying: that there was still time for her to find love again. But she didn't want anyone else! Couldn't Lorna understand that? Couldn't she see that love wasn't just about attraction, but connection too? That it was rare, a one-time deal? Mhairi knew it, Effie knew it. But Lorna, a spinster – what did she know of love?

Lorna's hand rubbed her back in circles as Flora wept; as if sensing her own ignorance in matters of the heart, she said nothing more. No words could make this better. No comfort could be given when beyond this heartbreak lay another calamity, too – for at a stroke, Flora's entire future had been swept away, her circumstances drastically changed. She was going to step onto the mainland penniless, unmarried and pregnant. She would be cloaked in shame and scandal.

All these months, she hadn't known why it should be that she should have such good luck and her friends such bad. Effie had never heard back from Sholto; Mhairi and Donald, already grieving their child, were to be separated after all . . . It had made her feel strangely nervous, this gross imbalance of fortunes, but she saw now that it had only been a matter of timing. Her loan of good luck had finally come to an end.

The debt was being called in.

Chapter Nineteen

30 August 1930

Three days later

Ten perfect fingers. Ten perfect toes. Flora cupped her baby boy's downy head in her palm as he greedily fed. They had each got the hang of it quickly and it was a relief for them both as her milk let down. 'You're a natural,' Lorna had smiled. She felt the weight of him against her stomach; it was already almost flat, deep contractions pulling her back to her old shape as he fed. Pregnancy fading as motherhood bloomed.

Her hand moved automatically in gentle caresses as she felt herself glow with love for him. It had been instant. All the sorrow, pain and horror forgotten the very moment Lorna had laid him on her belly. His cries had risen into the night sky, no louder than the wren, and she had gasped with disbelief that he had survived it.

She had screamed in distress as she had realized what was happening – her grief ejecting him from her several weeks too early – so certain that Mhairi's fate would become hers too. But things had been different this time. They hadn't been there alone; after several days of grumbling contractions, they had started in earnest early in the evening, last night, and

243

Lorna had arrived in time, as she had promised she would; she had monitored everything that could be measured, mopped her brow and for every one of Flora's cries that she couldn't do it, Lorna had quietly reassured her that she could. Mhairi had held her hand, just as Flora had held hers only a few weeks before, urging her to push when she just wanted to die; and when they had heard the first cry, all three women had wept with relief and joy that one of them had made it.

He was so small, so very perfect, a fuzz of dark hair beginning to sprout. She looked for signs of James in him but he was still so wrinkled and curled up, no sign yet of strong ankles and straight shoulders; only his eyes – gold-flecked hazel and not her sharp green – showed that he was his father's son.

His hand patted her breast lightly, as if understanding where his survival lay, and tears fell from her reflexively, splashing his cheek. She rubbed them away gently with her thumb but the tears continued to run and fall because she *wouldn't* be his survival. Not after today. These were their stolen hours together and the only ones they would ever know.

In the corner of the cabin, Mary cleared her throat. Flora looked up, her hand automatically cupping her son's head, keeping him latched onto her, keeping them as one.

But rupture was coming. The most unnatural division in the natural world.

Donald stood by the door, guarding it, his gaze on the floor. He was keeping others out, rather than her in, but he could scarcely look at her.

The baby pulled back, sated for the moment, one skinny arm pulling back in a sweep, the hand pulled into a miniature fist as he stretched and gave a small scream.

'He needs winding,' Mary said, stepping forward and

already reaching for him, assuming the duties – and identity
– of his mother.

Flora's grasp tightened on her child, instinct prevailing, her
heart rate accelerating.

No.

'Let me wind him, Flora,' Mary said in a placid tone,
standing before her. 'He'll need feeding again before long and
then you'll be back down here again. Go up on deck while
you can and show your face, else people will wonder.'

Flora didn't stir. She knew this was what had been agreed.
'It's the only way,' Lorna had whispered sadly as she had
wrapped the baby in her lambing scarf and carried him over
the ridge in the dead of night to the McKinnon cottage.

She looked at Donald, impelling him to meet her gaze. He
was a good man, suffering too. The pain in his eyes matched
her own and he took no joy in making her loss his gain. He
had had to be convinced that it was the right thing to do, Lorna's
implacable logic overriding sentiment for the good of the baby.
Without a husband, Flora had no viable way of providing for
her child, and the villagers still, mercifully, believed Mary to be
pregnant. They all had to be selfless, Lorna argued.

Donald nodded and she surrendered her hold on her child
with a gasp. Mary took the little bundle and settled him over
her broad shoulder, beginning to pace as she patted his back.
He screamed in protest and Flora felt every cell in her body
strain for him. She needed to hold her son in *her* arms. Feed
him from *her* breast . . . But a plan was already in place for
that too – Donald would use the ambergris money to secure
a wet nurse on the mainland; Lorna had contacts in the nursing
world over there. 'They're professionals,' Lorna had reassured
Flora, stroking her hair as she wept. 'He'll thrive and grow.'

She moved, tentatively, off the bed. She had been 'lucky

not to tear' but she was bleeding still, as was normal apparently, a thick pad fashioned from old dressings pressed into her undergarments.

'I'll get some air then,' she said quietly.

'That would be best, aye,' Mary said in a low voice. 'Show your face, make sure everyone sees you.'

Donald stepped aside and opened the door for her. 'Is she on board yet?' he whispered. Flora knew he meant Mhairi. These were their final hours together too.

'I'll check. I'll send her down here.' Flora passed him into the corridor, her body rigid with the effort it took to move through these motions. The door closed again with a decisive click.

'Flora.'

There was surprise in the word and she looked up to see Jayne sitting on the short, steep staircase that led up to the deck. She, too, was pale-faced, a haunted look in her eyes, and Flora wondered about Norman's silent beatings behind thick stone walls. The evacuation had taken a toll on them all.

Jayne straightened up, smoothing her skirt as she forced a smile. 'Were you in seeing the baby?'

Flora hesitated. 'Aye . . . he's a bonny wee thing.' Her voice was small, unlike herself.

There was a small pause, Jayne also seeming to struggle to find words. 'It's a blessing for them, at last.'

'Indeed,' she swallowed, having to cast her gaze to the floor as she endured the lie. 'Are you waiting to see him?'

'Oh—'

'Only I think they're trying to settle him to sleep.'

'Of course. I'm sure I'll catch them at some point.' Jayne's hands splayed against her skirt, the fingers stretching long as Flora's twitched against hers, unseen.

'Well, I suppose we should go on deck and . . . get some air,' Flora said after another pause, as Jayne made no move to leave.

She stirred, as if being roused. 'Aye. I suppose we should. Say our final goodbyes.'

Flora waited as the other woman began to climb the steps but she stopped and turned back again. 'Flora, I just wanted to say – I'm so awful sorry for your loss. James was a fine man and he loved you dearly. Hold on to that, won't you?'

Flora watched her go, feeling her heart pound. She wanted to tell Jayne there was flesh-and-blood proof of their love behind that door – but she couldn't hold on to him either. Memories were all she would have of either one of them; they were the only treasures she had left.

There were more faces than she had ever seen gathered in one place, handkerchiefs fluttering in the breeze as multitudes of hands waved a singular welcome. Cheers rose into the sky, men working busily on the quay as they wound the ropes around the bollards to tether the ship for its first call.

Flora glanced down at her own hands, clasped so tightly together that her fingers blanched. There was dirt and blood beneath her fingernails, she realized, and she curled them into a claw; her mother would have something to say about it if she saw. Family honour came down to such things: cleanliness, modesty, prudence. Flora pulled the red shawl tighter around her waist – she had lost the brooch securing it, somewhere in the move, and it kept working loose, threatening to betray her lack of both modesty and prudence at a stroke.

On deck, the passengers stood like chess pieces, chins up as the ramp was thrown down and their new lives lay before them suddenly, just a few steps away now. What had started as anguished cries of 'why?' following poor Molly's death had somehow led to this: a rampart on a summer's evening, strangers' greetings and a benign landscape where trees took root and crops could grow.

Life would be better here. Gentler. That was the promise of evacuation. They would no longer need to swing from ropes to eat an egg, nor save driftwood for coffins; they wouldn't be cut off from the rest of humanity for seven months at a time by monstrous waves; pneumonia would no longer be a killer.

And yet, hesitation gripped her with cold fingers.

Flora watched numbly as Ma Peg went first, assisted by Lorna down the short but steep slope. Some men in fine suits and bowlers were gathered in a cluster at the bottom and set apart from the other mainlanders by an officious calm. They didn't wave their hankies in the air but tipped their heads slightly. One of them began to speak to Ma Peg in a low voice – but it was Lorna who spoke back.

Flora glanced at her father as the first dislocation announced itself. There would be a price to pay for this easy life: the old ways were behind them now and that meant speaking English and not Gaelic, paying with coins and not favours. The younger generation, taught in the schoolhouse by the minister's wife, were well equipped to navigate the leap: they could read, write, perform arithmetic, and they spoke English with careless fluency. The middle-aged islanders – Flora's parents and the like – could certainly converse, albeit with grammatical errors; but for the older folk, a language barrier had sprung up on this crossing, and easy discourse with close neighbours would no longer be a given.

Another spark of panic zipped through her. Were they really all to scatter on account of failed crops, hard winters, a preventable death? She caught the tension aboard the boat as the islanders stood poised between two lives, and knew she wasn't the only one to feel this had been a grave mistake. The St Kildans had left behind not just their home but their whole world – a two-and-a-half-mile, cliff-walled island in the North Atlantic that had kept others out as much as it had kept them in.

She had always yearned for a bigger life – for the past year she had dreamt of little else with James – but now she craved the secret places of the cleits and cliffs, the familiarity of the humble cottages, the reassuring sight of the dogs sleeping in the grass and washing lines hung with clean linens stretching down towards the bay. If they'd stayed there, she could have raised her son there. To hell with the shame; knowing what she knew now, she would have endured anything to keep him with her.

Mad Annie and Old Fin went next, arms linked as if they were about to reel but for once, Mad Annie's dark eyes weren't dancing. Old Fin nodded his head as they walked, as if engaged in a silent conversation.

Flora dug her nails into her palm, steadying herself, as she watched Effie Gillies follow after with her father, the two of them tall and thin and as brittle as hazel sticks as they stepped into the crowd. Flashbulbs popped around them, the pressmen lunging and leaning in for their pictures, the mainlanders regarding Effie's long, tangled, sun-bleached hair and wind-burned skin with open curiosity. Flora watched them take in her rough, thick drugget skirt, pulled in at the waist by a bent nail, her calloused hands – developed from years of cragging – at odds with the daintiness of her bones. She watched the onlookers marvel at all the ways her best friend was 'wrong', and Flora wondered what they would say if they knew Effie dressed in boys' clothing most days and that this – in her boots and skirt – was her at her Sunday best? Or that Mad Annie was showing rare restraint to disembark without her pipe dangling from her bottom lip?

'I can't! I can't!'

Flora looked up at the sudden commotion to find Mhairi grabbing the bow rail. There was a collective intake of breath from the islanders on deck as their silent stoicism was interrupted. Dignity suspended. Flora felt her own heart hitch, all her carefully packed emotions suddenly pushing to the surface with a violence that felt uncontainable. She watched, breath held, while Mhairi's father grappled with her, as if her friend's fate still dictated Flora's own.

Ian MacKinnon tried to hoist Mhairi to her feet, but the girl was limp and overwrought, the enormity of the moment finally washing over her. From here, the boat would sail on to Oban and the few remaining passengers – the Big Gillies and the McKinnons – would tomorrow step ashore to their new lives twenty miles south of here.

From the corner of her eye, Flora saw Donald twitch as if to move – as if Mhairi's panic was a stray lightning bolt, leaping the crowd and striking bodies at random. But Mary, holding the newborn, stopped him with just a hand upon his arm, telling him without words that this – *she* – was not their concern. Not any more.

Donald's gaze lifted off Mhairi and met Flora's own, and she saw in his tortured soul the marbled mix of love and loss, of grief and gain that had sprung from these last few months. Arrangements had been reached – but at what cost? Flora saw the promise held in his eyes as they stared at one another across the deck: he would protect her son and raise him as his own. He'd be the father James could now never be; he'd be the father her son deserved. And yet it felt as if her heart might leap from her chest like a salmon swimming upstream and she could see in him the same instincts, twitching and quivering for release. An unnatural stillness was his only defence, as if a single movement would obliterate his resolve. Only his eyes betrayed his desperation. Only her finger, tapping against her skirt, betrayed hers.

Stop this madness, she wanted to scream, to lose herself like Mhairi. It didn't matter that everything was unfolding exactly to plan; nothing could have prepared them for how it actually felt, living through this and doing what must be done.

It's the only way.

Trembling, she watched Rachel MacKinnon usher her young brood down the gangplank, the baby strapped to her chest, as Mhairi was half-dragged behind them by her father, her red hair dancing like a flame as she tossed her head in anguish. Her younger brothers Alasdair and Murran, awed at first by their big sister's spectacle, instantly forgot the drama as they caught sight of parked motor cars, shiny and gleaming like beetles in the setting sun. Trophies of this new world. They ran ahead for a better look, St Kilda already just a memory for them.

'Boys! Get back here!' Rachel cried as they escaped their mother's skirts and darted into the crowd. Flora's gaze followed them, catching on the back of Effie's head as she and her father were led towards one of the cars; Flora willed her friend to turn back for a final look, but a slight tug on her hand from Bonnie was the cue to start down the ramp herself.

For a moment, her feet wouldn't obey; she was still inordinately weak and she felt heavy-footed in her boots after a summer barefoot on the grassy slopes, but her sister's small fingers gripped her own a little harder, as if in reassurance, as if she could feel how Flora trembled.

Their three brothers – David, Neil and Hamish – pigeon-stepped in an impatient arc behind her parents, but their father's limp meant they moved at a shuffle and Flora had a sense of them as a small herd being rounded into the sheep fanks back home. It felt somehow demeaning and she lifted her chin, staring haughtily but blindly into the crowd. In all her nineteen years, almost every face she'd ever seen had been either a friend, neighbour or relative – the distinctions were merely titular – but this was a land of strangers now and she had no care to look. The only face she wanted to see wouldn't be there.

Suddenly lights popped rapidly, one after another, the sky a symphony of explosions, screaming white, so that the MacQueens were blinded to their first steps on the mainland.

Stray voices babbled like water over the stones back home. 'Her eyes . . .'

'. . . hair . . . see how it shines . . .'

'. . . and so thick . . .'

By the time the dazzlement had passed and their eyes had cleared, it was impossible to tell who had spoken, but gazes fell upon her like weights. Flora turned her head away, not wanting to be seen. If they knew what secrets she held, what horror she was living through in this very moment—

'Where's Mathieson?' a voice behind her called. She didn't need to turn to know it was Hamish Gillies. 'MacLeod's factor?'

Flora flinched, drawn from her torpor. Amid the sea of strangers, her gaze found Mhairi's and behind her, Effie's too – stalled beside the car.

'Not here!' a man on the dock called back, passing along a bag.

The three young women stared at one another, held in frozen poses.

'He's got my money!' Hamish retorted.

'Not here,' the man said again, with a shrug.

Flora saw the puzzlement begin to settle on her neighbours' brows. Dawning realization. There had been so much commotion in the packing, so much high emotion on the crossing . . . the landlord's man on the ground hadn't yet been missed. 'The smack left after the *Dunara Castle* yesterday!' she called up carelessly, though it took all her strength to do so. The cargo vessel had left with all their worldly possessions last night.

She felt heads turn towards her once more, eyes settling upon her face with a rapture that befitted Cleopatra on her golden barge. The white flashes came again in a flurry and the factor was forgotten.

'Oban, then,' someone called, uninterestedly.

Flora looked back at Mhairi and Effie, both haunted and stricken by their dealings with the man, but in the next moment they were taken from her sight, the crowd swallowing them whole.

She was losing them. Losing everything.

'Keep moving now,' a voice said in her ear. Norman Ferguson – tall, broad-shouldered; a handsome man with an ugly temper; his wife silent beside him. 'Give them a show, Flora. We can't stop here.'

He was right. She wanted to turn around and run straight back up that ramp, take back what was hers and never let it go. Her body already ached with longing – but it was already too late. The past had slipped her moorings and disappeared over the horizon. This was the future now and she could no sooner reclaim her old life than blood could flow backwards.

She could only go on.

Thrusting her chin in the air again, she stepped into the sea of nameless faces – and felt herself disappear.

It took a couple of trips by car to transport the MacQueens – all seven of them – to their new home in Lochaline. Her parents separated for the journey, lest a calamity should befall them in the motors and a parent be needed, but the passage was smooth, speedy and almost disappointingly uneventful. In the space of mere minutes, they travelled past shops, an inn and a schoolhouse, along a rolling road up a hill, around a bend, to a leafy lane that reached out towards a distant heathered moorland. The explosion of space was an undulating and good-natured landscape, unlike the vertical cliffs of home, the dying sky silent but for the chirrups of unseen birds hiding in the trees.

No one spoke in the vehicles, all of them trying to absorb the barrage of new sights and sensations – the rumble of the motor beneath them, the smell of gasoline, the smooth yet soft leather seats. Flora stared out the window, seeing how the house doors were painted in different colours, unrecognizable flowers growing from small boxes on windowsills. She spied a horse grazing in a field, passed a bus and saw streetlights. In one six-minute journey, she saw more new things than in all her previous nineteen years – and yet, she was blind to it all. When she blinked, she saw her baby son behind her eyelids. When she closed her eyes or looked into the distance or glimpsed her own little brothers . . . he was all she saw. All she could feel. Her arms ached to hold him, to feel his weight against her.

Had the ship left harbour again? Was he drifting further from her with every passing moment? She thought of James floating in the blue and the pain of her losses flattened her.

She unfurled herself carefully from the car, feeling like a crispy autumn leaf in the spring blush. Her movements were laboured and with every step she worried about the padded cloth Lorna had pressed between her legs in a final act of mercy. But no one noticed her tentative hesitations. Not today.

They had stopped outside a short stretch of whitewashed conjoined houses, with three strips of lawn running down from the coloured doors – yellow, red and green – to matching painted wooden gates. The slate roofs appeared, to her eye, to have been put on sideways, running from front to back rather than across the width of the buildings, as at home, but it gave them an open, elevated aspect, as if mildly surprised. The property between the two ends was narrower, its roofline slightly lower, and was set back a little, as if it had been nudged out of position.

There were already two other cars parked on the verge, the yellow door at the far house left open. A red-haired girl suddenly burst through it in hot pursuit of her younger brother: Red Annie and Murran MacKinnon. In another instant, they were back inside the house again, but their squeals could be heard from the lane.

Flora felt the tension within her ease a little at the realization that Mhairi was but two walls away. A small mercy. She wondered where Effie had been taken. Would it be too much to hope that she and her father had been placed in the smaller property between the MacKinnons and the MacQueens? She thought she might somehow bear this if they were all still together.

Her parents were already standing at the green door with the man in the suit who had accompanied them; he was moving with efficiency, her parents with curiosity. Flora had missed his name – she felt as if she was underwater, voices

255

distorted, words shapeless – and she made her way slowly up the narrow path, after them. Unlike the torrid young MacKinnons, the MacQueen children – that bit older – walked in a slow-moving crocodile, following after the man in respectful silence as they passed through various well-sized and bright rooms. The biggest surprise was that the kitchen and sitting areas had been separated, split either side of a staircase that led to bedrooms upstairs. No one on St Kilda had ever had an Upstairs before and Flora stood at the foot of it, staring at the treads as if they led to the heavenly kingdom instead.

The kitchen had a range, indoor taps and a wooden floor, luxuries that had been unthinkable back home, where even driftwood or a washed-up whisky cask was considered treasure. There were radiators that heated the rooms and electric lights that switched on like magic. The room opposite was dressed with a large table, wooden settle and some chairs, a fireplace and cloth-covered settee positioned by the window overlooking a back garden. Upstairs were three bedrooms and a water closet. They had never seen a fixed bathtub before – at home, their tin tub was propped against the back wall and brought in front of the fire in the evenings. Flora watched, impassive, as the younger children squashed into it, their boots already abandoned at the front door.

'Get in with us, Flossie,' Bonnie implored, but even if there had been room, she wasn't up to playing and she removed herself to one of the bedrooms, lying down carefully on the unmade mattress. Her body relaxed into the unfamiliar soft-ness, vaguely aware that there was no prickle of horsehair as she allowed herself to grow heavy.

She stared at the wall, recognizing from the lilt of her mother's voice that she was pleased with what she saw, for this was all a distinct step up from what they'd known back home. Even her father was limping more quickly than usual, opening and closing cupboard doors and rattling open the windows as the man in the suit tried to run through the schedule for registering for work in the morning. The men had been found jobs at the Forestry Commission and were to report to the manager's office for eight o'clock; most of the women had to work too, for it would take more than one wage to support a large family this side of the water, and both Flora and her mother would be working at a local tweed factory. On St Kilda, weaving had been the men's job – the women carded and spun the yarn – and there'd been a collective hesitation when the news was first broken to them. Everything here was familiar and yet different, the world skewed off its axis by a few degrees.

Flora closed her eyes, her body and soul weary as she tried to block it all out. Her breasts were full, too full, of milk she could not rid herself of, a dull ache beginning to spread. A fat sunbeam was falling across her shoulders, trying to warm her, but she was cold inside. She had left the most vital part of herself behind today and she knew she would never recover from it. Her life from this point onwards would be feathered, warm and soft, a charade of dead-eyed smiles and cold beauty.

She felt something pressing against her hip and she stirred, reaching a hand into her skirt pocket. She pulled out the golden barrel that had been her talisman for so many months. But not any more. It was a reminder of all she had lost, the emblem of a life that would never now be hers. A bullet to the heart.

Chapter Twenty

'Psst – did y' hear?' Rachel MacKinnon said in a low voice, across the way to Jayne, her eyes tracking Mrs Buchanan in her office at the far end of the factory floor. 'There's talk of a ceilidh at the weekend.'

'Oh, aye?' Jayne asked back, looking pleasantly surprised, her grey eyes lighting up. 'Are we allowed to go?'

'Allowed? It's *for* us, they're saying! A welcome.'

'Och, that sounds grand. How thoughtful . . .' Then she pulled a face. 'Will we need to wear our boots?'

Rachel shrugged, her auburn hair loosely styled in a topknot; without the severe St Kildan winds to endure, the island women were already beginning to experiment with hair fashions – enjoying the privacy of sitting in front of their mirrors, in their upstairs bedrooms, as much as they did the finished result. 'It should probably be taken as a given now.'

'Aye,' Jayne sighed, disappointedly. 'Oh, and did I tell you? I ran into that Mrs Cameron in the churchyard last evening. She said . . .'

Flora sat at her loom behind them, hearing their conversation without listening. The rhythmic rattle and clack of the shuttles working the wefts was now the soundtrack to their days; already she yearned for the sound of the heavy slump of the waves on the shore in Village Bay. She missed the incessant cries of the seabirds and even the constant moan of the wind.

She didn't gossip with her co-workers. Grief for her lost fiancé gave her a pass of near-silence and the local women just smiled at her with pitying eyes whenever she walked by.

The loom beside her sat empty. Effie had handed in her notice after a single day. She had come to blows – quite literally – with Mrs Buchanan when she had turned up late the first morning, having assumed she would work with the men at the Forestry Commission. A drawn-out battle of wills had looked inevitable as Mrs Buchanan had instantly asserted her authority and Effie her independence, but to everyone's surprise, the young woman had walked in provocatively late the next morning and resigned her post instead. She had been offered a role working for the Earl of Dumfries and she and her father were relocating once again, to his Ayrshire estate.

She wasn't the only one gone. Lorna had travelled straight to Sutherland to be reunited with her family and Mhairi too had departed for imminent married life in Harris. The poor girl, still grieving her baby daughter, had been wretched with apprehension at what lay ahead and hadn't left her bed at all for the first four days after getting here. Flora wished she could have fallen apart too; she wanted to pull at her own threads and unravel herself, become nothing. She was a ghost of herself, but her family needed her to work. To keep going. Money was their master now and jobs were hard to come by. They were fortunate, she kept hearing from the local women, that roles had been found for them all.

How had it come to this? She remembered midsummer's day, not so very long ago, when her happy ending had shimmered as brilliantly as the ring on her finger and she had sat in Glen Bay with the girls, plucking the fulmars while making promises to them of full bellies and pretty dresses. But the world had inverted and her only comfort in these early weeks had come from curling around Mhairi at the end of each day as they lay in her bed and talked in low, hushed voices of all they had lost. Now, with Mhairi's departure, even that was gone.

Flora knew she appeared whole, but in truth she was hollowed out inside. Grief had dug its claws into her and left her deadened. Every morning when she awoke, she felt veiled with a numbness that made even her heart beat dully; and as she sat at the loom, she wished away the daylight, willing the moon to rise so that she could slip back into the oblivion of sleep. Only Mrs Buchanan seemed pleased with this new, docile version of Flora MacQueen who kept her head down and worked hard, her hands moving in a synchronized pattern and her feet operating the pedals; she didn't stir from the loom from the moment she arrived to the moment she left.

The St Kildan women had picked up their new roles quickly in these first few days here so that when they sat at the looms, they could scarcely be told apart from the locals except by the red plaid shawls they wore around their shoulders. Only when they moved away from the machines did they stand out: their home-made clothes didn't yet have the finesse of the mainlanders' wardrobes, their colour palettes too muted; their skin still too sunburnt and wind-whipped, their tread heavy as they moved about in boots all day.

In the afternoons, when the working day was done, they walked slowly through the village like a flock of hens, trying to get used to the coins jangling in their pockets and food being readily available to buy. Meat hung on hooks at the butcher's; fish glistened on ice on the fishmonger's shelves; fruit and vegetables in a rainbow of colours were heaped in baskets at the grocer's. Meanwhile, the men had taken to going to the public house for an ale before coming home for their teas; it was a ritual that would have been inconceivable back home but the reverend was no longer here to castigate them, having slipped into the mainland morass to his new posting in the Lake District. They had been released from his watchful eye, and life was already different – none of the St Kildans had unlooped a rope since they'd set foot on the mainland, and none had killed for their supper. There was something to be said for ease.

'Doctor!'

Flora was resetting the heddles when the word first came to her ear and she looked up, but the windows only allowed in light and were set too high to see through. Still, she knew the man's voice and she knew the tone. Something terrible had happened.

'*Please!* Someone help! Where's the doctor?'

The St Kildan women recognized the voice too because they left their posts and rushed towards the double doors with alarmed faces. Behind the glass walls of her office, Mrs Buchanan looked up from her desk with a scowl.

'Hai! Back to work, it's not your break-time!' she called as the women in red shawls congregated outside on the forecourt.

'David, what is it?' Flora heard Rachel MacKinnon ask as she got to him first.

'There's been . . . an accident,' he panted, his voice dropping now that people were spilling out onto the street, his plea answered.

'What? Who?' the women cried.

Flora strained to hear her brother but only stray words drifted above the hubbub. 'At the forestry . . . bleeding . . . We need the doctor!'

Flora began to walk towards the doors too; she felt her heart quicken but her feet were leaden. The birth was behind her – the milk had dried up, the bleeding stopped, her girlish figure returned – but her body still refused to do anything at speed.

'Miss MacQueen, what is the meaning of this?' Mrs Buchanan asked her crossly as she came and stood with her by the doors. She saw the St Kildan women's faces were white with fear, clutching hands as they talked in their huddle. David, always the fastest of the men on the island, was running again towards a white cottage with a black door on the other side of the road. Had he run all the way here? It was several miles to the forestry site.

They watched as he hammered it with his fist until a man in glasses opened it. The two exchanged a few rapid words before David stepped back and the man disappeared inside the house again for a moment, reappearing with a large leather bag in his hand. He strode towards a car parked on the street.

David looked back at the gaggle of women and made a beckoning motion to their mother. Flora's heart dropped and she pressed a hand to her mouth. Did that mean . . . ?

'I'll ask you again,' Mrs Buchanan repeated. '*What* is going on?'

David desperately scanned the crowd again, looking for another face. He stopped as he found her by the factory doors and made the beckoning motion with his arm once more. 'You'd better come too, Flora,' he called.

She felt her blood pool at her feet, her worst fears confirmed. '. . . My father's been hurt,' she whispered. And somehow, she ran.

They heard the cries before they saw the blood; the men had managed to get her father onto a long table and covered him with a sheet that they held above and away from his injury while they waited 'for the doc'.

'We were concerned with sawdust getting in the wound,' a moustached man said, crossing the yard in five strides as the doctor jumped out of the car. The foreman had a bushy moustache and thick forearms with bulging blue veins. On one was a ragged scar running the length of his elbow to his wrist. Another accident?

Flora, in the back seat beside David, watched through the window as their father cried out at the sight of his wife running towards him. Christina rushed to his side, clutching his hand in hers and kissing it over and over. 'There, there now, Arch,' she soothed him, smoothing his hair back from his brow. 'It'll be fine, you'll see. The doctor will take care of everything.'

'Aye,' Archie agreed, looking up at her as if *she* was the one who would save him, not the medic. He was panting with the pain.

David opened her car door and Flora looked up at him in surprise, for she hadn't noticed him stirring beside her; she had been transfixed, appalled, by the sight of her father laid out on high, his body hidden from sight by the sheet.

'Come, he needs us,' he said quietly, extending a hand and pulling her up.

Her body resisted, images of blood, of emergency, of disaster flashing through her mind. It was too soon . . . she couldn't endure another loss. She simply couldn't.

Her brother, seeming to understand her distress, tucked her hand under his arm and slowly led her across the yard.

The day seemed not to have registered this violent tear in its silken drape. The sky was sullen, sheep grazing in nearby fields, wildflowers winking in the grass, birdsong a melody that couldn't be caught. The ground was soft underfoot, even in boots; sawdust and chippings scattered thickly, vast tree trunks stacked like walls, denuded of their branches and leaves. There were various large outbuildings and some strange vehicles that seemed to be just giant wheels with a seat on top, chains attached to the back.

'Aren't we just so lucky we're here now and not back home?' Christina was saying, still gripping her husband's hand. 'You'd be in a tight spot over there.'

Archie nodded, closing his eyes as his wife's voice babbled like a cooling stream, passing no comment that no such injury could ever have occurred back there, on an island with no trees, with no mechanical saws.

Flora thought of Lorna, of her calm, capable manner and the way she exuded authority and confidence even in a crisis. She had always said she was 'just' a nurse, but she had done everything a doctor could do – nursing them through sickness and fevers, cleaning and bandaging wounds, delivering babies – and if anyone did die, it was always on account of lack of supplies or medicines, not medical expertise. Flora would have chosen Lorna over a doctor any day.

'Show me,' the doctor said, standing by his patient now. The men holding the sheet lowered it and Flora felt an icy wind whip through her. David immediately hooked an arm around her, her big brother holding her up as she fell back slightly; the whiteness of their father's face had served as a terrible contrast with the vast slicks of bright, arterial glistening blood pooled on the ground, but the injury itself . . .

Her father's right foot hung limply at a grotesque angle. It had never been good following a climbing accident in his youth when he had fallen on Connachair and his life was saved only by the rope tightening around his ankle. He had dangled, upside down, for more than an hour before help had come, but the damage to the nerves had been done and he'd walked with a limp ever since. It was a matter of personal pride that he didn't need a stick, but he couldn't climb well or run, and he had made a point of 'pulling his weight' by becoming the strongest rower instead.

'Tell me exactly what happened, Lennox,' the doctor said in grim tones, bending down to inspect the wound. The flesh of the lower leg had been badly mangled so that Flora could see bone through the flailed tissue. The cut wasn't neat either – no merciful sword strike but a jagged, raging mess. Someone had tied a rag around her father's knee and his leg was supported on a wooden block.

'Willie McIntosh and Barnaby Munro had just finished up on a fir in the prep hut . . .' The foreman pointed towards a long, low building with double doors. 'They were overdue their break so they set the misery whip down and went off. Callum here says a freak gust of wind blew in as they went out and the whip toppled – just as this poor fella came by. He couldn'a get out o' the way in time.'

There was a collective groan from the men at the bad luck of it all.

'What's a misery whip?' Flora asked her brother in a whisper.

'A two-man cross-cut saw,' David murmured. 'It can take them a day to saw through the bigger trees.'

'Oh.'

Everyone fell quiet as the doctor examined the wound closely, his eyes slitted as he observed the torn skin, muscles, tendons and ligaments. After a minute, he rolled up her father's sleeve and tapped firmly on his exposed elbow joint.

'You men did well to get the bleeding under control,' he

murmured, rubbing something Flora couldn't see into Archie's skin. He reached into his bag and pulled out a needle and a small clear bottle of liquid. Setting the bottle upside down, he pierced the cap and began to slowly draw.

'What is that?' Christina breathed as the doctor began to inject the liquid into her husband's arm.

'A sedative,' he murmured. 'I'll have to put some stitches in here to get him stabilized before we move him. It's a Grade Three laceration, a deep tissue injury. It's unfortunate it is so untidy; he'll need to be transferred to the infirmary for surgical treatment.'

'Where's the infirmary?' Christina asked, sounding scared but trying not to show it.

'Fort William. Reasonably close as the crow flies, but unfortunately there's a loch to cross.' He looked at Mr Lennox again. 'Get on the telephone to the Corran ferrymaster and tell him we've an emergency. He's to be waiting for us, north side, in two hours. He *must* be there, tell him. For as long as the wound is open, the patient risks infection.'

'Two hours?' Christina echoed.

'To the ferry. Then another hour on the other side,' Mr Lennox supplied as the doctor moved his attention off her, reaching back into his bag and pulling on a pair of rubber gloves. 'The journey used to be a lot longer with the horse-drawn ambulance, but we took delivery of the motor ambulance just last year. So that's something.' His attempt at optimism fell on deaf ears and he disappeared a moment later into an office at the far end of the building to make his calls.

'I'm afraid this will hurt,' the doctor said, immediately sousing the wound with a liquid that made her father cry out, his body arching and rigid.

Flora blanched; she had never seen her father express pain

before. David too dropped his head, unable to watch, his fingertips pressing into her shoulder.

'I'm sorry,' the doctor murmured, wincing as he continued to squeeze the bottle, clear liquid oozing into and out of the injury. 'But it must be done. It's necessary to clean the site as best we can; I don't want to sew in any foreign bodies . . . You should start to feel drowsy in a few moments.'

'Is my husband going to recover, doctor?' Christina whispered, clutching Archie's hands in both of hers. His return grip was already weakening, the fingers beginning to straighten as the sedative took effect. Within moments his eyes were closing, his body relaxing.

The doctor carefully threaded a curved needle. 'That depends on what you mean by recover. He should survive, provided there are no complications . . . but whether he'll ever walk again . . .'

His eyes met Christina's for a brief, apologetic moment, before he looked back down again and began to stitch.

Chapter Twenty-One

Mad Annie stirred the pot: chicken soup with potatoes, leeks and carrots. Except for the tatties, not a single ingredient would have been found on St Kilda and stomachs growled, feet pacing excitedly as the aroma filled the cottage. The islanders were quickly acquiring appetites for the new tastes available here.

But not Flora. Not tonight.

Their father was at the infirmary in Fort William, along with their mother, and every few moments Flora would get up to pop her head out to check that the telephone box on the opposite side of the lane wasn't ringing. Their mother had promised to call when there was news on his condition, and Flora and David were the heads of the household in the interim – or at least they had been, until Mad Annie and Ma Peg had come through from next door with the dead chicken and a basket of vegetables and taken charge. Flora had been grateful; she was no cook. Her years of shirking her chores suddenly revealed her to be wanting.

'It still won't be enough,' David said as she sat at the table with Bonnie, supervising her arithmetic. 'Both yours and Ma's wages combined still won't make up losing Father's.'

'But I don't understand! How can it not be enough? There's the two of us to the one of you.'

'Because women aren't paid what we are,' he said patiently.
'But why not?'

He shrugged. 'Because that's just the way it is here.'

Mad Annie gave a loud snort, setting down her pan with a bang and making clear her views on that matter.

'So then what are we do to?' Flora asked, slumping back in the chair. 'We've been here little over two weeks and already we're facing penury?'

'No. We just need to think of other ways to raise money,' he said thoughtfully.

'You mean socks?' Her heart dropped at the thought of more knitting. It had been one of the main advantages of moving over here as far as she was concerned: no more knitting.

'I don't think socks can help us in this case.'

'What, then? We have no skills of any use, no possessions of any worth—'

But before the words had left her mouth, her gaze dropped to the sapphire ring. She twisted it between her fingers, feeling sick at the very thought.

'No,' David said quickly, reading her mind. 'Not that, Flora. You'd regret it.'

Unlike most of the St Kildan men, her brother was sentimental. Flora knew the past was still very much alive for him, that he slept with Molly's shawl beneath his pillow. 'I'm sure I would – but a proud mind and an empty purse grow ill together,' she said flatly. 'Isn't that right, Ma Peg?'

'Aye,' the old woman said after a moment, stoking the fire with a pained expression.

Flora looked down again, still twisting the ring. It, the lipstick and a few letters were all she had to tether her to the great love of her life; to the baby she had given up, the husband she might have had, the life that would have been. Was she really to forsake this as well?

'There is another option,' Annie said coolly from her spot by the stove, one hand on her hip and still stirring the soup.

David looked back at her hopefully. 'Which is?'

Annie turned and jerked her chin towards Flora. 'Her hair.'

'Excuse me?' David frowned.

'I went for tea and a piece in the village yesterday.'

Flora sat back in the chair, waiting for the reveal. Mad Annie was a natural born storyteller and she didn't believe in getting to the point quickly if there was a scenic route to take instead. Mad Annie and Ma Peg's house – sitting between theirs and the MacKinnons' – had come with a bicycle found in the back garden and Annie had wasted no time in becoming familiar with it. Ma Peg's joints were too stiff for 'a new sport', but Flora thought Annie sometimes forgot she was a woman in her seventies, for she seemed to be relishing the adventure of cycling in and out of the village 'for provisions' every day. Flora saw her most afternoons as she made her way back from her shift: Annie puffing on her pipe as she pedalled along, her skirt tucked into her undergarments and her thin legs on show.

'The old dears were lamenting the plummeting prices for tweed' – she rolled her eyes, indicating she didn't consider herself in their age bracket – 'and they said some of the crofting womenfolk have been going to Glasgow and selling their hair.'

'*Selling* it?' Flora cried.

'Aye. It's made into wigs, they told me, which are like caps . . . but with *hair*.' She pulled a face of distaste but gave a shrug. 'They said there's good money to be made.'

'But why . . . why would anyone want to wear someone else's *hair*?' Flora asked, appalled.

'Sickness. And hair fashions, so they said,' Annie added. 'And you've got such lovely hair, Flora lass – so long and dark; that braid is as thick as my fist. They'd be bound to pay extra for yours.'

'Do you really think so?' David was looking interested.

'It can't hurt to ask. You never know, they might offer enough just to tide you over until you know more about your father's condition. Hair grows back, after all, but once that ring's gone . . . Hold onto it, lass.'

Flora was quiet in the face of her dilemma. Sell the ring or her hair? Memories or identity? It was hardly a fair choice – but what had been fair about any of the choices put to her recently?

A voice from the past drifted into her mind. *Beauty won't boil the pot, Miss MacQueen, now will it?* She sighed, knowing she had her answer.

Frank Mathieson had never been a good man. But he'd seldom been wrong.

'Mind!'

Flora spun on her heel, just in time to step back onto the pavement as a boy on a bicycle powered past. There was a basket attached to the front and an assortment of breads laid across as he stood on the pedals, muscles straining in his pale, skinny legs.

She watched as a tram 'caur' curled around the corner into the square, the tall, double-decked orange and green vehicle gliding smoothly on its rails. Faces at the glass looked past her, focused on more important matters; those that did notice her noticed too late, being whisked along and away before they could even turn.

Flora blinked. She had thought Lochaline a shock to the

system but here in the city, everything was doubly fast and loud and crowded. She wasn't used to so many bodies in one space, the way people walked past one another without greeting, much less knowing each other's names or business. The noise was disorienting too. No bird could sing over the sound of engines, or tram bells ringing, or street sellers' shouts as they proffered chestnuts and tobacco and newspapers.

And yet . . . it all made her heart quicken with nervous excitement. Everything in Glasgow was a feast for the eyes – bright fashions and grand sandstone buildings, glossy vehicles, shop windows displaying hats and gloves, shoes and handbags. Handbags! She had only ever seen them in magazine illustrations before now: special bags where ladies could keep a purse filled with coins, a comb for styling their set hair, a mirror, powder, a lipstick . . . Things that had never been needed back home and yet were vital here. Finally she glimpsed the limitlessness of what could be bought and done on this side of the water, possibility and potential shimmering like north stars on every street. She understood now how very, very small her world had been: puffins and ropes and sheep and a single street with only thirty-five other faces along it.

She tried to take it all in: how people walked so fast, swerving to avoid her at the last moment. She tried not to stare too longingly at the mothers pushing their babies in prams instead of swaddling them to their bodies with shawls. Because there were no shawls. Nor any wind either – not of any account, anyway.

She clutched the piece of paper Mad Annie had given to her by the gate this morning – it had a name and address on it, secured after another dawn dash on the bicycle – and turned into the street she was looking for, not fifteen minutes' walk from Queen Street station.

The premises was painted brown with gold lettering: 'Collinson Coiffure – 16 Miller Street'. In the window were large display cards illustrated with images of beautiful women modelling a variety of hairstyles. Flora stared at them, taking in the minute details of their different looks; they all seemed a little unreal to her, with their perfect white smiles and shining curls. They were dressed in fine gowns and looked as if they were going out for cocktails.

But she wasn't like them; she wasn't coming to be made more beautiful, but to be shorn like a sheep. She was forever on the wrong side of the fence.

A bell rang as she opened the door and stopped short, taking in the scene. Several ladies sat in chairs before mirrors, reading magazines; their eyes swivelled up towards her, though their bodies didn't stir. They were draped in matching cloths that covered their clothing and two of them had sets of rollers on their heads with black cables attached, which fed back into a machine on wheels. Women in white coats were attending them, fiddling with knobs and levers. Along the far wall was mounted a row of metal helmets, beneath which several more women were sitting. It was all a futuristic vision too far for Flora. They didn't seem to be in pain, but the image was so very unnatural—

'May I help you?'

Flora startled, turning to see a lady sitting beside a dainty white table. There was a large writing book open before her, and a typewriter. She wore red lipstick – as if it was nothing – and her fingernails too were the same bright red.

'Do you have an appointment?' the lady tried again as Flora stared at her, agape. '. . . Miss?'

'Er – no.' Flora collected herself. 'I . . . I was told to come here. For the wigs.'

'I beg your pardon?'

'For the wigs. You want hair, don't you?'

The lady's gaze fell to Flora's thick braid. 'Oh! You wish to sell your hair?'

'Aye,' she nodded. 'For money.'

There was a pause as the woman glanced across the room and made eye contact with one of the ladies in white coats. Flora watched her walk over to join them. It felt as if everyone in the room was staring and she knew her clothes marked her out, along with her desperation and coarse manner.

'Good morning,' the white-coated lady said, looking her over with interest. 'You wish to sell your hair?'

Flora swallowed, hearing the indignity in the words as they were spoken back to her. '. . . Aye.'

'Have you been told our rates?'

Flora shook her head, her fingers nervously playing with the sapphire ring she wore.

'We offer a pound for a six-inch ponytail – that's the shortest we'll take – and then a shilling per inch on top of that. It looks like you've got . . . twenty inches or so there.'

'So then . . .' Flora was too flustered to do the mental arithmetic.

'We'd have to measure it, but you'd be looking at £1 1s 2d.'

Flora swallowed with disappointment. Her father's wage was £1 11s 8d. 'I see.'

'Is that acceptable to you?'

Hair grown for nineteen years, sold for less than a week's wages. It hardly seemed fair. She remembered the pound James had paid to convince her to walk with him to McKinnon's Stone; she had known even then it was too much. Things had a way of balancing out in the end. '. . . Aye.'

'Then if you'd like to take a seat over here.'

Flora followed her across to one of the chairs facing a mirror and sat down. She looked at all the other women having their treatments and had the sense of eyes being suddenly averted.

'Yes, as I thought,' the lady said. She was standing behind Flora and holding a tape measure to her braid. 'There's nineteen inches from ribbon to tip, but on account of the thickness, we can offer for twenty.'

'Thank you,' Flora mumbled.

'I'll need to untie the braid first, just to check overall condition and cleanliness. I'm sure you understand. We cannot supply dirty hair.'

'Of course.'

She sat very still as the hairdresser unplaited the braid, spreading it out over her shoulders and back and beginning to brush it out.

'It's got a good shine to it,' the hairdresser said admiringly. 'And it's a true black, too – that's uncommon, so we can offer another inch for that. I had assumed it was a very dark brown.'

'Oh. No, my mother's hair is black too.' Flora looked up at her own reflection. Of course, she had seen herself in the small mirror at their new home, but in something of this size, with these lights . . .

'Well, it's certainly clean and healthy. In fact, it's . . . it's really quite lovely.' The hairdresser's voice trailed off as she lifted Flora's hair with one hand and let it fall in cascades, watching Flora's reflection too. A small frown wrinkled her brow. 'Are you quite sure you want to cut it?'

'Aye.' Flora's voice quavered and the hairdresser must have heard it, because she leaned in a little.

'You can change your mind. There's no obligation.'

'No. We need the money. My father was badly injured

yesterday and can't work.' She swallowed. 'I must do what I can to help support my family.'

There was a long pause as the hairdresser's gaze met hers in the mirror. 'Indeed. I'm sorry to hear of your father's misfortune.'

'Thank you,' Flora almost whispered.

The hairdresser straightened up and looked around to find the lady at the white table watching them. She cleared her throat. 'Well, if you're happy to go ahead, we'll pay you for a twenty-one-inch cut.'

Flora gave a nod of assent and the hairdresser brushed her hair back into a tight ponytail, moving with quick, deft strokes before securing it back again with ribbons.

Still Flora stared at herself as it was braided once more. Without vanity, pride or any sort of pleasure, she was seeing at last what other people saw, what James had seen and once loved – that she really was as lovely as she had been told. The arrangement of her features was perfectly symmetrical, her eyes so vividly coloured and sharply drawn, her lips plump and rosy pink – and all of it was framed, highlighted even, by her ebony sweep of hair.

Hair she was about to cut off.

The looks that had defined her all her life were about to vanish with a single snip of the scissors now in the hairdresser's hand. She would only know her own loveliness for these few final moments.

'. . . Very well, then, if you're absolutely sure,' the hairdresser said, holding the scissors aloft as if waiting to be stopped.

No, Flora wasn't sure; but she was already here, the scissors yawning wide and ready to snap. Tears pooled in her eyes and as she looked past her reflection again, into the room beyond, she saw the other women watching with tense expressions. This time they didn't look away.

She nodded. The hair would grow back, she told herself as she felt the tug on her ponytail, wincing at the sharp shearing sound as it took two, three, four cuts to decouple it from her head.

'There,' the hairdresser said, holding it up triumphantly. The braid had been tightly secured at both ends with blue ribbon, but Flora wasn't looking at that. She was staring at herself as her newly shorn hair – that which had been above the ribbon – lightly fell around her face, freed of all its weight.

'Oh,' the hairdresser said quietly. There was defeat in the sound. Regret too.

Flora watched how the hair settled bluntly at her jawline. Her neck, which she had never considered before, was suddenly exposed. Her hands flew to it, as if to protect her modesty, and she looked down and tried not to cry.

It didn't matter, she told herself. She was more than just a face.

Wasn't she? Was she? James had thought so, but he wasn't here any more.

A silence filled the room, everyone's breath suspended, and Flora knew what they were thinking: she had ruined herself. Thrown away her beauty without care or second thought.

She felt hands upon her cheeks, angling her head up carefully until she was looking back at her own reflection again. Tears visibly streaked her cheeks as the hairdresser turned her to face the right, then the left side of the room. She ran her fingers through Flora's hair again, watching as it tumbled back down.

'Yes,' the hairdresser murmured finally, 'I think we can do something with that.'

Chapter Twenty-Two

Flora walked back towards Queen Street station at a clip. The train was leaving shortly and she'd overstayed her trip. Her appointment at Collinson's had taken far longer than she had expected, for one thing. She'd spent two hours in the chair in the end, as Janice, the hairdresser, had cut, shaped and permed her hair into something not just acceptable, but *modish*; that was the word the other ladies had used as they watched what started out as a mercy mission become something altogether more exciting.

The silence in the room had quickly been replaced with a buzz of interest that grew into chatter as Janice had dramatically swept Flora's hair into a deep side parting, pulled back high along the hairline but shaped into soft waves at the sides and back; the hairdresser had spent an inordinate amount of time styling the hair to fall in a sinuous curve along Flora's right cheek, almost touching her eyelashes, and there had been a collective gasp as Janice had finally 'revealed' the finished look.

'She looks like a dark Carole Lombard!' someone had cried and the other women had agreed, a couple of them even clapping in appreciation. Flora hadn't known where to look when Janice had refused payment, saying simply that she had felt an obligation to 'restore some balance' to Flora's looks after her 'sacrifice'.

All the way back along Miller and Cochrane Streets, people stared at her even as they strode past at pace, but she didn't feel as alien as she had before. She had a sensation of settling into the landscape, like a fresh puddle slowly seeping into the ground and becoming a part of it. The city didn't terrify her as she had thought it might. There was something to see at every level – shoe-shiners on the streets, office workers moving behind glass windows, pigeons roosting on chimney pots on high roofs set several storeys off the ground. Scale, density, style – all of it was grander here.

'Roll up! Roll up! Read all about it!' a news-seller called out. He was standing by his cart outside the station and Flora glanced over as she started up the steps. He was waving a rolled-up copy of the *Scotsman* in his hand but she could clearly see the headline in thick black print: LAIRD'S FACTOR DEAD ON ST KILDA!

She stopped abruptly, feeling the earth shift beneath her feet so that she jolted forward a little as she read the words. Her heart began to pound in her chest, but she had forgotten to breathe. She felt caught between two worlds.

In a daze, she walked over to the cart, picking up the paper on top and scanning the words with a look of disbelief.

'Hey, lassie! Are you buying or not?' the news-seller snapped, snatching it from her hands.

Flora looked at him, then around her nervously, as if people could somehow see her connection with the drama. But no one broke stride; they all had busy lives, and she was just a pretty stranger in poor clothes.

She reached a hand to her pocket to fish out a penny to buy a copy, the news-seller putting out his hand in eager readiness – but she stopped again. If Frank Mathieson hadn't been worth spending a penny on in life, she wouldn't do it now in death. She would never forgive him the glee with which he had ripped James away from her that day in Glen Bay; it had been the beginning of her end.

She felt the past stir, a turning over deep within her, and she looked at the man with sudden intensity. 'Where's Blythswood Square, please?' she asked him instead.

'. . . What?' The man watched as her hand – and the penny – was returned to her pocket.

'Blythswood Square. How would I get there?' Suddenly she felt the city's unwieldy sprawl and her own insignificance. All these hundreds, thousands of people . . . she felt as small as a pebble on the beach back home. She stared up at the high roofs, her eye travelling over entire blocks of them. Somewhere, amid all these buildings, sat a townhouse like any other, save for the fact that it had once housed him.

This had been his world, his home, and – like Sophia Rushton before her – she wanted to see it.

The man, giving up on any hope of his penny, frowned at her from beneath his cap, seeing her evident bewilderment. '. . . Blythswood, you say?'

'Aye, sir.'

He took in the mismatch of her fashionable hair and lumpen clothes; she looked a woman of two halves, and he was quiet a moment, as if confused why someone like her should need to go there; but finally he turned and pointed the newspaper in the direction of the long street running away from them. 'Go a half mile . . .'

She walked until she found herself in a grand square with a lush green oasis sitting at its centre. The townhouses flanking the streets were glorious and dazzling, the square an homage to symmetry as one side perfectly mirrored its opposite in identical rows of classical architecture: tall windows that spoke of high-ceilinged rooms, ornate plaster-work and bag chandeliers that could be seen through the glass.

There was no way of knowing which house had been his, no way to tell them apart. All the glossy black front doors were double-sized and sat atop flights of stone steps with curved iron handrails. James had tried to describe it to her in one of his letters, detailing airy salons and elliptical staircases, but these words had meant nothing to someone who had grown up in a two-room stone cottage. Now, though, she saw what he had wanted to give her, the life they would have lived.

It was as if a silk veil had been hung over the streets and draped over the trees, for the noise of the city was muted so that she could hear birds singing; a dog was being walked on a lead over the grass. The natural world had a presence again amid the bricks and sandstone and concrete, and the air itself seemed rarefied in this closeted space. Even the people walking along the pavements moved differently, languid and elegant in their hats and gloves.

She crossed the road to the communal garden and peered between the bushes: people were sitting on benches with their faces turned to the sun, children playing games on the grass, their hard-edged shadows chasing them on the ground. These were leisured lives playing out before her, a social elite with concerns no more pressing than choosing which wine to drink at dinner that night. She knew for certain that not a single one of them had ever wrung a bird's neck or plucked a sheep – or probably even knitted a sock – as she stood by a tree, her fingers absently running over the rippled bark while she felt the slow, faint pulse of their lives here.

A family was emerging from a house on the other side of the square, a little girl in a yellow dress and white socks skipping carelessly down the steps; she made to sprint towards the square but her father caught her by the shoulder, as if in anticipation of her break. He bent to say something, perhaps to scold her, but Flora's view was obscured by two young women walking on the path in front of her and her attention fell onto them instead. Other lives to follow. They were wearing matching coats and hats – like uniforms – and talking in soft voices, pushing sleeping babies in prams.

Not quite asleep. One of the babies mewled, a tiny pink fist sweeping above the coverlet, and Flora gasped as if it had been a sabre swipe – memories surfacing, unbidden – but the young women were oblivious to her presence, six feet away in the shadows.

She moved away, still too fragile for such encounters, and her tears fell freely again at the thought of what would never be. She would never become the mother on the steps in a pretty dress, her handsome husband by her side; their son would never play on this grass . . . Like Mhairi, she had been damned, abandoned by a God she had defied. Donald had offered to forward their address once they settled in Oban but Lorna had advised against it – picking at scabs only delays healing, she had cautioned.

She walked back to the main street, trying to outpace dreams that would not die. She turned back towards the noise and the smuts, returning to where she belonged. She had to face up to it – James and their son were gone, and they were never coming back. The sooner she accepted that, the sooner her own life would go on. She had to find a way ahead without them, somehow.

She had to be brave.

She saw a shop sign up ahead of her as she walked –

. . . She had to be brave.

Flora pushed open the door, almost falling into the shop. A bald, bearded man was standing behind a counter talking with another customer. He glanced up uninterestedly at her arrival. He wore a black suit, like a mourner, and looked incongruously sombre in his surroundings. Everything around him seemed to glitter: under the glass cabinet were rows of timepieces and fob watches, brooches, bracelets and even a few small crowns; behind him were gilded mirrors, china vases and figurines, silver candlesticks, gilt-framed paintings; ornate crystal chandeliers hung on hooks from the ceiling . . . Flora had never seen so many *things* before, most of them entirely decorative and superfluous to need.

She hesitated where she stood on the door mat, not sure what to do next.

As if reading her expression, the pawnbroker murmured something to his other customer, who discreetly turned away and began to peruse the contents of one of the wall cabinets.

'Good afternoon,' the pawnbroker said flatly, bringing his attention to bear upon Flora instead. 'How can I help you?'

She hesitated, flicking her finger against her skirt nervously. 'I have something I . . . I wish to sell.'

'Then you've come to the right place.' The man stared at her with dull eyes, unaffected by her beauty and seeming not to care that her hairstyle belonged on a far better dressed woman. 'What is it you've got?'

She hesitated for a moment, then strode towards the counter, pulling the ring off her finger with a feeling of release.

'This.' She set it down roughly on the glass surface, refusing to look at it. Her emotions were running high and she felt flushed with adrenaline. She just had to do this and be done with it. Be brave.

The man's eyes widened slightly at the sight of it and he looked back at her with more interest. 'This is yours?'

'Aye,' she nodded, still not looking at it.

'You're certain?'

She frowned, a flash of indignation coursing through her. 'Of course I am . . . What are you suggesting?'

Her irritation seemed to reassure him because he gave a nod and picked it up, reaching for a small glass beside him. Flora watched as he settled the glass against his right eye, squinting hard as he held up the ring and began to examine it fully. For several minutes, he didn't pass a single comment as he looked at the setting, the stones, the band.

When he finally looked back at her, his eyes were hard.

'This is eighteen-carat gold with three premium-grade sapphires,' he said, openly looking her up and down for a closer inspection of her clothes, her incongruous hair. 'How did you come by it?'

'My fiancé proposed with it.'

'*Your* fiancé?'

The slur wasn't missed by her. 'Correct.'

'And now you're selling it?'

'Haven't you ever heard of a broken engagement?' she asked tartly. She didn't want this stranger's pity. And besides, her business was none of his.

'. . . It's good quality.'

Too good for her? She shrugged. 'Aye. He's rich.' Was.

He put his hands on the glass counter and gave a weary sigh. 'Look, lassie, this is a reputable establishment. The hoity-toity around here know they can trust me not to sell on

284

indiscriminately. You wouldn't be the first maid to come in here after pilfering from the mistress.'

Flora felt a flash of anger. 'I am no one's maid!'

She heard a sound almost like laughter, but it hadn't come from the pawnbroker and she glanced across to see the other customer struggling – and failing – to hide his amusement.

'Excuse me?' Flora asked. 'This is a private conversation.'

'Apologies,' the man said, tipping his hat. 'I really wasn't trying to listen in. It just . . . it just tickled me, that's all.'

Flora's eyes narrowed. 'Tickled you?'

He smiled at her, brown eyes crinkling beneath the rim of a hat; smooth-shaven, a wristwatch flashing at his cuff. 'That you were offended by being mistaken for a maid and not for a thief.'

'I'm neither.' She looked back at the pawnbroker. 'You hear? *Neither.*'

'No? Prove this is yours, then.'

'And how am I to do that?'

He shrugged. 'Have you a receipt?'

'Of course not. He proposed to me. He didn't buy me at auction.'

There came another laugh again that attempted to conceal itself as a cough, but this time she didn't look over; she was locked in a stare-down with the pawnbroker, who seemed completely unmoved by her indignation. Back home, her temper had been considered 'fearsome'; not so much in this big city, it appeared.

A thought struck her.

'I know!' she said, eyes widening. 'Here – is that proof enough for you?' she asked, holding up her hand so he could see her ring finger and the deep tan line. 'Would I have that if I had just now stolen it from the mistress? Well, would I? I've been wearing that ring day and night for a year.'

The pawnbroker happily conceded the point without further argument, drawing in a deep, slow breath as he considered his next move. 'Very well, then. I'll give you £2 18s 10d for it.'

Flora blinked, wrong-footed to have suddenly got what she'd come for. It was almost three times what she'd got for her hair.

'Right,' she said, still keeping her chin high and trying not to show her fluster. 'Well, then, that's good, thank—'

'Hey, hey, hey, not so fast!'

Both Flora and the pawnbroker turned in surprise as the loitering customer came rushing over. 'Surely you're not going to accept that offer?' the man asked her, with an incredulous look.

'What?'

He looked across at the owner. 'Dougie, even by your standards, that offer is insultingly low. It's an eighteen-carat-gold triple-sapphire ring, you just said it yourself.'

'Aye,' Dougie replied, looking displeased. 'And that's my offer.'

The man looked back at Flora with a disarmingly friendly smile. 'Miss, would I be correct in assuming that this is your first time in an establishment such as this?'

Flora stared at him through narrowed eyes, not quite sure what was going on. Why was this man getting involved? '. . . Aye.'

'I thought as much, as did my friend here. But you should know that there is a way business is conducted in these matters. You see, it's almost like a dance.'

'A dance?'

'Yes. Dougie makes you an initial offer. You laugh, refuse and state what you were looking for . . . *He* then laughs, before offering you a little more than originally . . . You laugh again, saying you won't settle for less than X . . .' He smiled. '. . . You see the pattern?'

'Aye,' she said warily.

'What usually happens is you end up with a number roughly in the middle of what you both wanted. But you certainly never, *never* accept the first pass. I mean, with a ring of this calibre, of course you wouldn't dream of accepting a penny less than six pounds.'

'Of course not,' she said quietly, even though she had no idea of the ring's value, but in his fashionable-waisted suit and trilby, this man looked as if he might; he looked rich, to her eye. 'Thank you for the advice.'

She looked back at the pawnbroker. 'I was looking for six pounds,' she said calmly, even though her heart was thudding so loudly, she was sure they must both be able to hear it.

She sensed the stranger grinning beside her, standing now with his ankles crossed and an elbow on the glass as he openly settled in to watch the negotiation.

Dougie's jaw pulsed but he didn't smile. In fact, he looked decidedly unamused. 'No chance. He's put fanciful notions in your head, missy. Three, and that's my final offer.'

Flora felt her courage leave her – she knew she was out of her depth in this. She looked over at her fellow customer. 'Perhaps I should let you negotiate on my behalf?' she said to him, seeing how his eyes were travelling over her face in that oh-so familiar way.

He hitched up his eyebrows. 'I'm flattered! Are you quite sure you want to entrust such a task to a complete stranger?'

'You couldn't do a worse job of it than me,' she shrugged.

The man regarded her for a moment before holding out his hand; a gold ring flashed on his little finger. 'George Pepperly. At your service.'

'Flora MacQueen.'

'Flora MacQueen,' he echoed, as if trying out the name for size while he shook her hand. A beat passed as he regarded her more closely now, seemingly seeing what the pawnbroker did not – a lost young woman, caught between two lives. Two different worlds. 'See?' he said finally. 'We aren't *complete* strangers now.'

Pepperly looked back at the pawnbroker and held out a hand for the eyeglass. 'May I?'

Reluctantly, it was handed over, and Flora waited as he too examined the stones. 'Hm . . . Good clarity, deep colour . . . very few inclusions.' He wagged a finger at Dougie. 'This is worth £5 15s any day of the week and you and I both know it.'

There was a silence. The pawnbroker looked furious. '£3 10s.'

'£5,' Pepperly countered.

'£4 on the nose.'

'£4 19s.'

'£4 10s.'

'Intriguing!' Pepperly said, not missing a beat as he turned back to her. 'What do you say, Miss MacQueen? Does £4 10s sound like a fair deal to you?'

She stared back at him. He knew perfectly well that she had no idea what a fair deal might be. Slowly, she nodded.

'I would be happy to ac—'

'Of course, you don't *have* to sell at all,' Pepperly said, interrupting her again. 'You do realize that, I hope? There are plenty of other options open to you.'

She looked at him in confusion. 'Options?'

'Pepperly,' Dougie said in a warning tone.

The customer ignored him, his attention entirely on Flora. 'For making money, Miss MacQueen. This beautiful ring must hold an extremely high sentimental value, no matter what tragedy has befallen your engagement; as you have just admirably demonstrated, you have worn it every day for the past year.' His eyes fell to the deep tan line on her finger. 'I fear you might come to regret selling it, sooner or later.'

'I won't,' she lied. She just had to do this and get out of here.

'Not to mention, what you would get for this would be spare change to what you could actually earn.'

'Earn?'

He reached into his jacket and brought out a small ivory card.

Behind the counter, Dougie gave a weary shake of his head and a small groan as he stepped back, sitting down on a stool she hadn't noticed before now and beginning to read a newspaper; the same edition she had seen by the station earlier.

George Pepperly – Theatre Impresario read the card.

'I don't know what that means,' she said, going to hand it back.

'No, no, keep it, it's yours,' he said quickly, holding up a hand. 'In case you want my number.'

'Why should I want that?'

'To call me!' he laughed, crossing his arms over his chest and looking intrigued by her. 'Believe it or not, there are a great many young ladies who would give a kidney to get hold of my private number.'

She rolled her eyes and went to turn away. 'I am not intere—'

'Does my name really mean nothing to you?' He seemed genuinely interested.

'Why should it?'

He gave a laugh as he looked her up and down, his curiosity growing by the moment. 'Tell me, where is it you're from exactly, Miss MacQueen? You're not from Glasgow, I can tell.'

She debated lying but didn't have the energy. 'St Kilda.'

'Ah!' There was a pause as he nodded, as if in perfect understanding. 'Well, now that makes sense . . . Of course it does,' he said, sizing up her clothing and stalling slightly at her new coiffure. 'It also explains why you, with a face like that, haven't been put in front of me before now.'

'Excuse me?'

He narrowed his eyes as he continued to scrutinize her. 'Can you act?'

'Act?' she asked, confused. 'What's that?'

Another laugh. 'Sing, then?'

This time her eyes narrowed. '. . . Aye.'

'Can you dance?'

She hesitated. '. . . Strip the Willow, Mairi's Wedding—'

She was stopped by his gale of laughter. 'That wasn't quite what I meant, but . . .' He nodded, as if agreeing with a voice in his head. 'Miss MacQueen, tell me – do you have dinner plans for tonight?'

She blinked. Did she look like someone who had dinner plans? 'I plan to catch my train.'

'Oh? Where to?'

'Why would I tell you such a thing?' she asked suspiciously.

'What I mean to say is, could you possibly delay getting your train until tomorrow?'

'No.'

'Because?'

'Because I need to get back to my family,' she said, not quite sure how her transaction had come to be hijacked by this man. 'We've suffered a misfortune and I'm needed back home. I only came down here today to help and now I must get back.'

Her irritation didn't appear to land because he leaned in again. 'Misfortune?' he probed.

'It's private.'

'But if I could help . . .' he persisted. 'And I do believe I could.'

Flora held her breath for a moment. 'Help' wasn't a word she had heard offered since they'd landed on the mainland. Work, earn, pay, on the other hand . . . 'My father suffered an accident yesterday and can't work.'

'Accident?'

He was nothing if not persistent, she supposed. 'A logging accident – with the misery whip.'

Both men winced.

'But he's alive?' the pawnbroker asked, interested now.

'Aye, but badly maimed.'

'And that's why you're selling this beautiful ring?' Pepperly asked, still holding the ring between his fingers.

She looked away. She couldn't trust herself to hold her resolve.

'If she's selling the rich fiancé's ring, either he's no longer rich or he's no longer her fiancé,' the pawnbroker chuckled, going back to his paper. 'In which case, she *wants* to be rid of it.'

'But she doesn't *have* to be, that's the thing,' Pepperly said, looking back at her. 'What if I told you that you could make more money in one night than this ring cost brand new?'

She blinked back, unimpressed. 'I wouldn't believe you.'

'Miss MacQueen, I could make you rich beyond your wildest dreams.'

She rolled her eyes. 'Well, that wouldn't be difficult, given that money means precious little to me. I'm a St Kildan, remember? I trade in feathers and wool.' She turned back to the pawnbroker. 'Thank you, mister, I'll acce—'

'I keep a suite at the Grand Central,' Pepperly said quickly, leaning over to catch her eye again.

But it was her hand that he caught – with his cheek. The slap resounded loudly in the small shop and she gasped in surprise herself, at what she had done.

There was a moment's stunned silence.

She pushed her hair back from her face, feeling fear creep up her bones. What had she done? Driving men to anger was never wise. 'I'll not be insulted,' she said quietly, snatching the ring from him and taking a step back, getting ready to run. 'I may be poor but I am no slut!'

'. . . And I'm very glad to hear it,' Pepperly replied after a moment, making no move to retaliate. 'Standards matter.'

She looked at him in confusion.

'I apologize if I caused offence. I was not – and am not – propositioning you, I assure you.'

'What, then?' Her cheeks burned with embarrassment.

'The room would be for you to stay there – alone, safely. I have my own home in the city where I fully intend to sleep tonight. I would simply like the opportunity to talk to you, at length, in a more . . . salubrious environment.'

'Hey!' the shopkeeper objected.

'Talk to me about what?'

Pepperly smiled, his eyes twinkling with delight, the handprint on his cheek already forgotten. 'About how I'm going to make you a star.'

She closed her eyes, letting the words settle for a moment. Even just a few months ago, they would have enthralled her – but she was no longer that girl. A red lipstick could no longer turn her head; sweet words couldn't steal her heart. She knew now that promises were like rainbows: inspiring but distant and impossible to catch. She had to live in the real world, the world where money was the master, not dreams.

She looked back at the pawnbroker. 'I'll accept your offer for the ring, sir.'

The man glanced back at the other customer in surprise, but he didn't hesitate to open up his till.

'Miss MacQueen, I'm not sure you understand the opportunity you're missing out on here,' Mr Pepperly said, leaning towards her. 'If you'll just place your trust in me, you'll become a rich young woman and all the trappings of fame shall be yours. Whatever your heart desires – furs, cars, jewels. You can buy your own sapphire rings.'

She winced, staring at her fingernails with intense scrutiny as she waited for the pawnbroker to count out the money they'd agreed. She didn't want rings. The only thing she wanted couldn't be bought. 'Are *you* rich?' she asked him, looking up suddenly.

He smiled, looking gratified by the question. 'Yes.'

'Then why are you here, in a pawn shop?'

'Ah.' He seemed amused to have been caught out by the contradiction. 'I'm settling a debt for a friend.'

'You're quite the Good Samaritan, Mr Pepperly,' she said with such outright suspicion that the pawnbroker laughed. 'Settling friends' debts. Making strangers rich.'

'Well, I wouldn't say I operate entirely from the goodness of my heart,' he conceded. 'I take my cut from every deal. The smart fellow's share is on every dish, as they say.'

'Aye. And I was always taught that the man that divides the pudding will have the thick end to himself.' It had been her father's firm opinion of the factor, for sure, and she was tired of being manipulated by cleverer, wilier, richer men.

The producer squirmed at her words. '. . . If you wish to negotiate terms, Miss MacQueen, I'm willing to be flexible on my commission. Far more flexible than usual.'

The pawnbroker placed the coins and notes into Flora's outstretched palm. She looked down at them – small change to Pepperly, perhaps, but still greater than anything she or her own had ever seen. Along with the money from her hair, it meant she had got everything she'd come for today – and more besides. 'No,' she said, looking back at Pepperly coldly. 'Thank you for the kind offer, but my mind is set.'

'Terms are, we'll keep the ring for thirty days,' the pawn-broker said. 'Then it'll be sold here or at auction.'

She swallowed hard. Tears misted her eyes. '. . . I'll not be back for it.'

'I've heard that before,' he sighed, reaching under the counter and retrieving a green leather ring box. Flora watched as he pushed the ring into deep folds of emerald velvet. Its quality rang out against the other jewels glistening under the glass.

She stared at it: her last thread of connection to James finally cut away. There was nothing to tie them to one another now. She was unmoored from him. Fully alone.

'Miss MacQueen, please—'

'Thank you for your help, Mr Pepperly. Good day.' And she turned away and left the store without another word.

Chapter Twenty-Three

'Flossie, is that you?'

Ma Peg's voice curled around the corner of the kitchen door before Flora could even untie her boots.

'Aye, it's me,' she sighed, feeling her feet spread against the ground as she shrugged off her jacket and shawl. The journey home had felt double the length of the passage out, but somehow she had kept herself glued together as she sat in a carriage of strangers, with full pockets and a broken heart. Scotland had keened in sympathy past the window in a vignette of umber velvet mountains, blackish pine forests and melancholy lochs. Only now, as she returned to the closest thing she had left to a home, did she feel herself begin to unravel.

She could hear the scrape and clatter of pans on the stove, floorboards creaking overhead as her wee brothers played upstairs. The cottage was warm, the electric lights already switched on for the evening and throwing out a cosy glow onto the lane, the smell of coal smoke drifting in tendrils back towards the water.

'You were gone that long I thought you'd decided on a trip to London instead,' Ma Peg was saying as Flora pushed on the open door and walked in. 'I had half a mind to—' The words cut off abruptly as Ma Peg straightened up from

295

laying the table to better absorb the sight of Flora's new looks. 'Och, lass.'

Flora's hands rose to her bare neck as she patted feebly at the hairstyle which made no sense here. Her long hair had been a symbol of her island wildness, a natural beauty that didn't rely on artifice, cosmetics and good lighting; the stylish women in the salon, with their painted nails and high heels, couldn't conceive of a room like this or a life like hers.

'They gave me extra on account of the good colour, length and thickness,' Flora said in a tremulous voice as she reached into her pocket and set the haircut money on the table.

Ma Peg crossed the room with her distinctive slow but stout waddle, placing her hands on Flora's shoulders and regarding her keenly. 'Well, you're none the worse for it, dearie,' she said finally, though Flora could see the sadness in the older woman's eyes that another layer of their St Kildan identity had been sloughed away. 'I daresay they could have taken the lot off you and you'd still have had five proposals of marriage on the train home.'

Flora raised a wan smile. 'Well, if I had, I'd have taken the rings straight to the pawn shop and exchanged them for this.' She reached into her other pocket and brought out the even greater fortune of coins and notes.

Ma Peg looked down at it in confusion before catching sight of Flora's bare ring finger. 'You sold your precious engagement ring?' she gasped.

'Money's what we need now, not love,' Flora said, ignoring the shock in her eyes. 'The money for my hair was never going to be enough and seeing as I was already there . . . I was on my way back to the station when I walked past and I asked myself, what good is sentiment when Father needs an operation? How could I prize jewellery for my finger over a working foot for Da?'

'Och, but pet,' Ma Peg consoled, looking pained. 'What a decision to have to make.'

'It was really very easy in the end,' Flora said, turning away from Ma Peg's gently enquiring gaze and walking over to the range as she tried to quell another swell of emotion surging in her chest. A pot of stovies was simmering away, smelling delicious, but she had no appetite. Food held no flavour for her, music no melody; the whole world seemed drained of pigment. 'Have you had any updates from the hospital?' she asked, stirring the pot listlessly for want of anything better to do.

'Aye. Your mother called a wee while back.' The phone box on the other side of the lane had become a source of much excitement to the MacQueen and MacKinnon children playing in the front gardens, and they screamed with delight any time it suddenly rang.

Flora looked back at her. 'What did she say? How's Da?'

'They're feeling more confident about the risk of infection now. This surgeon the doctor keeps talking about canna perform the procedure if there's any inflammation to the wound – but it's looking good, they think.'

'Did they say yet how much the surgery will cost?'

Ma Peg tutted as if the subject of money was all a nonsense as she resumed placing the spoons beside the forks on the table. 'No, but if that lot you've brought back tonight doesn't cover it, then I don't know what will!'

Flora said nothing. If her understanding of money was scant, Ma Peg's was non-existent; there was still every chance they would be far short of what they needed. She knew now the worth of a braid compared to a ring – but how did a ring compare to a surgeon's fees? 'Where's David?'

'Out back, filling the coal bunker with Annie. There was another delivery this afternoon.'

That was another cause of fiscal consternation. Back home, the peats were as free as the air they breathed. Here, they had to pay for their warmth.

Bonnie came running in, stopping abruptly at the sight of Flora's dramatic new look. 'Flossie! Flo—'

'Don't look so worried,' Flora smiled, crouching down to her and holding out her arms for a hug. 'It's just a haircut.'

'But . . .' Her little sister cautiously ran into her embrace and lightly patted the set waves, as if their neat symmetry confused her. 'Why's it all crinkly?'

'They're called waves and they're all the rage in the city. Everyone was wearing their hair like this.'

'What was it like there?'

'It was loud. And busy. With lots of motor cars. You have to watch out when you cross the road.'

Bonnie pulled a face that suggested she didn't like the sound of it. 'You look sad,' she said, examining her sister's face more closely.

'I'm not sad.'

'You *look* sad.'

'Well, maybe I am a little.' She felt Ma Peg's concerned scrutiny fall upon her once more; her grief for James accounted for her persistent low mood but she still felt fearful that she would somehow give away her raging sorrow for her lost son too.

'Let's sing a song,' Bonnie said eagerly, climbing onto a chair at the table and standing on it. 'That'll cheer you up.'

Flora went to turn away, her heart aching from all the pretence. 'Later, perhaps.'

Bonnie caught her by the hand. 'No, now.'

'I'm really not in the mood for singing just now, Bonnie,' Flora demurred. 'I've had a long day. And besides, don't you have schoolwork to be getting on with?'

'No! And anyway, that's when you should sing – when you *don't* feel like it. It'll make you feel better.'

'I feel fine enough.'

'Your eyes are sad,' the little girl persisted.

'They're not!' Flora snapped.

Ma Peg turned at the flash of temper. The last thing Flora needed was a closer inspection from the village matriarch. 'Och, all right,' she relented. 'A quick ditty, then. Just the one. Then we need to run the bath.'

'Shall we sing the Sailing Song?' It was Bonnie's favourite.

'If that's what you'd like,' Flora said, and Bonnie immediately launched straight into the first verse.

Flora looked into her little sister's eyes as they sang together, their voices blending harmoniously, effortlessly – they had sung together their whole lives: at bathtime, during storms, going to bed . . . Flora reached for Bonnie's hands to hold as they sang facing one another, Bonnie standing on the chair and their palms pressed together on one hand. Flora tried to take the other one too, but Bonnie pulled back, and Flora noticed she was holding something.

'What are you holding there, Bonnie?' she asked, dropping out of the song. Carefully Flora prised open her grip to find a shiny silver sixpence in the middle of her sister's palm. 'Where did you get this?' she frowned.

There was a small pause. 'The man gave it to me.'

Ma Peg, who was pouring milk into a jug, looked up abruptly. 'Man? What man?'

'The one outside.'

A throat was cleared. '. . . Knock-knock.'

Everyone startled at the sound of the unexpected male voice, just outside the kitchen. It wasn't David, they knew that much, and Flora's jaw dropped open as a hand appeared on the door, a signet ring flashing on the pinky finger.

'Good evening,' George Pepperly smiled, peering round.

'What are *you* doing here?' Flora shouted, such was her surprise.

'I'm afraid I followed you back here . . . I hope you don't mind.'

'Mind?! Of course I mind!' she cried, flabbergasted at his cheek.

'Flora, who is this man?' Ma Peg demanded, planting her hands on her hips, a wooden spoon within grabbing distance, the rolling pin within lunging distance. She spoke only Gaelic, of course, and Pepperly hesitated a moment as he realized the language barrier.

'Please – I can explain everything,' he said, holding his hands up but making no move to come further into the room. 'I mean no harm. I hope Flora will vouch for that, at least?'

Ma Peg looked at Flora for help – and Flora reluctantly translated a quick account of their meeting.

He looked at Flora apologetically. 'I couldn't just let you disappear into the ether, Miss MacQueen. That would have been a tragedy.'

'I hardly think so!' she scoffed.

'You don't know my plans for you yet.'

'You've only just met me. How can you have plans already?'

'Believe me – people in my industry dream of moments such as occurred this afternoon. Talent is around every corner, but stardust? That's an entirely different thing, and if one is ever so lucky as to happen upon it – as I did today with you – it's really very obvious what the next step must be.'

'Which is?'

'We launch you to where you belong – right into the strato-
sphere.'

She shrugged, rolling her eyes. 'I don't know what that
means.'

'Flora, what is this man talking about?' Ma Peg demanded,
interjecting herself bodily between them now. Once again,
Flora brought her up to speed.

'Flora, I'm a show producer,' Pepperly said. 'That's what I
do. And I would like to produce a brand new show around
you. In short, you'd be singing and dancing on stage, in front
of an adoring paying audience . . . At least, to begin with. But
if this goes the way I think it will, then we'd move into pictures
quickly. The talkies are really taking off.'

'Talkies?'

'Yes – and I'm confident the camera will love you. I know
a few influential people in the studios in Hollywood. In
America. I'd make some calls and get the ball rolling. In the
meantime, we'd start you on some acting and dancing lessons
too, although your singing – as I had hoped – is definitely
already there.'

'You've never heard me sing,' Flora protested.

'I had an instinct about it earlier; there's a melodic quality
to your speaking voice.' He nodded towards Bonnie and her
shiny coin. 'And I asked your sister on her way in here if she
would get you to sing, just so I could listen in. If it sounded
like a cat was being murdered, I'd have slipped away without
you ever knowing I'd been here, but now that I know you
have the combination of that face and that voice . . . I'm afraid
I really can't give up without a fight, Miss MacQueen.'

'A fight?' Ma Peg seemed to understand something of the
word, for she reached for the spoon.

'Figuratively speaking,' he said quickly. 'Look, I do understand this is a lot to take in, but all I am asking for is a little time to explain the ideas I have for you. Tell me, have you heard of Miss Baker?'

Flora shook her head.

'Josephine Baker is one of the biggest stars in the world right now,' he explained, undeterred. 'She started out, five, six years ago, in a show called the Revue Nègre, which was brought over to Europe from the United States. There are better singers, better dancers, prettier faces even, but she has presence. She has charisma. She has star power – just like you, Flora. People can't tear their eyes off her when she's on that stage. She could be up there singing the alphabet and no one would bat an eye, because *she* would be singing the alphabet. Do you see?'

'I . . .' She sighed. She felt so weary and worn down. 'Not really, no.'

'People are enchanted by you, Flora. You have a magnetic aura. People would pay just to be able to look at you.'

'No one would pay to see the likes of me!' she said dismissively. 'You should see the looks I got in the city today. They disapprove of me. I don't belong.'

'No, that's just it – it's not disapproval that makes them stare. They're fascinated, don't you see? I was fifty paces behind you the whole way back here and even dressed as a . . . a laundry maid, you outshone every woman you passed.'

'I'm not a maid!'

'Oh heavens, not again.' He winced. 'Better a thief than a maid, eh?' He arched an eyebrow in an attempt to share the inside joke, but she didn't crack a smile. 'What have you got against maids, anyway?'

'Nothing. But they're like . . . slaves, and I've my freedom.'

He looked at her, as if considering her point. 'Have you, though? Really?'

'Of course I have. What do you mean?'

'Things are different over here. I don't claim to know much about your home, but I know you lived off the land and had no need for money. I can see why you felt free. But here? Money is the god that rules us all.'

'Not me.'

He regarded her with outright scepticism. 'You sold your ring today, so that will buy you some time, I suppose. But what will happen when the money's spent? What else have you to sell?' He didn't look around the room to make his point. He didn't need to. 'How will you survive then?'

She hesitated. 'I have a job. I earn a wage as a weaver in a factory.'

'And do you feel . . . free there?'

She looked away, realizing she'd been tripped up.

No one spoke for several moments, before he reached into his jacket and pulled out a small paper booklet. He pressed it against the wall and began writing on it.

'What is that? What's he doing?' Ma Peg demanded to know.

'It's a banker's cheque – written out to cash for one hundred pounds.' Pepperly blew on the ink, waving the booklet in the air for a few moments before ripping out the top sheet and holding it towards the older woman.

She could read and understand the numbers she saw written there. 'One hun—?' For once, Ma Peg's voice failed her.

Outside, coming around the back of the house, they heard the low timbre of David and Mad Annie's voices. A moment later, the back door swung open to reveal the two rail-thin, lanky figures. They stopped in their tracks at the sight of Flora clasping Bonnie standing on the chair, Ma Peg armed with a wooden spoon, and a strange man holding out a piece of paper. David and Mad Annie, for their own part, were covered in coal dust, their blue eyes blinking pale against sooty skin; David was carrying a filled coal bucket, and Mad Annie's pipe dangled from her lip.

'What's going on here? Who's this?' David asked, immediately setting down his load and stepping forward as the man of the house.

'Don't worry, David,' Flora said quickly. 'There's no cause for concern. His name is Mr Pepperly. He's a show producer.'

'A what?'

'I met him in Glasgow today. He wants to make a singing and dancing show around me. He wants to—'

'I want to make her rich,' Pepperly interrupted, meeting David's gaze and regarding him, man to man. 'Flora said her father was badly injured and that he cannot work? This money here – this banker's cheque for a hundred pounds – is her freedom.' He waved the scrap of paper lightly. Flora couldn't fathom how something so nondescript could wield such power.

There was an astounded silence as the promise of one hundred pounds wafted through the room like a perfume, scenting their thoughts with promises and wishes.

Quickly, Ma Peg updated Annie on developments.

'What rot!' Mad Annie cried, breaking the spell and striding forth, snatching the piece of paper from his hands. Her eyes ran over it with studied intensity, giving no indication to their guest that she couldn't read. 'This is not a hundred pounds. I've seen bank notes, and this isn't one.'

'Take it to a bank and they will cash it for you,' Pepperly said calmly, seeming to catch the drift of their arguments.

Mad Annie's eyes narrowed and she looked back at Flora. 'Why would he do such a thing? Money's not free.'

Flora asked him the same question in English.

'It's an advance against future earnings, not a gift. I'm not a charity – I'm a businessman. I have utmost confidence that you will be a star, but my understanding was you need the money now, not later?' He didn't move a muscle as Annie turned the cheque over, looking for any clues that it might be a trap. 'Forget the pennies you've got to scrape together working on a loom or at the Forestry Commission. That cheque right there is your financial independence.'

'Let me see it, Annie,' David said, walking up to her and examining the piece of paper too.

Pepperly gave Flora a steady look. 'This is only a small advance against what you'd earn. You would be a rich woman within a year – able to provide for your father whatever the outcome of his accident. If he can't work again, it wouldn't matter – you'd be able to support him.'

Flora thought of the surgery they were trying to afford even now. If they could save Father's foot, he could still have a meaningful, active life.

But, more than that, another thought began to bloom in her mind . . .

'What's more, you could break as many engagements as you liked.' He smiled, unaware of the pain his words brought to her. 'You wouldn't have to marry for money, or position, or status – all those things would already be yours. Because let's be honest, that's how women are really owned, is it not? What is it they say – don't marry for money; you can borrow it cheaper?'

Flora translated for the others and Mad Annie's chin raised a little in the air. This was her kind of conversation. But Flora

305

was feeling something within herself beginning to stir at his words as well. True independence was something she had never dreamt of before now. She had longed for freedom from St Kilda, a bigger life elsewhere, but had always understood it to be possible only if she were attached to someone else, someone like Edward or James. Escape had always involved becoming a wife, but she had become a mother instead.

A husband would still provide the respectability of legitimacy, of course, but that no longer seemed as important as it once had. Not over here. What *did* matter was the pain that grew with each passing day at being separated from her son. She could feel herself dying inside. She had given him up to Donald in the belief that he and Mary could provide for her son in a way that she could not. But if what this man was saying was true – and he certainly seemed to have convinced himself of it – she would be able to provide for her baby herself.

She felt a judder of shock as for the first time, something like hope awakened in her. *Could* she get her baby back?

'You paint a rosy picture, Mr Pepperly,' David said, going to hand back the cheque, though the producer refused it. Unwilling to be beholden, her brother set it down on the kitchen table instead.

'Call me Pepper, please.'

David's eyes narrowed at the accelerated familiarity. 'It all sounds too good to be true.'

'For most people, yes, it would be. But Flora is not most people. She stands apart.'

Flora noted that her brother didn't argue with him on that.

'There's no light without shadow,' Annie interrupted, her voice rolling in low syllables as she addressed David. 'What are the pitfalls of this grand plan? Get him to speak plainly. I'm no fool.'

David recounted the command and Pepperly drew himself up as he looked away in contemplation. 'Well, I must admit it would be very hard work – particularly in the beginning, as we get the show set up. The days are long in rehearsal.'

David translated.

'No longer than the days on the fulmar harvest, I would wager,' Annie countered, as if it was a competition. 'What else?'

'. . . The hours are unsociable. Flora would be working late into the night.'

'Like during lambing season? Or on the gannet hunt?'

David shrugged and Mad Annie looked back at Pepperly for more obstructions, flicking her wrist impatiently for him to get on with it.

'And working with artistic types can bring its . . . frustrations. Tempers can be short, language colourful. She'd need to have a thick skin if the director flies off the handle, for example.'

David relayed the point in Gaelic.

'Ha!' Annie gave a small snort. 'He's clearly never met Norman Ferguson or Frank Mathieson. We've all dealt with far worse, you can assure him of that.'

Flora bit back a smile. Annie appeared to have no awareness that in matching the producer woe for woe, she was in fact removing any and all objections.

'Then I imagine her greatest sacrifice would be having to leave home. Here,' Pepperly shrugged. 'She'd go long stretches, perhaps even months, without being able to see her family and friends – and for someone from a close-knit community such as yours, I fear that might be quite a struggle.'

Flora considered the point as David translated for the older women. Once upon a time, even just a month ago, she hadn't been able to wait to disappear into her new life – but that had all changed in the wake of losing James and their baby. With Effie, Mhairi and Molly all gone too, the thought of leaving her family as well would have been too much to bear, even just yesterday morning. But her father's accident had changed their fates once more. The wheel of misfortune had continued to turn and their future had never been more uncertain.

She looked at Pepperly – a rich, self-assured, powerful man who had followed her all the way back here to make his case. That had to speak to his conviction in his own plan, surely?

'I'm sure there would be opportunities to see everyone,' Flora said quietly. After all, she had gone into the city alone today. 'It's not so very far to Glasgow by train.'

Pepperly looked at her, confusion quickly making way for clarity. 'No, no, the show wouldn't be in Glasgow.'

She frowned. 'Where, then?'

'Where else but the City of Light?' he asked, spreading out his hands.

They all looked at him blankly.

'Miss MacQueen,' he smiled. 'We'd be going to Paris!'

Chapter Twenty-Four

25 October 1930

Paris

'Levez les bras! . . . Lift . . . lift the arm . . .' the seamstress, Marie, said, looking up at Flora from her kneeling position on the floor with her mouth full of pins.

Flora did as she was told, trying not to squeal as she felt the sharp graze of a point along her skin. She stared at her reflection in the mirror, not quite able to believe what it was showing her: the fabric covering her – 'a mesh', she'd been told – was so fine it was like a fairy's fishing net, showing more skin than it concealed, so that from a distance she looked nude and as if she'd been sprinkled with stars. What would her mother say if she were to see her like this? Mad Annie? Ma Peg? Everything had been pinned to her body so that it clung like a shadow, only the merest of wrinkles at her elbow or knee as she moved; sitting down was almost an impossibility, but there was no time for that anyway. The nearest she came to it was when she was carried in, precariously perched on Marcel's shoulders, her legs dangling down the length of his bare torso, her arms spread wide and her head tipped back as Gilles, the director, shouted 'Prezonce! Prezonce!' at her.

In the pit, random notes from bows gliding across strings carried up to her, the orchestra bored and hungry for their lunch. Lights kept switching on and off, too, as the spotlight swung across the boards, looking for a fixed point on the stage and not – for the moment – her.

Pepperly was standing by the small desk set out just below the stage, talking intently with Gilles; both men were smoking cigarettes, their hats and overcoats set upon chairs in the front row. It worried her how sombre they always looked as they talked together – as if they were war generals in their bunker – their faces dramatically animating only when they directed their attention towards her. She was the 'star' – that was how everyone referred to her, and she felt eyes upon her all the time, both men and women: from the stagehands to the costume designers, the lighting men, the musicians, the dancers . . . She was supposed to like it.

'Alors, tournez,' Marie said, relieved of her mouthful of pins now and patting Flora lightly on the leg to impel her to turn.

Flora obliged, her eyes scanning the view as she slowly made a complete rotation. Two dancers kissing passionately in the wings, hands where they shouldn't be . . . the frame of the giant birdcage . . . a sound director positioning the cable of a microphone stage right . . . and back to the sumptuous red maw of the performance hall with its all-scarlet floors, walls, velvet chairs and matching boxes in the balcony. Only the gilded vaulted ceiling and pillars disrupted the cardinal colour palette. It was like being inside one of the Cartier jewel boxes Pepperly had opened for her in recent weeks.

'Bon, c'est parfait,' the seamstress muttered to herself. 'Tout fait!' she yelled across to the two men, getting up stiffly from her knees.

'But . . .' Flora stammered. 'The top . . . You said the top . . .'

She watched as the seamstress took several steps back, saying something to the director in rapid French, awaiting his judgement.

'Turn around, let me see,' Gilles ordered in his strong accent. 'Ah oui, c'est superbe maintenant, Marie. Pas plus de—' He smacked Flora on the bottom. 'See?' he asked, looking over to Pepperly, who had come over too.

'Yes, I agree. It fits much more closely now. The line is wonderfully sleek.' He looked at Flora. 'You're a vision under the lights.'

'But she said she would add more sequins to here,' Flora said, one arm strapped over her bosom, her modesty maintained only by the finest of margins for, in spite of the sparkling coverage, she was sure her nipples were still visible. Everyone seemed to find her modesty 'charming', as if it were merely a pose. The dancers themselves had costumes that were fully – shockingly – bare-breasted, their private parts hidden only by peek-a-boo feathers.

'And so she shall, stop fretting,' he reassured her. 'Gilles has this bee in his bonnet about the silhouette that needs to be addressed first. The rest will follow.'

'But we open tonight.'

'Exactly. Plenty of time,' Pepperly shrugged, drawing on his cigarette and closing his eyes blissfully as he exhaled a ribbon of dove-grey smoke.

'Deshabillez . . . Take it off . . .' the seamstress said, tapping her in that particular way of hers so that Flora gave a quarter turn and she could start to unbutton the tiny loops that ran down Flora's right side. An assistant ran over with a jade silk robe with cream fringing, wrapping it around Flora's body as the costume was peeled off her like a second skin.

Flora watched as the seamstress disappeared into the wings. She couldn't get used to the close attentions to her body. There had been a moment, early on in the fittings, when Marie had been on her knees, pinning, and she had stopped to trace a finger, low down on Flora's stomach. The seamstress's eyes had flashed up to hers, as if she understood something – but what? At the first opportunity, when she was alone again, Flora had rushed to the mirror and checked the spot she had traced, to find a single pink groove in her skin, like a rut in mud; she had never noticed it before and couldn't have said how long it had been there. Possibly all her life? There had been neither opportunity nor scope for examining their bodies back home. But why had it caught Marie's attention and what did it betray?

'Where are we at with the cheetahs?' Pepperly asked Gilles.

'Boucheron will be delivering at six on the dot,' the director pronounced, highlighting the words with precision. 'But they insist on a security guard.'

It had been, by all accounts, a protracted negotiation for the sapphire chokers that would grace the crystal-studded statues at either side of the stage. Pepperly was adamant that they must have the 'requisite sparkle'.

'After the business I've put their way?' he muttered irritably, rolling his eyes. 'Well, so long as they're in dinner dress and don't look like detectives about to raid the joint. Just make sure they're discreet.'

'Naturellement.' Gilles jerked his chin up. 'Did you hear back from London?'

Pepperly took a sharp intake of breath as though the question pained him. 'No. They're not returning my calls.'

Gilles looked irked, but then he shrugged. 'Their loss. They will be missing out on the hottest opening night of the twentieth century.'

'Hm,' Pepperly said, the sound a low growl in his chest. 'Don't let Josephine hear you say that.'

Gilles chuckled. 'Mais c'est vrai! Look at the frenzy we have here. Who needs *The Times* anyway?'

'Hm,' Pepperly intoned again, looking no less pleased as he held his cigarette between curled fingers.

Flora watched them talk as she tightened the robe's belt around her waist; she had quickly become used to the feeling of silk against her skin. Six weeks ago, it had existed purely as a concept in her mind; now she slept on it and dressed in it. Jewels, too, had become a rapid fancy and almost every other day, it seemed, Pepperly was opening up navy or red leather boxes for her to choose a sparkling bracelet or earrings or a necklace. They were borrowed, he apologized, but it made her 'look the part' at the places they frequented: the ballet, the opera, the theatre . . . Some days they had five o'clock tea at Angelina's, where tiny cakes in pretty colours were brought out on tiered stands. Pepperly had instructed her on how to eat them correctly – there was 'a form' to these things; she couldn't simply put them in her mouth – just as he had with croissants, and asparagus, and escargots, and myriad other foods that she had never even heard of before. The cakes were exquisite but her favourite treat was the hot chocolate drink that was so thick, the spoon stood upright in the centre of the cup.

Pepperly indulged her at every opportunity. 'I want to see a sparkle in those beautiful eyes, Flora. Where is it?' he would ask, watching her intently each time he presented her with a bracelet, or a bouquet of pure white roses. She would smile and coo but try as she might, the delight never seemed to move past her lips. Her heart was broken and she wasn't a natural actress, after all; she couldn't force her face to express emotions she didn't feel even though she wanted to please him, to make him proud. He was the closest thing to family she had here: if not a father figure, then a favourite uncle. He had never once looked at her with a lascivious eye, nor flirted, nor said anything risqué or inappropriate. It was a relief to be able to trust him.

For the first week after he followed her back to Lochaline, very little had happened. He had commissioned his best song-writer to work day and night for him on new material for the show while she stayed behind and began the process of saying goodbye – the doctor had been paid, bills met, her father visited in hospital and a few days later she had packed a bag with everyone's blessings. Pepperly had met her off the train at Queen Street with a bunch of fifty pink and yellow roses and, just like that, she had stepped into her new life. Hotels, trains, cars – everything was already arranged. She had to think about 'nothing but looking pretty', he had smiled, unaware of the shadows that lurked inside her.

Rehearsals had begun the very moment they arrived at the Gare du Nord. The venue had already been booked, the cast and crew hired and they all worked long days putting the numbers together into a show. Though she could sing and dance in a certain country style, she had never heard of the fashionable (and shocking) tango before now and had certainly never acted in her life. Gilles had his work cut out, but he seemed to see in her what Pepper had seen – some rare, elusive appeal – and he gave tireless instructions on how to make an entrance, command a stage, enthral an audience. Pepper had also hired singing and acting coaches, who were teaching her how to both protect and project her voice.

If it had all been thrilling, it was also exhausting: for the first month, she crawled into bed each night in the studio apartment he had rented for her in Montmartre. Life had been hard on St Kilda, but this was a different kind of work. She ached inside and out from her exertions as she learned to use her body in entirely new ways.

She was grateful for it – the intensity meant her nights passed dreamlessly and her days in a blur of choreography and song lyrics. She had practically no time to think of her lost child or lost lover; though her grief was still attached to her, with each day that passed, its grip loosened; it began to hang from her shoulders like a limp scarf instead of corseting her like a girdle. Her eyes might not sparkle but she found herself smiling along with the dance troupe's louche antics; her tummy no longer growled with constant hunger, and she found a comfort in satiated appetite. Crucially, she had a plan, and with every day that passed, she was now inching closer to, not further from, her child.

Every day Pepperly instructed her quietly and with dignity, teaching her how to move through society. She now knew when to use a salad fork, the correct form for greeting a duke, how to walk in high heels. She moved with ease in the crowded streets, holding her chin high the way he had shown her and not dropping her head as she felt the many stares begin to settle – as they always, invariably did. 'Let them see you,' he commanded as they 'promenaded' through the Jardins des Tuileries or past the Madeleine. 'Let them wonder about you . . . You're a star, Flora,' he whispered as he gave her his arm, a gentleman to a lady. 'Make them look.'

And she did. By the end of their first week 'on the town', as he put it, they had people constantly dropping by their box or their table, angling for an introduction to her – but Pepperly kept everyone at arm's length. He said she had no French and refused even to divulge her name. Speculation about her identity mounted quickly: it was assumed that she must be the star of his new show, and when tickets went on sale, they sold out within a single morning. By the end of the second week, Pepperly's social post bag had doubled as talk of his mystery companion grew; and in the third week, he moved Flora into a suite at the Ritz. She wore clothes by Madame Chanel and had acquired a habit of sliding her hand up and down the ropes of pearls that accessorized her outfits; Pepperly approved, saying it made her look 'fantastically bored' – which was a good thing, apparently. What he didn't know was that it was her self-soothing technique, much like rosary beads; a way of keeping her nerves in check.

Flora felt the new urge for a calming glass of champagne as she watched the organized chaos around her. 'Curtain up' was at nine o'clock. The press had been invited for this, the first night, and everyone's nerves were running high. Everything had to be just perfect. *She* had to be perfect. She had to somehow be the woman everyone thought she was from these curated glimpses, so carefully choreographed.

One of the trumpeters impatiently blew a jarring minor note, holding it for longer than necessary, and Pepperly checked his wristwatch, looking startled by what it showed him. The hours were beginning to run away . . . 'Right, everybody – time for déjeuner!' he called, clapping his hands. 'Reconvene ici at deux heures, s'il vous please. Ready to pick up with the fifth number. Cinquième! Paulette, remember the ostrich feathers this time, please!'

He turned to Flora, squeezing her arm affectionately. 'Take the car back to the hotel. Have lunch sent up to the room. Try to rest, Flora. It's going to be a long day.'

Everyone scattered like marbles on his cue, the hubbub of

316

laughter and conversation quickly dying away as the musicians, dancers and stagehands pushed through the double doors in pairs and groups, heading for baguettes and coffee at the café on the corner. Most of them smoked 'like trains' too, but it wasn't a habit Flora had yet been able to acquire.

She went back to her dressing room, where her clothes were draped over a chair, and began to get dressed again. There was a green silk chaise longue in one corner that she never had time to lie on; her costumes hung on a rail. An extravagant bunch of lilies sat on her dressing table; bright electric bulbs lit up the mirror with a harsh light and in the reflection, as she buttoned up her blouse, was a peeling poster of Charlie Chaplin on the back wall.

She was fastening the final button when there was a quick knock at the door.

'Message for you, M'selle MacQueen,' one of the stagehands said, peering round and holding out a slip of folded paper.

'Merci.'

He disappeared in the next moment and she opened it: *Call Effie.*

Flora straightened up with a frown. Had something happened? They had exchanged a couple of letters since her friend's relocation to Ayrshire, but to place a telephone call suggested there was a matter of some urgency.

Pulling her sleek knitted skirt over her hips, she hurried from the room and down the narrow corridor, heading for the stairs to the first-floor offices. She had only been up there a couple of times, but she knew they had telephones, and she sensed this couldn't wait until she was back at the hotel.

The door was ajar and she knocked quickly, lightly, peering in to find it empty. Everyone was at lunch, making the most of the calm before the storm. She headed straight for the telephone on the nearest desk; three secretaries worked in here, and there were some smaller half-glazed offices leading off the main space. Those doors were all closed.

Flora reached for the receiver and waited as the operator spoke to her in rapid French. Pepperly had taught her what to say, without needing to understand, and she read the number on the note; a few moments later and she heard the clicks down the line as the connection was made.

Distantly, a phone began to ring. She leaned against the edge of the desk, waiting and trying not to panic as she looked idly around her. Much like her dressing room, this was the sort of environment that had never existed on St Kilda, something she would have been unable to imagine before she found herself standing in it for the first time. Piles of paper towered on the desks, a printed silk scarf was draped over the back of one of the chairs, typewriters were fed with clean sheets and awaiting the first strike of an inked hammer; a basket of newspapers was on the floor and beside it, a small dog's bed. There was a shiny red apple on the desk opposite; a letter opener with a bone handle left on a pile of letters.

Flora reached for it; it reminded her a little of some of the knives back home—

'Dumfries House.'

Flora hesitated at the sudden, clipped tones. '. . . Hello? May I speak with Effie Gillies, please?'

There was a pause. 'May I ask who is calling?'

'Flora MacQueen.'

'Just a moment, please.'

Flora heard the sound of the receiver being set down, leather-soled footsteps receding along a hard floor.

She caught sight of a small vanity mirror tucked beneath the papers on the desk where she was sitting. She checked her reflection. Lipstick on teeth was a concern these days, a mainlander's worry –

Just then, a low, indistinct sound, muffled, came to her ear. She pulled back, feeling instantly guilty for snooping on the desk, and looked around her for the source, but the room was empty – there were no noises coming from the corridor or the stairs, only the far-off tone of a Scottish phone in her right ear. Had she imagined it?

She picked up the patter of running footsteps coming into earshot, but they were distinct from the others and she could tell just by the sound that her friend was barefoot. She smiled, comforted by this small token of constancy. Effie was still Effie.

'Flora?' her friend breathed – but not because she was out of breath.

'Aye, it's me, Eff. What's the matter? You sound worried.'

'I am. I can't talk long – the police are here.'

'Police?'

'They're back again, asking questions. About Mathieson.'

'What kind of questions?'

'Where was I that night? How well did I know him? Did he bring me gifts? Was I working with him, moving stolen goods?'

'Oh, Eff!' Flora realized she was whispering too, hushed by her friend's panic. 'What have you told them?'

'Everything we agreed. But you need to be ready, Floss; they'll come to talk to you too. It doesn't matter that you're over there in Paris. It's a murder investigation now.'

Flora winced. 'They don't think it was an accident?'

'No.'

She squeezed her eyes shut, trying not to relive the horrors of that night. 'Have you told Mhairi?'

'Well, that's the thing – *she* wrote to *me*. And it's why I've called you. There's something you need to know.' Flora could hear her swallow. She was nervous. 'Donald's been arrested.'

Flora's mouth dropped open, but she could make no sound. It was as if her voice had been snatched along with her soul. 'Donald . . . ?'

'Because of the ambergris business. They think it's a strong enough motive to kill.'

'But . . .' Flora felt a fear begin to settle in her bones. 'You mean he's in jail?'

'Aye.'

Flora tried to hold herself together, to stay calm even as her heart began to pound. 'How long will they hold him for?'

'Sholto says they'll either release him without charge or, if they press charges, he may have to stay in jail until the trial goes to court. It depends how strong they think the case is; Sholto says there's a chance he might be granted bail. We're heading to Oban this afternoon to meet Mhairi off the boat. She's on her way down from Harris . . . She's coming to give Donald his alibi.'

Flora felt a sharp pinch of unease. Why would Mhairi travel all that way to give Donald an alibi? They had already agreed he would say he'd been with his wife. 'But why hasn't Mary . . . ?'

'She told the police she didn't see him for several hours after midnight; she said she had the baby and then he went out. She got herself off the hook . . .'

'And landed him in it,' Flora whispered, now deeply troubled. Something was very wrong, she could feel it. 'You need to talk to her, when you get to Oban, Eff – make the woman see sense.'

Effie swallowed nervously down the line. 'We can't. That's the thing. Mhairi says she's gone. No one knows where she is.'

Flora felt the ground tilt beneath her feet, the world losing form. Gone? '. . . And the baby . . . ?' The words were just whispers, flutters of breath that fell from her without hope.

The silence that followed was agonized. Flora could hear in it the crackle of strain. 'We have to assume she's taken him with her. I'm sorry, Flora . . .'

'But you don't know where?' Pain twisted her voice into a higher pitch as she felt herself begin to fall apart. No. This hadn't been . . . it hadn't been the agreement. Donald was to raise the baby: he was a good man who had lost too much. He would pour all his love for *his* lost lover and *his* lost child into her son – that was the plan. That promise had been the only thing keeping her mind and body together. The thought of Crabbit Mary, somewhere out there without him, raising Flora's child as her own . . . For her to disappear with Flora's child just as she was striving to get back to him . . .

'No. Not yet, I'm sorry. I hope Mhairi might know more when she gets here.'

'We have to find her, Eff,' Flora said desperately, her voice cracking. 'We have to find Mary.'

'And we will. Sholto says he knows people. He has resources. I'll keep you updated, I promise. Are you still staying at that hotel?'

Flora felt her breathing become laboured as she dropped the receiver to the desk, where it lay like a dead crow. She planted her hands flat on the surface as her head hung low. This couldn't be happening. It couldn't be real—

The muffled sound came again and blankly, instinctively, she looked up, noticing that one of the office doors had merely been pushed to. From a first glance as she entered, it had appeared shut, but from here it was open sufficiently that a wide seam of the activities within was revealed: someone leaning back against the desk . . . the flash of a signet ring held low on something dark and moving . . . hair . . . Fingers in dark hair . . . She heard another sound now and this one was clearer – a groan, drawing out, urgent whispers . . . *'Yes . . . yes . . .'*

Flora felt a shudder of nausea rise up in her as she realized what she was seeing. Suddenly the entire world felt ruined – dirty, spoiled, shameful. No one was above hiding secrets, not even those she admired the most.

'Flora? Are you still there?' Effie's voice was far away, a metallic audio dot in the room.

She picked the receiver up again, unable to draw her eyes away from what she was seeing. 'Aye.'

'Are you still at that hotel?'

Flora looked back at George Pepperly and Marcel. She had tried to do the right thing by coming here, but what kind of place had she really run to? Who could she trust?

'Flora?'

Chapter Twenty-Five

'Flora, open this door – now.'

Pepperly's voice was low but she heard the urgency in it as she stood on the other side, watching through the peephole as he paced in the hotel corridor. He had been out there for several minutes and people walking past were throwing him wary looks as he tipped his hat to them, trying not to look as foolish as he felt. She knew that in a place like the Ritz, he couldn't risk making a scene. She had quickly learned that out here in the big, wide world, people's behaviour was constrained by a sense of place. Such a concept had not existed back home.

'I know you're in there. Open the door, please, or I'll be forced to ask reception to lend me their master key.'

She flinched, falling back a step as he rapped his knuckles hard on the wood again.

'Don't think they won't do as I ask – I'm paying for this room, remember. Now, open up.'

She stared at her side of the door, knowing she couldn't stay hiding in here forever, that she would have to face him sooner or later. She opened up and he blinked back, the two of them regarding one another in silence as he took in the sight of her reddened eyes and pale cheeks.

He strode into the room, taking off his hat and throwing it

onto the rose-pink silk sofa, then shrugging off his overcoat. 'Two o'clock, I said,' he began, turning to face her. 'Everyone's been waiting for you since two o'clock. That was three hours ago! You won't pick up the phone and then you keep me standing out there like an eejit? . . . You're not only being unprofessional, Flora, you're being rude too! What's got into you?'

'I'm sorry, Pepper, I can't.'

'Can't? Can't what?'

She stared at him, seeing the frustration in his eyes even though he was outwardly calm. He was a man used to crises.

'I can't do it. I can't be part of this.'

There was a pause.

'I see.' He lapsed into a thoughtful silence before nodding a little to himself. He walked over to the windows which gave onto a courtyard garden and put a hand to the taffeta curtains, looking out briefly, but she could tell he was blind to the sight of the statues and the city's autumn colours; his focus was entirely on what was inside this room. He turned back to her, stuffing his hands into his trouser pockets. His calmness was unnerving. 'And when you say you can't be part of this, you mean be part of the show that has been built entirely around you? Or . . . *this*?' His eyes swivelled around the sumptuous room, scented with fresh roses, the bed made in silk.

She froze under the weight of his accusing stare – it was like wearing a suit of lead.

He moved away from the window and slipped a hand inside his suit jacket to retrieve his cigarette case; it was silver, from Asprey. 'You know, it may come as a surprise to you to hear this, but you are not the first – and nor will you be the last – star performer to get cold feet.'

Cold feet? She wasn't sure she understood. Her feet were never cold.

'It's entirely normal.' She watched as he lit up, the tip of the cigarette beginning to glow. He jogged his eyebrows at a memory. 'I once had one young lady so terrified on her opening night that she tried to jump from the moving car on the way over.' He glanced at his wristwatch. 'But see here, we can go over all that at the venue. There are all sorts of . . . breathing exercises we can do. Not to mention a fresh glass of champagne to take the edge off. But we need to get your make-up done and if nothing else, the rest of the cast and the orchestra need to *see* you, so they're reassured that these past six weeks of hard work haven't been for nothing.' He arched an eyebrow as he regarded her with paternal disappointment. 'It's unnerving for them all, waiting and waiting for you to show. Gilles has been stretched to his limit trying to keep *their* nerves settled, I can tell you.'

Her stomach lurched at the thought of all the people she would be letting down; people she had come to regard as friends. He walked over to where her coat still lay in a heap on the floor from when she'd run in. He picked it up and flicked it, easing out the wrinkles; her shoes too, lying on their side, were brought over to where she stood. 'Come now. As they say, we must get the show on the road.'

Still Flora stared at him.

'Come now, Flora,' he repeated, more impatiently. 'Put this on, and we'll say no more about it. There's no real harm done by you missing this afternoon. I don't doubt the rest did you the power of good.'

She took a step back, seeing how his eyes narrowed at the refusal. 'I'm sorry, Pepper, it's not that my feet are cold.'

Slowly he lowered his arms, the hem of the coat puddling on the carpet like a matador's cape as he stared at her for a moment, before turning away in anger. She saw him catch sight of the suitcase on the bed and he whirled back to face her, seeing that this was, indeed, no joke. She really was leaving.

'I have to go back,' she confirmed. 'I'm needed at home.'

He rolled his eyes in exasperation as he walked over towards the ashtray on the table and flicked in his cigarette ash. 'Yes, yes, I'm aware – your father is convalescing, it's a difficult time. Even so, this is not the time to take a trip home! We have a thousand people coming to see you tonight! It's a sell-out!'

'I know—'

'And you also know the trade press are reviewing you. Not just you – the dancers, the musicians, all the people who have helped put this together. No-show equals no show. You're putting all their livelihoods at risk. Many of them have families. You aren't the only person with problems, Flora.'

'I know, but things have changed. I can't go on stage for you – not tonight or any night. I'm truly sorry.'

'You're sorry?' His eyes were cold now. 'Oh, I'm afraid I'm going to need a fuller explanation than that, Flora. If you want me to go back to the great Casino de Paris and tell them this is off, a few hours before curtain up, then I'm going to need something more than homesickness as an explanation!'

Her mouth opened but still the words stalled in her throat. How could she tell him what she'd done? The whole, awful story – how it had led her here and was now driving her from here too?

She watched him as he took a deep drag of his cigarette, impatient and irritated.

'It's a private matter. Nothing to do with my father.' She swallowed nervously, scarcely able to hold his gaze. 'I'm grateful for all you've done for me, but I have no choice – I've *got* to go back. If I could do anything to change it, I would. Of course I would.'

'You would if you could . . .' he muttered, flicking more ash into the ashtray. He straightened up with a sigh and stared at her for several long moments, reading the micro-expressions running over her face. 'Well,' he said finally, throwing a hand up in the air. 'Then if your mind is set, I suppose there's nothing more I can do. We'll just settle up the money you owe me and you can be on your way.'

She watched as he stubbed out the cigarette and walked over to the chaise, picking up his coat and smoothing lint off the shoulders.

'Money?'

'Yes. You need to repay me the money from the advance and I'll get my accountant to send you an invoice detailing all your food and drink expenses, the clothes, this place . . . The jewels were only ever on loan, so as long as they're returned you won't be liable for them.'

Flora stared at him, seeing how he pinched the top of his hat into precise folds and placed it neatly atop his head. Her heart had begun to pound, her blood rushing in her ears. 'What do you mean, repay the advance?' Much of it had already been spent – getting her father home from the hospital in the private ambulance, buying a wheelchair for him to get about, paying the hospital and doctor's bills, his medications . . .

'As per the contract you signed, all costs were to be netted off against profits. Now, obviously, with no show there'll be no income stream, much less any profits – we'll have to refund the ticket sales – but in the event you pull out for any reason, you bear all reasonable expenses incurred to this point. Theoretically I could sue you for breach of contract too, especially at this late stage, but I'm not a malicious man.' He lifted his hat courteously and headed for the door. 'Twenty-eight days' notice is standard for payment, just so you know.'

Twenty-eight days? To repay a hundred-pound debt?

'Pepper!' she cried as he put a hand to the doorknob. Her heart felt like it might leap from her chest. All colour seemed to have drained from the room.

He turned back to her. 'Yes, Flora?' He stared at her coolly but she saw the fire in his eyes. In the space of mere minutes, everything between them had changed, and there was a look there now that she had never seen before. They both knew that she had absolutely no way of reimbursing his costs.

'You know I can't afford to pay you back.'

'Yes, I do appreciate it's going to be a problem for you – but my conscience is clear. I have creditors to keep happy too, and if you're prepared to drop me in it with them without any hesitation, I fail to see why I should grant you any special favours.'

'But if I *can't* pay you back— '

'There's no such thing as *can't*, Flora. There's always a way. It's just a question of how low you have to go. When I met you, you were hocking the only valuable possession you owned. But what will you have to sell after that, eh? What do you have that men would think worth paying for?'

There was a pause as he let the implication settle in her mind.

'I offered you a way out; I saved you from that. My business proposition threw you – and your family – a lifeline, and now here you are, living in the Paris Ritz, on the cusp of making headlines with your beauty, your talent, your sophistication. I've given you everything I said I would. And now you're throwing it back in my face?' He shrugged again.

She swallowed, hearing the truth in his words but if he

only knew the horror of what other fate she faced – losing her child forever. 'What will happen if I don't pay you? If I can't?'

His eyes narrowed. 'Well, we don't have a formal debtor's prison system any more, but a presiding judge could still see fit to lock you up. Especially if many other livelihoods are impacted by your actions.'

Flora felt her blood run cold. If she too was locked up, Mary really could take her son anywhere in the time it could take her to get out again. She would have no way of ever finding them.

She was caught in a stalemate: stay here and lose her son, or leave here and risk her freedom.

She stared at Pepperly, knowing she had no leverage, no power, no freedom. Not unless . . . A thought came to her; a terrible one, but desperate times called for desperate measures.

'I'm sorry to have to do this, Pepper, but if you insist on holding me to the contract, then . . .' She swallowed as she watched a new suspicion dawn in his eyes. 'I'll be obliged to let people know what I saw today.'

Suspicion switched to utter shock that she would dare to blackmail him. 'And what *did* you see today, Flora?' he asked, drawing the words out slowly.

'You and Marcel, in the office . . . It's against the law, you know. Not to mention, a sin.'

A silence drew out and Pepperly looked confounded by her low blow – at least, until he burst out laughing. 'Oh, Flora! How very bourgeois you are!' he cried. 'Is that it? I thought you had more originality than that! Are you really such a simpleton that you will only live according to the rules set out by the church and by the courts? You may be from humble stock, but you have the face of a queen! I thought you had an innate sophistication that raised you above the dumb sheep you tended!'

Her cheeks burned as he stepped towards her. For the first time in their relationship, she felt a distinct sense of threat.

'Come now, Flora,' he said in a low voice. 'You should know that people in glass houses should never throw stones.' Without breaking eye contact, he ran his finger firmly along the right side of her belly, just as Marie had all those weeks ago. 'The body tells tales on us, even when the mouth stays shut . . . You have secrets too,' he whispered.

Tears filled her eyes. He knew about the baby. Somehow, that . . . tiger stripe had told Marie, and she had told him.

She nodded, unable to deny it now, as a solitary tear began to slide down her cheek. '. . . Yes.'

He turned away, as if her emotion bothered him, crossing the room and going to stand by the window again. A silence ballooned between them, their mutual threats having failed, their secrets bristling in plain sight. He still held all the cards but neither one of them spoke for several moments.

'. . . Do you want to tell me about it?' he asked finally, looking back at her.

She shrugged, feeling hopeless, tears beginning to fall readily. 'What's to tell? My fiancé died. And I had to give up our baby . . . I h-had to give him away.' She dropped her head in her hands, her shoulders beginning to heave as the thought of Mary disappearing with her child took root in her mind. Donald had been the only mitigating factor in their arrangement – but now he was in police custody, being questioned for murder.

'You've been through a lot.' If his words were understated, they were also kind.

'It's worse than that, Pepper: I had hoped to get him back

again, but the woman who's got him—' Her voice quavered. 'She's disappeared. I had a call today telling me she's gone. That's why I have to go back there, do you see? If I don't find my son now, I'll lose him forever.' This time her voice fully cracked into a sob and she was surprised to feel him lead her over to the sofa and sit her down.

'No, Flora. You're wrong. Lost is lost.'

She pulled back from him in alarm. She had thought he would understand! 'But—'

'This isn't a matter of time, but of resources. Money is what you need if you want to get your son back.'

Flora blinked, stunned by the simplicity of his words. Were they true?

'Now listen – I can help you, but only if you help me.'

'H-how?'

'I've put everything on the line for this production. I had big plans for you and I've put my money where my mouth is. I'll be straight with you: if this show doesn't go ahead, then I'll be ruined – completely financially wiped out – and my creditors might come after you instead. If they do, there'll be nothing I can do to help you.'

Flora listened, appalled, as he spoke.

'*But,*' he continued, patting her hand, 'if we make this thing a success, you'll have everything you need at your disposal to find your son and get him back again. You'll be able to hire the best private detective money can buy and there'll be nowhere in the world that woman can hide from you.'

She blinked, trying to take in his words; to believe them when every instinct was telling her to find her child *now*. 'R-really?'

'Yes. I can help you do that, Flora, I promise. But it's quid pro quo.'

'Quid pro . . . ?' she faltered.

He gave a stiff smile. 'You scratch my back, I'll scratch yours.'

The corridor fell silent as they walked back in, eyes dragging over them – her – as if their showdown could be read on their faces. Pepperly hadn't said a word on the journey over, staring out of the window at the raindrops wriggling down the glass. The darkening skies were grey and the city's soundtrack had become a sluicing of wheels through puddles, far-off thunder a drumbeat to a distant storm. Flora thought of St Kilda, alone and dark and silent in the ocean, providing shelter to the fishermen but no hospitality; not any more.

'What's everyone standing around for?' he barked, striding forward as people in pairs and groups jumped out of his way and fell back into their dressing rooms. The stage was now off limits as the front-of-house team made the final preparations – vacuuming, sweeping and polishing – before the doors were opened to the public and they finally had what he called 'bums on seats'.

Flora slipped into her dressing room behind him. Estelle, in charge of her make-up, was reading a magazine on the green chaise and she jumped up with a small squeal as Flora slipped off her coat.

'M'selle!' she gasped. 'You are here!'

'Yes.'

'But where have you been? We were so worried!'

Flora gave a wan smile; she felt completely drained. 'Just a touch of nerves. But I'm all right now.'

Outside, a babble of voices rose along the backstage area as the news spread that the star had returned. It was go-go-go as everyone rushed to finish getting ready and begin warming up.

She sat down on the stool in front of her mirror and stared at her pale image. It was quite evident that she had been crying and she saw Estelle pause for a moment, seeing it too, before reaching for her creams. In the reflection, the sequinned bodysuit hung from a hanger on the rail; the coverage over the décolleté had been filled in a little, not as much as Flora would have liked, but it wasn't as sparse as before. Marie had showed her this mercy, if not absolute discretion.

She closed her eyes as Estelle began applying the base for her make-up, warm fingers rubbing her skin in rhythmic strokes.

'Some refreshment for you, M'selle Flora,' someone said and she opened her eyes to see a waitress from the bar holding a tray and setting down a freshly poured glass of champagne.

'Merci,' she murmured, taking it. She knew she needed her mind to be clear and her wits sharp but, after this afternoon's dramas, she was tense. This was the only way she had to calm herself.

She took a sip, feeling the familiar fizz of the bubbles on her tongue. Even the sensation of it was rich. She looked back at herself in the mirror again, her features already beginning to dazzle as the make-up was applied. This was the world she belonged to now – even if she was a hostage in it.

Chapter Twenty-Six

The cymbals crashed and the red velvet curtain swept down in a dramatic flourish. The audience were on their feet before they were cut off from her sight but Flora held the pose, her body in profile and her head thrown back as she lay cradled on the two points of a glittering new moon. She arched her back and pointed her toes – all the pointers that Gilles had been drilling into her uppermost in her mind – feeling the white heat of the spotlight as it settled on her with dazzling intensity.

From the other side of the curtain, she heard the roars – 'Encore! Encore!' – as she jumped to her feet and ran to her marked position on the centre of the stage, where Marcel was waiting for her. By the time the curtain was pulled back again a few moments later, she was perched on his shoulder, elbows out and hands tucked under her chin coquettishly as he paraded her around. He was shirtless, his eyes heavily ringed with black kohl and his dark hair slicked back; under the lights he looked like a panther – silken, muscular and powerful. Flora wondered whether George had said anything to him about what she had seen, for his eyes had been hard as they had taken their positions on the stage earlier; but he had behaved with professionalism, making all his marks and lifts on cue.

She smiled so hard, she thought her face might freeze as she looked out at the audience – trying and failing to see past the glare of the footlights. Further back, faces could be discerned in the dim light but not identified, and tears shone in her eyes as she soaked up the adulation, wishing she could feel happy. That it had been a triumph was indisputable and the applause seemed endless, cheers and shouts still coming as Marcel carried her first one way, then the other; single stems of roses were thrown onto the stage and she could see Gilles standing in the wings, clapping too, laughing as tears rolled down his cheeks.

'Paris adores you, chérie,' Marcel murmured as he finally dropped to his knees in the heroic style and she slid off his shoulder. He must have been exhausted and yet he made her appear weightless, stepping back balletically with his arms outstretched so that she might glide forward and take her final bow. She pressed a hand to her heart as Gilles had taught her to do, then dropped her head graciously, and the curtain this time came down with a final swish.

Immediately the backstage area erupted, the dancers all running to hug one another, everyone crowding around Gilles and cheering him. George was somewhere on the other side of the curtain, in the audience, and Flora stood alone by the velvet drape, breathless and panting from her efforts; her skin felt damp from the heat of the lights, the mesh bodysuit itchy against her skin. She waited a moment for a happy look or a kind word from someone – anyone – but no one was looking her way.

She was being punished.

If she had just made the show a success, she had also almost torpedoed it. She wouldn't be forgiven in a hurry, nor would she be trusted.

'Brava, m'selle,' one of the stagehands mumbled, managing to pass her the silk robe without meeting her eye.

'Merci,' she murmured, covering herself and hurrying back to the dressing room. She slammed the door shut and climbed onto the green chaise while the sound of champagne corks popping carried through the walls, everyone laughing and celebrating. She could hear them making plans to go out dancing whilst all she wanted to do was catch the next ferry back to Dover—

There was a knock at the door.

'Not now!' she pleaded, but it was flung open the next moment and in trooped a line of porters, all with armfuls of bouquets. Flora looked on in despair as twelve, thirteen . . . fourteen extravagant arrangements were laid on the dressing table and, when that was full, along the floor.

'I guarantee there'll be triple that amount by the time you arrive for make-up tomorrow,' a voice said. She looked up to find George standing by the door, his overcoat slung over one arm, the other hand in his trouser pocket. He waited for the porters to file out before coming fully into the room. A bottle of Dom Perignon had been set in an ice bucket and he poured them each a fresh glass.

'Félicitations.'

'Félicitations.'

They both took deep swallows; the champagne tasted bitter now and the tension in the room was thick as Flora waited for his verdict. The audience had liked it – but had he? Had she done enough to guarantee them the box-office sales they both needed so badly?

'Well,' he shrugged. 'It's official – you're a sensation.' He gave her a token smile, but she saw the disappointment in his eyes. For all the success and plaudits, the victory had been tarnished by this afternoon's showdown. They had struck a truce but neither of them could take back the threats they had made, and she sensed something in their relationship had irrevocably changed. The innocence of their partnership had been lost.

'Just as you said I would be,' she said haltingly.

'Yes.'

There was a silence, all their closeness, the familial intimacy that had built up over almost two months, gone at a stroke.

She knew she had to do more. 'Pepper . . . I owe you everything.'

'Yes, you do.' He took another sip of champagne and looked steadily at her, then appeared to relent a little. 'You look tired; you should rest. You worked hard out there tonight.'

'I really tried my best.'

'It was enough. They loved you. The manager's already asking about extending the run . . .'

Flora felt her heart drop as she looked at him in alarm.

'But I've told him no.'

She felt a spike of renewed hope, just as there was another knock at the door.

'Come in,' he said.

The door opened and Marie walked through, barely able to see over the bundle draped in her arms. Flora watched in silent wonder as she hung a liquid silver satin gown on the rail, followed by a fur coat so plush, her hand would fully disappear in the pelt were she to touch it.

Marie met her eye with a certain sheepishness and Flora wondered if she knew her part in today's proceedings. Her indiscretion had cost Flora dearly.

'Merci, Marie,' George murmured as she left again. 'Madame Vionnet has been so kind as to lend you this gown for the evening.'

Flora looked at him. This evening? Why should she need a gown when all she was going to do was roll into the car, get back into the hotel and climb into bed? She was too tired even to eat.

'We're going for dinner. At Maxim's.'

She had heard of it, of course she had. Even a St Kildan newly arrived in the city soon heard of Maxim's.

'Oh. Thank you, but I'm not hungry,' she demurred.

'That's fine,' he shrugged, pulling out a cigarette and lighting it. 'The food's incidental anyway. We're not going there to eat.'

'Then what are we going there for?'

'To be seen.'

She blinked, feeling aghast at the thought of getting herself revved up for another one of their soirees.

'But . . .'

'It's business, Flora. This is how things are done in the industry. You need to be seen. We need to create buzz – and after what everyone's just seen here tonight, your arrival at the most exclusive restaurant in the city will be the crowning touch. They'll be expecting to see you there. Besides, there are people I need you to meet: producers, directors, scouts. They came in especially for the show and they're flying out again tomorrow; we can't afford to wait.' He took a deep drag on the cigarette. 'There's one chap in particular keen to meet you – an executive producer, my main money man; he's had a run of hits lately and he's got the Big Five studios' ear.'

'But it's so late now. It's . . .'

'Eleven, yes. But no one who's anyone dines at Maxim's before ten thirty anyway.' He rose, draining his glass and setting it down among the bouquets. 'I'll be waiting round the front for you. I've arranged for some photographers to wait there too, so be ready for them with a smile. And wear the sable – let it drop off one shoulder. The French love a little *insouciance.'*

An-what?

She watched as he pulled a slim red box from his coat pocket and set it down on the counter with a pat. 'Just borrowed, mind, so be careful with them . . . I'll see you in half an hour.'

The door closed softly behind him and she stared at it in despair. She wandered over to the dressing table and opened the Cartier box: rubies. A bracelet and earrings, set in open-work platinum and alternated with diamonds.

She went over to the rail too, plunging her hand into the fur and rubbing it against her cheek. She had never known anything so soft and she felt the urge to wrap herself in it, to curl up like a fawn and sleep in it beneath the moon.

But she drew her hand back quickly, refusing to be seduced; she knew now the cost of these luxuries. It was all a masquerade. None of this was really hers but she would be paying for it all, one way or another.

George would see to that.

'Bonsoir, Monsieur Pepperly,' the man said, inclining his head respectfully as he held open the car door while George stepped out. There was a moment of calm but as Flora's foot, then leg, emerged, the photographers' flashbulbs began popping.

'M'selle Flora!' they called, having possession of her name now, each one wanting her attention and direct eye contact for their publications.

Flora did as she had been instructed in the car and stopped for a few moments, holding her poses and smiling as brightly as she could manage. This was the night on which her new life began, Pepperly had told her – these were the moments that would cement her future glory. She had to act the star here, in this glare, as much as she did on the stage.

'Flora, come,' he said presently, indicating their time was up. 'Always good to leave them wanting more,' he added under his breath as the door to Maxim's was opened and they stepped inside.

'Ah, Monsieur Pepperly, an honour to see you again – and on such a night as this! The grande salle is alight with excitement about your new show.'

George smiled, looking satisfied. 'Merci, Albert. May I introduce you to M'selle Flora MacQueen? You're going to be seeing a lot of her in the coming weeks.'

'An honour, m'selle,' said the maître d'hôtel, taking her hand and kissing the back of it lightly. 'Please – allow me to show you to your table.'

Flora held her breath, clutching the sable closed with one hand as she walked between the two men into a room that was beyond all her imaginings. She slept each night in the eighteenth-century splendour of the Ritz, and she had sat in a box amid the baroque magnificence of the Paris Opéra; but here was a modern glamour that took her breath away. Golden walls were decorated with giant frescoes of nymphs; huge oval mirrors were framed with gilded swirls that reached like the tentacles of jellyfish; richly painted glass roof tiles cast a low, atmospheric light.

The noise level was high as two hundred people laughed and talked over one another, bottles of champagne wedged in silver ice buckets, small electric lamps set on each table – but there was an audible break in conversation as their entrance was noted, people leaning in to whisper as they passed. Their progress through the room was slow, almost stately, as people clamoured to catch Pepperly's eye.

'Pepper, good to see you—'

'How was Berlin?'

'Heard the Revue's gone down a storm!'

'Return my calls, will you? Paramount's on my neck—'

'First thing tomorrow,' Pepperly grinned, shaking one man's hand enthusiastically. 'I may have something.'

'Your usual table, sir,' Albert said, stopping at a large, round table set for eight in the centre of the room. Five men were already seated there and they jumped up as Flora and George approached.

'Good to see you fellas,' George said, immediately pumping their hands with a jollity that had been missing on the car ride over. 'Glad you could join us.'

'We wouldn't have missed this for the world,' one of them drawled. He had an American accent and a thin, dark moustache. 'Pleased to meet you, ma'am. Charlie Buck at your service.'

'Good evening, Mr Buck,' she replied as he kissed the back of her hand, distinguishing himself from the rest with his keen manners.

'Flora, meet Robert Kinney; Johnny Adler; Jimmy Cripshank; Ronald Wilson.'

'Call me Ronnie,' Wilson said when it was his turn to kiss her hand.

'Ronnie,' she obliged.

'You have a beautiful accent, Miss MacQueen,' James Adler said. 'Very . . . soft.'

'You really weren't pulling our legs,' Charlie Buck said, jogging George, who was standing beside him, with his elbow. 'She's more beautiful than Cleopatra.'

But before she could reply, a waiter stepped forward. 'Your coat, m'selle?'

Flora allowed the sable to slip off her shoulders, revealing the mercurial silver satin dress hidden beneath. It clung to her body, a deep scoop at the back revealing bare skin, and she wished that she still had the long hair of her girlhood; instead her chic bob left her exposed, eyes boring into her as a chair was held out and she took her seat among the men. She felt gazes run down the very length of her and back up again, looks being swapped. She tucked her hair behind one ear, the ruby bracelet twinkling under the lights. Once, she had liked being seen, being recognized as the most beautiful woman in any room, but now she felt somehow . . . vulnerable, like a rare orchid everyone wanted to pick.

'Eddie's running late,' Jimmy Cripshank said as the waiter began pouring champagne. 'Traffic, apparently.'

'Plus ça change,' George muttered with a wry look. Flora sensed she was missing an inside joke.

'You know, you always get the best tables, Pepper. If I ever come here without you, they place me on the right side,' Ronnie said, sitting back in his chair, fingers interlaced.

'Right side?' Charlie Buck sucked through his teeth. 'Social Siberia, old man.'

'I am a habitué,' George shrugged. 'Loyalty is valued here,' he added, pointedly looking across at Flora.

Robert Kinney leaned in, drumming his fingers on the table. 'You know, this place is all it's cracked up to be too. I heard someone say they've a million bucks' worth of wine in the cellars under here.'

'Here, and a couple of other locations,' Pepperly said.

'So it's true, then? A million bucks' worth?'

The other men laughed. 'Why? Are you planning a raid, Kinney?' Charlie Buck teased.

Flora looked around as the men talked. Their eyes kept settling upon her and then lifting off again, like restless birds. She knew she was being scrutinized: how she held her glass ('always the stem', George had shown her), how she sat, her profile, her laugh . . . The past few weeks' instruction had been preparing her for this moment and outwardly, it was all going to plan. In fact, it couldn't be going better. She was relieved they didn't seem much interested in talking to her, only looking.

'I saw MGM took a hit on the Buster Keaton movie,' George said to Jimmy Cripshank.

'Yep. Yep, they've been giving Sedgwick hell all summer about the above-line figures.' He looked at Flora. 'Pardon my French, Miss MacQueen.'

Flora blinked, unaware any French had been spoken.

'What's Kitty Sullivan's contract?' George asked, looking interested.

'Seven projects over three years. But Fox have been making a play, so they might buy her out. They think she'd look good opposite Fred Winters.'

Ronnie laughed. 'I think she'd look good under—' He stopped himself abruptly.

'Do you smoke, Miss MacQueen?' Charlie Buck asked, proffering a cigarette from his gold case.

She shook her head. 'No. Thank you.'

There was a small silence as the men either lit up or reached for their drinks. Flora felt no compunction to move at all; her conversation wasn't necessary, merely her presence.

'. . . Reckon Paramount will sell her?' George asked, striking up the conversation once more.

'Might have to,' Joe shrugged. 'They went in too big on constructing all those movie theatres and audience figures are going down. They're at about, what, a thirty per cent drop?'

''Bout that,' Robert Kinney agreed.

'They need some liquidity – and a hit. Fast,' Jimmy Cripshank murmured.

'Things are getting bad over there, huh?' George asked.

'Like you wouldn't believe. Watch out – it'll make its way over here too.'

'Already has. We're all feeling the squeeze.'

'Yeah, but it hasn't *really* started to bite here yet.' Cripshank gestured around the opulent room, one eyebrow raised sardonically at the women in velvet and satin and furs, jewels and crystals gleaming, men in white tie and polished patent shoes. 'Y' know?'

George smiled. 'Are you saying you think the industry is a duff? We should all get out?'

'Hell, no! Pardon my French, Miss MacQueen,' he said again, covering her hand apologetically with his own. 'We just can't afford any more turkeys. If we want audiences to come back, we need to invest in top-quality sets, first-rate scripts . . . and talent.' He looked across at Flora. 'I mean, can you think of a man alive who wouldn't pay his last dime to look at that face?'

'I know quite a few dead fellas who'd pay it too,' Ronnie chimed in, making them all laugh.

'Well, well, well: you've started without me, I see.' The cut-glass English accent cut through the relaxed American vowels and everyone looked up. Flora felt the man's presence right behind her chair, and the hairs stood up on the back of her neck; given her bare skin and short hair, he might even be able to see them.

'Experience has taught us not to let the fizz go flat waiting for you, old boy,' Robert Kinney quipped. 'Bad traffic, was it?' His knowing laugh suggested it wasn't.

George pushed back his chair and shook the newcomer's hand enthusiastically. 'So you made it. I'm glad you could join us. There's someone I want you to meet.'

'Pepper, old boy!'

George stepped back to create a space beside Flora for the movie mogul to step into. Flora found her hand being clasped and lifted before she could even see his face.

But she knew that voice. And as his head tipped down, his lips upon her hand, she recognized those blond curls too.

'Actually, we've already met,' Edward Rushton smiled, lifting his head and looking straight into her eyes. '. . . How are you, Flora?'

Chapter Twenty-Seven

An old friend. That was how he treated her as they ate a three-course dinner, reminiscing about 'times past' as if they'd had more than a single eventful day together; as if his parting words hadn't been shot through with blood, fists and hatred.

But all their worlds had changed since then: James had died; Edward was living in Hollywood; she was the toast of Paris; passions and tempers had long since cooled. Perhaps it had been, for Edward, exactly as James had warned her: he was quick to love and just as quick to move on, the high drama forgotten once his attention was caught by something new. Flora didn't care either way. Edward's fond smiles made up for George's lingering coolness, his jokes a respite to the day's tears. She felt warmed up from the inside as he told stories about her home.

'I feel rather honoured to have the distinction of being the man who introduced Flora to her first ever . . .'

The men all waited, transfixed, as an innuendo hovered.

'. . . picnic.'

'What?' Ronald laughed. 'Surely not?'

'Oh, believe me – when I say it was another world on St Kilda, what I really mean is, it was another time. Eighteen-eighty, in fact.'

They laughed again.

'No cars?' Ronald asked.

'No cars? No horses!'

'Well, radios then, surely.'

'Not even a postal boat! One of the old boys told me they didn't hear of Queen Victoria's death for several weeks. Nor of the sinking of *Titanic* for over a month.'

'No!'

'Oh! That was a distinct step-up by all accounts. Apparently, a century earlier, it had been a full year before they heard of the Battle of Waterloo!'

The table was in uproar, the men slapping their hands on their thighs, cigars shaking in their fingers. Flora laughed too. She could see how it seemed funny to them, the *quaintness* of isolation.

'Just extraordinary!' Joe marvelled with a sigh, looking at her with fascination. 'And yet, to see her sitting here, dressed in . . .'

'Vionnet,' George supplied helpfully.

'Indeed! Vionnet and . . .'

'Cartier.'

'Cartier jewels.' He laughed. 'She looks as if she grew up in Bel Air!'

'Well, cream always rises to the top,' Edward said, looking at Flora proudly. 'I knew the moment I saw her that she was destined for greatness.'

'As did I,' George chimed in quickly, not wanting to lose his claim to any proprietary deals.

The two businessmen smiled at one another as if in understanding. If Edward had met Flora first, it was George who had brought her here, to Paris.

'But . . . when I saw you last, you weren't anything at all to do with motion films,' Flora said to him, using her voice at last. 'You were wanting to invest in that man's business. Oh – what was his name? When we were having dinner on the deck. You and your father . . .'

Edward thought back for a moment. 'Oh, you mean Cecil Hatry!'

The men roared again at the mention of this name. They were five bottles into a 'particularly good' Malbec and had started on the brandy. 'Old Hat-Trick Hatry? Christ, man, you didn't fall for it, did you?' Joe Carter frowned.

'Nearly. Very nearly. But a . . .' He glanced at her. 'A good friend had reservations about his funding, and – trusting his judgement – I pulled back from my pledge. In the nick of time, it turned out.' He shrugged. 'So, with the money suddenly freed up, I turned my attention to Hollywood instead before Father could object. All rather serendipitous, really.'

Flora stared at the table, feeling her heart tighten at the brief allusion to James. She wanted to ask Edward what he knew of the accident – who had told him? Had there been a funeral? Did any of his family know about her? Did they know he had proposed with his mother's ring? For the first time, it struck her that they were unaware James had a baby son, out there in the world somewhere, being raised by a woman who wasn't his mother.

Oh, God – the feelings were surging inside her like storm waves again and it was all she could do to remain in her chair. Her fingers gripped the edge of the table as she reminded herself that this dinner, with these men, was the only way she could get him back. They controlled the purse strings, and money would give her the power she needed. It was the god she must worship if she was to find her child.

'What did Hatry do?' she asked, trying to look interested.

'Committed corporate fraud on a colossal scale,' Edward

smiled. 'He forged over a million pounds' worth of securities as collateral for the financing of a project that would amalgamate the British steel industry.'

'Oh,' Flora murmured, even though she had no idea what securities or collateral were. She could feel George's gaze upon her and she knew he could tell that she was out of her depth. Ordinarily this would have been one of his teaching opportunities; but if their *contretemps* today had thrown up a wall between them, her acquaintance with Edward seemed to have pulled her further out of his sphere. Suddenly he was no longer the man who exclusively controlled access to her – it had been made quite clear to everyone around the table that Edward had known her first, and she felt a new anxiety in George's gaze.

'What did he get in the end?' Charlie Buck asked.

'Fourteen years,' Edward replied. 'Two, hard labour.'

'Damn.' Charlie winced and sucked his teeth. 'That'll hurt a man used to the finer things. It all came to court pretty quick, as I recall.'

'Well, he confessed. To Cecil's credit, he knew the game was up.' Edward reached for the humidor that had been set on the table and selected a cigar. 'There's something to be said for coming clean when you're caught with your hand in the biscuit jar.'

Flora's eyes flickered towards him – the words had felt somehow pointed – but he was focusing on cutting his cigar.

'Well, Hatry's loss was certainly your gain,' Robert Kinney said, toasting his glass in Edward's direction. 'You've got the Midas touch in Tinseltown, that's for sure.'

'What can I say? It suits me there – the weather, the lifestyle . . .'

There was a pause.

349

'The question is, do you think it will suit Flora here too?' George asked him, getting at last to the point of this dinner. Everything – the best table at the best restaurant, the fur, the jewels, the gown, the champagne . . . all of it had been geared towards softening any resistance to Phase Two of his master plan.

The men fell silent, all eyes on Edward. Flora realized that he, out of all of them, was the one who held the power. It was his opinion that mattered.

She swallowed as she met his gaze, awaiting his verdict. He had once promised to be the one to bring her into this bright, shiny world. Perhaps this wasn't how he had envisaged it but she could see now, from the way his eyes sparkled when he smiled at her, that those ambitions hadn't entirely faded.

'Well, there's no doubt the camera would adore her,' he shrugged, his fingers pressed together in a steeple as he considered her beauty objectively. 'And we've all seen tonight that she can sing and dance. Acting, though, she remains untested. An unknown risk, and the new wave of films is far more rigorous in its demands.'

'I've got Flora working with Christophe Balzac three days a week,' George said. 'Now the show's up and running, we can increase that to five.'

'Balzac? He's good,' Cripshank said, looking impressed.

'And he's very pleased with Flora. He believes she'll have good range.'

Behind him, the band started up and several couples took to the dance floor. Flora saw how they moved in perfect synchronicity, bodies pressed together as they whirled and laughed. She had been instructed in the foxtrot and waltz as part of her dance training.

'If Balzac thinks she can deliver, then as far as I'm concerned she's the whole package. There's no doubt she's got presence. Wouldn't you agree, boys?' Robert Kinney asked. 'Let's get her over!'

But he was getting ahead of himself.

'Ed?' George asked. It was Edward's say-so he wanted.

'I have one condition,' Edward said, slowly raising an eyebrow, his eyes locked upon Flora.

'Oh?' George cleared his throat, looking tense.

Edward pushed back his chair and rose, gallantly holding out a hand. 'I get to have the first dance.'

'Well, I think we can say that was a successful evening!' Charlie Buck said as he was helped into his black astrakhan coat, cigar still clamped between his lips. Flora was enclosed in her sable again and clutching it tightly; the rain had stopped but there was a distinct chill in the air, heralding the city's gradual slink into winter. Cars and taxis rushed past, the roads busy even at this late hour, whisking glamorous incumbents back to plush homes and elegant apartments.

The door to a 1925 Rolls-Royce Phantom was held open by George's driver and Flora automatically went to his side. Everyone was saying their goodbyes, pumping his hand with zeal, all pleased with the night's business. She smiled and offered her hand to be kissed once more as the men bade their adieus and those flying back said they would look forward to seeing her next in the Golden State.

Edward came and stood in front of George, and Flora felt a rush of panic that he was about to leave. There had been no opportunity for them to talk privately at all; even when they had danced, the music had been too loud to speak over and people had constantly interrupted them, a few even trying to 'cut in'.

'Well,' George said, holding out his hand, 'I'll be in touch about the details for coming out. As I said, we have a three-month commitment to oblige here—'

'Yes, yes,' Edward said distractedly. 'See here, why don't I drop Flora back at her hotel?'

'That's not necessary.' George's reply was quick but firm.

'Not necessary, no, but I think we'd both like the opportunity to talk a little in private. We're old friends, after all.' He looked at Flora, seeming to read her mind. 'Would you like that, Flora?'

She knew from Pepperly's expression that she should say no, that this was a chance to demonstrate her loyalty after a testing day. She also knew no real good could come of stepping back into the past. But Edward was her first and last link to James, and even if the temptation to grab onto it was self-destructive, she found herself nodding in reply.

George stiffened, registering it as a rejection. Did he sense his control slipping?

He tried again. 'I'm afraid it's been a very long day – and Flora and I, too, have things we need to discuss.'

Edward laughed, leaning forward and slapping him on the shoulder. 'Give the poor girl a break, Pepper! There's plenty of time for that tomorrow. Don't spur the willing horse and all that! You don't want to wear her out on day one!'

'Shall we have breakfast together and discuss things then?' Flora suggested to George, trying to build a bridge. 'We could order some pastries from Angelina's?'

'Angelina's?' Edward chuckled, reaching over and squeezing the back of her neck affectionately. Flora fell still at the unexpected touch. 'You really have schooled her in the art of living well.'

George looked between them both, visibly unhappy, before relenting. 'Very well, then.'

'À demain, Pepper,' she smiled over her shoulder at him, as Edward offered his arm and led her away. She felt the satin dress swish against her legs as they approached a pale blue Bentley purring softly on the cobbles. The door was held open and she slid in, Edward smiling as he came around the other side.

Flora felt the tension inside her begin to ease for the first time all evening as they pulled away. She was finally alone with the man who knew James almost better than anyone, and she could feel his ghost sitting between them. It was all she could have, but she'd take it anyway.

'My, my,' Edward said as they walked into her room, throwing down his coat and taking in the splendid decor – cream walls and rose taffeta drapery were set off by gilded rococo mirrors and urns of fresh flowers, the pale grey carpet like velvet beneath their feet. 'Old Pepper really did see the bright lights when he set eyes on you, didn't he?'

'He was certainly persuasive,' she said, slipping off her high-heeled shoes with relief; they were not a part of this new life she would ever enjoy, and she let her toes spread as she headed straight for the comfort of the soft sofa. She curled up, grateful to relax at last.

'Remind me – where was it you met him? He did tell me . . .' he asked, walking over to the window and peering into the courtyard, now moodily lit. His silhouette was immaculately tailored, his movements more mannered than she remembered from the island as they had walked along the beach. California living clearly suited him – he was even more striking with a tan, his blond hair brightened by the sun.

She still couldn't believe *he* was George's money man – producer, benefactor, sponsor, fairy godfather, 'however you want to think of it', George had said in the car on the way to Maxim's as he had impressed upon her the importance of this dinner. And yet her memory of Edward's soft, pale feet somehow undermined the image of him as powerful Hollywood power broker. It was difficult to believe that he had the final word in all of this. Harsh though it might be, compared to James, he'd always seemed something of a fool.

'Glasgow.'

'Ah, yes.' He turned back to her, looking impressed. 'Glasgow's a big city for an island girl.'

'Aye.'

'What took you there?'

She swallowed, not wanting to lie. 'I went to have my hair cut.' It wasn't an *un*truth; she simply stopped short of telling him she'd then sold the hair that had been cut. From this new, elevated vantage point, from this silk sofa, it seemed so . . . undignified.

'He said you met in a pawn shop?'

'Oh, maybe . . . I don't really remember.'

He squinted, thinking hard, jabbing a finger in the air. 'No, it was – I recall he said he helped you to negotiate a better deal . . . Typical Pepper, just can't help himself.' He looked back at her and she saw a growing puzzlement in his expression.

'What?'

'Well, I don't mean to be disrespectful, but what did you have of value to pawn?'

Flora felt her cheeks burn at the blunt enquiry, though it wasn't an unreasonable question given what he knew of her background. But how could she tell him she had been hawking James's engagement ring? Did he even know they'd been engaged? She had no idea what Edward knew about how far

354

things had gone between them. James's name hadn't been mentioned by either of them over dinner, but they both felt it hovering in the air – and this conversation inched him closer into becoming real again. Alive once more, if only momentarily.

Edward suddenly squeezed his eyes shut, shaking his head quickly and putting a hand out, as if to stop her from saying his name. 'Good Lord – I'm sorry. Forgive me, Flora, that was unspeakably rude! Don't answer that.'

He wandered over to the cocktail cabinet and had a good look at the contents before turning back to her with a mischievous grin she recognized. 'What do you say – a White Lady for a nightcap? For old times' sake?'

How could she refuse? Old times' sake was why they were both here, after all. She had questions to ask and no doubt he did too. 'Well, so long as it's a small one.'

He glanced over with a sympathetic look. 'You must be dropping.'

'I am weary,' she smiled, feeling the burning exhaustion in her limbs. She had been whirled around the dance floor for at least an hour and the show itself had been physically draining, but it was the ache in her heart that ran her flat. It was taking everything she had to stay here, to sit still and smile while her baby son—

Flirt, George had instructed her. *Sparkle. Be light.*

'Well, this will give you a little buzz before sleep. You've earnt it. Did you enjoy Maxim's?' He poured and mixed the liquids, stirring with assurance.

'It was wonderful,' she sighed, twirling a wrist fancifully. 'The room was so beautiful. And all the ladies in their evening gowns—' She stopped as she saw him smirk. 'What?'

He hesitated, as if startled to have been caught. 'Oh . . . nothing.'

'Please – say,' she insisted.

'Well,' he shrugged. 'There's just a saying that Maxim's is a place where women are seen, but never ladies . . .'

Flora blinked, catching the drift quickly.

'A stupid distinction. I . . . I shouldn't have laughed, it's a silly thing,' he said quickly. 'Far too much brandy, clearly. I'm sorry for being so crass. Hollywood does rather blunt one's manners.'

She stared at him, feeling somehow unnerved by the observation as he brought over the cocktails in striking waisted glasses. He sat down with a groan on the other end of the sofa, revealing black silk socks. 'Cheers.'

'. . . Cheers.' She drank a few sips, trying not to shudder; she had forgotten the sour taste, having quickly grown accustomed to champagne.

'Funny, isn't it?' he murmured after a moment, stretching one arm along the back of the sofa and looking idly around the room. 'Us . . . being here together . . . The Paris Ritz!' He laughed. 'Who'd have thought?'

'I know. Every morning, when I wake up, it's such a shock to find myself here. I canna get used to it.'

He looked across at her understandingly. 'Your world's changed a lot since I saw you last.'

'Aye, it has. But so has yours. You live in America now.'

'It's not the same, though. We're divided by a common language but that's largely it,' he demurred. 'For you, though, nothing at all is as it was.'

She looked down at her hands. 'I suppose that's true.' Truer than he would ever know.

'. . . Was it hard, the evacuation? I read about it in the States.'

'You did?'

'Yes. Didn't I tell you that once – that you St Kildans have a reputation the world over? I feel sure I did. You're no ordinary islanders.'

She marvelled at the thought that people should care about the fate of their thirty-six-strong community. 'Well, yes – it was hard saying goodbye for good. So much happened in that last year . . . It was difficult leaving people behind, for one thing.'

'Oh? I thought everyone left?'

'Aye, they did. I meant . . . leaving behind the recently departed.'

He frowned. 'Who had recently died?'

'My friend Molly Ferguson, for one.'

'Molly F—?' He looked shocked. 'Wasn't she the girl who taught Sophia to knit?'

'Aye.'

'But what happened to her? Don't say it was a climbing accident?'

'Pneumonia. We had heavy snow early in the season and there was a drama with the sheep; she caught cold and . . . never recovered.'

He looked dumbstruck.

'It was her passing that became the reason for the decision to request evacuation, actually. If we'd been on the mainland, with access to a hospital, Molly most likely would have survived. It just didn't seem . . . reasonable any more, that we should all be living with such risks.'

'No, I can see that,' he murmured, looking upset. 'My God, the poor girl. She was a lovely thing.'

'Aye. One of my closest friends.'

They were quiet for a moment, letting a respectful silence build.

'And what about that other friend of yours?' he asked. 'The tomboy dressed in boys' clothes and climbing cliffs.'

'Effie? Believe it or not, she is working for the Earl of Dumfries now. He's an avid egg collector and . . . well, she knows birds' eggs,' Flora shrugged, wishing her friend's name hadn't been raised in this particular conversation. Would Mhairi have arrived with her by now?

'Hm. It sounds very different to becoming a Hollywood star.'

'I'm not that yet,' she protested.

'Oh, but you will be. George knows it. I know it. You know it too, in your bones. I said from the start that a face like yours needed to be seen by the world, didn't I?' He joshed her hand with his as he joked, wanting acknowledgement.

'Aye, you did,' she conceded, noticing that his hand didn't withdraw.

He looked at her, his smile fading a little. 'I just . . . Well, it never crossed my mind that *this* would be the set-up if we were to be over here together. A business arrangement.'

'I know,' she murmured. 'It's all so strange.'

James shimmered between them like a ghost, almost solid, almost real. She could see Edward sense it too, his gaze meeting hers as they finally came to the moment they had both been waiting for all night.

He gave a small smile. 'It brings us, I suppose, around to James. He's not even here and yet still he is somehow looming large over us.'

'Aye,' she said, with a small, sad smile back, summoning her courage. 'I . . . I miss him so much, Edward. There's been no one I can talk to about him. No one who knew him. Not like you.'

Edward's smile became fixed upon his mouth as he saw

358

the tears gather in her eyes and she knew it must hurt him – or at least his pride – to hear her talk about James this way, even after all this time. After all these changes . . .

'When did you hear?' she asked him.

'Hear?'

She swallowed. 'That he'd died.'

Edward stared at her, as if her words were arrows and she realized his grief was still as raw as her own; for a moment she thought he wasn't going to answer at all, but then he jumped up suddenly and walked over to the fireplace, trailing a hand along the mantel. '. . . In the summer . . .' He cleared his throat, composing himself. 'We weren't on speaking terms, so . . .' His fingers tapped on the marble. 'But mutual friends . . . passed it on, you know.' She could tell by the strain in his voice that it was a difficult subject for him to talk about; whatever tensions there had been between the two men, they had been old friends, after all.

'Yes.' She looked down, not wanting to remember how she had learned the news – and what it had led to.

'What exactly happened between the two of you?' he asked, his gaze moving around the room before finally settling upon her.

She bit the inside of her cheek, feeling emotions rise along with memories. 'He came back . . . a couple of times.'

'To St Kilda?' He looked surprised. 'But I understood access wasn't possible after the summer?'

'That's true, but the first time he came back was . . . just a couple of weeks later, while the sea was still calm. He sailed over with Sir Thomas Lipton.'

'Ah, of course.' Edward looked away for a moment and she could see that he was hurt. 'Handy, having so many friends with boats,' he murmured.

Flora didn't know what to say to that.

'. . . And the next time?'

She looked down, feeling her cheeks grow pink at the memory. 'It was just before Christmas. He came by seaplane – from Iceland. They were just about to move up to Greenland.'

There was a long pause, as if Edward was coming to understand the effort his former friend had made in order to see her. '. . . I see.'

'We loved each other, Edward. It wasn't . . . it wasn't just a fancy.'

'No?'

She wondered whether that made it better or worse for him. 'He asked me to marry him – and I accepted.'

Edward blew out through his cheeks suddenly and whirled on his heel, turning away from her. 'Christ, right . . . I see.' He tapped his fingers on the mantelpiece again, clearly agitated by the news.

She didn't know what to say. His unsettled reaction had thrown her. All evening, his behaviour had been nothing but friendly – as if he really had moved on, and was no longer bothered about his brief flirtation with an island girl.

'My apologies, Flora,' he murmured over his shoulder as the silence lengthened. 'It's rather a lot for a fellow to take in, is all. I had no idea things had . . . progressed like that. Naturally I mourned the friendship *I* had lost. The betrayal felt unforgivable and it was difficult for me to forget the way he went about things. So underhand . . .' He swallowed. 'And Sophia was devastated, of course. My entire family . . . It was a difficult time, you understand.'

'Of course . . . I'm so sorry. We never wanted to hurt anyone. It was just somehow . . . there, between us.'

He nodded and when he finally turned back to face her, it was with an inscrutable expression, all his own pain hidden.

'Well,' he said finally, trying to raise a smile. 'I won't be a sore loser and wallow in hurt pride. I made my peace with things a year ago. I lost him long before everyone else.' He walked back over to the sofa and sat beside her again, resting his hand upon hers. 'But I'm very sorry for you, Flora. It's a terrible thing to lose someone so dear.'

'Thank you,' she whispered, although somehow she still felt as alone with her grief as she had before. They had been united by a common loss and she had hoped to find in Edward a sort of kinship – but Edward had grieved the loss of James many months before he'd actually died. It wasn't the same thing.

'At least . . .' He gestured to the room. 'Well, look at you now: in Paris, living every young woman's dream.'

She knew he was trying to sound encouraging, but his words rang hollow to her ear. What did she care for sitting in silks in Paris when James was dead and her child lay in Mary McKinnon's arms, in some distant, unknown place?

'Flora.' She felt the pressure of his hand on her arm and as she looked into his eyes, saw his open adoration, still. 'Let me take you to lunch tomorrow.' His finger stroked lightly over her bare skin and the small gesture made her want to leap up, to move away.

'But I thought you were leaving,' she murmured.

'I'll push it back a few days. I can see that you need a friend. A proper friend. Someone who really knows you.'

Did he 'really know' her?

'Truly, there's no need,' she demurred.

'But look at the two of us, sitting here together. Fate's

brought us into one another's lives for a second time. That must mean something, surely?'

His finger still stroked her skin but an intensity had come into his eyes now too, and she realized with sudden alarm what was coming next. Smoothly, he slid closer to her on the sofa, reaching over and kissing her before she could protest.

His lips tasted of brandy, his tongue pressing into her mouth and urgently filling her, another hand running up her thigh, rumpling her dress. She pulled back and he smiled, as if pleased by her response – even though she hadn't responded. Her lips hadn't kissed his in return and she had felt only panic as he invaded her body.

She wasn't ready. She wasn't sure she would ever be ready for him.

'Edward—' she gasped as his grip tightened around her arms.

There came a sound at the door, a key slipping into the lock, and they turned to find Pepperly standing in the doorway, still wearing his evening coat and hat.

'Pepper!' Flora exclaimed with relief.

'I . . . I . . .' He was out of breath and looked wild-eyed as he took in the scene of them together, on the sofa.

'George?' Edward frowned, sitting up. '. . . What brings you here?'

'I . . .' Pepperly straightened up, taking off his hat as he stepped into the room. 'I forgot to mention . . . *The Times* wants an interview with you, Flora.'

Edward blinked. 'What, *now*?'

'No – God, no.' The producer shook his head brusquely. 'Next few days or so, they'll confirm nearer the time.'

There was a confused pause.

'And this couldn't wait until breakfast tomorrow?' Edward

asked, sounding displeased. He had pulled back and had one arm slung across the back of the seat again as he reached for and cradled the last of his drink.

'Well, I . . . didn't want to forget,' Pepperly bumbled. 'So much going on and whatnot, at the moment.'

'Indeed,' Edward agreed, watching him with a suspicious look as Pepperly strolled towards the windows and blindly looked out, already knowing what he would see. '. . . I wasn't aware you had a key.'

Pepperly shrugged. 'Well, it's my name on the bill here, after all. I thought Flora might already be asleep and I didn't want to disturb her by knocking.'

'Very thoughtful of you, old boy,' Edward nodded, a faint smile flickering on his lips. The two men regarded one another for a moment. George made no move to leave again, for which Flora felt peculiarly grateful; she was reminded of James loitering on deck and on the stairs that night on the yacht, determined to thwart Edward's heavy-handed romantic manoeuvres.

The strange encounter held for a few long moments, growing increasingly awkward, until Edward finally threw back the last of his cocktail and set it down on the table. 'Well, I ought to be heading back. You've had a busy day, Flora – you must get some rest. I'll collect you at noon tomorrow, shall I?'

'What's happening tomorrow?' George asked proprietorially, ever concerned about losing his cut.

'We're having lunch together,' Edward said, adjusting his cufflinks. 'I've decided to stay in town for a few more days.'

'Ah, sorry, no can do,' George said flatly. 'We'll be in rehearsals all day. Gilles wants to polish up some of the numbers.'

'Does he? I didn't notice any problems.'

'Delighted to hear it!' George smiled. 'Everyone's a true professional, after all. Smile through it, eh? Even so, there are one or two kinks that need to be ironed out.' His tone was firm.

'I see.'

There was another pause and Flora sensed a slight friction between the two men, though they smiled and spoke with apparent ease.

Edward turned back to her. 'If lunch is an impossibility, Flora, then keep your diary clear after dinner tomorrow. There's something I'd like to show you.'

'Oh?' George raised an eyebrow.

'Not you, old boy! You know Paris like the back of your hand – and besides, I'm told there's precious little *you* haven't seen in this city.'

George's smile became fixed, and Flora sensed a trace of threat in the words. Did Edward know what Flora knew about his private life?

'I'll walk out with you, shall I? Seeing as you're just leaving,' he said as Edward rose, smoothing his trousers.

Walk out, or escort from the premises? Flora wondered, getting up too.

Edward planted a kiss on her cheek, catching her gaze. 'Sleep well, Flora. Don't let him work you too hard – I want you fresh for our rendezvous tomorrow. You won't be disappointed, I promise.'

Pepper was silent as he followed Edward out of the room. At the doorway he turned and gave Flora a single nod, his glance sweeping the room as if searching for potential threats. Then he stepped out to the corridor and disappeared, with Edward, back into the night.

Chapter Twenty-Eight

'Bonjour, M'selle MacQueen – votre petit déjeuner. Voudriez-vous que j'ouvre les rideaux?'

The words tinkled like musical notes, charming but meaningless, an assemblage of sounds. Flora stirred, hearing indistinct noises around her: a spoon clinking on a saucer; voices in the corridor outside; the swish of the curtains on their rail.

Light spilled in, a gentle slump rather than a rush, suffusing behind her eyelids. She blinked, groggy, unable to pull herself from the depths of her slumber. The bed was too soft and she felt sunken, as if she was underground . . .

'Merci.'

The sound of the male voice made her eyes fly open and she lifted her head from the pillow just as the door softly closed.

George was standing by the fireplace, several newspapers rolled under his arm. They stared at one another for a moment and she saw in his eyes some of the residual hurt caused by yesterday's showdown; scar tissue forming over a wound.

'How are you feeling?' he asked stiffly, going over to the tray that had been left on a small table. He poured some tea from the pot, bringing a cup back to her and setting it down on her bedside table.

Reluctantly she hauled herself to a seated position. Behind him, she saw her dress like a silver pool on the floor. She had climbed into bed mere seconds after he and Edward had left the previous night, but sleep hadn't come easily as she lay in the dark, troubled by Edward's sudden kiss.

'Fine . . . Tired.' Her body ached, her head heavy from all the champagne, and she sank back into the pillows again, pulling the sheets up around her and curling into a ball. She thought again of her lost baby, somewhere out there without her, and she felt exhausted in body, mind and soul; she just wanted to sleep and sleep . . .

'Well, the reviews are in,' he said, collecting his own teacup and beginning to pace slowly. He glanced back at her to check she was still listening and not drifting off again. She blinked in reply.

'*Paris-soir* called you a "tour de force". *Le Populaire* are calling it the "battle of the savages".' He raised a sceptical eyebrow. 'They're pitting you against Miss Baker, which is good, I suppose – you've heard of her "Danse Sauvage"? Although I'd have liked a more upmarket tone.' He went back to the papers with a tut. '*Variety* – the one whose opinion we really care about – says, "The lustrous Miss MacQueen radiates such star quality, it's only a matter of time before Hollywood comes calling," and *Le Monde* has declared you the most eligible young woman in Paris.' He threw the last paper down with a slap, looking mildly satisfied. 'What do you say to all that?'

But her eyes had closed again and she was slipping down under the covers.

'Flora!'

She forced them open, blinking at him. 'I'm sorry . . . what?'

He frowned. 'You should eat something.' He went over to the tray and brought her a pastry. 'Sit up.'

Flora sighed, heaving herself up the mattress again with effort. She took it from him wordlessly but saw that it was the hazelnut cream cornet – her favourite – a small nicety that passed unspoken from her favourite uncle, her only friend here.

'You're so good to me,' she said quietly, picking at it. 'I should never have said what I said to you yesterday. Of course I'd never tell anyone what I saw.'

George, pouring himself more tea, fell still, his back to her.

'Do you . . . love him?' She asked the question tentatively. From the very start, the balance of their relationship had been entirely weighted towards her – teaching her, showing her, guiding her. They had never once gone near his own personal life, his past or future hopes.

He turned back to her, his expression bemused. 'Of course not.'

'But . . .'

'Sex isn't love, Flora. It can be companionship. Or lust.' He shrugged. 'And sometimes it's just a stress release.'

'Oh.' She had never heard anyone speak so candidly about the act before; back home it simply went unmentioned, buckled to matrimony and what the reverend called the Christian duty to reproduce. Though of course, there were occasionally 'mistakes' outside of marriage – such as those made by Flora herself and by Mhairi, not to mention Flora's cousin Kitty. But several times over the years, she had also accidentally happened upon some of the younger men, either in a cleit or behind a wall, engaged in solitary pleasure. To her shame, she had never averted her gaze.

'But seeing as we're getting personal at breakfast . . . may I ask what happened to your fiancé?'

She felt her body sag. It wasn't a question she would ever be able to answer without physical pain. 'It was an accident.

He was part of an expedition to the Arctic and their ship got trapped in the ice. The hull was breached, and . . .'

'He drowned?' he said for her when the silence lengthened.

She nodded, looking away.

'Was his body recovered?'

She shook her head quickly.

'But you're sure . . . ?'

'Of course! It's not something that could be mistaken!'

'No, no, I only meant . . .' He held his hands up apologetically as a small silence blossomed. 'How did you come to meet him?'

'Actually, James visited St Kilda with Edward and his family. Their fathers were old friends and they'd both gone up to Cambridge together.'

'Ah.' Understanding dawned across Pepperly's face. 'So you met him and Rushton at the same time?'

'Aye.'

'But you chose your James fellow over Rushton?'

She hesitated, surprised he should have guessed that there had been a love triangle between the three of them. '. . . It was tricky,' she conceded.

'I'm sure it was. Although it's a lot less tricky now, if what I walked in on last night is anything to go by.'

Flora felt her cheeks burn. 'That wasn't . . . I didn't . . . know he was going to do that.'

'No?' Pepperly gave another of his small, bemused laughs. '*I* did. Why do you think I came back?'

Flora swallowed. 'He was just a little drunk and emotional, that's all.'

Pepperly watched her. 'And does Rushton know about the baby?'

'Of course not!'

'Don't jump down my throat, Flora!' he snapped back. 'I've got to be in full possession of the facts, that's all. Until we were all sitting at dinner, I had no idea about your past history with Rushton, and yet he's my main investor. It isn't irrelevant to the situation at hand.'

She swallowed back her indignation. 'No, I suppose not.'

'Hm. Make sure you make no mention of it to him. Best not to give him any . . . leverage.'

'Leverage?'

But he wasn't listening. 'Tell me, what precautions do you take?'

She looked at him blankly.

'Have you a diaphragm, is what I mean?'

'A what?'

He rolled his eyes. 'Well, question answered. Don't worry, I know a doctor here who can help out.'

'Pepper, I have no idea what you're talking about. Why would I need a doctor? I'm not ill.'

He sighed, coming to sit on the end of the bed, his teacup still in his hand. For several moments he just looked at her. 'Now that Rushton's staying in town for a few more days, we need to be realistic about what's around the corner. I'm doing what I can, but I won't always be able to . . . rescue you.'

'Rescue me?'

'Yes. Like last night.'

She frowned. 'But I didn't need rescuing last night.'

'No? And what do you think would have happened if I hadn't turned up when I did?'

'Edward would have left and I'd have gone to bed.'

He sighed again, looking as if he was choosing his words carefully. 'Look, Flora, possibly – because the two of you are "old friends" – he might have been satisfied with just a kiss

369

last night. But he's joining us at Le Boeuf after the show again tonight and then taking you on somewhere. And he will be expecting more than a kiss then, I can assure you.'

'What?' She blinked at him in disbelief. 'Well, he won't be getting anything at all!'

He put a hand out and patted her foot over the covers. 'Flora – he won't leave Paris until he's got what he wants.' He took in her expression. '. . . Don't look so horrified. It's not uncommon in this industry. This is how business gets done. The casting couch often helps . . . confirm a hunch.'

'A hunch?'

'Exactly. Men like Rushton are taking huge risks with their own money any time they invest in one of these projects. Sometimes – very often, in fact – it's these "little extras" that help a deal over the line.'

Flora could only stare at him. 'Pepper, I don't think you understand. Edward would never . . . he would never be so improper with me. Last time we met, he wanted to *marry* me.'

'Yes,' he replied, unperturbed. 'Because back on St Kilda, the only way he could possibly have gotten you off the island and into his circle – by which I mean, into his bed – was by proposing to you. But now you're already here, and . . . Well, to put it in very crude terms, I own you and he owns me.' He shrugged at the bald intimation.

Flora stared at him. 'What do you mean, he *owns* you?'

'Shows need financing, Flora. You know money doesn't magically grow on trees! He's my principal backer. I need him on board with my projects – and the moment I told him about you, he was *on board*. Which, of course, makes perfect sense now.'

'You told him about me specifically?'

'Yes.'

'You mean, you gave him my name? You told him where I was from?'

'Naturally. It all added to the legend – a beautiful island girl comes to the big city . . . He's been waiting for months for this to come together. He gave me carte blanche with the budget. Who do you think gave me the green light to put you up here?' He gestured to the opulent room.

Flora fell quiet as she absorbed this, remembering Edward's mild amusement as he had surveyed this room last night, the way he'd laughed as he'd learned of her expensive breakfast habits – a habit he himself had paid for. He had been waiting for her all this time? She felt as if she had been caught in some kind of trap.

'Stop looking so horrified,' George chastised her. 'He's not a monster! But it's important that you understand his expectations. He's a key player in this industry and . . . well, it pays to keep him happy. If he were to pull the plug, it would hurt us both.'

Flora could hardly believe what she was hearing. 'You're saying he'll expect me to lie with him because he's financed the show?' She drew her legs back on the bed, pulling the covers to her chin. 'No! I won't do it.'

A look of disbelief travelled over George's face. He looked confounded that the logic of his words had missed their mark. 'Why not?'

'Because I don't love him! Why else?'

'Love?' he scoffed after a moment, as if he couldn't believe his ears. 'What have I just been telling you? Sex is always a transaction, be it in marriage or business.'

'That's not true.'

'Flora, you – as a beautiful woman – know better than anyone that you've been trading on your looks all your life.

371

You know damn well that you're a prize, something to be won, and you dangle that over every man you meet. But there has to be a winner in the end. Someone was always going to get you.'

'And it was James. I accepted James because I loved him!'

'And now he's dead.' Hs words were like a slap. 'I'm sorry to be so direct, but those are the facts – and Rushton is still in the race. He won't give up, Flora, especially now, with his tactical advantage over both of us. If you turn him down, you'll risk losing everything you've come by – and I do mean everything. I saved you, but by extension it was Edward who saved you. Is it really so bad if he asks for something in return? Something you've already freely given?'

'I can't believe you're saying these things to me,' she whispered.

'No? Would you rather I'd left you to work it out for yourself as he takes your dress off you this evening?'

Flora didn't reply. She watched as he rose from the bed and crossed the room.

'It's time to grow up, Flora. This is Paris – it isn't chic to be bourgeois. I'm trying to help you, as I always have. I don't want you to come to any harm and there's absolutely no reason you should – but if you run, he'll only chase harder.'

She stared at him, appalled by what he was telling her. Her act on stage was in fact no act at all. She was a songbird, imprisoned in a jewelled cage by the man who owned her.

'Let him have you and he'll move on quickly, I assure you.'

He reached into his jacket pocket and pulled a thick wad of francs from a money clip, tossing it onto the bed beside her. 'There's a boutique on the Rue Saint Honoré. Buy yourself some *appropriate* nightwear.' He looked disapprovingly at her heavy, undyed linen nightdress; woven by her father, hand-sewn by her mother, it smelled of home. 'They'll have a selection to choose from.'

'So this is his money you're giving me, to buy clothes to seduce him in?' she asked, picking it up angrily. 'Isn't that just a bit pathetic?'

'Whether it is or it isn't, it's his money that will keep this show on the road and enable you to locate your son,' he said, stating the facts in the terms she would best understand. She fell back and he walked slowly back to the armchair to retrieve his hat. Flora watched as he set it carefully on his head.

'Where are you going?' Her voice trembled.

'To the theatre.' He glanced over at her. 'Don't worry, you're not expected.'

'But you said to Edward—'

'I was giving you an alibi, Flora. As I said, I'll do what I can to run interference between the two of you, but I can't stop everything altogether. And, if he senses that's my game, the consequences will be dire, I have no doubt.' He headed for the door. 'Rest while you can; now we're up and running, you need to conserve your energy.'

'Pepper, please,' she whispered, as he reached for the door-knob.

He looked back at her. 'It's just business, Flora. Don't make it personal when it's not.'

She watched him go, the door closing behind him with a soft click.

But it would always be personal to her, she thought. It was impossible to think of going to bed with Edward when she still belonged to James. He remained with her, even in death and her heart had become like a fossil – impermeable now, and indelibly imprinted with the shape of something that had gone before, refusing to ever let it go.

Chapter Twenty-Nine

Flora stood at the boutique window, staring in. The signs meant nothing to her: *Le Trousseau – La Lingerie – La Layette*; but she studied the posed mannequins styled in silk and lace-trimmed nightgowns, their hands splayed in upturned positions and wistful gazes directed into the distance.

Was this . . . was this what was expected of her? In spite of the Egyptian cotton sheets she now slept on, her old rough nightdress from home had become a comfort to her as she drifted into sleep each night. Sleep had been her only refuge as her entire world was upended – the only place left where she could be with James and their son – but seemingly even that couldn't be protected any longer.

She saw a figure pass behind her in the glass and turned around quickly. During her walk over here, she'd had a sense that she was being watched – almost preyed upon – but when she looked back, there had been no one she could pinpoint as observing her directly. Pepperly had warned her that some people might recognize her from the newspapers or from posters for the show, perhaps without quite knowing why she looked familiar. She was used to being stared at, but fame was a different proposition, she was beginning to realize. And she wasn't at all sure she liked it.

A man in a hat and overcoat nodded politely as he passed

her, his gaze sliding to the seductive attire in the window display and then straight back to Flora. She could almost see the connection link up in his mind's eye – her, in those scraps of nothing – and she quickly pushed on the door and disappeared inside.

A bell overhead sounded her arrival.

A woman behind the counter looked up, and from the way her eyes widened, Flora knew she had recognized her too.

'Bonjour,' the woman smiled, looking delighted as she came round the desk and stood before Flora. 'Comment allez-vous, m'selle?'

'Très bien, merci,' Flora smiled, repeating the common phrases George had taught her when they'd first arrived in the city. She held out her hands apologetically. 'Désolée, je ne . . .'

'Ah, bien sûr, d'accord, d'accord, vous ne comprenez pas?'

Flora smiled blankly.

'Ah . . . how may I help you?' The woman's English was heavily accented, but Flora supposed her own was too. She pointed in the direction of the window.

'Ah oui, la peignoir? Négligée? You wish to try?'

Flora simply nodded, wondering if her shame could be read on her face.

'Toute suite, m'selle. I come back straight now.'

She disappeared into a back room, leaving Flora alone in the shop. The walls were lined with shelves, mannequins standing in the room like cocktail party guests. She ambled slowly, her gaze tripping over brassieres and girdles, a few corsets of the older style; there were some nightgowns in heavier cotton, and short bed jackets with marabou collars and long silk ribbons. Everything was cut in a gentle palette of ivory, primrose, apricot, pale pink or ice blue.

She came to a corner dedicated to children's clothing: piles of perfectly folded jumpers with ornate cable knits, poplin shirts trimmed with coloured rickrack and mother-of-pearl buttons, tiny bootees . . . They were clothes she could now afford, gifts she could give. The irony wasn't lost on her that she had been forced to give up her child on account of penury – but now that she had money, she had no child on whom to spend it.

She realized her breath was coming faster – too fast, feelings surfacing – and she turned quickly away, just as the shopgirl returned with a selection of nightwear draped over her arm. Flora watched as she arranged the pieces, hanging them from full-height silk privacy screens. The fabrics were buttery silk, liquid satin, and a chiffon that was completely translucent.

Flora stared at it in horror. The thought of standing before Edward in that . . .

'Do you like?' the assistant asked, stepping back so that Flora could move closer and inspect them. Lightly, she trailed her hands over the fabrics, seeing their sumptuous handle and how they refracted the light, the intricate hand stitching even more beautiful up close. Each item was exquisite, possessing more beauty than she had ever expected to be hers; and yet she could take no joy in knowing she must wear it for a man she did not want. She closed her eyes for a moment, feeling a wave of nausea, her body protesting just at the thought.

This is Paris. George's words drifted through her mind. *Let him have you.*

Women did this all the time, she told herself, though it might be dressed up in different guises. *Sex is always a transaction*: getting a business deal over the line, the prize of a good marriage – and the tax on a bad one. It was difficult to imagine Donald and Crabbit Mary ever having desired one another. Their marital bed had lain cold for years, Mhairi had told her in confidence.

She handled a pale lemon silk crêpe-de-Chine gown, seeing how it fell in narrow folds; the bust was criss-crossed with deep lace and threaded with a black velvet ribbon. She knew just by looking at it that the colours would be offset perfectly by her dark hair. She would look beautiful, even when she didn't want to be.

'This one,' she said, swallowing hard and stepping back.

'You wish to try on?'

But Flora shook her head.

The shop girl looked surprised, but she nodded and smiled. 'Bien sûr.' Carrying the gown to the counter as if it was fragile, she laid it out carefully and began to wrap it in layers of tissue. Flora stood patiently as she waited, her attention falling to the objects displayed beneath the glass counter.

She blinked and stared at the accoutrements of the rich: lace-frilled bloomers to cover a nappy; handkerchiefs embellished with embroidered flowers . . .

'And that too, please.'

The shop girl looked surprised as she saw what Flora was pointing to. 'Ce-la?'

Flora nodded, feeling her heart quicken again as the silver baby rattle – glinting like a knife, wounding her – was plucked from the cabinet and wrapped in tissue too, bound in ribbons and placed like something precious on top of her other purchase. One necessitated the other, she thought, staring down at it as the girl rang up the bill. If she had to wear that négligée, the rattle would be emblematic of her reasons. It was the reminder she needed that she could endure anything; she had lived through far worse than a night with a man she didn't love.

She would surrender herself to save her son. To get back to him . . .

She paid with the plentiful supply of francs George had given her and headed back towards the hotel. With every step, the shopping bag tinkled lightly, breaking her heart, but she kept walking across the Place Vendôme. Tonight, it would be done.

And then, God willing, she would be free.

'Ah, M'selle MacQueen,' the manager at reception said, catching her attention as she crossed the marble floor. '. . . Your guest is awaiting you in the salon.'

She stopped walking. '. . . My guest?'

Surely it couldn't be Edward – not already? Although it wouldn't be very surprising to find he had been trailing her around the city, lurking in shadows, still watching and waiting for her? Catching out Pepperly's lies?

'A Monsieur Bonner from *The Times*. Shall I take you to him?'

'Oh.' She exhaled with relief. She had forgotten all about the interview. George had only mentioned it in passing last night, not even giving her a time; he had been too busy trying to 'save' her. 'No, I can find him, I'm sure.'

The hotel's public spaces were grand, but after ten days of living here, she no longer felt intimidated by them. The staff knew her name and always looked at her admiringly when she passed through the lobby. George had told her that self-assurance was two-thirds of success, and nothing spoke of confidence like holding one's chin in the air.

She walked into the gilded salon, where velvet sofas sat amid potted ferns. A man in a tailcoat was softly playing the grand piano. The assorted guests were mainly – at this hour

– women in pairs, drinking from dainty cups, but there was one man sitting alone near the windows overlooking the Place. He was dark-haired, with a thick moustache that covered his top lip, and he wore a limp overcoat of visibly inferior quality to anyone else's in the hotel.

'Mr Bonner?' she asked, as he saw her approaching and rose courteously.

He tipped his hat. 'Pleased to meet you, Miss MacQueen. I'm Mr Bonner, from *The Times* newspaper in London.'

'Aye – hello.' Back home, *The Times* had been considered The Authority on All Things Important on the mainland. The idea that she was being interviewed for its pages felt almost . . . ridiculous. 'I hope you haven't been waiting long.'

'Not at all.'

She held up her shopping bag with a guilty look. 'I'm afraid I wasn't . . .'

'You weren't expecting me?'

'I just wasn't quite sure of the time. I understood you weren't covering the show, but then . . .'

He gave a small, apologetic smile. 'Well, when we saw the reviews . . .' He shrugged.

'Of course . . . Are you happy to do the interview here?'

'If you are.'

'I'll have some coffee sent over,' she said, catching the eye of the maître d'. 'Or tea?'

'Tea would be much appreciated.'

'Du thé et petits fours, s'il vous plaît,' she murmured.

'Bien sûr, M'selle MacQueen.' With a nod of the head, he was gone.

Bonner looked around the salon with an admiring expression. 'I see the rumours are true – you have become an overnight sensation.' He smiled, his moustache splaying as his lips stretched. 'Staying at the Ritz seems due reward for headlining the biggest show in Paris.'

'Oh, aye,' she nodded. 'I'm very lucky.'

'Although I'm sure you've worked very hard for your success.'

'It's been a busy time getting the show ready, aye.' She set the bag on the floor, hearing a last tinkle, and her heart flinched in silent reply. Her hands went to her hair, fussing slightly as she tried to compose herself. 'I apologize – I must look frightful.'

'If it's any consolation, your "frightful" is most people's "on a good day with a following wind".'

'You're very kind.'

'I mean it. Even on St Kilda when your hair was still long, you possessed a rare beauty that had no need of hairstylists and make-up artists.'

Flora stared at him, her hands falling back to her lap. 'St Kilda?'

'Yes.'

'You speak as though you'd seen me there.'

'I did . . . I was there on the day of the evacuation, and I remember you quite well, Miss MacQueen. Don't worry,' he said quickly, holding up his hands. 'I take no offence that you don't remember me. I'm scarcely memorable to my own mother.'

She stared at him in amazement. He'd been to her home?

'Wait . . .' Vaguely, she recalled the brouhaha surrounding a reporter; he had tried to stay behind on the isle as the villagers left. Norman Ferguson had found him hiding out in one of the cleits by the dyke. No one could understand the logic behind it. The *Dunara Castle* was scheduled to drop anchor a few days after they left, but that landing was weather-dependent and, it being so very late in the summer, there was every chance it would be delayed if not cancelled altogether. He might have risked being stranded there for weeks – or worse. The island men had taken a very dim view of the 'prank'.

'Was it you? As tried to stay behind?'

'Indeed.' He seemed pleased with himself.

'But why? You might have starved to death if the weather had turned.'

He gave a small chuckle. 'Well, I hope my employers would have called in a favour with the Royal Navy or some such if it had looked like it was coming to that!'

She did remember him now. Details of that awful day drifted back in snippets: she had glimpsed him sitting on the deck as she had been there with Mhairi, just before they hauled anchor. A stranger in their midst. But she had barely been capable of much coherent thought during those hours.

'But why did you want to stay? Surely you were there to cover the evacuation. What was there left to see after we'd gone?'

His smile was enigmatic. 'Actually, I was looking for evidence of Frank Mathieson's criminal enterprise.'

She stared at him in utter bewilderment. '. . . What criminal enterprise?'

He hesitated at her mildly scoffing tone. 'Did you know the Earl of Dumfries is a close friend of your former landlord, MacLeod?'

'I did know that, aye.'

'Well, the earl's steward – a Mr Weir – has recently been arrested on suspicion of theft and of handling stolen goods. It is believed that Weir and Mathieson were working together: stealing to order from their respective estates for a circle of private clients overseas. America, I believe.

'I'd been onto Mathieson for a while – a tip-off put me on the trail originally, and I'd been investigating for five months when word came of your evacuation. I'm convinced Mathieson and Weir were smuggling stolen items onto the isle, and then Mathieson – or a third party – was hiding them in the cleits, moving them on once the heat had died down.'

'And that's why you stayed behind?'

'*Tried* to stay behind.' He shrugged. 'But perhaps it was just as well I was unsuccessful, or I might have found myself in more trouble than I'd bargained for. I would have been in a tight spot, being found on an abandoned island with the dead body of the man against whom I was conducting a criminal exposé.'

Flora stared at him. 'I don't know what to say. It all seems so . . . unlikely.'

'You don't believe Mr Mathieson was capable of such things?'

'I'm not saying that—'

'Then you *do* think he was capable of them?'

'I'm not saying that either,' she said curtly. 'But I won't speak ill of the dead, Mr Bonner.'

A waiter appeared beside them, bearing a large tray set with a teapot, milk jug, two cups and saucers, and a small tiered stand of petits fours.

Neither one of them spoke as the waiter began to pour. 'Tea and a piece' was much the same routine wherever you were, she had found; the teapot might be Limoges porcelain, the 'piece' rose-petal macaroons, the tea leaves a rare Ceylonese blend specially formulated for the Ritz, but the ritual here was just the same as at home with their Lipton's brew and the smell of Black Twist tobacco in the air. And it always came with a helping of honest conversation.

Mr Bonner withdrew a notepad and pencil from his coat, preparing for the interview as the waiter served. He held it up with a questioning arch of his eyebrow and she nodded her consent, waiting until they were alone again before resuming the conversation.

'Your former landlord has been much in the press himself lately,' he said. 'He's been very exercised about his factor's death.'

'Naturally. It's a terrible thing, what happened to Mr Mathieson.'

Mr Bonner reached for his cup and took a sip of tea before looking back at her. 'It was a brutal attack, from what I've heard. The police have already questioned several people of interest.'

'Well, that's good. As they should. A man is dead, after all.' Slowly she returned the cup to her lap, trying not to let her hand tremble or betray her wild curiosity. 'Who, exactly, have they questioned?'

He pulled back slightly. 'I probably shouldn't say—'

'Please, Mr Bonner. Anything you say here will go no further, I promise, but I'm far from home and of course, this concerns my friends and neighbours.'

He blinked, looking reluctant to gossip – until she smiled at him. It always worked.

'Well, I do know that one person of interest was a young woman named Effie Gillies.'

Her smile faded in a trace, even though it wasn't news to her. 'Effie wouldn't hurt a fly.'

'She's a skilled hunter, I believe.'

'*Hunter?*' Flora scoffed. 'Of puffins, perhaps. Frank was double her size!'

'The police feel she has a clear motive,' he shrugged.

383

Oh, God. What did they know of Effie's motives? Did they know the truth about Effie and Frank's 'relationship' – about the night of the storm, when she and Mhairi had been attacked? The jumping of the broom . . . ? Flora sat straighter, thrusting her chin in the air as she tried to hide her mounting panic. 'Which is?'

'Allegedly, a priceless book from the Dunvegan estate was found underneath her bed at Dumfries House. Weir has pointed the finger at her, saying *she* was the one involved with him and Mathieson.'

Flora looked at him in horror. Effie had mentioned none of this.

'It's her word against his at the moment; the earl's family is siding with Miss Gillies, and Weir has been sacked from his position. But the police are convinced he's telling the truth on one count: that there was a third party involved.'

'And . . . do the police think he was murdered by his accomplice? This third man?'

'Or third woman,' he corrected her, reminding her of Effie's inclusion in inquiries. 'They're looking at all angles. Mathieson was an unpopular man. He had enemies on the isle and it appears many of the islanders had motives.'

'No, they didn't,' Flora rebuffed. 'I know every person on that isle and none of them could have done this. None of them were criminals.'

'Anyone can commit a crime in the right circumstances, Miss MacQueen.' He paused. 'Donald McKinnon certainly seems to have had reason enough to kill Mathieson. From what I've heard, the two of them were constantly at logger-heads. They had come to blows several times in the preceding months, I understand.'

Flora swallowed down the panic she felt whenever she

thought of Donald's arrest. It was tied far too closely to her own fate, her own heart. 'Donald just . . . he didn't like the rates the factor was offering. He said Mathieson was under-cutting us. But that's not a reason to kill someone.'

'Maybe not; but apparently it wasn't just the rates causing friction. Donald also stole something valuable belonging to Mathieson and sold it out from under him.'

She looked at him steadily.

'You mean the ambergris?' She was determined to show him they had no secrets. 'Donald didn't steal that. It was no more Mathieson's than it was mine, or Effie's, or Ma Peg's. He retrieved it from a whale that had burst in our bay and tried to sneak it out under all our noses as a cure for his mother's gout! He took us for fools – but he didn't like it when Donald took *him* for one back and sold it direct to the big boss at Salvesen Whaling. Mathieson would dish it out but he couldn't take it.' She could still hear the echoes of Mathieson's threats that day back in July, the savage fight between the two men and Donald's eventual victory over his old foe.

'Hm. It sounds like all-out war between them.' Bonner frowned, seeming almost to read her mind. 'Men kill over money all the time, Miss MacQueen.'

Flora pulled herself back. In trying to defend Donald, had she achieved the opposite? 'Actually I know for a fact that Donald didn't kill Frank.'

'How?'

'His wife was in labour the night Frank was killed.'

'Yes, yes – that was certainly *her* alibi. But if he . . . how can I put this delicately? If he was a devoted father, it seems he was a less than devoted husband. He and a Miss MacKinnon – with an "a", no relation – were having an affair. Were you aware of that?'

Flora held her breath as another secret fell out into the open, a shadow crawling on the ground reaching for her now-scrubbed, pretty feet. She looked away. 'I prefer to keep my nose out of other people's business.'

The reporter didn't care two hoots about her sense of propriety. 'Well, it transpires he was with his mistress that night and not his wife as she gave birth.' Flora felt her heart pound as the truths – and half-truths – came thick and fast. He was a hair's breadth away from her own secret. 'Miss MacKinnon's statement has been enough to see him released on bail – at least for the moment – but one has to question her moral rectitude and therefore her reliability under oath.'

Flora bristled at this. He knew nothing! His facts painted a very different picture to the truth. 'Perhaps we'd better get back to the real reason you're here, Mr Bonner,' she said, forcing a blank smile as she rearranged herself on the sofa. 'Tawdry gossip from a remote Hebridean isle is hardly likely to be of interest to your readers, after all. They want the glamour of gay Paris.'

'Your dazzling life now certainly contrasts starkly with your humble origins,' he agreed. 'But you're quite right. I'll come to the point of my visit.' He picked up the notebook and pencil, flipping to a clean sheet, and looked up at her. 'Miss MacQueen . . . Did *you* kill Frank Mathieson?'

'. . . What?' The word escaped her like a bark.

'A witness alleges you had a combative relationship with the deceased. Is that correct?'

Witness? What witness? 'Who . . . who said that?' she whispered, disoriented. What was happening here? He was supposed to be asking her about the show. George had said . . .

'I can't reveal my sources, I'm afraid, but I understand

Mathieson tried to meddle in your engagement with a Mr James Callaghan. Is that the same Callaghan who was recently awarded the Polar Medal for Arctic services?'

Flora stared at him. Where was he getting all this information?

'Did he break up your engagement, Miss MacQueen?'

'What? No!'

'And did you kill him for that?'

'No! You've got this all wrong . . .'

'Well, that's why I'm here, you see. I want to hear your side of things.'

She blinked, pulling her gaze away from him and looking around the room at the ladies sipping on afternoon tea, oblivious to the nightmare engulfing her. She tried to catch the eye of the maître d', but his back was turned. 'You need to leave.'

'Just tell me about Mathieson. Why did you hate him so much?'

'Leave now, or I'll call someone to take you out.' As calmly as she could, she rose to her feet. She wouldn't let him see her tremble at his accusations. 'Monsieur!' she called to the manager.

Bonner watched her intently, as if reading her panic. Slowly, he picked up his hat and stood too. 'Just one comment for the readers, Miss MacQueen, that's all I need. What have you to say in your defence? . . . No? Nothing? The police will be coming to interview you, you do know that?'

She did know it. Effie had already warned her. She just hadn't warned her about *him.*

'Monsieur!' She waved her arm as the manager turned and caught sight of her.

The reporter reached into his coat pocket and pulled out a

card. 'My number, if you decide you'd like to make a statement. Be on the front foot, so to speak.' He set it down on the table when she made no move to take it from him. 'You're a public figure now, Miss MacQueen. Different rules apply. Do yourself a favour while you can; this exclusive will be running in tomorrow's edition and then the whole of Fleet Street will be beating on your door. I'm trying to help you get ahead of the pack . . .'

'I said get out!' The words burst from her before she could stop herself. Every head turned in their direction – but he wasn't the one embarrassed by the scene.

He gave a shrug. 'Just think about it. You can call me any time – day or night,' he said, as the manager approached with a stern expression. '. . . Yes, yes, I'm leaving . . . Think about it, Miss MacQueen!' he called over his shoulder. 'This isn't going to go away!'

Flora watched as he was escorted out, the memories of that terrible night playing through her mind on a loop: blood in the moonlight, screams in the silence. She could never forget it, never unsee the events burned on her soul, no matter how much she tried. Life and death had been locked in an interplay that night – like the eagles' mating dance, plummeting claw to claw, head over tail, through the St Kildans' final starlit sky.

Chapter Thirty

'Curtain up in ten, m'selle,' the stagehand said from the doorway as Flora sat at the dressing table, having her make-up applied. She looked composed, but she had already finished two glasses of champagne and was on her third, her nerves friable.

After Bonner's ambush she had paced in her room, deeply unsettled, trying to calm herself. What did they really have to pin on her? So she had disliked Mathieson? That didn't make her a killer. They couldn't make her guilty by association, either. Instead she had come to a fragile conclusion that her new, starry profile was an opportunity for the ambitious reporter to provoke further interest in his big break case. Glamour and murder went well together, and he wanted headlines.

Even so, she couldn't be sure of exactly what he knew – and her feeling of paranoia, the sense that she was being watched, had only deepened. A small crowd had gathered on the Place Vendôme to see her walk the short distance from the sanctuary of the hotel door to her waiting car this evening, and every stare upon her had felt loaded. She knew she had to tell George what had happened; he had managed her reputation with a sniper's precision until now, and there was simply no way a report in *The Times* linking her to a sensational murder could be transformed into good publicity.

She took another sip of champagne and shifted distractedly in her seat, her leg brushing against a bag at her feet. The nightgown was inside, wrapped in layers of tissue and tied with a ribbon. She couldn't even look at it – how would she be able to meet Edward's eye at dinner, knowing what he intended? Pepperly had been right; she had been naive. She remembered now all the smirks and verbal slips that had passed her by the previous night; the innuendos that had occasionally slunk past the men's manners as their glasses were steadily refilled.

Maxim's: where women are seen, but never ladies. Nor gentlemen either.

She turned her hands over in her lap as the red lipstick was applied to her mouth, regarding her reflection dispassionately. The woman staring back at her in the mirror wasn't her: not a daughter, sister, friend. Mother. She was a fantasy, one of the sirens Edward had referenced that first day on the beach as he grasped for anything and everything that would make her his.

And now she so nearly was.

'Voilà,' the make-up girl smiled, setting down the powder brush and looking satisfied. 'Tout fini.'

'Merci, Estelle.' Flora rose as the girl began to pack up, walking over to the rail and reaching for her first costume: ropes of pearls covering a brassiere, looping down over her bare torso towards a sash that girdled her hips, covering the very bare minimum.

She stepped into it carefully, taking care not to catch one of the ropes. One pull, and hundreds of beads would scatter everywhere.

'Vous êtes prêt, M'selle?' Marie asked, walking in with the gown sent over by Pepperly for her to wear tonight: emerald silk with straps that criss-crossed in front. The sable already lay, opulent, across the chaise, ready to be grabbed on the way out the door.

Marie set down tonight's jewellery box on the dressing table and came over to fasten the hooks on the back of Flora's costume. Flora stood patiently as she tugged and pulled the one-piece, making sure it sat exactly right.

'Alors, bien,' she said at last, satisfied, and wandered out again as the five-minute call was shouted down the corridor. Flora heard the stampede of feet exiting the other dressing rooms, the troupe getting into their positions as the orchestra finished its fine tuning.

She checked her reflection one last time, taking another sip of champagne to calm her nerves. As she turned away to join the others, her eyes fell to the jewellery box Marie had delivered. Usually the boxes were long and narrow, for bracelets, or broad for necklaces – but this one was as small as a robin.

Curiosity got the better of her, and she opened it.

She fell back, the box toppling onto its side, the sapphire engagement ring it held clearly on display.

How . . . how could this be here? Blood rushed through her head as she tried to understand what she was seeing. It just didn't make sense!

Until it did.

Slowly, she stepped forward, picking it up again.

George. He had been there when she'd sold it. He had been there because he was settling a friend's debt. A Good Samaritan, she had taunted, but it had been true. This . . . this was just another kindness, on what he knew was going to be a difficult night.

How long had he had it, she wondered, rubbing her fingers over the stones? Had he bought it immediately after she'd left the shop – or had he gone back for it, held onto it for all this time? Had he only understood just how precious it had been to her when she told him her full, awful truth this morning? She slipped it onto her finger and immediately felt something of James's memory come back to her, as if the gold encircling her finger could be his arms around her once more. After losing everything that had connected them, she had something of him back again, and it emboldened her. She could still reclaim something even greater of him – of them – too.

She just had to be brave.

She kissed the ring, feeling something inside her lift again for the first time in months. Like sap rising after a bleak winter, it was the first stirring of life – of hope returning – and she ran from the dressing room, towards the bright, dazzling lights.

Mirrored walls magnified Flora's image around the room as she was led to the table where George, Edward, Robert Kinney and Charlie Buck were already waiting, the men all rising to greet her like an old friend – although only one of them really was. Kisses were planted familiarly on her cheek but she kept her gaze demurely averted as she settled into her seat, aware of the stares penetrating her skin as her coat was taken from her and her gown revealed. The hubbub of conversation dipped and then rose in a crescendo throughout the room as her presence was noted by the patrons, her name carried through the room as if on a wave.

'Congratulations on another stellar performance, Flora,' Charlie said, toasting her as their champagne was poured. 'I wasn't sure it was possible but I would say tonight's show was even better than last.'

'Thank you. We ironed out some kinks in rehearsal today,' she smiled, her eyes bright as the lie slid from her tongue, echoing Pepperly's own words last night. But it was true: the show *had* been even better tonight. His gift had revitalized her in her hour of need, bringing a dynamic edge she hadn't been able to find before. She had seen James in every face in the crowd – he was everywhere and nowhere at once – and, for the first time since leaving St Kilda, her smile had reached her eyes as the memory of him flickered inside her, an inter-mittent shadow she could glimpse in the lights.

'You most certainly did. You practically left scorch marks on the stage!' Edward said, catching her gaze and holding it with the same provocative stare of their first ever meeting.

As then, she didn't look away, even though he repelled her now. Last night, at the dinner table, she had mistaken his manner for nostalgic sentiment, but now she saw everything clearly: in his eyes was not affection, but anticipation. Long-delayed and exquisitely drawn out, his victory – over her, over James – would be all the sweeter when he finally got his reward. Knowing that he was the power behind her throne, that he had been waiting for this night for months, made her feel like prey in green silk. Served up to him – meat on a plate. Everything was on his terms now.

But she would take what she wanted from him too. He served a purpose he couldn't even guess at.

He looked away first, with a smile – as if he had read something of her surrender in her eyes – and leaned forward to tap his cigarette ash into the ashtray. He looked handsome in his dinner suit and she remembered something Effie had cautioned that very first day on the beach: *a dimple on the chin, the devil within.* True, after all.

She closed her eyes briefly at the memory of her dear, fierce friend, always so plain-spoken; always so brave. She missed her – all of them: Mhairi and Molly too – with an intensity she had never foreseen. Theirs had been an age of innocence. That couldn't be said of her situation now.

'I must say that dress looks sensational on you, Flora,' Kinney said. 'The colour's perfect for you.'

She brought herself back to Paris, opening her eyes again and regarding the businessman with a cool gaze. 'Thank you. Although it's not mine, of course, just borrowed, like everything else,' she demurred. 'Sometimes I think I'm just a walking shop display.'

'Ooh, does that mean you're for sale, then?' Kinney laughed, attempting to flirt. 'Because I'd most definitely buy!'

The others laughed, but it was Edward who laughed longest and loudest. Pepperly shifted position in his chair, looking awkward.

'I say – what's that?' Charlie Buck leaned forward suddenly, reaching for her left hand as he caught sight of the ring. He looked at her with a less-than-pleased expression. 'Have you been snapped up?'

Kinney inhaled sharply. 'That could be a problem,' he murmured, leaning back as he looked across at Pepperly beside him. 'The studios aren't fond of . . . baggage.'

'Actually, it's just a gift,' Flora said, smiling as she openly gazed upon it, admiring her splayed hand. 'Pepper got it for me.' She looked over at him with gratitude. Could he see what it meant to her? She hadn't yet had a chance to thank him; he had left his car outside the Casino for her tonight, travelling over with Kinney and Buck instead as they discussed business after the performance.

'But it's on your ring finger,' Buck pointed out.

'Yes. It holds sentimental value, that's all.'

She saw Edward glance between the two of them; he too seemed less than happy, though he passed no comment. For a moment she wondered whether he had recognized James's late mother's ring; but if it had been in a vault in London for so many years, that seemed unlikely.

Pepperly, beside her, was looking uneasy.

'I heard a rumour Duke Ellington's coming out later,' Kinney said, changing the subject as the jazz band fell into a new song.

'Really?' Pepperly tried to look interested.

'You hadn't heard? I thought you knew him?'

'I do, but I didn't know he was in town,' Pepperly shrugged. 'I can introduce you afterwards if you like. He's a great fellow.'

'Blast. That's a real shame, Pepper, I'd have liked to meet him; but we'll have to shoot straight after dinner,' Edward said, his gaze coming to settle directly on Flora. She felt a shift in his energy – as if the ring had provoked him in some way.

Kinney frowned. 'Not running out early on us, are you?'

'I'm afraid so. Flora and I have made plans.'

This statement was met with a short silence.

'Actually, about that,' Pepperly said, looking apologetic. 'I think it might be best if Flora had an early night. She's been working non-stop and I need to keep my brightest star shining. We've a full performance schedule to get through, so until she's used to how tiring that can be, it's best if we pace things.'

'That would be . . . exceedingly unfortunate, Pepper,' Edward said after a long moment. 'I'd been hoping to run some lines with her. I've arranged a screen test here in Paris for the day after tomorrow, you see. I've been speaking to David Humber at MGM. They're about to greenlight a project and I've persuaded them that Flora fits the bill. They were excited to see what she's got. But if you think she's not up to anything . . . extracurricular to the show, I'll let him know.'

Pepperly didn't respond immediately, and Flora felt her heart begin to pound. She understood perfectly well what was happening; they all did, Buck and Kinney staring into their drinks as the ultimatum dangled.

Slowly, she reached over and covered his hand with hers. His rescue efforts could only extend so far. As he had warned her over breakfast, he could limit her interactions with Edward, but he couldn't prevent them altogether. She must be her own white knight. 'You're sweet to worry about me, Pepper, but I feel perfectly well,' she told him, communicating with her eyes.

'. . . Well, if you're sure.' Pepperly's voice was thin; he was no actor either. 'It does sound like too good an opportunity to turn down.' He looked at Rushton, his paymaster. 'Can you give us a clue about what the project is?'

'Not yet.' Edward shrugged, a finger tapping the side of his glass. 'They're keeping it under wraps until the leading man's firmed up. You know how it is. Standard stuff.'

'Of course.'

Pepperly reached for his drink and took a long gulp. Flora watched the bubbles disappear along with her last hope as Edward's gaze settled upon her once again; any subtlety of intention was gone and she could feel his lust like a heat. He had been deterred first by James and then, last night, by George. She knew he wouldn't be denied a third time.

'I'll try not to keep her too long, Pepper,' he smiled, reaching for his drink. 'But I can make no promises.'

The Bentley drew up outside a pale limestone townhouse in the seventh arrondissement. Streetlights dotted the night with golden pools, the boulevard wide, although there were few people about at this hour. Flora glanced around at the buildings topped with grey mansard roofs and trellised balconies and knew it was a moneyed district. Safe – from some dangers.

'Come,' Edward said, almost gallantly, squeezing her hand as the driver opened the car door for her. He had been talkative, almost garrulous, the whole journey over here, his hand settling upon her every few moments as he recounted a story or pointed out a landmark, as if she had just arrived in the city this morning instead of six weeks ago.

Flora followed him inside the building, her narrow heels tap-tapping across a marbled lobby, the bag swinging in her grasp.

'You live here?' she asked him as he pressed a button for the lift. She had expected a hotel.

'After a fashion. We don't own the apartment, but my parents took a long lease thirty or so years ago. If ever we come to the city, this is where we stay. We prefer it to staying in a hotel. More intimate. It's a home away from home, you might say.'

The lift arrived at the lobby – it was like a cage – and he stepped back for her to enter. Playing the gentleman. *He* was a terrific actor, she realized.

'What exactly have you got in there?' he asked her, pulling the grilled door across and looking down curiously at the bag.

She stared out at the floors speeding past as they travelled up. She was caged again; a songbird unable to fly away, even through an open door. '. . . Something appropriate. I'm told.'

The bold comment stripped away his mannered pretence that this was a seduction and not a business transaction, and he fell silent for the rest of the journey to the eighth floor.

He led her wordlessly along a narrow corridor and she watched his key slide into the lock, knowing this was her last chance to run. Once she stepped into that apartment and the door closed behind her, there would be no rescue.

She didn't stir.

'Well, here we are. Chez moi,' he said, as they stepped into a tall-ceilinged apartment. The walls were peppermint green with violet borders, a large mirror splayed with angular sunrays above a curved marble fireplace. Against the far wall, a striking bronze statue of a woman holding a ball stood on an onyx plinth between a pair of French doors that led onto a balcony.

'It's very chic,' she said, surprised. From what she remembered of his mother, she wouldn't have put her down as an art deco sophisticate.

'Only recently completed. My parents gave it to Sophia to update. They thought it would be a good project to occupy her.'

Flora glanced at him, inferring that his sister had needed distracting from her broken heart, but Edward was crossing the room, turning on table lamps. All the furniture was slope-edged and sitting low to the floor; a thick rug covered older parquet floors.

She looked around her. Several doors led off the living room, and she wondered which were bedrooms – which was his. She let the bag drop beside an armchair and slipped off the sable, waiting. Now that she was here, just let it be done.

'A drink?' he asked, turning back with a smile that grew as he saw her in just the gown. He had forgotten, it seemed, her hostility in the lift; he had convinced himself of his own hospitality. In his mind, at least, he was a gentleman and this was real.

'All right.'

He faltered a little, as if noticing how she stood – still, limp – in the middle of the room. She knew she had always unnerved him somehow.

'And some music, I think.'

He walked over to the gramophone; the sound horn bloomed into the room like a giant silver flower. 'Perhaps some Duke, seeing as we're missing out on the real thing?' he asked, his fingers tripping over a thick collection of vinyls.

'If you like.'

'No, I know – how about some Adelaide Hall?' He looked up at her expectantly.

She nodded. There was a stilted silence as he shuffled the vinyl from its sleeve and set it on the turntable, a loud scratch booming as the stylus dropped down. The room filled with a caramel voice. If velvet could be a sound, this is what it would sound like, Flora thought, mesmerized.

There was a faint crackle in the background that served to smother the blistering silence as Edward wandered over to the drinks trolley and began mixing them something strong.

A golden light fell in past the lace curtains at the French doors, and Flora wandered over with a dull curiosity. Was it a full moon? She had lost track of the lunar wanderings in the night sky. It had been something she had taken for granted back home. There, the North Star, the Plough, Venus were all the villagers' companions, everyone always outside far more than they were ever in. But it was the opposite here – life was led indoors and, even if she ever was outdoors late, the sky was dim here, with no sign of star-studded canopies above.

She put a hand to the curtain and looked out . . .

'Oh!' she gasped, her jaw dropping down as she was met with a wholly unexpected sight.

Edward looked pleased by her reaction, her *froideur*

forgotten in a moment. 'You see why I had to bring you here?' he grinned.

She looked back at him. 'It's . . . so beautiful!'

'Go out!' he said excitedly. 'Have a better look. I'll finish mixing these and meet you out there.'

Flora turned the handle and stepped onto the balcony, awed by the sight of the Eiffel Tower, maybe half a mile away, shimmering in its lights. She had passed it many times by day, but had somehow never caught it at night. And from this vantage point . . .

She stared, transfixed. In a curious way, something about it reminded her of the yachts at night on Village Bay – strung with lights in otherwise pristine darkness, they were a faint echo of this dazzling display. Pale imitations, perhaps, and yet . . . She felt something on the breeze, her past reaching for her.

She startled, turning around suddenly. There it was again – that feeling of eyes upon her back; it was like a warmth on her skin, a breeze in her sleep. She stared around at the neighbouring buildings, lights on in some of the rooms, deserted balconies . . . A cat prowled on the wall of one, flicking its tail as it walked before leaping effortlessly onto a higher ledge.

She willed herself to remain calm. She didn't think *The Times* would have a budget that extended to covering Bonner's expenses in an area like this. Besides, he couldn't possibly know she was here; no one could. That was precisely Edward's intention.

'This was why we couldn't stay for Duke to play,' the man himself said, stepping through the open door and handing her her drink. 'They switch them off at one.'

As if that had been his reason, she thought with disgust. It had merely provided him with an excuse.

Lightly, he toasted her with his glass. 'To reunion.'

'. . . Reunion,' she murmured, pointedly not taking a sip of her drink but turning back again to the light display.

He stood closer behind her and she felt his hand rest upon her hip, lightly at first; his breath against her hair. She heard his breathing deepen as he inhaled her scent, the pressure in his fingertips increasing as the seconds ticked by. She felt his head move against her as he began to nuzzle and she closed her eyes, knowing it had begun . . .

She shuddered. It was an instinct she couldn't control and he pulled back with a frown.

'Are you all right?' he asked, in an offended tone.

She took a steadying breath. *Don't run. He'll only chase harder.* She forced a smile. '. . . Just a little chilly.'

'Oh. Well, here – let me give you my jacket.'

'No, I . . .' She swallowed. 'I might just go and change into . . . something more comfortable instead.' She looked back at him and saw the way his eyes lidded at her words, his lips parting. She could see how much he wanted to kiss her, to claim her body.

'Now that sounds a fine idea.'

'Where should I . . . ?'

'First door on the left.'

She nodded, handing him her drink, and slipped past, back into the apartment. Adelaide Hall enveloped her again like a fur coat but there was no comfort to be found here. She took the bag and stepped into the room he had indicated. It was a bathroom – marble clad with a mirrored wall, perfumed toiletries stored in lidded glass jars.

She put the bag on the counter and pulled out the tissue bundles. The négligée slipped free of its ribboned trusses, formless and slippery in her hands. She unbuttoned the straps of her gown and let it puddle at her feet before pushing her silk French knickers down over her hips. She stared at her reflection in the mirror, her eye falling to the single tiger stripe on her lower tummy.

She pressed a finger to it, feeling a surge of love at the idea that she had been branded by her baby after all. Something of him remained on her body, if not within.

She pulled the négligée over her head and stared at her reflection again, now that she was dressed to be undressed. When she had lain with James, they had only cared about taking their clothes off; the desperation to put their bodies together had been a primal urge that had overwhelmed them both. There had been no charade, and she had never been more herself than in those moments.

This, though – this was all an elaborate, empty farce. Motions and artifice. A dead dance.

She could hear Edward moving about in the next room, awaiting her: the tinkle of glasses, the light clatter of silver tongs on ice, the record being changed over. He was humming . . .

She reached for the smaller tissue-wrapped packet in the bag. She opened up the rattle and pressed it hard against her palm, feeling its ridges and edges and trying to imprint it into her skin as if it was something she could wear. An invisible tattoo, reminding her of who she really was . . . why she was doing this.

She opened the bathroom door and stood in the doorway, letting him absorb the sight of her in flimsy primrose silk and ribbons.

'Flora,' he said, his voice thick. He had taken off his jacket and unfastened his bow tie so that it dangled at his neck, the top button undone. 'Come here.'

It was a command, as if he was reminding them both who held the ultimate power here, but she wasn't so sure it lay with him. She could see from the rise and fall of his chest that he wouldn't have control of himself for long. His fingers flexed as he savoured at last the sight he had been imagining for so long.

She moved towards him, feeling the hem of the gown trail on the rug and find resistance there so that it dragged a little, pressing the silk against her body. She stopped when they were toe to toe, looking at him, waiting.

She felt almost as if she had left her own body and was watching herself from the ceiling. He reached an arm forward and cupped the back of her head; with the other, he splayed his hand across her throat so that her head was tipped back slightly – he held her there for several moments, staring into her eyes, before running his hand slowly down her body: between her breasts, over her stomach, his fingers curling as he got to the mound at the top of her legs. He held them there, establishing ownership.

Her own fingers pressed against the grooves on the fleshy pad below her thumb, the rattle's indentations holding firm, like a fossil. She would not lose shape. She would not lose herself.

He leaned forward, his mouth falling upon the saddle of her neck, and she closed her eyes. *Let him have you.*

His hand, lower down, began to move, pressing against her more insistently, and she felt his breathing become more ragged—

There was a knock at the door.

Edward pulled back in surprise, as if such a thing had never happened before. He looked at her, his cheeks flushed, his eyes burning. 'Who's that?'

'I have no idea,' she replied, just as bewildered.

His eyes narrowed. 'Did you tell Pepper to do this? To come after you?'

'Of course not. How could I have done? I had no idea where you were taking me. I *still* don't know where I am.' Much to her own dismay, it was the truth.

He considered this for a moment as another knock came, this one more insistent.

'Well, hadn't you better answer it?' she asked him. 'It might be important.'

'How?'

She shrugged. 'The building could be on fire?'

He groaned but pulled away from her, rearranging his trousers and running a hand through his hair as he strode angrily over to the door.

'Yes?' he demanded curtly as he threw it open. Flora saw his hand drop from the door jamb and he took a stunned step back. 'What in blazes . . . ?'

'Edward? . . . Who is it?' she asked, just as a fist sailed through the doorway and her question was answered.

Chapter Thirty-One

'You're *dead*,' she whispered, feeling her blood run cold.

James stared back at her with the same anger that had driven him to send Edward sprawling. 'Unfortunately for you, I'm very much alive,' he said, stepping over Edward's outstretched legs and coming into the apartment. She saw his eyes run over her fashionable haircut and the flimsy nightgown, reading the very clear message it sang out. He looked at her as if he couldn't believe what he was seeing – but she didn't trust her own eyes either. His form was altered too. He had lost weight and there was a tension about him that hadn't been there before. If he wasn't a ghost, he looked haunted.

She took a step towards him, wanting nothing but to throw herself into his arms, to feel for herself that he was real – but he stopped her with a look that could have cut her in half and she knew what he must be thinking, finding them together like this. She knew exactly how it appeared.

'Get out, Callaghan!' Edward said from behind him as he staggered to his feet. Bleeding from the nose, he pointed to the door. James didn't move. If Edward wanted him to leave, clearly he would have to bodily eject him.

The moment held until Edward looked away, surrendering to the invasion. He slammed the apartment door shut, blotting his nose with his fingers and seeing how the blood was spotting the new rug. 'Fuck!' he spat. 'What the hell are you doing here?'

'Isn't it obvious?' James's gaze was still fixed on Flora. 'I came to see the show. I wanted to see with my own eyes what the fuss was all about.' He shook his head as if in disbelief, his eyes travelling over her body again. 'You're quite the sensation, Flora, even making headlines in London . . . Impossible to escape you, it seems.'

She blinked, hearing the cold glint of sarcasm in his voice, but she couldn't reply; she couldn't stop staring at his face. That handsome, angular face she had kept in her mind's eye for so many long, lonely months – and now here he was, *not dead*, and he was looking at her like he despised her. Was this a dream? Or a nightmare?

Edward grabbed a white napkin from the ice bucket and pressed it to his nose, his head thrown back. 'Spit it out, Callaghan! What do you *want*?'

James's eyes never left hers. 'It's quite simple really. I want Flora to tell me to my face why she no longer wants to be my wife. Call me old-fashioned, but I don't propose marriage to every girl I see.' His eyes were cold. 'I want to hear from her why she called off the engagement – even though she's still wearing my ring.'

She gasped as she remembered it glittering on her finger. *He* had given it back to her? She recalled Pepperly's bewildered expression at the dinner table earlier.

'James . . . I didn't . . . *I* never called off anything—'

'That's not what your neighbours said.'

Her *neighbours*? His every word was like the thrust of a sword. Everything was happening too fast – she could scarcely catch her breath, much less make sense of it all. 'James, they told me you were dead,' she repeated. 'They said the ship sank.'

'Sank?'

'Yes. That it got caught in ice and the hull was breached.'

He let a beat pass. 'We were stuck for three days in the ice. Three. It was an inconvenience at most.'

'But . . .' She felt panic rising in the pit of her stomach. 'We were told you'd perished. That's what we were told! All of us. Even Edward, he—'

She stopped as James's lips curled into a sneer. 'Oh no. Rushton never thought that; not for a moment.' Sarcasm dripped from his words, a new, offhand cruelty she'd never seen in him before. 'He saw me very much alive at our London club only last month – and he wasn't too happy about it. You got quite a petition going in my absence, didn't you, Rushton? Trying to get them to blackball me.'

'Fuck you!' Edward snarled. It seemed to be all he could say.

'You allowed me to go on believing he was *dead*?' Flora whispered to Edward in disbelief. He simply shrugged, and she realized that his treachery didn't surprise her after all. She would have expected nothing else from a man of his type. He was an opportunist – in business as well as pleasure.

She looked back at James with renewed urgency. 'James, you've got to believe me,' she beseeched. 'I never called off anything. I thought you were dead.'

'If you thought that, then why did you write me that letter?'

'*What* letter?' Her hands splayed in front of her in bewilderment. It was as if they were having two entirely separate conversations.

'Asking me to meet you off the boat in Oban.'

She caught her breath, feeling disorientated. 'I didn't write any letter to you! I thought you were dead!' she cried. 'How many times do I have to say it?'

He blinked, a small doubt starting to register. For the first time since he'd entered the room she saw something like a thaw in his eyes, as if he was beginning to hear her. Believe her. A glimmer of the old James, her James, ran across his face.

'James, please. I'm telling the truth,' she begged. 'Please!'

He relented, a tension inside him seeming to release suddenly and he nodded. 'Then we need to talk. We need to get out of here, Flora.' He held a hand out to her and she moved towards him, feeling the same urgent need for his touch that Edward had felt for hers.

But Edward, quick as a cat, sprang between them.

'Not so fast!' he said, gripping her upper arm and holding her back. 'You're not going anywhere.' Flora winced as his fingers dug into her skin. 'It's a shame to have to put it in such crude terms, but you're mine now.'

'No!'

'Oh, yes. Money is god on this side of the water, Flora – and you, sweet girl, owe me lots of it.'

Flora swallowed. All of Pepperly's cautions rang in her ears as Edward played his trump card.

'Let go of her.' James's voice was low.

Edward snapped his head round to face him. 'Things have changed while you've been gone, Callie. Forget that ring on her finger; she's not yours any more. I *own* her.'

'I'll settle everything.'

Flora looked over at James with a gasp. He had said the words without hesitation. 'James—'

Edward smirked. 'No, it's really not that straightforward. I'm afraid it's quite a debt, old boy,' he tutted. 'Pepper went to town on launching her. If I pull the plug now, there will be no more ticket sales to offset the costs. She's liable for all of it.'

James took another step closer, looking down upon him. 'I said I'll settle it.'

A silence drew out as Edward saw his pulled fist, recognizing the further physical threat to his own handsome bone structure. He knew better than anyone that James had boxed for Cambridge.

Slowly, he nodded. 'Yes . . . I've heard things are going especially well for you now. That jolly of yours with the Eskimos wasn't such a waste of time after all.'

Flora said nothing, but she felt his grip loosen around her bicep until eventually he released her. She drew her arm in and began rubbing it, as if sloughing off his physical contact.

'Flora, get your things,' James said, not taking his eyes off his former friend.

Neither man stirred as she darted into the bathroom and shoved her clothes into the bag, the silver rattle safely packed under her dress. Picking up the sable and her shoes, she returned to stand by James's side, breathless.

'Send me your invoice, Rushton,' James muttered, placing a hand on the small of her back and moving her towards the door, keeping his body between her and Edward all the way.

Flora didn't say a word as Edward, his dinner shirt splattered with blood, watched her leaving in her nightgown, still unconquered. She stepped out into the corridor and James closed the apartment door behind them.

Immediately she turned to him. 'James—'

But the words were torn from her as he pushed her against the wall and kissed her, right there, his hands in her hair, their bodies pressed together. Making her his again. She felt the world contract between them: all the distance and time that had forced them apart was swept away as she was transported back to their last moments together on St Kilda. *I'll come back for you*, he had whispered to her in the cleit. Now she inhaled his scent, remembering how it had felt being with him the last time they were together.

'I've missed you,' she breathed as he pulled back and kissed her cheeks, her brow, her nose, her eyes. 'You've no idea how I've missed you.'

'I have some idea,' he murmured.

'No,' she protested. 'I thought you were *dead*.'

'And I thought you no longer loved me. That's worse. I'd rather be dead than unloved by you.'

She smiled at the twisted logic as he kissed her over and over.

'We have to go somewhere,' she panted, looking up and down the corridor. 'We can't stay out here, like this.'

He trailed his fingers over her hip and up her side as he reached into his pocket and held up a key with the other hand. She watched in astonishment as he slid it into the door of the apartment . . . next door.

'But . . .' she whispered as he opened it up.

'It's how our families first met. We're neighbours here,' he smiled, pulling her inside.

'Did he touch you?' he asked jealously, kissing her, pulling her towards the bed.

'No.'

He groaned with relief. 'I want to kill him.'

'No . . . you stopped him in time.' They fell together onto the mattress, limbs intertwined. The kiss deepened and she felt the connection between them surge, somehow stronger in spite of all they had lost. She wanted to lose herself in him and never be found again, but she pulled back, panting. This was no ordinary reunion. He'd returned from the dead and everything had changed. He had no idea just how much.

'Where are you going?' he protested as she clambered off the bed and moved away, putting a much-needed distance between them. She tried to gather her thoughts. There were things he had to know.

Her too. She had questions that needed answers. '. . . How did you even know I was with him?'

He watched her closely, his eyes tracking her every move, as if he would never let her out of his sight again. 'I didn't. I arrived in the city last night and went straight to your hotel – it was late, but I needed to see you and I'd heard where you were staying.' He sighed and shifted his position, leaning back on his elbows. 'When I saw *him* coming out, of all people, my heart sank. I was afraid that was why you'd left me – to be with him after all. But I couldn't be sure. He'd come out with another chap, so I decided to follow you around today, to see if you were with him.'

That feeling of being watched . . . the sound on the balcony. This balcony. 'That was you?'

He shrugged. 'Every time I saw you, you were alone; I still couldn't work out what was going on. So I paid someone I saw coming out of the stage door to drop the ring to you before the show; I wanted to see if you would wear it. When you did, I felt some hope that you still cared after all.'

Flora listened in silence. It really *had* been his face she had seen in the crowd tonight. Not a wish, or a hope, or a dream – really him.

'I tried going backstage to see you afterwards, but you had already left before I could get there. I happened to see the same girl I'd paid earlier, so I paid her again to tell me where you'd gone. Then I took a cab to Le Boeuf and waited outside – and that's when I saw you coming out with him.' He sighed again as he looked down at his feet. 'It was my worst fear confirmed. I followed you, but I already knew where you would go. Rushton's a creature of habit and it wasn't difficult to guess he'd make his move here. Believe me, he's seduced many girls by showing them the lights from that balcony.'

Flora stared at him, hardly able to take in what she was hearing. She didn't care about Edward's ploys. 'But how did you come to have the ring?'

'I saw it by chance in the window as I passed the shop, soon after I returned home.'

She was horrified by the thought of what he must have felt, seeing his mother's ring in a pawn shop window. 'I had to sell it, James, I had no choice. We had no money—'

'I know that now,' he said, seeing her distress. 'At the time, though, it seemed to me you'd simply had a change of heart.'

'But I hadn't! I wouldn't!'

'Well, that's not what I was told. Everyone had disembarked at Oban and there was no sign of you. When I asked them where you were, they said you didn't want to see me; that the engagement was off . . .' He stared at her with pained eyes. 'When I saw the ring in the window, I hated you. Or at least I tried to.'

'But this makes no sense – I never did any of those things. I never wrote asking you to meet me in Oban, and I never called off the engagement. I don't know why anyone would say otherwise.' She frowned. 'Who was it you spoke to?'

He shrugged. 'I don't know her name. Some woman. Rather bad-tempered-looking. She was carrying a newborn—'

Flora's head whipped up and she recoiled as if he'd scalded her. *No . . .*

'Flora?' he asked, concern in his voice as she stepped backwards, her fingers pressed to her mouth as she tried to make sense of it. Everyone in the village had heard what she had heard: that James's ship had sunk. If Mary had seen with her own eyes that he was alive, why would she have said such a thing?

She felt a sudden sickness in the pit of her stomach that she couldn't explain, an uneasiness that made her want to drop to the floor. She had a sense of a picture coming together – and yet pieces were missing. She paced, beginning to feel frantic as her mind rushed to make connections.

'Flora, tell me what's wrong.' He sat up now, planting his feet on the floor as he watched her.

She looked back at him, knowing she had to tell him what she had done. 'There's something you need to know.'

He looked nervous. 'Very well. What is it?'

She swallowed, knowing she couldn't sugarcoat her words. Would he hate her? Could he ever forgive her? '. . . I had a baby. Our baby.'

'*What?*' The colour bled from his cheeks at the stunning announcement.

'I had no way of telling you. And then, when . . . when I was told you were dead, the shock, I . . . I went into early labour. Brought on by the distress.' She watched his eyes run over her face, a look of utmost dread on his own. 'We had a little boy.'

'Had?' She heard the trepidation held in that one word.

'I had to give him away.' She heard her voice rise as her panic – her pain – grew. 'To a couple who were desperate for a child of their own. It was the only way. We were about to

413

come over to the mainland and I had no money – no one to support us – and I knew I couldn't get work with a baby. If I was to arrive there as an unmarried mother, we'd have floundered. I had to do the best thing for him. Giving him up was a mercy – you see that, don't you? At least this way, he would grow up with a happy family that wanted him.'

But even as she said the words, she knew that wasn't strictly true. Donald and Mary would never be happy together.

A deep groan escaped him as he dropped his head into his hands, his body hunched as his fingers twisted hard in his hair.

'Please say something,' she whispered, as his silence grew.

'This is a lot to . . .' He swallowed, looking up to meet her eyes. 'And are you telling me . . . the baby that woman was holding – it was . . . it was *our* child?'

Flora nodded, seeing his despair as he absorbed the fact that he had greeted his own child – his own flesh and blood – in another woman's arms. A fresh moan escaped him as he fell onto his back, his hands over his face. 'She stood there, with my child in her arms, and lied to my face about you calling off the engagement?'

Flora couldn't even answer him. Too many questions were swirling in her mind.

'Why would she do that? What have I ever done to her? What have *you* done to her?'

'That's what I can't understand,' she said desperately. 'I had no quarrel with Mary. I gave her our child, for God's sake!'

He looked back at her with sudden understanding, sitting upright again. 'So then that's it! She saw I was alive and feared that if I found you, and you knew it too, we'd take the baby away from her.'

414

Flora stared at him. Of course. It was suddenly so obvious.

Mary had already lost the baby Mhairi had promised to give her. Her husband's illegitimate child had been her best chance of being a mother, until Mhairi had made the grave mistake of lambing the late-tups. When their daughter had been stillborn, there had been only one hope left. But that meant something else too . . .

'Oh, James . . . she *planned* it.' Why else would Mary have pretended her pregnancy had continued for those three weeks after Mhairi's baby had been lost? 'She actually planned it!'

James looked at her intently, seeing her panic rising. He jumped up from the bed and held her firmly by the arms. 'Flora, we've got to go and get our son back. You made the best possible choice under the circumstances, I know that – but everything has changed now. We're together again and we must find our baby boy.'

She blinked, tears coming to her eyes as the horror of the situation began to overwhelm her. This had been planned. *Plotted*. It was grotesque. Monstrous. 'But we can't,' she said, beginning to cry. 'Effie rang me yesterday: Mary's gone. No one knows where!'

A flash of anger, such as she had seen in the apartment next door, crossed over his face as their luck continued to plummet. His hands dropped from her and he took a step back. 'But *someone* must know. A friend? A neighbour? Think, Flora! People don't just disappear without trace.'

'. . . Mhairi? She might know something,' she stammered, remembering Effie's phone call. 'She had a letter from her. She was on her way down from Harris yesterday to give Donald an alibi.'

He frowned in bewilderment. 'Who's Donald?'

She wiped her tears with the backs of her hands. 'Mary's

husband. He's been arrested.' Seeing his blank expression, she shook her head dismissively. 'It's a long story.' She glanced around, an idea coming to her. 'Is there a telephone here?'

'Through there.' He led her into the living room and lifted the receiver.

'The Royal Hotel, Oban. Ecosse,' she said to the switchboard operator. James watched her as the dial tone sounded in her ear. '. . . Hello – Miss Gillies' room, please.'

There was an agonizingly long pause. Flora's fingers twitched as she waited for her friend to pick up. 'Effie!' she gasped as Effie came onto the line at last.

'Flora?'

'Eff, I'm sorry for my haste, but I must know urgently – have you heard any more about Mary?'

'Aye.' Effie hesitated, and Flora knew that whatever was coming next couldn't be good. 'Mary told the neighbours she was going to Canada. Sholto and I went round and spoke to them today.'

'. . . *What* . . .' The word was just a breath; no colour, no shape.

'Apparently she booked onto the RMS *Empress of Scotland* – three third-class tickets to Quebec City. Donald's beside himself. He had no idea. He got bail, only to find she's taken the baby and the ambergris money and left the country.'

Flora's legs began to tremble. The receiver fell from her hand, Effie's voice dropping away to become a tinny staccato in the background.

James bent to pick up the receiver. 'She'll call back,' he murmured, before replacing it on its cradle with a concerned look. 'Flora, what is it? What's happened?'

'She's gone to Canada. Three tickets to Quebec.'

'Quebec?' A look of horror crossed his face but he reined

it back in the next moment, his eyes becoming intense as he thought fast. So cool in a crisis. 'All right, then we'll . . . we'll sail over there too. Next and fastest crossing we can get, and we'll . . . hire a private investigator once we're over there. They won't be moving quickly with limited funds and a newborn. Her husband will need to look for work—'

'That's just it,' Flora said quietly. 'He's not with them. Donald's been in police custody. He's only just out on bail.'

James frowned. 'Well, he can't leave the country if he's on bail.'

'No. She went without him.'

'So then she took someone else?' James asked. 'But who?'

Flora lifted her head at the simple question. Who would Mary have taken?

She stood in silence, sudden clarity spreading in her mind like the dawn light as she saw, from a distance, what she hadn't been able to see up close: that there *was* someone else involved in all this. Someone who had always been involved.

Someone who had access to the post bags and could easily have dropped in a forged letter.

Someone who had given and withheld information at her own discretion.

Someone with a bag of special tonics that she had said would calm – but in fact might have done other things as well.

Someone who had found a way to move everyone off the island and scatter them like marbles into the ether.

Someone who was behind every secret. And behind every solution.

Snapshots of daily life clicked through her mind: *Mary won't lie with him . . . staying overnight, just to be sure . . .* hands held behind the cottage . . . *an old maid . . .*

What did she know of love?

It was a secret that had lived out in the open, too bold to be taken at face value back home. But Flora was more worldly now, not so naive. She had seen things: George and Marcel, in the office . . .

'Lorna,' she said, seeing it all at last, her eyes filling with tears as she looked back at him. 'Oh God, she's taken Lorna with her . . . James, they've got our baby.'

Acknowledgements

We're three books into the four-book series now and certainly, for me, it's not getting any easier! It is a lot of fun though, carrying a plot over several stories and characters. As ever, what you read in terms of characters and their actions is fictitious, but the books are wholly embedded in historical fact, which is why I must admit to manipulating the timeline on one important account in this story.

The British Arctic Air Route Expedition was real and the team did sail on Shackleton's old ship, the *Quest*, but the expedition took place in 1930–31, not 1929–30. However, if you can imagine for a moment how difficult it is to find a way to bring a character back to St Kilda in the very depths of winter, without anyone else knowing . . . well, you can also imagine why I desperately needed to borrow their Gipsy Moth seaplanes and relative proximity in the Faroes and Iceland! But for that one year's discrepancy, it was an absolutely perfect fit and, sometimes, writers have to exercise the 'artistic licence' that lies at our disposal, so long as we give full disclosure.

Real-life timings were much more fortuitous with Cecil Hatry, the disgraced businessman who really was jailed in January 1930 for his illegal manoeuvrings over the conglomerated steel endeavour.

Deep thanks are owed to my publisher, Gillian Green, for

steering this book into its current shape. The first draft looked very different indeed – it didn't run in chronological order but in back-and-forth sections, and several vital reveals were held back until the final scenes. Gillian had the vision to help me condition it into the fine beast now held in your hands. No mean feat. Everyone needs a stiff drink when my first draft lands in their in-tray!

To the Pan team, too: thank you for every effort you make on my behalf to ensure that my efforts don't go unrewarded and instead find their way onto bookshelves up and down the land. I know there's fierce competition out there and that every new account, promotion and sale is a triumph! In particular, I'd like to thank James Annal, art director extra-ordinaire, who has spent countless hours creating stunning covers and fashioning a strong brand image for the series – thank you, I'm so grateful, please don't get your voodoo doll of me out of your drawer! And Lucy Hale, who has steered the concept for the series from the start and is its greatest champion, your confidence is infectious and gives me hope when I find myself standing in the shadows of doubt. Thank you.

To Amanda Preston, my agent and good friend, we're the definition of teamwork. There is simply no question of doing my job without you. As a grown woman myself and a mother of three, I like to think I'm a fully functioning adult, but you somehow always know when I'm having a panic or feeling wobbly and you rally me back to competency! Never retire.

Finally, my gorgeous family. They're used to this now and they know I'm more likely to be found in the study than in the kitchen, but they support me no matter what, and every effort I go to is for them. Writing is my passion, but they are my life – and what a life it is.

Karen Swan is a *Sunday Times* top three bestselling author and her novels sell all over the world. She writes two books each year – one for the summer period and one for the Christmas season. Previous summer titles include *The Spanish Promise*, *The Hidden Beach* and *The Secret Path* and, for winter, *Together by Christmas*, *Midnight in the Snow* and *The Christmas Postcards*.

Previously a fashion editor, she lives in Sussex with her husband, three children and two dogs.

Follow Karen on Instagram @swannywrites,
on her author page on Facebook,
and on Twitter @KarenSwan1.

The Secret Path

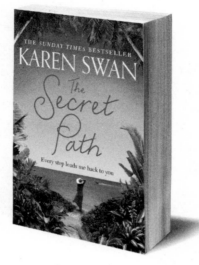

'Deliciously glamorous, irresistably romantic!'
Hello!

An old flame. A new spark. Love can find you
in the most unlikely places.

At only twenty, Tara Tremain has everything: she's a trainee
doctor, engaged to Alex, the man of her dreams. But, just when
life seems perfect, Alex betrays her in the worst way possible.

Ten years later, she's moved on – with a successful career and
a man who loves her. But, when she's pulled back into her
wealthy family's orbit for a party in the Costa Rican jungle,
she's flung into a crisis: a child is desperately ill and the
sole treatment is several days' trek away.

There's only one person who can help – but can she trust
the man who broke her heart?

The Hidden Beach

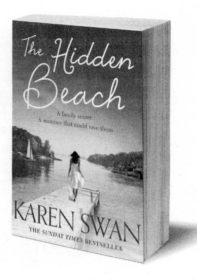

'**Novels to sweep you away**'
Woman & Home

Secrets, betrayal and shocking revelations await
in Sweden's stunning holiday islands . . .

In Stockholm's oldest quarter, Bell Appleshaw loves her job
working as a nanny for the rich and charming Hanna and
Max Mogert, caring for their three children.

But one morning everything changes. A doctor from
a clinic that Bell has never heard of asks her to pass on
the message that Hanna's husband has woken up.
But the man isn't Max.

As the truth about Hanna's past is revealed, the
consequences are devastating. As the family heads off
to spend their summer on Sweden's idyllic islands, will
Bell be caught in the crossfire?

The Spanish Promise

'The perfect summer read'
Hello!

The Spanish Promise is a sizzling summer novel about family secrets and forbidden love, set in the vibrant streets of Madrid.

One of Spain's richest men is dying – and his family are shocked to discover he plans to give away his wealth to a young woman they've never heard of.

Charlotte Fairfax, an expert in dealing with the world's super rich, is asked to travel to the troubled family's home to get to the bottom of the mysterious bequest. She unearths a dark and shocking past in which two people were torn apart by conflict. Now, long-buried secrets are starting to reach into the present. Does love need to forgive and forget to endure? Or does it just need two hearts to keep beating?

The Greek Escape

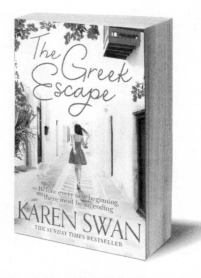

**'A beautiful setting and steamy scenes –
what more do you need?'**
Fabulous

Set on an idyllic island, *The Greek Escape* is the perfect
getaway, bursting with jaw-dropping twists
and irrepressible romance.

Chloe Marston works at a luxury concierge company, making
other people's lives run perfectly, even if her own has ground to a
halt. She is tasked with finding charismatic Joe Lincoln his dream
holiday house in Greece – and, when the man who broke her
heart turns up at home, she jumps on the next flight.

It doesn't take long before she's drawn into the undeniable
chemistry between her and Joe. When another client's wife
mysteriously disappears and serious allegations about him
emerge, will she end up running from more than heartbreak?

The Rome Affair

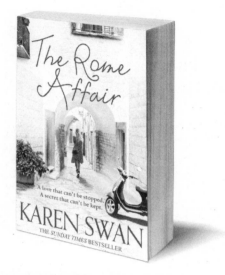

'Enthralling and magical'
Woman

The cobbled streets and simmering heat of
Italy's capital are brought to life in *The Rome Affair*.

1974 and Viscontessa Elena Damiani lives a gilded life, born to
wealth and a noted beauty. Then she meets the love of her life,
and he is the one man she can never have. 2017 and Francesca
Hackett is living la dolce vita in Rome, forgetting the ghosts
she left behind in London. When a twist of fate brings her into
Elena's orbit, the two women form an unlikely friendship.

As summer unfurls, Elena shares her sensational stories with
Cesca, who agrees to work on Elena's memoir. But, when a
priceless diamond ring found in an ancient tunnel below the city
streets is ascribed to Elena, Cesca begins to suspect a shocking
secret lies at the heart of the Viscontessa's life . . .

Summer at TIFFANY'S

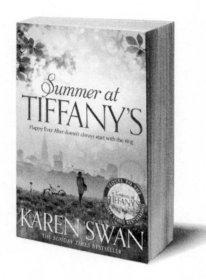

'Glamorous, romantic and totally engrossing'
My Weekly

A wedding to plan. A wedding to stop.
What could go wrong?

With a Tiffany ring on her finger, all Cassie has to do is plan her dream wedding. It should be simple, but when her fiancé, Henry, pushes for a date, Cassie pulls back. Meanwhile, Henry's wild cousin, Gem, is racing to the aisle for her own wedding, determined to marry in the Cornish church where her parents were wed. But the family is set against it, and Cassie resolves to stop the wedding.

When Henry lands an expedition sailing the Pacific for the summer, Cassie decamps to Cornwall, hoping to find the peace of mind she needs to move forwards. But, in the dunes and coves of the north Cornish coast, she soon discovers the past isn't finished with her yet . . .

There's a Karen Swan book
for every season . . .

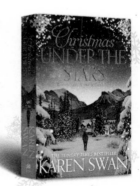

Have you discovered her winter stories yet?